To Chris.

Enjoy! Iris



# MY LADY MARIAN

Iris Lloyd

Published by New Generation Publishing in 2018



First Edition



**www.newgeneration-publishing.com**

Cover design by Jacqueline Abromeit

ISBN 978-1-78955-335-2

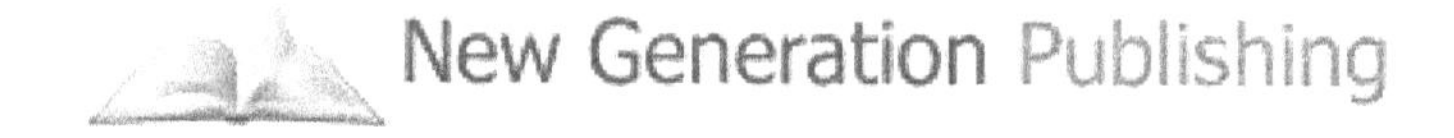

Dedicated to

Cynthia

my sister

who challenged death as bravely

as she had challenged life

*Acknowledgement*

My thanks to Alice Wickham,
Editor of New London Writers online magazine,
for her assistance with the manuscript

## About the Author

Photo by Nigel Perrin

Born in Clapham, London, Iris moved to Queensbury, a newly-built north-west London suburb, with her parents and younger brother before the war. They survived the first night of the Blitz, while visiting her grandparents in Clapham, and shortly afterwards were evacuated with her father's firm to Chesham, Buckinghamshire. They had been there about ten days only when an enemy plane dropped bombs along the road, killing a woman just a few houses away. While there, Iris attended Dr. Challoner's Grammar School in Amersham (then co-ed.)

On returning home at the age of 14, her sister was born. Iris trained as a shorthand/typist and worked in various organisations, including the BBC and as secretary to the Editor of Children's Books at Macmillan's publishing company.

Having taken dancing lessons since the age of three, she joined the chorus of a small touring professional pantomime company at the age of 17, and later wrote, choreographed and directed eight pantomimes for her church youth club and another nine in co-operation with a friend for his amateur dramatic society.

Marriage followed and a move to Berkshire, then the birth of two daughters and three grandchildren, and early widowhood. During those years, she taught dancing to children and later tap dancing to adults. She continued writing, including being correspondent and dance critic for the local newspaper.

Attaining the age of 70, Iris decided it was time to write her debut novel and based it on an archaeological site on top of the Berkshire downs north of Newbury that she was helping to excavate. And so the story of BRON began in the late Roman era and continued through five novels, all of which were self published. Two stand-alone novels followed and now her eighth, MY LADY MARIAN.

Now 87, Iris has hung up her tap shoes but continues to write and hopes you will enjoy the story of Marian.

Author contact:

e-mail: iris@irislloyd.co.uk

website: www.irislloyd.co.uk

Previously published:

BRON Part I, *Daughter of Prophecy*; Part II, *Flames of Prophecy*; Part III, *The Girl with the Golden Ankle*; Part IV, *The Scarlet Seal*; Part V, *Pearl and Amber*.

*Flash Black*

*Hunterswick Green*

# CHAPTER 1

*Place: Greenwich Palace on the Thames*

*Date: Autumn, 1524*

"Sir William Forrester, Sir Philip Forrester and Lady Marian de Booys," announced the steward as he ushered them into the audience chamber.

Marian had been looking forward to this moment for weeks but, now that it had arrived, was unable to motivate her legs and stood as if glued to the floor.

At the far end of the room, on a däis, sat his majesty King Henry VIII of England and Katharine, his Queen. The Queen was relaxing against the back of her throne-like chair, hands clasped across her heavily-embroidered stomacher. Two ladies-in-waiting were standing in attendance behind her. The King, lolling by her side, was inclining his head to speak to her and she was smiling up at him and nodding agreement.

The whole country had rejoiced at their coronation but that was a year before Marian was born. She thought they must be very much in love. The King was a handsome man, obviously very tall. His thick dark hair was escaping from beneath his black velvet hat. His moustache grew down to meet the beard that sprouted beneath his lower lip and covered the whole of his jawline.

As the royal couple were ignoring the three supplicants waiting respectfully by the door, Marian had time to look around. Sir William had described the audience chamber many times but she was quite unprepared for the splendour that now surrounded her – the tall windows with their heavy blue drapes, the colourful wall tapestries showing scenes of the King and his retinue hunting a stag in the forest, the glittering crystal chandeliers. Her eyes then returned to their majesties, whose magnificent apparel and rich jewels were such as she had never imagined.

The steward coughed discreetly and the Queen looked in their direction. His majesty turned his head, the motion fluttering the white ostrich feather crowning his hat, but he remained leaning towards his wife.

The steward withdrew then, closing the door behind him.

Marian looked back at her step father, who smiled and nodded reassuringly.

"Marian, they're waiting for us to approach!" Philip whispered and she willed her legs to walk the length of the room, Philip and Sir William following. Pausing at the foot of the däis, she curtsied as she had practised, while the men bowed low.

The Queen leaned forward, placing her elbows on the arms of her chair.

"Come closer, child, and let me look at you."

Marian took a step forward and wobbled another curtsey then stood, eyes lowered, surveying the polished oak floor.

The Queen spoke over the girl's head.

"Her révérence leaves much to be desired, Sir Villiam."

Sir William Forrester, an Esquire to the Body of His Majesty, acknowledged the criticism with a smile and an inclination of his head.

The Queen returned her attention to Marian.

"Don't be nervous, girl. Look at me."

Marian raised her chin and gazed steadily into the blue eyes of the woman with the strange accent seated above her. She saw a face that she could not describe as beautiful but it was a kindly face with a straight nose and a full-lipped, sensitive mouth.

*"Cómo te llamas?"*

Marian was puzzled and must have looked it because the Queen smiled and translated, "Your name?"

"Marian, your Majesty."

"And she is your ward, Sir Villiam?"

Sir William bowed low again. "Yes, your Majesty, Lady Marian de Booys."

"And, by placing her in our service, you think she vill learn much to her advantage as she grows towards vomanhood?"

"I am certain of it, your grace."

"How many years have you, Marian?"

"Fourteen, your Majesty."

"Would it pleasure you to serve us here at Greenwich Palace?"

Marian's broad smile rendered her reply unnecessary. "Oh yes, your Majesty, if it please your Majesty."

"I think it pleases us very much. She is a credit to you, Sir Villiam."

He acknowledged the compliment with a slight bow of the head. "It is very gracious of your Majesty to judge so."

"We do judge so, do we not, sire?"

The Queen laid a hand on the arm of her husband and the rays of the autumn sun, streaming through the windows, kindled the jewels on her fingers, scattering splinters of rainbow light.

The King regarded the girl standing before them. "The decision is yours, my dear Katharine," he said.

"Sir Villiam, I understand that you also desire to introduce your son to us?"

"He is sixteen and would serve faithfully in whichever position his majesty chose to place him. Stand forward, Philip. As you see, he is a comely lad, strong and capable."

He urged forward his golden-haired son, who came to stand by Marian, taller than her by several inches. The boy's bow was as graceful as his father's.

The Queen nodded. "You speak truly. He is a handsome young man. And the couple are betrothed to be married?"

"Yes, your Majesty, and will be, as soon as my son reaches the age of eighteen."

"So, how say you, husband? Will you engage him as one of your squires?"

The King stroked his beard. "We are conscious of the love and dedicated service that has been rendered by you, Sir William, and your lady Margaret – God rest her soul –" He paused to make the sign of the cross – head to heart, left shoulder to right in the Holy Catholic tradition – then continued, "– the love shown to our mother church of Rome and to ourselves. We trust this same loyalty has been nurtured in your son?"

"Indeed it has, your Majesty."

"Then yes, I am agreeable to such an arrangement. Now we have other matters requiring our attention. Introduce him – Philip, is it? – to privy councillor Lord Bathampton and say that we wish him to instruct the lad in the etiquette of the court before assigning him any duties. And the girl, madam?"

"I will choose one of my ladies to undertake her instruction."

"Send her to the Boleyn girl."

"Lady Mary?"

"No, her sister, Anne. Of all your ladies, she is the most highly spirited and the responsibility may steady her."

"I will do as you suggest, sire. Then, Lady Marian, in time, you may become companion to our daughter, her royal highness The Princess Mary. She is eight years old and in need of a young companion. Would that please you?"

"Oh, yes, your Majesty, very much."

The Queen nodded agreement then waved her hand in dismissal.

"You may retire, Sir Villiam, with the young people. It shall be arranged as ve have pronounced for both of them."

"Thank you, your Majesties. We are very grateful."

The audience concluded, Sir William and his son and adopted daughter made their révérence and backed away until they reached the door, which was opened for their departure and closed behind them.

They were now standing in the ante-room, which was crowded with supplicants awaiting an audience with their majesties. Uniformed stewards were answering questions and trying to satisfy complaints about the delay, at the same time ushering them into an orderly line and keeping the noise down to a reasonable level.

Sir William beamed. Nearing forty years old, he was still a handsome man, with only a few hints of grey in his dark hair and beard.

"Well, children, there we have it, just as we hoped. Now it is up to each of you to make of this great opportunity what you will. As we have discussed, Philip, in two years' time you will partner me in the management of Forrester Hall and the estate, in preparation for the day when you will become Lord of the Manor in your own right. But not yet, eh? I have a lot of living to do before that time comes."

"Of course, Father."

Sir William became aware that his ward had remained silent and raised her chin to better study her face.

"Tears, Marian? Come now, my child, what ails you? Are you not delighted at the prospect of serving her majesty the Queen and becoming companion to Princess Mary?"

"Yes, Sir William, but I shall miss you, sire, and Philip and our home."

"For two years only, Marian, then you will enter the Hall again as Philip's wife – Lady Marian Forrester. That will please you, will it not?"

"I want nothing other than that, Sir William."

"You're a good girl, Marian." He bent to kiss the top of her head. "As you know, because I have told you many times, on his deathbed, hours only before he passed to his heavenly reward, Sir John – your beloved father and my dearest friend –expressed the wish that one day you and Philip would marry –"

"Yes, sir."

"– and that has been my intention from the moment my dear wife and I took you into our home to bring you up as our own daughter."

"No more tears, Marian," Philip interrupted. "As my wife, you will have to show you are made of sterner stuff."

"Yes, Philip."

Sir William smiled at his son. "You're being too hard on her, Philip. She will learn – and from Lady Anne Boleyn, it seems. Marian, we will all three see each other from time to time as we go about our duties around the palace, and I shall be kept informed of the welfare of you both. Now we must find Lord Bathampton, but I am not sure what to do with you, young lady."

At that moment, the door behind them opened again to allow one of the Queen's ladies to approach.

"Sir William, her majesty has asked me to take Lady Marian to Lady Anne Boleyn. Have no fear, she will be well nurtured. We are taking from you a child but will give you back a woman. You'll see."

Sir William bowed. "Lady Jane, the prospect pleases me. Farewell for now, Marian, my dear. Do as you are bid and don't waste a moment of your time here."

"No, sire. Goodbye. Goodbye, Philip."

The lady-in-waiting laughed. "Don't look so forlorn, Lady Marian. I promise no one is going to eat you. Come." She took the girl's hand in hers. "Come. Let us go and surprise our Lady Anne."

Marian's last glimpse of her guardian and his son vanished when her escort guided her around a corner of the gallery and the pair were lost to view.

# CHAPTER 2

Bewildered by the maze of galleries and passageways they traversed, Marian knew she would never be able to find her way back to the audience chamber where they had left the only family she possessed.

The pretty lady whose hand she held looked down at her.

"Our first task will be to dress you in something more becoming than that sack you're wearing."

Marian blushed, conscious of her best but inappropriate brown dress with laced-up bodice, suitable for her previous rural life but obviously not for the English court.

She was further dazed by the number of gentlemen and ladies passing in both directions, some flamboyant in court finery and some in priestly garb or their dark robes of office. The ladies stared at Marian, now acutely embarrassed by her appearance. Most bobbed a curtsey while the men acknowledged Lady Jane Seymour by murmuring her name and giving a nod of the head, though some were too preoccupied to do either.

The couple halted outside a stout wooden door guarded by two of the King's young men-at-arms who stood, feet apart, gripping long, ceremonial battle-axes in front of them. They stood to attention as Marian and her lady approached then one of them raised the latch and opened the door, allowing the women entry.

Marian was immediately conscious of peals of light laughter and saw across the panelled room, seated before a large window, six of the most beautiful ladies wearing the most splendid gowns she had ever seen – apart from her majesty's – most of them black velvet trimmed with gold braid and lace, with adornments of gold crosses and pendants.

Engrossed in sharing confidences, at first they were unaware of the approach of the newcomers. However, as the pair drew nearer, one of the ladies, her gown cut low across her breast, revealing olive skin, laid aside her embroidery hoop and stood.

"And who have we here, cousin Jane?"

"May I present Lady Marian de Booys? Marian, this is Lady Anne Boleyn."

Marian bobbed a curtsey, remembering the Queen's critical comment and hoping she didn't look as awkward as she felt.

"Anne, may I have a word with you?" Lady Jane asked confidentially.

The two young women drew to one side, their heads close together. Marian, left on her own, caught snatches of their whispered conversation and the words, "Am I a nursemaid now?" Acutely embarrassed, she studied the speaker.

Lady Anne was of slender build, medium height, with hair that was dark brown, almost black. Noticing Marian watching them, she turned her back before continuing the conversation.

The other ladies had ceased their activities, needles becoming idle and a game of chess abandoned.

"Oh well, if his majesty wishes it –"

"It was the King who suggested –"

Lady Anne moved towards Marian, her dark eyes reflecting her wide smile.

"So, little Marian, it seems that her majesty wishes me to take you in hand and make a lady of you. Looking at you, i'faith, I'm sure I don't know where to begin. However, you have a pretty face, Marian, and that's a start and I enjoy a challenge. By the time I've finished with you, we shall have all the young men of the court at your feet – and not only the young ones, I daresay."

She crossed to a small table on which stood a handbell and shook it so that it pealed with a light tinkle. Marian wondered who was being summoned.

"Come and meet some of her majesty's ladies-in-waiting."

There were sufficient chairs for the three newcomers to join the circle. Marian was discomforted to find herself the centre of attention as the young women introduced themselves.

Lady Joan Dereham, her brows drawn together in a disapproving frown, asked, "So, tell us why their majesties have afforded you this special honour."

Shyly, but gaining confidence when her audience appeared genuinely interested, Marian told them about her happy childhood in a small manor house in Hampshire with her parents and two brothers, but how her mother and a longed-for baby sister had died during the birth pangs, and how her brothers and then her father had succumbed to the pox.

On his deathbed, her father had beseeched his oldest friend, Sir William Forrester, to take her into his home and bring her up as his own daughter. He had said he would die in peace if he knew that one day she would be married to Sir William's heir, Philip, and become Mistress of Forrester Hall and so be provided for during the remainder of her life.

At this point, they were interrupted by a young waiting girl who had answered the bell.

"You rang for me, my lady?" she asked of the assembled ladies, not knowing which one she should address. Lady Anne stood and indicated that Marian should do the same.

"Kate, we have a guest – Lady Marian de Booys." The girl bobbed a curtsey. "First we must feed her so instruct cook to serve our meal in an hour's time. Then ask the housekeeper on duty to set aside a bed chamber that is not being used and to light a fire in there to ward off the autumn chills. She should order the preparation of a fragrant and hot bath with towels and castill soap. Then send for the dressmaker to measure Lady Marian for gowns that befit the station she is about to occupy. Until her gowns are made, she will require a cast-off or two. She is not very tall, as you see, and they may need shortening. You will remember my instructions?"

"Yes, my Lady."

The girl dropped a deep curtsey and left the room. Lady Jane Seymour said she must report back to the Queen and also left.

For the next hour, the ladies questioned Marian about the life she had led at Forrester Hall and the personage of Sir Philip, her future husband.

"Is he as handsome as his father?"

Marian could not understand why some of the ladies exchanged mischievous glances when they mentioned her guardian's name. She had never thought of her step father as handsome, though the ladies obviously thought that he was.

"Describe him to us."

As they resumed their embroidery, Marian replied that Philip was blond with blue eyes, and a straight nose, and wide mouth and, yes, he was very handsome. She had noticed that the servant girls and young women from the village followed him with their eyes whenever the family went to church or visited their neighbours in the county, or rode out to the farms, taking victuals to the poorer tenants.

"But he has eyes only for you, Marian?"

"I can't say that, exactly," Marian admitted with honesty. "Sometimes his eyes stray if the girl is specially pretty. Then Sir William is very sharp with him, if he notices. But I know 'tis of little consequence. We will be married in two years' time and then he won't look at any of the other girls."

She noticed the ladies exchanging glances again.

"Marriage is for always, isn't it?" she asked them.

"Of course," Lady Anne assured her.

"And you're in love with your Philip, are you, Marian?" asked Mary Boleyn, Anne's elder sister.

“I love him as a brother,” she answered, “and I am sure I will love him as a husband when the time comes. It was my father’s wish and I would not disobey him.”

At the end of an hour, a servant came to summon them to their meal and they took Marian with them through a door into a room decorated with light linenfold panelling with tall windows that looked out over gardens stretching down to the River Thames. A long trestle table had been laid with a variety of dishes, some of which Marian had never seen before.

She was invited to sit next to Lady Anne and copied the manners of the company, waiting until a servant had shaken out a linen table napkin and had placed it over her shoulder before choosing which dishes to accept.

The ladies described the meal as ‘light’ but Marian thought it would feed her for a week at home. She was offered sliced venison, mutton, badger and other meats, various fish fresh from the river, and fine white bread, all washed down with ale. There followed apples, pears and plums from the palace orchards.

When she had eaten her fill, Lady Anne made her comfortable on a couch, surrounded her with cushions and lay a light coverlet over her, suggesting she should have a rest before her bath.

Marian insisted she wasn’t tired but the next she knew she was being shaken awake to be informed that her bath was ready.

After another walk along galleries and corridors and up a flight of stairs, they reached the bed chamber that would be hers for the next two years.

A circular tub, draped with sheets to protect her bare skin from the rough wooden sides, had been placed in front of a marble fireplace. Servants were heating water in large iron kettles hung from a chimney crane over the blazing fire, then filling the tub.

On a wooden plank across the bath were laid a scrubbing brush, pumice stone, a bar of white soap, a washing cloth and a phial of scented oil.

Two of them helped her undress, throwing her clothes onto a wooden chest that stood at the end of a large four-poster bed, and tied up her long and unruly fair hair. They held her hand as she stepped into the tub and slid down into the fragrant water. For a while she lay there, indulging the pleasurable sensation of warm water on bare skin, filling her lungs with the relaxing aroma of garden herbs. Lady Anne was kneeling by the tub, one arm resting on the edge, leaning over to dangle the fingers of her other hand in the water and swishing them backwards and forwards.

“When did you last have a bath, Marian?”

Marian had to think about that and finally answered, "It must be about a year ago."

While the young attendants rubbed her all over with the castill soap and she stood and sat as requested, Lady Anne asked what she thought of the King.

"He looks like a king," Marian answered. She had been more impressed with the Queen than her husband.

"Handsome, isn't he?"

"Mmm, yes, but he's rather old."

Lady Anne laughed delightedly.

"He's thirty-three."

"That's old," Marian said decisively and was playfully splashed all over by her new friend. She giggled and was about to splash back but decided against it when she considered the black velvet gown the lady was wearing.

Anne now rested both arms on the edge of the tub and lay her chin on them. Her expression became more serious and a pale pink flush began to spread over both cheeks.

"And what exactly did his majesty say when he suggested you should become my pupil?"

"He said that you were the most spirited of all the Queen's ladies and the responsibility might calm you down."

Marian had considered this a criticism but thought Lady Anne looked pleased with the answer. She next asked, "How did he sound? Was he serious, do you think, or just teasing the Queen?"

"He sounded as if he didn't mind that you had spirit."

"And what did her majesty say?"

"She said she would do as he suggested."

The attendants had moved away to fetch a large towel.

Anne whispered, "Little Marian, are you good at keeping secrets?"

"Oh, yes, my lady. Philip told me never to tell anyone when he chased me into the shrubbery and tried to put his hand up under my skirt, and I never have, until now."

Lady Anne sounded amused. "And did you let him?"

"Oh, no!"

"You will one day, when you are a little older. Do you think you could keep a secret of mine? It's a very big, grown-up secret and no one must know about it but you may be able to help me."

"Yes," Marian replied breathlessly, excited that this courtly lady was not only going to confide in her but wanted to enlist her help.

"Then I will tell you, but not today."

She stood as the attendants returned to help Marian out of the tub and envelop her in the towel.

"The seamstress has arrived, Marian. I will talk to her while they wash your hair."

Marian was asked to kneel on a footstool and lean over the tub so that her hair could be washed and rinsed with clean water before being rubbed as dry as it was possible to get it. She was taken across to a small table where Lady Anne and a little woman with a bird-like face were seated, deep in conversation.

"Ah, Marian, come and meet someone who can work miracles. Mistress Fettiplace, this is Lady Marian de Booys."

The little woman bobbed a curtsey then studied the girl with interest, reaching out and running her fingers through Marian's still wet hair.

"One gown in green, I think, to complement your hair and match those green eyes, and the second in bronze. Now the young ladies will dress you in these undergarments and I will measure you."

First to go on was a white loose-fitting shift, then woollen stockings that reached just above her knees and were kept in place with ribbon garters. Her corset was stiffened with whale bone.

"Now I measure you," said the seamstress, her movements quick and precise.

When all was measured to her satisfaction, she beckoned to a young girl in attendance, who slipped a farthingale over Marian's head. Marian wriggled and laughed as the three parallel rows of bent willow, designed to give her skirt its shape, swayed around her. The seamstress lifted the lid off a box and held up a gown in pale blue. As instructed, Marian raised her arms above her head and the dress was soon in place.

"It needs taking up two inches. I will stitch it now. Onto the table with you, my dear, and it will be finished in a flash."

Marian was helped from foot stool to the table top and rotated slowly as the seamstress with her needle raised the hem. Then she was helped down.

"I have a second gown here for you to wear until the new ones are finished. I will take it away with me as it will also need shortening by an inch or two."

So saying, the little lady packed up her box and bags and left the room.

For the remainder of the day, Lady Anne made sure that Marian was kept well occupied. She was introduced to other ladies-in-waiting as they came and went between their duties for the Queen; she made friends with the Queen's two black spaniel puppies who could only be told apart by their velvet and kid collars, one pink and one blue; and she was allowed to fill small containers with seed for the singing birds in their cages. Then Lady Anne found her a piece of material held in a wooden hoop and some fine silks to demonstrate her embroidery skills, which were pronounced far from satisfactory.

"You cannot be allowed to embroider linen for your trousseau with stitches as ugly as those," Lady Anne told her decisively.

After a supper of bread and cheese and ale, Marian was glad when her bedtime was declared. Lady Anne went with her to her chamber where two young personal maids helped her undress and don a white linen bed gown.

"Are you tired, Marian? You should be. You've had a busy day."

"Yes, my lady." Marian climbed into the high bed, glad to snuggle down between the sheets, and wondered how far away in this huge palace were Philip and Sir William. Shyly, she asked that the bed curtains should not be closed around her as she wished to see the candles suspended from the ceiling in their circular metal fitting and the comforting light from the fire as it burned low.

"Tomorrow will be just as busy, as you are to have a lesson with the dancing master – and I hope he will teach you how to curtsey, which will please her majesty next time she honours you with an audience."

"I love to dance," murmured Marian and was asleep almost before Lady Anne and the maids had left the room.

# CHAPTER 3

The dancing master threw the door open in response to their knock, beamed jovially and invited them into the long gallery with its highly polished floor, tall windows and mirrors at intervals around the panelled walls.

Not much taller than Marian, he reached only to Lady Anne's shoulder. He was very slender and wore a black doublet with long sleeves and full puffed trunks; beneath them his stick-like legs were encased in black silken hose. His dancing shoes had pointed toes, unlike the square-toed shoes of most of the gentlemen at court, and they were decorated on the insteps with gold buckles. As he skipped back into the room, waving his arms about, directing them to follow him, Marian thought he resembled a busy black beetle.

"Ladies, ladies, *bon jour*," he squeaked at them, "good morning, good morning, good morning. What a splendid morning!"

"Good morning, monsieur," Lady Anne greeted him.

"So, my lady, you have brought me a new pupil. What is your name, new pupil?"

"Marian, sir," replied Marian, trying not to laugh and looking across to Anne, who shook her head in reproval as he danced away from them, his back turned.

"Lady Marian de Booys," Anne told him, "but you may call her Marian."

He pirouetted round to face them. "And I am Monsieur. So, what would you have me teach you, Marian?"

"To curtsey, please, sir – monsieur."

"Her majesty has requested it," Lady Anne explained.

"Then you shall learn to curtsey as no one has ever curtsied to her majesty before! No one. We will have you curtseying to the envy of the whole court."

Lady Anne moved across to a chair and sat to watch, leaving the new pupil stranded in the centre of the room. Marian looked across at her beseechingly.

"Just follow the dancing master," Anne said. "He's the best in all England."

The little man stood in front of his pupil, facing her. "Stand up straight, arms by your sides, head up, shoulders down, feet slightly apart," he instructed her. When she was standing quite still and poised to his satisfaction, he continued, "First we warm our muscles and loosen our joints or dancing –" and he executed an intricate ballet movement, "– dancing, *c'est impossible*".

Then he took Marian through a series of exercises, instructing her to roll her head in a circle, hunch and relax her shoulders, clench and unclench her fists, bend from the waist, which she found difficult in her corset, bend then straighten her knees several times, and finally rotate each ankle in turn in both directions.

"That is good. Do you feel stretched now, *ma petite*?"

Marian had to admit that she did.

"Now, Lady Marian, stand up straight again, straighter, look up! Chin up! Delicately take hold of your gown on each side, curving your arms, so! Display your gown, yes, yes, display yourself, let us see our beautiful Marian, yes, yes, that is good. *Maintenant, faites glisser votre pied*, so! Your right foot, slide it round in front of you then stand on it, firmly; it becomes your rock."

Marian did so and wobbled.

"Again, Marian, again," he instructed her and at the fourth attempt she managed to stand firmly on her right foot.

"Now place your left foot behind the right, like so – anchor the ball of the foot firmly to the floor and bend both knees. No, no, no. Again, Marian, again."

Five minutes later, he was pleased with her. "With practice, you will curtsey lower – lower than most of the ladies of the court because you are so young. Now bend your neck and look down at the floor, honouring her majesty, respecting her position as sovereign lady Queen of England, wife of our illustrious and beloved King, but then, Marian, then –" He paused theatrically. "Then you will look up! You are an obedient servant but you are also a young woman with your own thoughts and ideas, so reveal your soul to the Queen in your eyes and in your smile, your bright smile. So!"

He illustrated by grinning beatifically and in that moment Marian warmed to this eccentric little man who wanted her to make her own way at court.

Lady Anne clapped her hands in delight.

"I'faith, Marian, you will undoubtedly win the heart of her majesty!"

"But you must practise, practise, practise," her tutor said, "every day until it becomes second nature."

"I will bring her to you every morning," Lady Anne promised, "until you decide there is no further need."

He nodded. "*C'est bon!* Now to the first dance you must learn – the *Pas Quatre*. Its first movement has only four steps. It is danced with a partner round the perimeter of the hall. Place your left arm on my right arm, thus. Now right foot point forward, point behind, step forward and close left foot to right foot. Repeat with the left foot, then twice more and for the fourth time use the last two steps to turn round to face the other way. *Voici, mademoiselle*."

By the end of an hour, Marian had mastered both movements of the new dance.

"What will you teach her tomorrow, monsieur?" Lady Anne asked.

"There are many dances she must learn," the dancing master observed. "The *Pavane,* the *Galliard*, but not the *Volta*. Definitely not the *Volta*. We shall see. But it is not good that she dances alone. She needs a partner, my Lady."

"Do you think your betrothed, Sir Philip Forrester, would partner you, Marian?"

"He could be asked. He may accept."

"And mayhap another couple, my Lady, to keep them company? Are there two other young people you could suggest?"

"I will give it some thought and ask the other ladies," Anne said. "Now we must leave, Marian."

She bobbed a curtsey to the dancing master, who acknowledged her with a courtly bow, bending low over his forward-stretched right leg and sweeping his right arm across it almost to the floor.

"Now, Marian, if it please you, your curtsey, as I showed you."

Marian became very serious and offered him a curtsey as she had been taught, bowing her head towards the floor in deep respect then lifting it and giving him a radiant smile that was reflected in her green eyes.

"You have quite won my heart, *mademoiselle*," he said, "and I am very much looking forward to tomorrow's lesson."

# CHAPTER 4

When Lady Anne came to waken her, having insisted that she should rest for an hour after their mid-day meal, Marian was conscious that her lady looked different. Her flushed cheeks and shining eyes animated her face and rendered her quite pretty, and Marian caught some of the nervous excitement that was fluttering her lady's delicate fingers around her throat and over her breast.

"Marian –" She paused to regulate her breathing and started again. "Marian, I thought you might like to walk with me in the knot garden."

"Yes, my lady."

"The fresh air will do us both good."

It was a fine day and the sunlight glinted off the water in the ornamental pond, which was churning and splashing beneath the fall of water from the fountain basin above. Lady Anne seemed preoccupied so Marian stayed silent.

As they trod the gravel paths between the maze of low-cut hedges, she delighted in the aroma of lavender, mint and marjoram and the vibrant colours of poppies, wallflowers and sweet william in the flower beds.

"I want to show you something," Lady Anne said, "in the far corner of the garden."

"By the crooked tree?"

"Exactly so."

They slowly made their way over to the tree. Its roots were a tangled mass above ground and the gnarled trunk was twisted and contorted.

"It's a yew tree," Lady Anne explained, "and very old – much older than the palace and the garden."

"Is it a magic tree?" Marian asked, looking up into the dark green covering of needle-leaves, hoping not to see a pair of yellow eyes malevolently staring back at her.

"It's a very magic tree," Lady Anne confirmed, "and a very secret tree. See here, Marian, there is a cavity where the trunk squirms, large enough for your fingers. Give me your hand and let me guide it round the trunk just here – can you feel it?" Marian nodded. "Put your hand inside."

Marian did so and exclaimed, "There's something there!"

"What is it? Pull it out and let's have a look."

Marian took hold of the object and was surprised to discover a brown leather pouch in her hand.

"Open it, Marian. Let's see what you've found."

Marian excitedly pulled at the drawstring and opened the mouth of the pouch, reached her hand inside, and brought out three flat discs of marchpane covered in gold leaf.

"Two are for you and one is for me," said Lady Anne. "I put them there myself."

"Thank you so much," Marian managed to say as the sweet almond paste and gold leaf dissolved in her mouth. Anne, who was chewing, said, "No one else knows about the cavity and you must not tell a soul."

"Oh, I won't," Marian promised. "Is this your special secret?"

"It's part of it. Now we must return as Mistress Fettiplace is coming for a fitting of your new gown."

Instead of the rich green material that Marian had been promised, the gown slipped over her head was of plain white cotton.

The seamstress laughed to see her disappointment.

"It's a pattern," she said with her head on one side, "before I cut the green taffeta. Then I will have your measurements for all time – I am sure this will be the first of many gowns for you. Now stand quite still while I adjust the waist a little and put in a tuck here – and here."

When she had completed her tucking and pinning, Lady Anne asked, "Mistress Fettiplace, do you know of any young people at court who might make dancing partners for Lady Marian?"

The little lady stood, her forehead puckering, her fingers twitching as if already pleating and sewing, then her face brightened.

"Yes, I do. Lady Dereham's young sister, Alice, has recently come to court, and there is a personable young man who is scribing for Lord Bathampton, Richard Mordaunt by name. I believe both are slightly older than Lady Marian."

"Thank you. I will make enquiries. There you are, Marian, two friends for you already. If their majesties are agreeable, the young couple as well as Sir Philip will join us tomorrow morning for your next dancing lesson."

# CHAPTER 5

When they entered the gallery on the following morning, they found the dancing master talking to a young lady. He crossed the floor to welcome them with a delighted smile and bowed low.

"Lady Anne, and *ma petite*, what a pleasure to see you again. May I introduce Lady Alice Dereham, who has come to dance with you, Marian?"

Marian crossed towards the young lady and they curtseyed to each other.

"I'm very pleased to meet you, Lady Alice," she said. "I hope we can be friends."

"That would please me, Lady Marian."

"Please call me Marian."

"And you shall call me Alice."

Marian smiled. The girl standing in front of her appeared older by about two years. Her appearance was quite remarkable by reason of her red-gold hair, several locks of which were escaping from beneath her coif, which was set well forward, probably in an attempt to contain them.

The hood of the coif matched her gown, a cheerful bright red. Marian hoped her own new green gown, when it was ready, would make her feel less dowdy than she felt in her borrowed blue.

To Marian, though, the girl's greeting was less than friendly. The look in her dark blue eyes was almost hostile and her thin lips were set in a tight line that did not readily relax into a smile. Marian wondered whether she had come to the dancing class voluntarily or had been sent by her older sister, whom Marian had already met. That lady, too, was not the friendliest of the ladies-in-waiting, seeming to resent Marian's privileged status.

Suddenly, though, a change came over the girl's face. Lines that had crossed her forehead disappeared, the look in her eyes softened and her lips broke into a warm smile as self-consciously she ran her fingers over her kirtle to smooth the red brocade. Marian turned and saw that Philip had just come through the door.

"Philip!" she exclaimed and crossed to him, kissing his cheek. "I'm so happy to see you!"

"As I am to see you, Marian. So this is where you've been hiding."

"Philip, come and meet Lady Anne Boleyn, my new friend," she said, taking his hand and drawing him across the room to where Lady Anne now sat. He bowed low.

"You tell the truth – he is quite as handsome as his father," Anne said, clapping her hands together as she appraised him from head to toe. "Truly, Marian, you are a lucky girl, and so are you, Sir Philip, if I may say so."

"I know it," he replied and smiled at Marian, who felt her heart swell with pride at his handsome looks and her good fortune.

"Philip, come and meet Monsieur, our dancing master – Lady Anne says he's the best in all England – and this is Lady Alice Dereham. Alice, may I introduce you to Sir Philip Forrester – you may know his father and my guardian, Sir William. Philip and I are betrothed to be married."

For an instant, in a reaction so subtle that Marian almost missed it, the girl's eyes darkened into pools of deep indigo, but then they lightened again and Marian wondered whether she had been mistaken.

"Betrothed? Are you, indeed? Then Lady Anne is right, you are a lucky young woman."

Unaware of any undercurrents, if undercurrents there were, Monsieur complained, "We await our fourth dancer – and here he comes, master Richard Mordaunt, if I am not mistaken."

"You are not mistaken, sir, I am Richard Mordaunt," acquiesced the young man who was standing in the doorway.

"Then you are also welcome."

While all the introductions were being made, Marian had opportunity to appraise the newcomer and liked what she saw – a dark-haired, serious young man, a few years her senior, dressed, as she would expect, in the black doublet and hose of a scribe on the staff of privy councillor Lord Bathampton. A black feather fluttered as he doffed his hat and bowed to the assembled company. He then laid hat and cloak on a chair before pronouncing himself ready to proceed – "Though I profess that I will prove a very inept pupil," he added.

*An exceedingly handsome young man, though modest*, was Marian's estimation of him and she turned her head, wondering if Alice agreed, but Alice was still staring at Philip. However, he seemed unaware of her appreciative interest and took Marian's hand again, leading her to the spot indicated by Monsieur.

"Now, Richard, please bring Lady Alice to stand behind them, just so, and I will teach you the *Pas Quatre*, which little Marian learned yesterday. Tomorrow, we will have musicians, today I count."

The lesson proceeded with a deal of mistakes and much laughter, but by the end of an hour, all four were dancing without error, if not as gracefully as Monsieur would have liked.

"Splendid! Splendid!" he exclaimed. "Tomorrow, the *Pavane*, which you will soon master, though the *Galliard* is another matter. Till tomorrow then, *mes enfants*."

"Monsieur," said Richard as he retrieved his cloak and hat, "my master wishes me to ask how many days I will be cavorting here – he calls it 'cavorting' – which is preventing me from attending on him."

"You may tell Lord Bathampton," the little man replied, "that his majesty is holding a masque a week today – is that not so, Lady Anne?" She nodded. "I will have you all ready to partake in the most popular of the dances by then, after which you will no longer need my daily tuition."

"A week, then?"

Lady Anne interrupted them. "I very much regret, Richard –"

"I understand, my Lady. I am aware that I will not be allowed to dance at the masque. That's all right. I will probably need the extra time, anyway, to catch up on my work."

"If it is of any consolation," said Monsieur, "neither shall I be allowed to take part but I shall be watching from the gallery."

Alice pouted and complained, "If Richard is not there, Monsieur, I shall need another partner."

For the first time that Marian noticed, Philip looked directly at the red-headed girl.

"I doubt you will be in want of partners, Lady Alice," he said.

# CHAPTER 6

"Sir Philip," said Lady Anne when they had left the gallery, "will you walk with Marian and me in the knot garden this afternoon, if you have no other duties?"

"I have none that will suffer by delaying for an hour or so. Thank you, that would give me great pleasure," he said.

A few hours later found the three of them traversing the gravel paths and enjoying the beauty of the afternoon.

Philip was at his most charming and was explaining to Lady Anne the plans he had for the Forrester estate and manor, once he was partnering his father in its management, and she was listening to him with great interest.

Marian felt so proud of Philip. Today he was dressed in a deep blue doublet with sleeves slashed, showing his white shirt beneath, his matching cloak casually thrown back across one shoulder beneath a hat decorated with a jaunty white feather. She looked forward to the day they would be wed and she would spend her days under his care and protection.

"Just listen to him, Marian. He has such plans!"

"Marian has heard it all before," Philip smiled. "She has no need to concern herself with such matters."

"But I want to concern myself with such matters if they are important to you and your tenant farmers, Philip. I know that, if the estate increases the size of its flocks and turns more land over to grazing, as you have just described, those who have had their strips of land taken from them will not be able to feed their families."

"It's wool that brings in the money, Marian, and it will feed and clothe you in the manner you have come to expect. As my wife, you need have no worries about how the estate is managed."

"And your father – ?"

"My father belongs to the last generation. I shall persuade him to gradually hand over the management of the estate to me."

"It's too lovely a day for you two to be out of countenance," Anne complained. "And look, here comes Lady Alice to improve our humours. I hoped she would join us."

Philip's frown cleared immediately as he turned to greet the newcomer but Marian's greeting was less gracious. She was irritated at the way he always dismissed her opinion when she offered any ideas of her own.

Lady Anne was gradually leading them towards the old yew tree and it was not long before she interrupted their chatter to draw their attention to its age and twisted appearance.

Lady Alice decided she would like to draw it. “I will ask my drawing master if I may do so,” she said. Lady Anne agreed that was a splendid idea and asked to see the drawing when finished.

Marian opened her mouth to tell them about the cavity in the trunk but then remembered her promise. She longed to prove to Philip that someone was treating her like an adult and to show Alice that she was Lady Anne Boleyn’s confidante, but revealing the secret would only prove that she wasn’t an adult and couldn’t be trusted. So she shut her mouth tightly and bit on her lower lip to prevent the words from slipping out of her mouth.

When they turned away from the tree to walk back, she looked at Lady Anne, who surprised her by smiling and winking at her, and suddenly realised that she had been put to the test and had passed it. So that was the reason the three of them had been invited to walk in the garden. She nearly laughed out loud and did not mind that Philip and Alice walked side by side in front of them and were deep in conversation.

That evening, Lady Jane Seymour spent an hour patiently teaching her how to play chess.

“The aim of the game is to try to checkmate your opponent’s king.”

“Checkmate?” asked Marian.

“Try to stop him escaping,” Lady Jane explained.

By the end of the hour, Marian was yawning.

“Marian, dear, you are not in checkmate even if your king is,” Lady Anne joked. “You can escape to bed at any time. Jane, she must be up early in the morning for her next dancing lesson.”

“Then bed it is, Marian. We shall continue the instruction another time.”

Marian hadn’t realised how tired she felt and was glad to take the advice of the ladies and prepare for bed. When she was comfortably settled beneath the sheets, Lady Anne came into the room and sat on the edge of the bed, stroking the long fair hair which overlaid the coverlet.

“Marian, I believe that now I can let you into my very special secret.”

“I can keep secrets,” Marian said.

“I know you can. I have seen you can. So I will tell you.”

She waited until the last maid had exited the room, bearing a chamber pot, then whispered, “You see, I have a friend, a very special friend, but we cannot be seen together –”

“Why not?”

"I cannot tell you why because that could put you in a very difficult situation and I do not want for you to be in any way complicit. So you must not ask me or try to find out. I leave messages for… my friend… and my friend leaves messages for me."

Marian sat up.

"In the hole in the yew tree?"

"Exactly so. The messages will be left in a pouch –"

"Like the one you left with the confectionery?"

"Yes, just like that. So, if I sometimes give you a leather pouch, will you leave it in the tree for me, when no one is about?"

"Yes, of course. That will be very exciting. And she will leave messages for you?"

Lady Anne hesitated before replying. "Yes, she will."

"You can trust me," Marian said, snuggling down again. "I won't let you down and I won't breathe a word to a soul."

"To no one, Marian – do you understand? Not to Philip or Alice or any of the Queen's ladies – no one."

"No one," Marian promised.

"You're a good girl, little Marian," Lady Anne said and kissed her on her head. "I will see you in the gallery in the morning."

# CHAPTER 7

Marian could not contain her excitement on the morning of the royal masque and was chattering so inconsequentially and so loudly that one of the ladies-in-waiting asked her to calm down and concentrate on the sampler she was stitching – with greater effort than skill, it has to be said.

Lady Anne had described all that was to happen. The evening would begin with supper in the long dining room then the company would retire to the great hall for the entertainment, after which there would be dancing until the early hours of the morning. Everyone would be masked so that no one knew who anybody was. Then Lady Anne had laughed and said that, i'faith, everybody knew who everybody was, though there were some delightful surprises on occasions.

At some time during the evening, Marian would be presented to their majesties, when she would have the opportunity to demonstrate her very special curtsey.

As the hours dragged by, Marian became more and more nervous, surrounded as she was by the chatter and laughter of the Queen's ladies. She caught snatches of their conversation, much of it about the young men of the court, some of which made her blush. Marian knew that she would be partnered by Philip and mayhap by his father, but Lady Anne told her that she should accept any invitation to dance, especially now that she had learned the steps.

Her new gowns had been delivered several days before but she had not worn either of them, not having made up her mind which she would wear to the masque.

"You must rest this afternoon," Lady Anne told her, "so that you look your loveliest this evening, and don't eat anything all day so that you can do justice to the feast."

Marian nodded enthusiastically.

"But first I have an errand for you, Marian. I desire that you visit the yew tree – do you understand?"

Marian nodded again and Lady Anne handed her the brown leather pouch.

"Be sure no one sees you. Report to me on your return."

Marian decided to commence her walk in the rose garden and spent some time among the many coloured and delicately-scented flowers before passing into the knot garden.

There were few people out in the grounds this afternoon as many were preparing for the evening by resting. She knew that the ladies-in-waiting were spending time with their tweezers and their maids were mixing and pounding egg whites, vinegar, talcum powder, lead, vermilion and other ingredients to paint their faces and lighten their hair.

"You have no need yet, Marian, to whiten your face or flush your cheeks and lips or lighten your hair. You are perfect just as you are," Lady Jane Seymour had told her. "There will be time enough to learn how to make all those ointments once the wrinkles and blemishes start to appear."

Marian walked a circuit of the knot garden, to make sure she was quite alone, before approaching the yew tree for the second time. Reaching her hand round the gnarled trunk to find the cavity, she pushed the pouch into the hole then walked away without giving any impression of haste.

She felt very honoured that her lady had trusted her with this errand and wondered what she had written to her friend and why they could not meet in public. On her return, she found Lady Anne and reported that all had been accomplished as requested.

After lengthy deliberation with her own maid, Marian decided to wear the bronze gown for the masque. The square-necked kirtle and undersleeves were designed in a beautiful brocade shot through with gold thread, with an overgown of plain bronze satin. Her hood was of the rounded French style preferred by Lady Anne, beaded with gold. Her gold mask covered only her eyes.

"You are so young," Lady Anne said wistfully, "and so beautiful. The young men will not be able to take their eyes off you. Come, let us proceed to the ante-room and find your Philip so that he can escort you to your place at table."

The conversation and laughter in the ante-room was quite deafening until King Henry and Queen Katharine with their entourage, all suitably masked, made their regal entrance. The assembled company fell back to make a pathway for them, bowing and curtseying as they passed, acknowledging their smiles and gracious comments. The royal party walked through into the dining room and the company began to follow.

After Marian had found Philip and his father, Lady Anne left to join her sister. It was the first time that Marian had seen her guardian since their arrival at court and she would have flung her arms round his neck if it had not been for the august company around them.

"Is it really you, Marian?" asked Sir William with obvious pleasure. "But how you've grown up since we last met. I would not have thought it possible if I hadn't seen you with my own eyes."

"You look ravishing," Philip added. "Will you take my arm, my lady, and allow me to escort you to our places at table?"

"Gladly, Sir Philip," Marian laughed and laid her hand on the cream sleeve of his doublet. Sir William was partnered by Lady Agnes Mortimer, an elderly woman, one-time lady-in-waiting to the King's mother, Queen Elizabeth of York.

The King and Queen sat at the high table with their various ministers and attendants. Lady Anne, dressed this evening in royal blue and silver with silver mask, was seated next to her sister, near the Queen. The remainder of the company sat at three tables that ran at right angles along the length of the room.

Marian once again gazed at the splendour around her. Heavy damson damask curtains beneath draped pelmets were drawn across the windows. The pewter displayed on the side boards round the room and the portraits above the huge, vibrant tapestries glowed in the light of the roaring fire in the huge fireplace.

Above them, cut glass chandeliers hung from high wooden, painted beams and along each side of the ceiling flags of St. George, their red crosses centred on white backgrounds, wafted gently in the rising heat from fire and candles.

Displayed at intervals along the length of the tables were replicas of castles and mansions of marchpane, meringue and other sweetmeats, with candles concealed in their interiors so that light flickered through the tiny windows. The candles had to be doused during the meal as they began to melt or burn the walls, emitting sufficient smoke to cause those sitting nearby to cough and choke.

Marian turned her attention to the lords and ladies in their fine clothes, displaying a riot of colour. Among them was Alice, dressed in red, as she usually was, and masked but unable to hide her flaming hair. Beside her was Lady Joan Dereham, her sister, of similar complexion but with hair colouring that appeared faded in comparison, and altogether less flamboyant.

Lady Anne had tried to describe the feast to come but Marian was not prepared for the procession of meat dishes that followed the boars' heads with apples in their mouths and the platters bearing all manner of delicacies.

"Select only a little portion of whatever takes your fancy," Lady Anne had said and she was glad to follow this advice, choosing morsels of familiar beef, mutton, pork and veal but then daring to select pieces of swan, peacock, crane, stork and gulls and unfamiliar fish varieties such as eel, sturgeon and lobster as well as small salmon pasties. Silently, she thanked Lady Anne for having shown her how to use the silver knives and spoons provided.

To follow there were three courses of jellies, candied fruit and pastries, all washed down with fruit juice, wine and ale in silver tankards.

Marian had just decided that she would not need to eat anything more for a whole week when chairs were scraped back and the company rose to listen to a loyal address read from an illuminated scroll by one of the King's privy councillors, who Philip whispered was his mentor, Lord Bathampton. The company then raised their drinking vessels to toast their majesties before following them through to the great hall.

By now, she was beginning to relax as Philip led her to a chair then stood behind her to enjoy the entertainment.

All the hired players wore colourful, elaborate costumes and masks. There was a team of acrobats and tumblers, and a jester in red and yellow with curly-toed shoes and a horned headdress adorned with bells. A small company of actors presented a short play in which one wore a donkey's head, and musicians delighted the company by entertaining on hurdy gurdy, drums, stringed instruments, recorders and crumhorns.

As the entertainers finally bowed, their majesties led their guests in a standing ovation, and then it was time for the dancing. The animated conversation quietened as the orchestra introduced the overture to the *Pavane* and his majesty, resplendent in gold, led his Queen onto the floor, bowed to her in a most chivalrous manner, received her révérence, then stood regally as other courtiers and their ladies gathered in place behind them. Philip brought Marian to join the dancers.

When all were ready, there began the stately and processional *Pavane*, the steps slow and measured, the company turning to face all four directions and sometimes moving backwards, following his majesty's lead.

Marian noticed Alice, who had found a partner in spite of her voiced fears of not doing so. She was radiant, her cheeks flushed with excitement and wine and the pleasure of dancing with a handsome young man. Marian guessed her own hot cheeks were similarly glowing.

There followed the *Pas Quatre* and again Philip asked Marian to dance with him. She was pleased to do so as he was a considerate and gentlemanly partner.

During the pause after the dance had ended, the King led the Queen back to their throne-like chairs and they sat to watch the proceedings. Philip also led Marian back to where they had been sitting with Sir William and Lady Agnes Mortimer, the elderly lady he had partnered for supper. She had said she was too old to be dancing and was content to sit and watch.

"Marian," Philip said, "I wish now to partner Lady Alice. Please excuse me." And he was gone, abandoning her.

"Marian, my dear," said Sir William, standing before her and bowing, "if my son has relinquished the privilege of taking you into the next dance, then please allow me."

"Thank you, Sir William," acquiesced Marian, glad of his offer and taking his arm.

"But, before we dance, I think we have a pleasant duty to perform. We must let her majesty see how well you have learned to curtsey. Lady Anne has been fulsome in her praise of your accomplishment."

Marian was not so sure, now that the time had come, that she wished to draw the Queen's attention to her curtsey. Mayhap she would topple over!

"Courage, Marian," Sir William said, smiling at her reluctance. "All will be well, you'll see."

He led her across the floor and approached their majesties.

"Courage, Marian," he said again then brought her to face the Queen and bowed.

"Your Majesty, may I again present to you my ward, Lady Marian de Booys. You may remember that you graciously placed her in the care of Lady Anne Boleyn, who has been most kind and is teaching her the manners of your majesties' court."

"I remember, Sir Villiam," said the Queen.

"You also said that her révérence left much to be desired. She has taken your Majesty's criticism to heart and would like to show you the improvement. Marian –"

*Take hold of your skirt with both hands, slide your foot to the right, left foot behind right foot, no wobbling, bend low – lower – look down at the floor, then chin up and smile!*

As Marian rehearsed the words in her head, she carried out the actions. Her chin came up and she looked straight into the eyes of the Queen and gave her the most radiant smile, which was not difficult as she was very grateful to this gracious lady who had placed her in the care of Lady Anne.

The Queen was delighted. "That is indeed an improvement, Lady Marian, and quite the most deferential and beautiful curtsey I have ever received. Again, if you please."

Surprised, Marian repeated her curtsey.

The Queen turned to her husband. "Well, your Majesty, what do you think of that?"

"It is as you say, my love, quite the most beautiful curtsey we have ever received. And I suppose we have Lady Anne Boleyn to thank. Please excuse me, my dear."

He stood and signalled to the musicians, who began to play the tune for the *Sarabande*. No one moved as the King left the side of his Queen and moved down the hall to stand before Lady Anne Boleyn. He bowed and held out his arm to her. She placed her hand on his sleeve and he led her onto the floor. It was not until then that other gentlemen led their partners into position, ready to commence the dance.

"Lady Marian," said the Queen, seemingly unruffled, "ve shall name that curtsey after you, and I vant it taught to all my ladies – though I doubt they can reproduce that captivating smile of yours."

"Thank you, your Majesty. I – we –" Marian trailed off in confusion.

"We are very grateful to your Majesty." Sir William finished the sentence for her. "Now, with your permission –"

"Of course, take her onto the dance floor. As I said before, she is a credit to you, Sir Villiam."

As they moved in time to the music, Marian watched the King dancing with Lady Anne and thought he seemed much taken with her.

She looked for and found Philip and Alice and had the same thought, that Philip seemed much taken with Alice, and could not help a feeling of disquiet rising in her chest.

Although she was enjoying dancing with her guardian, she suddenly wished she was dancing with Richard. The wish surprised her. Then she realised that she had been thinking a lot about Richard lately.

"You are dancing very gracefully, Marian," Sir William complimented her. "The dancing master has taught you well."

Thinking about pleasing the dancing master made her remember that he was watching from the gallery above, and she looked up, and there he was, his head barely visible above the balcony rail, nodding in time to the beat of the music.

She was surprised to notice that he was not alone and that Richard was with him. When he saw her looking up, he waved.

She averted her eyes and tried to concentrate on the steps, disconcerted to feel her heart beats quickening and pounding against her chest.

"I spoke too soon," smiled Sir William. "That was the first mistake you've made. No, don't apologise, there's no need."

When the dance was over, they returned to their seats.

"Can you see Philip?" asked his father. Marian shook her head. Philip seemed to have disappeared and so had Alice. Sir William frowned.

"He won't be far away," Marian said lightly, glad of the opportunity this gave her. "Sir William, will you excuse me? The dancing master is up there in the gallery, watching the dancing. I would like to go up to him as he can't come down here, just to thank him for making possible such a very happy evening."

"Of course but don't be long or you'll miss the *Volta*."

"He doesn't approve of the *Volta* so wouldn't teach us the steps."

Sir William laughed. "I would be very surprised if he had. You're much too young. Look, everyone is standing to watch."

"Where are the steps up to the gallery, sire?"

"Over there in the far corner. Ah, here we go!"

As the musicians struck up a lively tune and everyone who had not stepped into the centre of the room to dance surged forward and closed ranks to watch, Marian pushed her way to the rear of the company and gained the staircase.

At the top of the stairs, she was met by the dancing master, who squeezed her hands in his then pumped them up and down in welcome.

"Marian, my dear little Marian, how gracious of you to come up to say *bon soir*. Are you enjoying the dancing?"

"Very much, monsieur, and thank you, because it is you who have made the evening so enjoyable for me."

"Then I am *très heureux*. But come and greet Richard – he's here with me."

"Yes, I saw him."

"Richard, look who has come to visit us."

As she crossed to greet her erstwhile dancing partner, she hoped they wouldn't notice how the heat from the candles and climbing the stairs were combining to make her quite breathless.

"I'm surprised to see you, Richard."

"I'm not supposed to be here but I had finished my work and managed to slip away without anyone noticing."

"I'm glad you did."

"How could I not come to watch you?"

Marian laughed. "So you recognised me, even though I am masked?"

"It was not difficult. I just had to look for the most beautiful girl in the hall."

Marian felt her cheeks burning.

"Monsieur, did you see me curtsey to the Queen?"

"It was a beautiful moment, Marian, a moment *par excellence*! I was so proud of my pupil."

"Her majesty says she wishes you to teach all her ladies to curtsey in that fashion."

The little man's eyes lit up and he smiled broadly. "Then I have a lifetime's work ahead of me – some of them are so – so – oh, the English word eludes me. They are not all as graceful as you, Lady Marian. But come, *mes enfants*, and watch the spectacle they make of themselves in the *Volta*, these foolish young people. They do not wish to dance, only to take hold of each other and make donkeys of themselves!"

The three of them moved across to the rail of the balcony and looked down. It was as the dancing master had described. The young courtiers had their hands on the waists of their ladies and were lifting them into the air, the ladies resting their hands on the young men's shoulders and jumping as high as they dared. There was much laughing and whooping and revealing of ladies' ankles and calves.

The dancing master snorted his disgust and walked away, saying he did not wish to see any more and he would return when it was all over and the gentlemen and ladies, if such they be, had regained their senses.

"Where's Philip?" Richard asked her.

"Over there."

From her viewpoint, she had just noticed him, standing at the back of the crowd. He was in animated conversation with Alice and had his arm round her waist.

"Does that not displease you, Marian?" Richard asked.

"Yes, it does," she answered, "but it is of no consequence, whatever Lady Alice might think. When he reaches eighteen, we will be married, which was the wish of both our fathers. Nothing will prevent that. Then he will settle down."

"If you were my betrothed, Marian, I would have no desire to look at anyone else. Does he not know how fortunate he is?"

"It seems not, Richard."

He opened his mouth as if to complain further about Philip's cavalier attitude towards her but shut it again and was silent. It was, after all, not his place to criticise those above his station but Marian was grateful that he had wished to do so.

The *Volta* had ended and the dancers were returning to their seats or leaving the room to find refreshment or the cool night air in the gardens.

The King had watched the *Volta* with great enjoyment, to judge by his hearty applause, and now led the Queen onto the floor to dance *His Majesty's Pleasure*. The melody had been composed by the King himself and the dancing master had created steps to fit the musical pattern. It was a slow and stately dance where, after every six bars, the men moved on to the next lady in the circle.

"Come, my pupils, let's dance to *His Majesty's Pleasure*," enthused the dancing master and took Marian's hand and led her into the figures. On the sixth bar, he guided her forward to dance with Richard.

Neither spoke or even looked at each other, suddenly shy after their last exchange. Richard passed her back to the dancing master, who was beaming with delight, and in turn handed her again to Richard.

"My lady Marian," he whispered, "There are words in my head – nay, in my heart – that should not be said –"

"Then best not to say them, Richard, or we may both be sorry."

What was she saying? He was gazing at her so intently. She desperately wanted to hear those words, though she knew she should not.

"The music has come to an end, *mes enfants*," the dancing master was saying from miles away. "Richard – Lady Marian –"

Richard was first to break the spell. "Yes, yes, of course." He released her hand and bowed.

She curtsied. "Thank you, Richard. Thank you, monsieur."

She moved across to the balcony rail and held onto it, steadying herself, surprised to feel tears welling in her eyes.

Below them, Philip had returned to his father and they seemed to be having a heated argument.

"I must go back as they will be wondering where I am," she said, turning away, and ran along the gallery and down the staircase, pausing at the bottom to take several deep breaths before joining her guardian and his son. Both looked as though the storm, whatever had caused it, had not passed and neither spoke except to welcome her back.

Philip now seemed in no mood for dancing but Marian was flattered to discover that a lot of young men wished to dance with her, and not only the young ones.

Among the older men was Lord Bathampton, the privy councillor who had read the illuminated address at the table. He was tall and of a solid build, with dark hair turning steely grey.

He spoke first to Philip but after only a moment abruptly turned away, leaving him in mid-sentence, and asked Sir William for permission to take his ward onto the floor to dance the *Almain*.

Sir William looked taken aback and, before he could reply, Marian had been swept in among the dancers. As the musicians began to play, her partner introduced himself and said he was scrivener to Cardinal Thomas Wolsey, Archbishop of York. He asked her name.

"Marian, my lord."

"A pretty name for a very pretty young lady," he said.

In spite of the compliment, Marian felt ill at ease in his company. His eyes, also steely grey and without warmth, rarely left her face throughout the dance and several times his fingers found their way onto her wrist and arm and once lightly brushed across her breast – so lightly it could have been accidental but she was sure it was not. She was glad when the dance was over and he brought her back to her seat. She thought that Sir William seemed glad to see her return.

As the evening wore on, the dances became more and more energetic, the rhythms increasing in speed. The men laid aside their swords and began trying to outdo each other with their hops and jumps and leaps. By now, very few masks were still in place.

"It's not dancing as I know it," complained Sir William.

Out of the corner of her eye, Marian saw Lord Bathampton again making his way across the floor towards them.

"Please, sire, may we go now?" Marian asked Sir William.

"Are you tired, little one?" She nodded. "Then yes, of course we may, though we should take our leave of their majesties before doing so."

They stood and Marian saw Lord Bathampton stop in his tracks, pause for a moment, then turn and walk away.

"I think I will stay," Philip said, suddenly brightening.

"No, sir, you will not!" replied his father, so vehemently that Marian looked at him in surprise. Suddenly, she had an inkling of what their argument had been about. "You will come with us to say good night to their majesties, then we will escort our Marian to the ladies' wing and you will retire to your room."

Marian thought Philip was about to disobey his father but he lowered his head and mumbled, "Yes, Father."

Marian again delighted the Queen with what her majesty was now calling the Lady Marian curtsey, and the three of them left the masque.

Marian could not sleep for a long while as she mulled over the happenings of the evening – the Queen's delight in her curtsey, Philip and Alice together, the King and Lady Anne together, dancing with Richard and then dancing with Lord Bathampton. Thoughts of him made her shudder.

She finally fell asleep, wondering in the darkness what Richard had wanted to say to her and why, oh why, had she stopped him from saying it?

# CHAPTER 8

Marian determined to pluck up courage and ask him at the very next opportunity.

"My lady," she said three days later as they sat at their easels, brushing pale blue watercolour onto paper prior to dabbing it with a soft cloth to give the impression of clouds.

"Concentrate, Lady Marian," the art master reproved her. She produced the required effect and, when his back was turned, tried again.

"Lady Anne, when is the next dancing class?"

"I regret there will not be another."

"Whyfor?"

"I will tell you when the class is finished."

Marian was greatly mystified. When the tuition had come to an end and they were walking back to the women's wing of the palace, Marian prompted, "Now you can tell me."

"I know you'll be disappointed but there are not to be any more dancing classes."

"But why not?"

"Your guardian has asked that they cease."

"But he knows how much we enjoy them. Is it something I've done?"

"No, no, little one. You have done nothing amiss."

"Then I don't understand."

Lady Anne took her hand. "I think it is more to do with Philip." She paused. "And that little hussy, Alice."

"Oh." Marian had an inkling now of the problem. "Philip doesn't mean anything by it."

"But clearly Sir William thinks his behaviour is inappropriate. He does not approve of their friendship."

"And Richard?" Marian asked in a very small voice, pleasureable anticipation slipping away from her.

"Even if your guardian changes his mind, Lord Bathampton won't. He says his scribe is neglecting his duties."

"Then how can I – we – see Richard again?"

"You can't. It was simply a useful arrangement that has now come to an end. He is not of your social standing, Marian, and you should not be thinking about him."

But Marian *was* thinking about him, and thinking about him a lot.

"Oh, what a long face! You're too young to be so low in spirits. You'll soon forget about the dancing classes and that young man – believe me, I know. And I have some good news for you, sweetheart. Her majesty has been pleased to take a personal interest in you, Marian, and has commanded that I arrange a full programme of tuition for you. In future, my dear, you will be kept very busy. I hope you understand how fortunate you are."

Marian said she did understand this. She learned that she was to take lessons with the little Princess Mary. When they were not learning arithmetic, reading, writing and spelling, they would be out in the butts endeavouring to shoot a straight arrow or spending time with the falconer and his birds. For relaxation, Marian would be taught to master chess, card and dice games.

Horse riding was not new to her but she was to be schooled to join the hunt. Lady Anne confided that the King loved to hunt but the Queen did not share his enthusiasm and stayed away, which was advisable anyway in view of her many pregnancies, all of which had proved disappointingly unproductive except for Princess Mary. Everyone knew that the King longed for a son to follow him onto the throne.

Occasionally, Marian walked with Philip along the earth towpath by the side of the Thames. The river presented an ever-changing panorama of interest. When the tide was high, its murky waters lapped against the grasses and water weeds close to their feet but, when the tide was low, they looked over muddy banks littered with detritus from the sailing boats, rowing boats and wherries that plied their trade up and down the river.

Then out came the mudlarks, some as young as three or four years old, like an army of worker ants, squelching through the mud, scavenging and sorting and carrying home treasures that might sell for a farthing or less.

Philip and Marian enjoyed each other's company on these walks but were always chaperoned. Philip chafed at this restriction.

"What do they think we're going to get up to," he asked in exasperation, "in full view of the palace windows? If we could escape into the shrubbery, that would be a different matter, but there's no chance of that. Don't look at me so severely, Marian. We're to be married so what would it matter?"

"If you're suggesting what I think you're suggesting, Philip, it would matter to me."

"Do you intend to come to my bed a virgin, Marian?"

"Of course."

"That's very commendable and a very intriguing prospect, but whether you come to me before or on our wedding night makes little difference."

Marian hung her head and did not reply.

"And what about that scribbler, Richard?"

She brought her head up sharply, too sharply she realised, and demanded, "What about him?"

"Don't think I haven't noticed the way you looked at him."

"That's nonsense. I don't look at him in any special way."

"Touched a sensitive spot have I? Well, you won't be seeing him again, now that my father has put an end to our dancing lessons."

*And neither will you be seeing so much of Alice*, she thought but didn't say so.

Throughout the busy weeks, Lady Anne asked her on several occasions to take the leather pouch and hide it in the cavity in the yew tree. A day or so later, she was sent to retrieve it and bring it back with all speed and secrecy. Now that her literacy skills were improving, Marian was sometimes tempted to read the notes within, but knew she was being trusted and refrained.

However, on one occasion when she had been summoned to Lady Anne's chamber and had responded with alacrity, she found Anne adding the final words to one of her letters. Signing it 'A' with a flourish, Anne blew on it to dry the ink then folded it hurriedly but not before Marian had read, though the wording was upside down from her perspective, the inscription, "To H, my dear love".

Not a woman, then, but a gentleman friend! Marian was greatly surprised as this possibility had never occurred to her. As she made her way to the knot garden, she searched her memory for any gentleman at court with the initial 'H'. The only name that came to mind was Sir Henry Norreys, who served in the King's Privy Chamber, but he was married and she had never noticed that he and Lady Anne paid particular attention to each other. Who then? She could think of no other gentleman with a Christian or surname beginning with the letter 'H' and puzzled over it for the remainder of the day.

Two days later, having been sent to retrieve the pouch, she perceived a familiar figure at the far end of the knot garden, a figure dressed all in black. For a moment she was unable to move, her heart pounding most alarmingly. Then she began to walk forward, willing herself not to quicken her pace.

He had seen her and waited for her, standing where he was by the yew tree, making no effort to conceal the leather pouch clutched in his hand.

"Richard! I'm so glad to see you."

He made no move to approach her but bowed very formally.

"Richard?"

"My lady?"

"Richard, why the formality?"

"How else would you expect me to greet you?"

"As a friend, as we were at our dancing class."

"We are no longer at our dancing class, Lady Marian."

Marian felt tears wet her eye lashes. Had she been mistaken in thinking he held her in special affection? In that moment, she was acutely aware of her feelings for him. She looked at the pouch in his hand.

"Are you acting as messenger today? Were you about to hide the pouch? I have been sent by Lady Anne to collect it."

He handed it over and said, "Lady Anne? I guessed as much."

"Richard, do you know who the messages are from?"

"I am given them by Lord Bathampton, but I think they are not from him."

"From whom then? Lady Anne said they are from a friend and I believe he is a gentleman with the initial H, but who, is a mystery to me."

"Have you not guessed?"

"No, how could I?"

She waited for his explanation but he remained silent.

"Why won't you tell me?"

"Because I cannot put you in a position where you might need to be silenced."

"What are you talking about? I don't understand."

"It is treason I am talking about! I would not have you understand. But now I must leave. People would gossip if they saw you conversing with me and that I could not allow when our meeting has been so innocent."

She touched his arm but he moved it away.

"Richard, the last time we met, in the gallery on the night of the masque –"

"When we danced together. How could I forget?"

"You wanted to say something to me but I stopped you. I didn't mean to stop you. I don't know why I did."

"You stopped me because we both knew that those words should not be said."

"But how shall we have another opportunity when we do not meet at the classes any longer?"

"We are young, Marian, and life has a great deal in store for us, I'm sure, and our friendship cannot be part of that. You will marry Philip and who knows where I shall go? Mayhap I'll be the King's first minister one day."

"But us, Richard, where does that leave us?"

"It leaves us here, Marian. We were friends once but that's over. You are Lady Marian de Booys, betrothed to be married, and I am just a scribe with inky fingers."

Marian's fingers tightened round the pouch in her hand as she drew herself up to her full height, controlling the tears that were threatening to betray her.

"I'faith, Richard Mordaunt, I hate you," she said, "and I hope never to see you again!"

Then she turned and fled from the garden, running instinctively, unable to see the paths clearly because of the tears now blurring her vision, suddenly aware that she was in love with this young man with all the love that her fourteen-year-old heart could hold, and that she was unlikely ever to see him again.

She almost collided with Lady Joan Dereham.

"Steady there, Lady Marian. Why the hurry? Are you crying?"

Marian cradled the pouch in her fist and put her hand behind her back. "No, my lady, it's just that the wind had blown dust into my eyes."

"I've seen you walking the knot garden several times. And what is that you're hiding behind your back? Secrets, Marian?"

"No, my lady – " Marian's thoughts raced and she blurted out the first explanation that sounded at all believable "– just a beautiful pebble I picked up to show Lady Anne."

She ran on but turned back as she reached a door into the palace and found Lady Dereham looking after her, a puzzled expression on her face.

When she handed over the pouch and recounted her meeting with her inquisitor, Lady Anne's cheeks paled a little.

"Marian, this is becoming dangerous, for you and for me. This will be the last time I shall ask you to perform this errand. I will find another messenger. But thank you for your loyalty and remember – not a word, nary a one, you do understand?"

"Yes, of course, my lady."

"Good. Now I have a surprise for you. I am to take you to meet her royal highness, Princess Mary. If she likes you, you will become one of her ladies-in-waiting for the remainder of your sojourn in the palace. I will remain as your mentor and you will be able to come to me at any time if you have any problems, but her majesty wishes me to return to her service. She has been very lenient in allowing me all this time off from my duties, but now she wants me back. Are you pleased?"

"Oh yes, my lady."

"Her royal highness has other attendants so you won't be left on your own with her. Now, off to your room and I will call for you in one hour."

Alone in her room and lying on her bed, Marian wanted desperately to sleep, to shut out all thoughts of Richard and the stupid things she had shouted at him. She didn't hate him and of course she wanted to see him again – and often.

Any feelings she had for him and any he had for her, if he did, would make no difference to their situation. She was not about to disobey Sir William, whom she also loved and to whom she was very grateful for all the care and affection he had shown since the death of her father. And she certainly was not about to turn her back on her father's wishes. She and Philip would be married in due time and nothing would change that, not even her feelings for Richard. She did not see why she could not marry one man and love another. From the chatter of the Queen's ladies, she had gleaned that this happened all the time.

Then her thoughts turned to the notes in the leather pouch. Who were they from and why had Richard been so mysterious, talking about treason? Suddenly she had a vision of the King dancing with her Lady Anne at the masque. She had thought at the time that he was paying her an inordinate amount of attention as they danced together – his eyes never leaving hers – but then he was courtly with Lady Jane Seymour and all the ladies with whom he danced. But with Lady Anne it had been different, she was sure.

Sudden comprehension made her sit bolt upright. She remembered Anne's written inscription: "To H, my dear love." Could it be? Was Lady Anne's 'dear love' his majesty the King? No, no, surely not. That would not be right. Under the nose of the Queen? She was letting her imagination run away with her.

Mayhap it was as well that she wouldn't be seeing as much of Lady Anne in future and would be spending more time in the royal schoolroom. Mayhap, just as well.

# CHAPTER 9

*Place: Greenwich Palace*

*Date: November, 1524*

No one else was there when Lady Anne ushered Marian into the schoolroom. It was on the second floor of the palace, a small, plain room with a large table in the centre around which were arranged forms for pupils and a chair for the master.

"Her royal highness will be here soon," Lady Anne said.

"May I have a look round while we wait for her?" Marian asked and, on receiving a nod of assent, she began to explore.

On the table were ink horns, goose quill pens, sheets of rag paper and two pen-knives. Marian picked up several cards showing drawings of objects with their initial letter displayed – 'A' and 'a' for 'Apple' and so on.

She moved to the other end of the table and was playing with a counting frame when the door opened and in walked a little girl followed by Queen Katharine and two of her ladies.

Marian curtsied her special curtsey, as she always did before the Queen, which never failed to please her majesty, and she was asked to curtsey again to the princess, who accepted the révérence with great solemnity.

Mary was rather a plain child, with very fair skin, pale blue eyes and hair the colour of sand that has been covered by the tide. She had inherited none of her mother's regal authority nor the handsome features of her father.

"Lady Marian, come and meet my daughter, Princess Mary. You vill be good friends, I am sure. Her royal highness has been looking forward to having a companion during her lessons. Ladies, you have my leave to retire now."

Both ladies-in-waiting curtsied and left the room.

"Be seated, children. I vill be tutoring you both today. Ven you are ready, ve vill begin with the Lord's Prayer."

Together they recited the Lord's Prayer in Latin then the Queen examined them on their knowledge of the Catechism, especially the Ten Commandments, followed by reading aloud some of her majesty's favourite psalms.

Marian discovered that the young princess's knowledge far exceeded her own. However, her majesty was so patient and desirous of teaching her the tenets of their Catholic faith, and the princess found it so amusing when she had to help Marian towards the correct answers, that the new pupil was not discomfited.

After a drink of warm milk and a biscuit brought by a serving girl, there followed a lesson on arithmetic. Marian discovered an ability that she didn't know she possessed and, in her turn, took pleasure in helping the princess to reach the final figures.

When the Queen saw that her daughter was tiring and in need of sustenance, she brought the lessons to a close.

"May Lady Marian come tomorrow morning, please, mama?"

"Certainly."

"I would like that very much, your Majesty," replied Marian. "Thank you."

"And every morning, mama?"

The Queen ruffled her daughter's hair. "Yes, every morning. Tomorrow your tutor will be examining you in words and their spellings and will engage you in copy writing. Have you a fair hand, Lady Marian?"

"I believe so, your Majesty."

"Then you shall help the princess. She has little penmanship – eh, Mary?"

"Mama says my writing looks as though a worm had crawled across the page."

"A vorm, yes," repeated the Queen, looking affectionately at her daughter. "But we hope that she vill improve when she has the beautiful cyphers to copy that her tutor has requested from the scribes."

Marian smiled at the Queen's description of her daughter's writing.

"Come now, Mary, let us find his majesty and you may tell him how vell you have learned your lessons this morning. Marian, vait here and I vill send one of my ladies to escort you back."

When they had gone, Marian sat at the table and began experimenting with numbers, as the Queen had shown her, writing them in columns of hundreds, tens and units then adding them together or taking one figure from another, using her fingers and the counting frame to check her answers.

She was so absorbed in her task that she was quite unconscious of the door opening and closing again or of the figure that was standing hesitantly at the other end of the table.

"Lady Marian?"

"Oh!" Startled, she looked up then said again, "Oh!" and was embarrassed to feel herself blushing.

For a moment there was silence between them before Richard explained, "I've brought these written cyphers for her royal highness." He held out a scroll of vellum.

"May I see them?" Marian asked him. "The Princess Mary and I are taking lessons together now."

"Of course."

He untied the red ribbon that secured the scroll then weighted one end with a glass paperweight and unrolled it along the table. On the vellum had been inscribed all the letters of the alphabet in both small and capital cyphers, with space beneath for copying them.

"Richard, the letters are exquisite."

"I took great pains in scribing them," he said. "If her royal highness copies them well, she will no longer write as if a vorm was crawling over the paper."

They both laughed at his imitation of her majesty's manner of speaking but stopped abruptly, aware of perceived disrespect.

"I'm so glad to see you again, Richard," Marian said. "I – I didn't mean those stupid things I shouted at you."

"I'm happy to hear that, my lady."

"Do stop calling me your lady!" Marian stamped her foot in exasperation. "Are we not friends again?"

"I would never be allowed to address you so disrespectfully."

"Then I allow you!" Marian replied with passion. "I've missed seeing you."

"But I have seen you. The windows of the scriptorium overlook the gardens and the Thames path. I have sometimes seen you walking there with Sir Philip."

"Then you have been spying on me?"

"No, Marian," Richard replied. "I am just happy to watch you."

Marian reached across and laid her hand on his as he leaned on the table but withdrew it hastily as the latch clicked and the door opened to admit one of the Queen's ladies.

"Lady Marian, I have been sent by her majesty to escort you back. I believe she thinks you might get lost on the way."

Marian laughed to cover her confusion. "Thank you. She may well be right."

As she followed her escort through the door, Marian could not resist a backward glance but Richard was concentrating on rolling up the scroll and would not look at her.

Now, when she and Philip were strolling in the gardens or along the towpath, she would look up at the palace windows but there were so many and she had no idea where the scriptorium was, not even on which floor it was situated. She was desperate to meet Richard again and cajole him into saying the words he was withholding from her.

It was the Queen who fulfilled her desire in an unexpected way. She decided that the princess was not making the progress she should with her cyphers and requested that the young man who had scribed them for her should be in attendance during their next writing lesson.

Marian could not believe her good fortune. When Richard walked into the schoolroom, she sat with head bent over her work and pretended not to notice his presence, although her heart was playing games inside her breast, a blush rose to her cheeks and the palms of her hands became clammy with perspiration.

The tuition progressed. Frustrated that he was preoccupied with the princess and not paying her any heed, Marian tried to attract his attention by dropping her quill pen on the floor then noisily moving her end of the bench away from the table so that he could retrieve it for her. When he made no effort to do so, she huffed a little then coughed several times so that the Queen asked if she was feeling quite well and sent one of her ladies to bring a jug of water and glasses.

Embarrassed, Marian decided she had better stay quiet. She was further disconcerted when the lady-in-waiting returned with the water and she had to take the drink that she did not want.

She looked across to where Richard was leaning over the princess's shoulder, guiding her hand to form the long letter 's' with the ascender curving to the right and the descender to the left. The princess's head, bent low over the vellum, obscured his face from the Queen but Marian could see his expression clearly and was annoyed to observe a wide grin on his face. She wanted to huff again to show her indignation but thought better of it.

When, after several attempts, the 's' had been scribed to the satisfaction of the Queen, Marian asked if he would help her. He came to her shoulder and looked at her work and pronounced it an excellent copy of his cyphers, requiring no amendments. Marian was even more cross.

The Queen thanked him for his careful attention to her daughter's script and dismissed him.

However, happily for Marian, her majesty sent a request to Lord Bathampton for master Richard Mordaunt to attend future lessons.

On these occasions, Marian was in a ferment of anticipation, hoping that somehow she could speak to him privately. He was always courteous towards her but never made any attempt to engage her in conversation, no matter whether the Queen or only one of the tutors was present. Marian felt she had lost control of the situation and Richard was in charge, and was not at all pleased.

Gradually, Princess Mary's scribing improved and the day came when the Queen decided that the services of master Richard Mordaunt were no longer required.

Encouraged by her mother, the princess thanked him most cordially whereupon he bowed and expressed his great pleasure at having been of service to her royal highness.

"It pleases me that the vorm has disappeared," the Queen said, "and I can now read my daughter's writing. Come, Mary. Your lessons are finished for the day. You may go, master Richard, after we have left."

Richard bowed again and, to Marian's astonishment, requested permission to stay longer as there were one or two errors in Lady Marian's script that required attention. Her majesty nodded acquiescence and the royal party swept out.

"You find fault with my cyphers?" Marian asked, not knowing whether she should be offended or delighted.

"You think your scribing is perfect, my lady?" he countered.

"Of course," she replied. "You said so yourself."

"Then let me show you where you are at fault."

He came to her then and stood behind her and lent over her shoulder, placing his right arm over hers and his right hand over hers. Marian felt a shock of excitement tingling its way up her arm and into her heart.

She let his hand guide her own and stared as the letters formed beneath their fingers.

"There!" he said. "Isn't that what you wanted to hear?"

The words were almost jumping off the vellum. "I love you".

"Yes," she whispered, "Yes. And I love you."

Then he sat beside her and took her in his arms. She raised her face to his and their first kiss came so naturally that they repeated it again and again.

Held in his arms and with her head resting against his chest, Marian said, "Richard, there must be somewhere we can meet sometimes, in secret if we must."

He was silent for a moment then whispered, "Marian, there is somewhere – if you are sure."

"I'm sure. You know a place?"

"Yes, the scriptorium. It is a room where documents are stored, a library of scrolls and precious books. People seldom go there and then only the scribes. We could meet there."

"Will I be able to find it?"

"I will draw you a map."

He released her and pulled a sheet of paper forward and deftly drew a plan of a section of the floor above with the room marked. While the ink dried, he described how to reach it using a back staircase.

"I will be able to access the room at any time without suspicion but it will be more difficult for you," he said. "How will I know when to be there?"

"I could leave you a note somewhere in here," Marian suggested.

They both prowled about the room and saw no obvious hiding place for a message until Richard noticed a knot hole at the back of an oak beam that would not be visible to anyone seated at the table.

"In there," he said. "Don't sign it, just write the initial letter of the day – T2 if you mean Thursday and not Tuesday – and a time, and I'll be there. Now I must go."

The intoxication of keeping this secret between them urged Marian to discard any pretence of propriety.

"Don't you want to kiss me again?" she asked. "I shall burst if you don't."

So he did.

# CHAPTER 10

When she regained her chamber and the reality of the situation gradually replaced the euphoria, she felt very guilty. She remembered reciting the Ten Commandments before the Queen earlier that morning. 'Thou shalt not commit adultery.'

Surely a kiss was not committing adultery? But she was betrothed to Philip and had promised him that she would come to the marriage bed a virgin, and she intended to keep that promise. But she had wanted so desperately for Richard to kiss her.

But would those kisses send her to Hell? The priests were always warning against bodily passions.

She made up her mind that it would not happen again – but she would meet Richard in the scriptorium occasionally and talk to him and get to know him better. There was no harm in that. But no kissing! Definitely no kissing! Suddenly, life seemed rather dull.

Tutors came and went as the lessons in the schoolroom progressed – reading, writing, spelling and grammar, Latin, arithmetic, landscape painting and singing. The young princess had a sweet voice in a middle range that blended well with Marian's higher register.

"Your singing master tells me you have learned a new song," the Queen said during one of her regular supervisory visits to the schoolroom.

"Marian and I sing together," the princess told her mother.

"All the better. May we hear it?"

Their singing master bowed, picked up his lute, nodded to his pupils, and started to play. After a few bars of introduction, the two young, clear voices began to sing the chorus:

*"O! The merry, merry greenwood,*
*The merry, merry greenwood.*
*The very merry green, green wood.*

*"We scrambled through the greenwood*
*In the Springy month of May*
*And gathered wood anemones*
*And primroses, all gay,*
*And sought the tiny violet*
*And spent long hours in play,*

*Then rambled, scrambled homeward,*
*To dream the night away.*

*"O! The merry, merry greenwood,*
*The merry, merry greenwood.*
*The very merry green, green wood."*

Her majesty beamed with delight and clapped her hands in appreciation then crossed to her daughter and kissed her.

"There are other verses, your Majesty," said the singing master with some embarrassment, "but I considered them not suitable…"

The Queen nodded. "I know it," she said, "and you are right to leave them untaught and unsung."

"Truly?" thought Marian and was curious to know what the other words were. Perhaps Lady Anne would tell her. Perhaps not.

The Queen turned again to the girls, who were holding hands and smiling at each other.

"You have sung well, young ladies!" she exclaimed. "I'faith, you have a sweet voice, Lady Marian, and everyone knows that her royal highness has a musical gift. You have taught them well, singing master, and the King shall hear of it."

A couple of music lessons later, Marian was presented with an opportunity to satisfy her curiosity and did not hesitate. Their singing master apologised profusely to the princess and said he had forgotten to bring with him the music and words of a new song he wished to teach them and it would take him but a few minutes to retrieve the sheets.

As soon as he was out of the room, Marian moved across to the satchel that he had left on his chair with his lute. The princess was occupied in transcribing the notes of a melody from her head to the written stave system of five horizontal lines and four spaces that had recently been brought over from France, and was paying no attention to what Marian was doing.

She opened the satchel and rifled through the song sheets inside until she found the words of *The merry, merry greenwood.*

The first stanza she knew, about innocently scrambling through the greenwood in the Springy month of May. Quickly, she read the next three verses, which gave a fairly explicit account of two lovers and their antics during Summer and Autumn until they thought it expedient to *marry in the greenwood in December's falling snow.*

Marian smiled, her curiosity satisfied, and understood why their singing master would not teach the remainder of the song to the princess.

She replaced the sheet in the satchel and was looking over Princess Mary's shoulder by the time their tutor returned, none the wiser that someone had interfered with the contents of his satchel.

Four weeks had passed since Marian and Richard had met and she longed to talk to him again. She caught glimpses of him in the gallery at Mass on Sunday mornings when she stood below with Sir William and Philip but that did not satisfy her. His absence chafed her heart.

However, the remedy lay with her and one Wednesday morning, when she found herself alone in the schoolroom, she penned the cryptic message "S 10 ½" and left the note screwed up in the knot hole of the beam.

How slowly the remainder of Wednesday, then Thursday and Friday passed. Marian didn't even have the distraction of walking in the gardens with Philip. He seemed to be avoiding her and she couldn't understand why.

Saturday dawned – at least, Marian guessed it had dawned but she couldn't tell because of the mist and low, dark clouds and the rain pelting against the mullion windows of her bedchamber. However, she brightened considerably when she thought of her assignation with Richard later that morning.

It served no purpose to consult the sun dials on such a morning so she kept her eye on the huge astronomical clock on one of the towers in the Clock Courtyard, which her windows overlooked, and at a quarter past the hour of ten, she left her chamber, telling her maids she was on an errand for Lady Anne.

She had committed Richard's instructions and map to memory, and made her way to the stone staircase and climbed to the floor above. At the top, she looked along the corridor, and seeing no one, began to walk along it, counting the doors on the right as she went.

*Five*, she thought. *The next but one.*

She had just reached the sixth door when someone called her name.

"Lady Marian!"

Looking ahead along the corridor, she was aggrieved to see Lord Bathampton approaching.

"Lady Marian," he said again, drawing nearer.

Marian dropped him a perfunctory curtsey.

"My lord," she said.

"What a pleasant surprise, my lady. So, what brings you to this floor?"

Marian trotted out the same excuse she had used to her maids. "I have an errand to perform for Lady Anne, sire."

If he asked what errand, she would say it was a personal matter. However, he seemed satisfied with her answer, almost as if he really had little interest in why she was there. He took another step towards her and his eyes narrowed, reminding her of the fox that Sir William had recently shot on the estate. It had been prowling round the brushwood fencing of the chicken run with just such an expression on its wily face. She shivered inwardly.

"Have you ever seen inside the scriptorium, my lady?"

"No, sire."

"Then you should. It is crammed full of documents dating back several hundreds of years – laws and statutes and ordinances and proclamations and all the miscellanea emanating from the governance of this realm back to the time of King Alfred, and some before that. It is supremely interesting."

"I am sure it is, sire," Marian replied, hoping to escape from his presence as soon as possible.

"Would you like me to show you, my lady? I was on my way there and it will take but a few moments to reveal to you its treasures."

Marian hesitated, looking past him and hoping that, if Richard arrived and saw them conversing, he would withdraw.

"Come," Lord Bathampton urged her, placing his hand beneath her elbow. "Come. It will take but a few minutes."

Marian felt unable to resist without an unseemly struggle and allowed him to guide her to the next door along, which he opened then ushered her inside, turning to close it behind them.

Although she had been told by Richard, and now by Lord Bathampton, how comprehensive were the records deposited there, she had had no conception of the extent of the collection.

Along the centre of the room ran several long tables, polished to a high gloss, on each side of which benches were placed.

On both sides of the room, running at right angles to the tables and with aisles between them, were row upon row of shelving, stacked from floor to ceiling with scrolls of all sizes and thicknesses, each tied with a red ribbon, many with large red wax seals dangling over the edges of the shelves.

"Impressive, isn't it?" Lord Bathampton said, following along behind as she walked the length of the aisles, reverently touching some of the scrolls.

As she rounded the end of one aisle to gain access to the next, he was quick to pass her, blocking her path, so that she collided with him. She jumped back, apologising, and felt herself flushing in embarrassment and apprehension.

"I'm sure you've had enough of admiring the collection, Marian – may I call you Marian? Come, sit with me for a while." He indicated a window seat at the foot of a tall window.

"I think not, sire," Marian said. "Please let me pass."

She made as if to dodge him but he stepped to the side and blocked her way again, then moved in close, placed his arms round her, and began to press his body against hers.

"Has anyone ever told you how beautiful you are, my dear? Has your betrothed ever shown you how not to waste all that beauty? Come and sit on my lap, Marian, and I will pleasure you with sensations you knew nothing about before my fingers were exploring your secret places."

Marian was aghast at what he was whispering in her ear and struggled to free herself from his close embrace.

"Please, my lord, let me go!" she pleaded.

"You want to play, do you?" he grinned, pinning her arms to her sides, his face, the colour of red wine, close to hers. He was using his bulk to gradually push her against the shelves, which were digging painfully into her back. His breathing quickened and his arousal was obvious, even to Marian who had had no experience of such matters.

"A kiss, my lady Marian, a kiss, my beauty."

Both heard the door open and close and he jumped away from her as if he had been stung by a horse fly.

"Is anyone there?"

It was Richard's voice!

"We're here!" Marian called, not wishing to speak his name and reveal that she was expecting him.

Lord Bathampton wiped spittle from the corners of his mouth with the back of his hand and straightened his clothing.

"Not a word, do you hear?" His threat was like grit in her ear. "Not a word or I'll tell everyone what a strumpet you are!"

Richard appeared at the end of the aisle they were occupying.

"Is everything all right? Lord Bathampton? My lady?"

"I was just showing the young lady the extent of our collection. What are you doing here, Richard?"

"I came to study, the better to understand some of the work the Cardinal entrusts to you and which you ask me to copy." There was no hesitation in Richard's answer and Marian guessed he had prepared it for such a contingency.

"Very well. Then at the same time you can find for me Rastell's new English Law Lexicon. Bring it to me straight away and see that Lady Marian leaves. She is on an errand for Lady Anne Boleyn."

Saying that, he turned his back on Richard to face Marian and with lips barely moving hissed, “Remember – not a word!” then he strode out of the room, leaving the door wide open. After an interval, Richard went across and closed it, having first ascertained that his lordship had vacated the corridor.

Marian was still standing where he had left her, too shocked to move. When she heard the door close, she began to sob, her chest and shoulders heaving.

Richard was at her side in an instant and put his arms around her. Then her tears began to flow.

“My lady – Marian – what’s the matter? Please don’t cry so.”

“Oh, Richard, it was all so disgusting!”

He pulled her close to him. Her arms slipped around his waist and she clung to him with her head against his shoulder.

“What did he do to you?”

“Nothing because you came in, but he would have – I don’t know. He was trying to get me to sit on his lap.”

“The devil he was!” Richard exclaimed. “You must tell Sir William or Lady Anne.”

“I cannot,” Marian sobbed. “He threatened to blacken my name if I told a soul. It would create such a furore and would be his word against mine, and who would believe me? And how could I explain my presence here?”

“Come and sit down,” Richard said, gently leading her to the window seat. He produced a linen kerchief from inside his doublet. “Dry your eyes. I am so sorry. It was my fault for suggesting that we meet here but I thought we would be safe. This must not happen again. We cannot meet like this.”

She raised her head and looked up at him, still clutching the kerchief. “But, Richard, we *have* to meet. You know I love you.”

“And I love you too, Marian, but, as I have said many times, you are betrothed to Sir Philip.”

“What difference does that make?” Marian protested. “Yes, I will marry Philip but I will always love you.”

“That’s an impossible situation, Marian.”

“But we could stay friends and meet sometimes. I would just want us to meet sometimes.”

“You ask too much of me. How could I bear it in the dark hours of the night, knowing you were in his arms and not mine?”

Marian felt heat rising all over her body and knew her face must look ugly, flushed red and streaked with tears, but Richard seemed not to mind.

“I would rather go into a monastery!” he suddenly declared.

"You – in a monastery?" Marian repeated and they began to laugh together in spite of the gravity of their situation.

"I must go," Marian said.

Richard sighed and went to open the door for her.

"I must stay and find that book for him. But be careful of Lord Bathampton, Marian. He has a certain reputation. It will do you no good to be seen in his company."

"Don't worry about that!" she replied defiantly, returning the kerchief. "I hate him and I won't go anywhere near the man!"

# CHAPTER 11

Two days later, Marian received a missive brought by a young page, a summons from her guardian, bidding her attend him in his chambers. She was immediately fearful. Had word leaked out about her tussle with Lord Bathampton? Had he blackened her name already by lying about her to Sir William?

With trepidation, she responded straight away and was surprised to see Philip waiting for her outside his father's door.

"Philip!" she greeted him, running over and giving him a chaste kiss. "How good to see you. I've missed you. Where have you been?"

"Where haven't I been?" he grumbled. "I wanted to meet with you, Marian, but each time I asked permission, my Lord Bathampton found another errand for me to run or I was called to a fencing lesson or a wrestling bout – not that I don't enjoy them, because I do."

"And are you very accomplished at wrestling and fencing, Philip?"

"Moderately so and I am improving all the while. Lord Bathampton allows Richard Mordaunt to be my opponent. I can wrestle him to the ground without very much effort but he is a better swordsman than I am." He paused then added with pride, "You see standing before you a fully-fledged squire now, Marian."

"You've attended the ceremony?"

"Yes, in the chapel. I swore my fidelity on a sword consecrated by the Cardinal. Now I wear my own suit of armour for my jousting lessons instead of having to borrow someone else's. It's very splendid. My father is very proud of me, though he would never say so. And you, Marian, what has been occupying your time?"

Marian told him how busy she had been and of all her learning and acquired skills in company with the young princess.

"My sewing and embroidery are improving and I have begun to lay aside table and bed linen in my marriage chest."

"I'm glad to hear it – your handiwork could do with some improvement!" he said, grinning at her. She raised her hand to playfully punch him in the biceps but he caught her arm by the wrist and held it in a strong grip. She laughed and tried to wrestle her arm out of his grasp but stopped when she saw the way he was looking at her chest.

"I'faith, Marian," he said, "I do believe you've grown into a woman. When did they happen?"

For some time, Marian had been conscious of her swelling breasts, which her new green gown did nothing to hide, and was self-conscious but flattered by the sudden interest her step brother was taking in them. He let her hand drop and she was much amused when he turned away and knocked on the door of his father's chamber to hide the colour reddening his cheeks.

They heard Sir William's invitation to enter and Philip opened the door, allowing Marian to walk in ahead of him.

Sir William was sitting in his wooden armchair by the fire, chatting to someone in the facing chair – a lady, Marian was surprised to see. He rose immediately and came towards them, embracing Marian and placing his hand on Philip's shoulder.

"Marian, how are you? We haven't seen much of each other since arriving at court but I receive regular news of you from Lady Anne. Come to the fire both of you. I believe you know Lady Joan Dereham."

The woman in the chair turned towards them with a broad smile. Marian wasn't best pleased and wondered what she was doing here but bobbed a curtsey while Philip bowed.

She asked courteously after Lady Dereham's sister.

"Lady Alice is very well. I will tell her you were asking after her. Very kind."

Sir William indicated that Marian and Philip should sit in two chairs that had been placed there for them. They sat and waited expectantly for whatever it was he was about to tell them.

He passed his fingers through his hair and Marian thought he looked very distracted. She wanted to reach out and smooth away the creases from his forehead but sat quite still, as did Philip.

At last Sir William spoke. "The King has decided to set out on one of his progresses, visiting his home counties, and wishes to spend the Christmas season at Forrester Hall."

There was a stunned silence so he continued, "We will be leaving Greenwich Palace in two days' time to travel home and begin making preparations."

"How many in the company?" asked Marian.

"Probably two hundred," Lady Dereham answered.

"Two hundred?" Philip sounded as though he could not believe his ears. "But Father, we can't –"

"We have no choice," Sir William interrupted him. "As I have no wife, her ladyship will advise us, though I intend that you should take on some of the responsibility, Marian, my dear. What do you say to that?"

"I don't know what to say, sire," Marian replied.

"I will help you, Lady Marian," Lady Dereham promised. "At your age, you cannot be expected to order your household for such a prestigious occasion without help."

"The journey will take the best part of two days by carriage," Sir William continued. "Lady Dereham will travel with you, Marian, and your maids will follow in a second conveyance. Philip and I and our escort will ride on ahead and begin to make ready. When you arrive, Lady Dereham will be on hand to advise on her majesty's sleeping and toiletry requirements. I know what the King expects."

"This is a major undertaking, Father," Philip said, anxiety evident in his low voice and troubled expression.

Sir William stood and turned his back to the fire, his arms folded across his doublet.

"Yes, it is, son, but we will rise to the occasion – with the assistance of my lady here."

"Does Lady Anne know?" Marian asked.

"Yes she does, and she will be in the Queen's entourage, but your mentor will be Lady Dereham."

That lady smiled up at him, a winsome smile that seemed to please him but troubled Marian.

"Very well, you may go now. You will need to start making ready for the journey."

Philip and Marian stood and made their obeisance.

"We shall all meet again at Forrester Hall, young people. Lady Dereham, I should be glad if you would stay a while as we have much to discuss."

"Gladly, Sir William."

"Philip, find a steward and have him bring me a flagon of red wine and two goblets. Lady Dereham and I will toast the visit of their majesties to Forrester Hall."

"Yes, Father."

Philip and Marian withdrew and faced each other outside the closed door.

"Well, Philip."

"Well, Marian."

"This is very serious a matter."

"I know it. I wonder whether Lady Alice will be travelling among the Queen's ladies."

"Fie, Philip! You pay too much attention to that young lady!"

"Are you jealous, sister?"

Marian tossed her head. "No, of course not."

Philip chuckled. "I think you are." He took her hand, gently this time. "But there is no need. You are prettier by far than Lady Alice." He moved closer and looked down into her face. "And how beautiful are your eyes! And you tell me you are not jealous! Isn't that what's making them so intensely green?"

Before she could stop him, he had taken her in his arms and was kissing her passionately on the lips. Marian struggled from his embrace.

"Philip, behave! You are playing with me now!"

"Yes, I am, and enjoying it! Come, Marian, another kiss."

"Be serious!"

"I am being serious. We are betrothed, are we not? So I am allowed a little licence." He lowered his voice to a whisper. "But I can wait till we are at home – not so many prying eyes. Farewell, my Marian. I will see you at Forrester Hall. Now to find a steward."

He turned and strode away, leaving Marian feeling very confused. She couldn't say she hadn't enjoyed that kiss because she had and there was a strange feeling in the pit of her stomach. Then she remembered Richard.

*Oh dear*, she thought, *life is so very complicated.*

# CHAPTER 12

*Place: Forrester Hall, Berkshire*

*Date: December, 1524*

At dawn two days later, a pair of carriages set out from Greenwich Palace for Forrester Hall. Sir William, Philip and their escort had left on horseback two hours earlier.

Marian and Lady Joan Dereham occupied the leading carriage with four maids in the second, to which was roped the cart containing all the baggage. They were accompanied by six mounted knights and their squires, with four grooms to facilitate the nightly change-over, two to each pair of horses.

The weather was bright and dry but extremely cold. Happily, the carriages were roofed but icy winds swept through the open sides and Marian and Lady Dereham withdrew into their layers of beaver furs, both of them more than grateful for two hot bricks wrapped in sheepskin on which to rest their feet.

In spite of a plentiful assortment of cushions and bolsters, the journey was extremely uncomfortable as they were jolted and jarred along the uneven, rutted roads.

Marian was not sorry that conversation became impossible, but so was sleep, and there was little to occupy them except gazing out at the beautiful Thames valley scenery of fields, marshes, streams and woods, the tree branches bare. They became used to the peasants staring at the entourage as they drove through their thatched-roofed villages with sturdy Norman churches.

The White Hart Inn at Cranford Bridge was their first stop, where the horses were fed and watered and the men enjoyed pots of beer round a roaring log fire, while the ladies sat at little wooden tables drinking tankards of ale and waiting for the foot-bricks to heat up again in the ashes.

They were soon on their way along the road leading to Bath, making for The Bear at Maidenhead, where they ate a mid-day meal of mutton cooked in beer. Then on to Reading, where the men-at-arms obtained for the company a night's lodging at the Crown Inn.

The women arrived exhausted and stiff-limbed and again had little to say to each other except for a few commiserations about their shared discomfort.

They were too tired to do justice to the rabbit pie and Marian was glad to retire to her chamber and prepare for bed. After her maids left the room, she was soon asleep, lulled by the scent of the herbs they had scattered between the sheets.

Next morning, after breakfast, they were on the road again and were glad to stop at Woolhampton before reaching Speenhamland. From there, the whirlicotes turned north towards the Ridgeway and within a few miles came within sight of Forrester Hall, set among the gentle undulations of the Berkshire downs.

Marian's heart beat faster at the sight of her home. Lady Dereham said she wished to have a clearer view of the house and ordered the horses to be reined in so she could climb out and look down on the estate.

"How many acres does Sir William own?" she asked.

"Ten thousand," Marian said with pride. "They encompass the church, Forrestram village down there in the valley and St. Jude's monastery." She pointed out each feature as she spoke.

They stood on the road for several minutes, appreciating the view below them, laid out like a painting on an artist's canvas. The Hall was looking its best with its brick frontage garnet-red in the wintry sunshine, gleaming a welcome from its mullioned windows on three floors in the main house and four and five floors in the two towers.

Behind the Hall lay a large ornamental lake fed by a small stream and around it well-kept lawns stretched towards brown arable fields to the north, thick woodland to the west and the tiny church and village to the east. Further away, the monastery with its surrounding gardens, fish ponds and trout farm was also built of local red brick but at this moment was in cloud shadow and appeared somewhat forbidding.

Marian looked at Lady Dereham, whose dark eyes were shining.

"Isn't it beautiful, my lady Dereham?" she asked.

"It certainly is – and all that we see belongs to Sir William?"

"Yes. It was given to Guillaume de la Forêt by King William the Conqueror after 1066 but the family changed its name to the English 'Forrester' a long time ago."

"You are a very fortunate young lady, my dear, to have become a ward of Sir William."

"Yes indeed, and I do acknowledge it, my lady."

"And how does Sir William manage his household affairs without a wife to support him?"

"He retains a housekeeper and steward and a very faithful staff and soon I will be old enough to take on the responsibility."

"When you and his son marry?"

"When I marry Philip, yes."
"In two years' time?"
"Yes."
"Then you will become mistress of the estate?"
Marian was becoming a little uncomfortable, having to answer all these questions. It was also bitterly cold, standing on the edge of the escarpment with the wind blowing round them from the north.
However, she was mindful that she had to be polite to this woman for whom she had little liking but who had come to the Hall on the express instructions of Queen Katharine, to help Marian prepare for the coming invasion by the court. And she recognised that she would need a lot of help if all was to be accomplished in a manner that would bring credit to her guardian. She was prepared to suffer many irritants if it would promote his standing in the eyes of his sovereign and the Queen.
"It will be as you say," she replied. "Shall we return to the carriage, my lady?"
"Of course."
They were soon ensconced once more on the bench seats in the whirlicote. While the maids were tucking the furs around them, Lady Dereham asked in a tone that suggested it was of little consequence, "Sir William has said in the past, but I have quite forgotten the details – how long has he lived without a wife?"
"Lady Forrester passed away ten years ago, when I was but four years old. I do remember her, though. She was a beautiful lady."
"I do not doubt it."
She waited until the maids had clambered out of the coach and had returned to their conveyance before asking, "Ten years? A long time for a man to be without the comfort of a wife, much too long." Marian thought she added under her breath, "Yes, much too long."
They relapsed into silence as the whirlicote moved forward, following the road as it dropped down towards the entrance to the estate park.
*What has it to do with her?* Marian thought resentfully as they passed between the stone pillars surmounted by two lions supporting the Forrester coat-of-arms. *It's no concern of hers how long Sir William has lived without his lady wife. We are very happy as we are. Her questions are so strange.* She resolved to speak to Philip about it as soon as she could get him on his own.
She was out of the whirlicote almost before it came to a halt in front of the steps leading up to the porticoed entrance of the Hall. In a haste that was most unseemly for a young lady of her station, she raced across the courtyard towards a middle-aged woman of ample proportions who came

hurrying down the steps to greet them, stumbling into arms stretched out to envelop her.

"Lady Marian, my dear young lady, how happy I am to see you again – and looking so well!"

Marian laughed. "It's been less than four months, Marmy, but I've missed you, too."

As a toddler, she had been unable to pronounce the name of the housekeeper, 'Mistress Malmesbury', and her affectionate attempt had never been corrected.

The woman released her, curtseyed and moved aside as Sir William hurried down the steps.

"Marian, my dear, you made it in good time. Welcome home! And you, Lady Dereham." He made a sweeping bow to Joan Dereham, who had followed sedately to the foot of the steps. "Welcome to Forrester Hall. I do hope you will take pleasure in your time here."

"Thank you, Sir William. I am sure I shall."

He motioned to several servants who were hovering around, awaiting instructions, and they busied themselves collecting the valises from the carriages and taking them up the grand staircase to the next floor, where Mistress Malmesbury was directing them to the ladies' chambers. The four maids were conducted to the servants' quarters in the basement.

After instructing his grooms to take care of the visiting grooms with their horses and carriages and to show the escort to their quarters above the stable block, Sir William led Marian and Lady Dereham across the hall to sit at a side table where a meal of bread, cheese and ale had been prepared.

After they had eaten, my lady said she wished to rest awhile but Marian was far too excited at being home and spent only a few minutes freshening her face and hands before running down the stairs and going in search of her guardian.

John, his steward, directed her to Sir William's study so she raced back up the staircase. Hurrying along the landing to the left, she opened the door of Stephen Tower and ascended the spiral stone staircase. Hearing voices in his study, she knocked gently on the door. It was opened by Philip, who embraced her fondly and drew up a chair next to his, facing Sir William across his large mahogany desk.

"So, Marian, my dear, how have you and Lady Dereham fared? I hope you have become friends on the road. You get along well?"

"Tolerably well, sire."

Sir William seemed amused at her answer and the laughter lines round his mouth and eyes deepened a little.

"You must be friends, Marian, for there is much to be accomplished before their majesties and the court arrive. You will have great responsibilities placed on your young shoulders and will need Lady Dereham's advice and assistance."

Marian nodded her understanding.

"I have already been in consultation with John and Mistress Malmesbury," continued Sir William, "and between them they will organise the affairs of the house – the sleeping arrangements and such. There will likely be two hundred in the party and many of the servants will have to take rooms in the village. That will all be arranged. I totally understand the King's requirements and Lady Dereham will see to it that everything the Queen needs is provided."

"Father has delegated to me the organisation of the horses and carriages," Philip explained with pleasure. "That means the rides over the estate and the day spent hawking! Of course, I shall need to consult with the head groom."

"The final decisions will be mine," said Sir William, running a hand through his hair, a habitual gesture when he was perplexed or anxious.

"What can I do to help?" Marian asked. "I want to help."

"And so you shall. I will make you responsible for all the menus. Together, you and Lady Dereham will supervise all the ordering of supplies in consultation with cook. Can you do that?"

"That's a great responsibility," Philip said. "Are you capable, little sister?"

"If I am not now, I will make myself capable," Marian insisted, straightening her back and sitting up in her chair. "I will learn all I can from her ladyship and cook and we will not let you down, sire."

Sir William smiled at her with affection and some of the anxiety disappeared from his face.

"And what about entertainment?" Marian asked.

"We will have to think about that when all the practical decisions have been made," Sir William replied, a frown returning to his forehead.

"Sire, I have an idea," said Marian, her face brightening. "Why don't you send for Monsieur, the dancing master? I'm sure he will be able to take on that responsibility – don't you think so, Philip?"

"That's an inspired idea, Marian."

"Yes, it is," confirmed their father. "I will certainly request his majesty's permission to send for the little man. Now you two run along. I have a great deal of work to do. I will see you at our evening meal. And Marian, do be pleasant to her ladyship. There is much of importance resting on this visit."

“Of course I will, sire.”

Urged by her love for him and wanting to spare him as much worry as she could, Marian hurried round the desk and planted a kiss on his cheek.

“Please don’t worry, Father. All will be well, you’ll see.”

Sir William smiled. “I couldn’t leave it in better hands,” he said. “Philip, please find John and send him to me.”

When they had done so, Marian asked Philip to walk with her around the lake.

“I have something to speak to you about,” she said.

They left the house by the door from the orangery, crossed the gravel terrace, descended the flight of stone steps and stepped onto the lawn. Both were glad of their fur-lined mantles and Marian pulled hers close round her and drew the hood over her head. She had already discarded the headgear she wore at court and her long fair hair was flowing freely round her shoulders.

They reached the lake in silence and began to follow the sandy path around the perimeter. Resting on the grass, a cob and pen with their brown-feathered cygnet, born last Spring and as big as its parents, hissed at them as they passed. Marian hissed back.

Laughing, Philip asked, “Well, what is it you want to speak to me about, Marian?”

“It’s Lady Dereham. We stopped on the road to look out over the estate, at her request, and she kept asking me so many questions about Father.”

“What sort of questions?”

“How long he had been widowed, how he managed without a wife, how big was the estate – those sort of questions, personal questions.”

Philip began to chuckle.

“And how did you answer her?”

“With the truth, of course. I said he would have no need of a wife once we were wed and I was mistress of the estate.”

Philip seemed amused. “I expect she was not at all pleased with your reply!” He then became very serious. “And so you shall be – mistress of the estate,” he said, “in spite of this lady and all the other ladies.”

“What do you mean?”

“Don’t you know? How innocent you are, Marian. Our father has considerable wealth and he is a widower and the ladies at court seem to regard him as handsome, in spite of his age. So –”

“So what?”

“They think he would make a desirable husband – and my lady Joan Dereham stands first in line.”

"She wants to marry Father?" Marian was aghast.

"That's my reading of affairs," Philip said. "She fancies herself mistress of Forrester Hall – and you, my dearly betrothed, stand in her way."

Marian remained silent, turning all this over in her mind, meantime watching the antics of the ducks which were waddling to the edge of the lake and plopping into the water as the human interlopers approached.

"Then she has no reason to like me," she said slowly, "in spite of her pleasant demeanour."

"None whatsoever."

They had reached the wooden bridge and began to cross it, pausing half way to admire the colourful fish in the clear water below. Marian looked up towards the distant vista of the Hall – her home and her inheritance when she married.

"Is it possible that Father will – I mean, does he know?"

"Of course he knows. He enjoys all the attention and it sometimes brings him – er – advantages. I wish him good fortune in these encounters."

"So he may marry?"

"We must conspire together and make sure he is never lured into doing something he wouldn't wish to do, merely to preserve his honour – or a lady's honour. But no, I don't think he is ever tempted. He is still in love with my mother, may she rest in peace."

"Amen to that," said Marian. "Then, Philip, you think that love – true love – can survive a long absence?"

"I am sure of it."

Marian nodded. But at that moment she was not thinking of Sir William and Lady Forrester.

# CHAPTER 13

The next two weeks passed in a frenzy of activity. Everyone at the Hall knew what was expected of them, including the army of young women who came up from Forrestram village with their mops and pails, brooms, brushes and cleaning cloths.

Walls, windows and floors were cleaned and chimneys swept; curtains and hangings were taken down from windows and four-poster beds and, together with rugs, were hung on rope lines in a back yard and soundly beaten; and tapestries and carpets were carefully brushed and cleaned and darned where necessary. Then dust sheets were whipped off and stored away, used candles were replaced and furniture, paintings, clocks and ornaments were dusted and polished until every room gleamed a welcome.

The royal couple would be bringing their own beds, linen, tapestries and plate but, for the rest of the party, table porcelain and cooking utensils were washed, and quantities of cutlery cleaned until it shone, in case anyone had forgotten to bring their personal knife and spoon with them.

Table linen was washed, starched and ironed and sheets, pillow and bolster cases laundered and aired and beds made up. Nothing was left wanting and, when all was accomplished, Forrester Hall had never looked so splendid as it awaited the arrival of the King and Queen of England and their court.

In the kitchens, Marian, again wearing one of the gowns that Lady Jane had described as 'a sack', with the assistance of Lady Dereham and cook, had written endless lists of menus and supplies to be sourced and purchased. They checked the quality and quantities of non-perishable goods delivered and placed orders for meat, fish, eggs and other fresh items to be brought to the Hall on the correct day, even to the purchase of porpoise meat, a favourite of the Queen, which would be served at the high table only. Barrels of ale had already arrived by cart from the monastery for transfer to the cellars.

Cook was relying on women from the village to work under her instructions in preparing and cooking the various dishes. Young men had been hired and given superficial training in basic skills so that they could act as servers at the lower tables, leaving the experienced staff to serve the high table.

In the stable yard, Philip, grooms and stable hands had been fully occupied in grooming the horses and preparing the saddlery and other tack that would be used, and had hired horses from neighbouring estates to make sure there were sufficient for the day's hawking for the King and his companions.

Finally, the dancing master had arrived by carriage and assured Sir William that he had everything in hand as far as entertainment was concerned. He brought with him a simple-minded fellow he had met along the way whom he thought could impersonate the Christmas Lord of Misrule if only the lad could be prevailed upon to take instruction.

As far as could be ascertained, nothing had been left to chance. All was prepared and anticipation was high as one and all awaited the arrival of their majesties.

On the day the procession was expected, a young lad on horseback had been stationed at a high point on the downs to watch for the progress of the royal entourage so he could gallop back to the Hall and warn of its approach.

It was spotted early in the afternoon three days before Christmas and, when the procession arrived three hours later, everyone waiting was in a fever of anticipation.

Sir William stood at the foot of the steps with Philip and Marian behind him. The whole household lined both sides of the steps and stretched back into the hall. Another line of able-bodied young men spread out along both sides of the frontage of the building, ready to handle valises, bags and packages and carry them to the respective chambers, guided by John, who had a plan of the upper floors in his gloved hands.

As the King then the Queen alighted from their separate whirlicotes, there was a flurry of obeisance from everyone. Sir William stepped forward.

"Welcome, your majesties, to my home," he said and flourished a courtly bow.

"We are very grateful for your hospitality, Sir William," said the King, looking all around him with interest, and the Queen nodded agreement.

"It is we who are grateful, your Majesties, for the honour you bestow on us," Sir William replied. "May I present to you my son, Sir Philip, and my ward, Lady Marian, both of whom you have met previously."

He stood aside and allowed Marian and Philip to come forward. While Philip bowed, Marian curtseyed in the manner that had always delighted the Queen.

"Sir Philip." The Queen acknowledged him with a nod of her head. "And little Marian." She turned to the King. "You remember the young people, your Majesty?"

“Of course,” he said as they bowed and curtseyed again, though Marian wasn’t sure that he did.

“Your Majesty, I had hoped to see the Princess Mary with you,” Marian was emboldened to remark.

The Queen replied that she thought it best to leave her comfortably at Greenwich in the care of her nursemaids. “You will see her soon enough on your return to the palace,” she said.

Next to come forward was Lady Dereham and, after her, Sir William introduced his steward, housekeeper and cook. The royal couple were then escorted into the Hall and to their chambers, where they were offered facilities to refresh themselves before sustenance was served.

Once their majesties had left the drive, the Queen’s ladies and King’s attendants were assisted from the next twenty whirlicotes and all escorted to their chambers. The Queen’s baggage and chests were lifted from the carts and delivered to her on the floor above. The King’s effects were conveyed to his rooms in the West Tower, which he was taking over in its entirety.

Marian was delighted to see Lady Anne Boleyn and Lady Jane Seymour among the ladies-in-waiting. They greeted her with great affection and would have engaged her in idle chatter but she said she had to go as she had so much to do.

“Busy as a pretty little bee,” Lady Anne laughed. “When you are free, come and see me in my chamber. I have a surprise for you.”

Marian thanked her and said she would visit her as soon as she was free to do so.

While this was happening, Philip supervised the staff who were directing the escort of knights and their squires to rooms above the stable blocks. The visiting grooms were taken to the horse boxes where they would be sleeping on straw with their seventy or so horses, and the carriages were manoeuvred into the outhouses that had been cleared out and cleaned in preparation.

Servants formed a constantly moving line as they carried six hundred pieces of tagged baggage from the carts and hefted it onto their shoulders to deliver to the correct owners, with very few errors. The carts were then manhandled to stand outside in a field until they were required for the homeward journey.

There was also great activity at the rear of the column as the families who were hosting more than one hundred servants in their own homes collected their guests and took them and their bags down to the village, from whence they would walk to and from the Hall each day.

The entire procedure took three hours to complete but at last there was peace in the driveway, though a great deal of noise and bustle on every floor inside the Hall.

Marian had looked in vain for Richard and had come to the disappointing conclusion that he had not been included in the company. Neither had she seen Lord Bathampton, which surprised her but was also a cause for relief.

The simple soup and bread meal that evening, acknowledging the fasting of the court during the four weeks of Advent leading up to Christmas Day, passed with only a few minor incidents. Marian noticed a goblet of wine knocked over and a basket of bread dropped onto the floor, much to the delight of the Queen's spaniels. However, good humour at the tables meant that, once profuse apologies had been made, no one was disciplined and news of the mishaps did not reach the royal ears.

King Henry and Queen Katharine were tired after their long progress and once they had retired, everyone else went gratefully to their beds, to the relief of the servants who had to clear up and prepare for breakfast next morning.

"Marian, if you are not needed, come up to my room in ten minutes," Lady Anne whispered.

Most of the ladies-in-waiting were doubling up in chamber and bed with few exceptions, one of which was Mary Boleyn. Marian wondered about this and why she had not been allocated the same room as her sister, who was sharing with her cousin, Lady Jane Seymour. Both were in their night attire when Marian arrived.

"You have such a beautiful home, Marian," commented Lady Anne as a maid brushed her hair in long, even strokes, making it gleam black in the candlelight.

"Tell us," added Lady Jane, "who is the formidable gentleman whose bust tops the alabaster pillar in the alcove along the corridor?"

"That is Sir William's grandfather, who built the Hall a hundred years ago. I used to be afraid of him when I was a little girl. He has such piercing eyes."

Lady Anne sent both maids off to their lodgings in the village, then said, "Now for the surprise I told you about. Come over to the bed."

She pulled aside the bed curtains and, as she did so, Marian gasped. Lying on the coverlet were two gowns, one in black velvet and gold, like those of the ladies-in-waiting, and another of a delicate eau-de-nil silk.

"They're beautiful!" Marian exclaimed. "Are they yours?"

"No, ninny, they're for you!" laughed Lady Anne. "Mistress Fettiplace has made them for you, especially for Christmas, as you can't keep wearing the two you have. Try them on!"

They helped Marian out of her bronze gown and into each of the others. Of course, they fitted perfectly and suited her colouring well.

"Just wait till Sir Philip sees you in those!" Lady Jane laughed. "Our Lady Alice will have her nose quite put out of joint!"

"Is Lady Alice here?" asked Marian, somewhat deflated. "There were so many courtiers arriving that I didn't have opportunity to see everyone."

"She's sharing a room with her sister," Lady Anne said. "How have you been faring with Lady Dereham?"

"Tolerably well. In fact, she is being very pleasant to me and to everyone on the staff. I have been very surprised."

"And how is she faring with Sir William?"

Marian bristled. She had been very concerned that her guardian and Lady Dereham had been spending a great deal of time in each other's company. However, she had reasoned that that was to be expected in view of the number of arrangements that had to be made to ensure the success of the royal visit – "Though it will bankrupt me!" he had complained. Marian had been included in many of their discussions, but not all, and not those that had taken place in his chambers in Stephen Tower late in the evening, when much laughter had been heard and she guessed much wine had been drunk.

"She and my guardian seem to enjoy each other's company," Marian said guardedly.

"And do you take pleasure in the prospect of welcoming my lady as your step mother?" Lady Anne teased.

"No! That shall never happen!"

"To be mistress of this house is your destiny, is it not?" asked Lady Jane.

"It will be so when Philip and I are married."

"Then let us hope that nothing prevents it."

"Now off to bed with you," said Lady Anne. "You must be as tired as the rest of us. I think you will find that what everyone needs is a quiet day tomorrow."

"Good night, my ladies," said Marian. "I cannot tell you how grateful I am."

"My maids will deliver the gowns to your chamber tomorrow," Lady Anne promised.

As Marian left, Lady Jane was moving round the chamber, snuffing out the candles.

# CHAPTER 14

*Place: Forrester Hall, Berkshire*

*Date: Christmas Eve morning, 1524*

Everyone had recovered by the morning of Christmas Eve. When a band of young men and women servants arrived outside the Hall mid-morning, carrying armfuls of greenery gathered from hedges and woodlands on the estate, a crowd was waiting to greet them.

They came singing Christmas carols in which everyone joined – *A Babe is born in Bethlehem, For Joy the Christmas Bells ring true,* and others, more bawdy – as they bore swathes of holly, mistletoe, ivy and yew into the Hall to decorate walls, doors, fireplace and grand staircase.

Marian stood on the stairs, viewing the bustle below with great excitement. She was joined by Sir William, who had emerged from Stephen Tower especially to honour the Christmas traditions. The King and Queen, with their attendants, were watching from the landing above.

Then a shout went up, "The yule log is coming!" and those who were not standing on chairs or on the tops of ladders hurried outside again.

Ten minutes previously, it had begun to snow, the flakes laying a thin, white covering over the driveway. The little procession left drag marks as three heavy horses, iron chains clanking, strained to pull three huge oak tree trunks to the steps at the front of the Hall. There, the largest was unchained and set upon by two lads who wielded a powerful saw, backwards and forwards, backwards and forwards, until it had been divided into large logs and the heavy air was thick with the fresh, natural aroma of sawn wood.

Willing hands helped drag the logs into the Hall and across to the stone fireplace, where the largest was placed on the ashes of last year's yule log with much of its length protruding into the room.

The other two trunks were hauled away into storage.

Behind the heavy horses had come two smaller and lighter, pulling a cart load of branches sawn into smaller logs for the fireplaces in the bedchambers. These were unloaded and carried by young servants to the floors above.

Sir William made a decision to light the yule log straight away as the temperature was dropping fast, so he requested their majesties to offer the first lighted taper.

The royal couple descended the staircase amid the cheers and applause of their excited subjects. King Henry was obviously in a jovial mood and waved his hand expansively to the assembled company, acknowledging their greeting.

The log was sprinkled with wine, salt, powdered borax, copper sulphate and other chemicals to colour the flames, then a candle was brought from which to light two tapers and their majesties applied them to the kindling. The rags and twigs caught fire and it was not long before the log began to release red sparks up the chimney.

It would take several hours to catch fire in earnest and for the flames to burn bright yellow, violet, apple green, vivid green and blue, and for the hall to warm, but all those standing around like ancient fire worshippers were happy to know that Christmas had begun in truth.

By now the snow was falling thick and fast and Philip and some of the young courtiers donned hooded cloaks and ran outside for a snowball fight. Marian would have joined them but Lady Dereham whispered that she was needed in the kitchens to check the progress of the mid-day meal, and please to follow her.

She was about to obey the summons when a man's voice she recognised and feared spoke her name. She clenched her fists to steady her breathing and her resolve not to flee before she slowly turned to face him. Lady Dereham also turned.

"Lord Bathampton," Marian said, bobbing a perfunctory curtsey. "I was not aware you were here." What she really meant was that she had hoped against hope he was not in the company.

"As an Esquire to the Body of the King, you should have guessed I would be staying close to his majesty. I am disappointed that you thought otherwise. It is a great privilege to be in your home, Lady Marian. I hope there will be opportunity for you to show me around the house and grounds before we bid farewell. That would give me great pleasure."

"Of course, my lord, Sir Philip and I would be glad to do so."

"Cook is waiting for you," Lady Dereham reminded her impatiently and moved away.

Marian turned, longing to quit his presence as quickly as possible, and tried to follow her but Lord Bathampton caught her by the arm.

"Leave me if you must, sweet Marian, but I will keep you to your promise. However, the presence of Sir Philip will not be necessary, I think."

Marian felt his voracious eyes consuming her inch by inch. There seemed no part of her that she could hide from him.

"And if you feel the desire," he whispered hoarsely, "you will know that my chamber is in the West Tower, which has been taken over by his majesty."

"I am aware of it, my lord," she said, wrenching her arm out of his grasp and turning, fled to the kitchens, knowing there was no way she would allow herself to be alone with that man ever again.

That evening, everyone was abed in good time, in anticipation of the Christmas Mass in the chapel early next morning, which would be followed by a day of feasting and revelry.

# CHAPTER 15

*Place: Forrester Hall, Berkshire*

*Date: Christmas Day, 1524*

The snow had continued to fall steadily and was lying several inches thick by the time the company assembled in the great hall, where the yule log had been burning all night.

Sir William guided their majesties, who led the procession along the corridor leading to the chapel, and made sure they were comfortable in the front row of chairs. He then sat behind them with Philip, Marian and Lady Dereham.

On both sides of the central aisle, the ladies-in-waiting and King's attendants, with their furs and cloaks clasped tightly around them, filed into the other rows until the chapel was full. The royal servants and house servants were crowded onto benches in the gallery.

Sir William's priest, Father Anselm, officiated, supported by an assistant priest who administered the chalice. Father Anselm was a sincere man of God. He gave a very moving sermon about the divine love that had suffered the blessed Lord Jesus to leave His heavenly splendour to be born as a human baby, live a human life and then die on the Cross in the agony of a human body, to save all those present and all the world from the consequences of their sins.

After their majesties had received the sacrament of bread and wine, the ladies and gentlemen of the court came forward to the altar rail to receive the offering. When the last communicant on the ground floor had returned to his place, the servants came down from the gallery in their turn.

Philip murmured his surprise when Marian suddenly gripped his hand where it lay on his open Bible. He turned towards her to ascertain the reason then followed the line of her gaze.

"So," he whispered grimly, "the scribe is here and you did not know it."

Flustered, Marian removed her hand.

"No, I didn't," she whispered back.

"Then we are both well content," Philip said. "You have your scribe and I have Lady Alice."

"Philip, I'm sorry."

"Forget it, Marian, 'tis of little consequence."

*Not to me*, she thought.

She had not seen Richard since their meeting in the scriptorium but he did not once look her way.

The service over, everyone followed their majesties to the great hall for the feasting and merriment. Marian had chosen to wear the black and gold gown she had been given by Lady Anne and was conscious of many glances of approval from the gentlemen in the company. The only look of admiration that displeased her was that from Lord Bathampton and she made sure that she stayed close to Philip when he was in the vicinity.

All the chatter and laughter and wishing each other Christmas cheer was drowned out by a fanfare of trumpets from young men placed above them on each step of the staircase as a large silver bowl, its contents steaming, was carried with great deference to King Henry. A chorus of carollers followed, singing,

*"Here we come a-wassailing,*
*Among the leaves so green,*
*Here we come a-wassailing,*
*So fair to be seen."*

The King, followed by the Queen, drank deeply from the bowl of spiced and sugared ale that had been whisked together with apple purée, their mouths then being covered in the 'lambswool' of froth floating on top. Their majesties laughed heartily as their faces and the King's beard were wiped clean, and the whole company joined in the merriment.

While the silver bowl was passed from mouth to mouth, two large wooden bowls also came from the kitchens. Servants were despatched, one group to tour the village with the offering and the other to tour the apple orchards and splash the liquid over the tree roots to ensure a good harvest next year. All the while, the voices of the singers regaled the company:

*Love and joy come to you,*
*And to you your wassail too,*
*And God bless you and send you,*
*A happy New Year,*
*And God send you*
*A happy New Year.*

Those who had drunk from the bowl then seated themselves in order of precedence, in great anticipation now that the Advent fast was over.

The tables were decorated with roasted peacocks flaunting their feathers, as well as boars' heads with apples in their mouths, displayed on gold and silver platters which had been carried into the hall high on the shoulders of the waiting men.

When all were seated, the food began to arrive – swans from the lake baked in pastry coffins, pickled pigs' feet and ears (a delicacy favoured by the King), roast venison from the forest, a rich meaty broth made from boiled hares from the fields and Christmas minced meat pie.

Turkeys had been introduced into England the previous year and had become very popular and Cook surpassed herself with her final savoury offering. She and her lackeys had spent many hours stuffing turkeys with farm geese which in turn had been stuffed with pheasants stuffed with chickens stuffed with partridges stuffed with pigeons, with layers of chestnuts, force meat and bread stuffing between each bird. To the birds had been added onion, clove, celery, thyme, parsley, salted pork fat, salt, pepper and coriander and all had been stewed in pots over a fire for twenty four hours.

Lady Dereham had remarked earlier that the kitchens in the palace cooked as many as seventeen birds stuffed one inside another, but Cook had replied that Sir William's coffers were not bottomless and the household had to eat after the royal party had gone on its way. She hoped that their majesties would find her recipe acceptable and Sir William would not be discredited.

Marian was particularly nervous as the vegetables were served – the winter cabbage, leeks, carrots and onions – for which she had been responsible. She had also been responsible for the preserved and sugared fruits that were layered on tall, silver stands, as well as various cakes, puddings, jellies and tarts. As it was all disappearing before her eyes, washed down with copious amounts of wine and ale, she presumed there were no complainers.

For the final two hours she only picked at the dishes offered and marvelled at the stamina of those around her who were still tucking into the sumptuous fare, principally the King and his nobles.

At long last, he banged on the table with a wooden spoon and called for silence, which took some time to achieve. Standing a little uncertainly, his words slightly slurred, he grasped his goblet and bowed deferentially to the Queen.

"Your majesty, my lords, ladies and gentlemen, it affords me great pleasure to thank Sir William Forrester for his generous hospitality and to congratulate him on his fine Christmas board. I give you – Sir William."

Everyone followed their monarch's lead in raising their drinking vessels and chorusing, "Sir William!" before putting them to their lips and consuming every last drop.

Then the tables were cleared and the leftover food conveyed to the kitchens for the servants to enjoy. What they could not consume would later be taken down to the monastery and village for the monks and nuns and peasants to devour, though it was known to upset many stomachs for days afterwards.

The elderly men and women courtiers who had fallen asleep in their places were woken up so that the trestle tables could be removed and the benches pushed back along the sides of the hall, making space for entertainment and dancing. Their majesties were conducted to two dark-wood chairs facing down the hall.

It was now that the dancing master came into his own. While the meal was being digested in each stomach, a play was performed about a wife who rampaged into an inn to find her husband in bed with one of the serving wenches. While he lay on the bed (several benches pushed together) protesting his innocence and the girl trembled beneath them, hidden by the dangling sheets, the betrayed wife revenged herself by throwing his outer garments into the fire. This raised great guffaws of mirth as the flames consumed his doublet and hose and he was forced to walk 'home' in his underclothes.

Then the simpleton the dancing master had acquired along the way took a turn at singing and dancing and tickling the ladies under their chins with peacock feathers. His antics were reminiscent of the Lord of Misrule, whose upside-down reign the King had banished from court many years previously.

The incompetent young man was soon booed from the assembly and was replaced by a jester in a red and yellow costume. He was applauded as he performed each rhyme, trick and riddle.

Coloured ribbons, lace kerchiefs and apples were produced from the capacious sleeves of the ladies or from beneath the soft hats of the gentlemen. Lord Bathampton looked greatly discomfited when he was asked to stand and was accused of trying to hatch the duck egg he had apparently been sitting on. His protestations that ducks didn't lay eggs in winter went unheard by most amid laughter at his embarrassment.

Then the clever fellow turned somersaults and back flips along the length of the hall, without his hands touching the floor, until he came to where Marian was sitting between Philip and Sir William.

"My lady Marian, please excuse me, but the dove you are nursing so carefully is wishing to be set free!"

Everyone looked towards Marian in expectation as he reached towards her coif and seemingly took from beneath it a pure white dove which he threw into the air. It soared upwards towards the ceiling, flew round the hall once, then landed on a rafter and began to coo softly.

"You see," the jester said, "he is singing the praises of her majesty the Queen and of all the beautiful ladies in the hall, yourself included."

Everyone clapped loudly and thought that was the culmination of his act, but he had one more puzzle for them. He returned to the centre of the floor, bowed low to their majesties, and began to recite.

*"My first is in pheasant and also in hare,*
*My second in table but not in chair.*
*My third is in Katharine and also in Queen –*

begging your majesty's pardon –

*My fourth is in emerald and in tourmaline.*
*My fifth is in holly and ivy and yule,*
*The whole has the love and respect of this fool!*
*Who am I?"*

There was a moment's silence as the company began to puzzle over the riddle, followed by an eruption of babbling as words and letters and possible answers were suggested, then a name was on many lips but no one would speak it aloud until the King slapped his thigh and shouted, "By my oath, I have the answer! The answer is 'Henry'! Am I not right, fool? Has not your King worked out the riddle?"

"He has indeed, sire, he has indeed!" replied the jester and turned another somersault.

Then everyone began chanting, "Henry! Henry! His majesty King Henry!" and clapping and laughing and stamping their feet until he held up his hand for silence.

"Fool, I perceive that you are not such a fool as you present to us."

He looked round the hall and addressed the company. "I perceive that this fool is in truth a very clever fellow."

Then he turned his attention back to the jester. "I will make sure that you are well rewarded. Now off with you and let the dancing commence!"

The young man skipped and cartwheeled his way from the hall amid the congratulations and well wishes of those he passed, and the musicians struck up the introduction to the first dance.

After being partnered by Philip, Marian was besieged with requests, from many of the young courtiers present, to allow them to escort her into the next measure. Most of them had drunk far too much ale and were clumsy in their attempts to put their arms round her waist or entice her into one of the corridors leading off the hall. She managed to extricate herself from each compromising situation without giving offence and reflected that she had learned a great deal since arriving at court.

However, when she saw Lord Bathampton approaching, she turned to Sir William and her green eyes sent him an appeal that he couldn't ignore. When Bathampton asked if he might take Marian onto the floor, Sir William apologised profusely and said she had just accepted him as her partner. Lord Bathampton bowed stiffly and walked away, to Marian's great relief.

"Marian, is anything amiss?"

"Sire, he – that is – I – his attentions are not welcome."

"Then he shall be warned – if you are certain you are not mistaken."

"There is no mistake, sire."

"I can see you are frightened of him. I will attend to it."

"Thank you, Father."

Sir William kept his eye on her for the remainder of the evening as Philip was nowhere to be seen. Neither was Lady Alice, Marian noticed, and wished so much that Richard was there to dance with her.

Lord Bathampton came nowhere near them after his first approach, releasing Sir William to partner many of the ladies, Lady Dereham receiving more than her fair share of his attention, to Marian's mind.

The company danced until it was almost dawn, when the King decided enough was enough and he was away to his bed. The musicians packed up their instruments and everyone else, sated with the best food and drink, retired in good spirits.

Sir William looked round the hall.

"Where *is* Philip?" he asked as he had done many times that evening.

"I don't know, sire."

"That boy!" he muttered in irritation, so quietly that Marian only just heard him.

Before wishing her a good night's sleep, he thanked her for the part she had played in making the day such a success.

"My little Marian is growing up fast," he said. "I hope my son realises what a fortunate young man he is."

As before, when Richard had made the same remark, Marian was not at all certain that he did.

# CHAPTER 16

Contrary to expectations, the King was out of bed at eight o'clock next morning, prepared for the day's hawking that Sir William had promised him. This was to be a diversion at which the women were not welcome.

Before ten o'clock, twenty-one nobles and their squires were astride horses and waiting impatiently in front of the Hall together with trained spaniels from the kennels with their handlers.

The King had brought his falconers with him and his birds were being challenged to compete against Sir William's. The falconers in both teams were also waiting for his majesty to arrive, reins in one hand and their falcons, merlins and fractious goshawks balanced on protective leather gauntlets on the other.

At ten o'clock precisely, the King, Sir William and Philip, mounted on thoroughbred horses, joined them.

The silver stirrup cup in the shape of a stag's head was passed around, the horns sounded a fanfare, and the horses and their riders trotted off along the drive, all anticipating an exciting day's sport.

Deprived of their male companions, and finding the Hall suddenly quiet, the Queen decided she would enjoy a game of skittles. Marian conducted the party to the skittle alley and summoned servants to set up nine wooden pins.

Having practised for ten minutes with the wooden balls and finding she was in good form, her majesty decided that she would make the game into a competition among her ladies.

"Lady Marian, we need someone to score for us," she said, "if my ladies are not to quarrel among themselves and – dare I suggest it? – cheat a little."

The ladies-in-waiting laughed, seeming to agree.

"Is there anyone who springs to mind?" the Queen asked.

Then Marian had an idea.

"Lord Bathampton has brought two scribes with him. As his lordship is away hawking with his majesty, the young men are likely to be enjoying free time today. Master Richard Mordaunt you already know, your majesty."

When the Queen looked blankly at Marian, she hastened to remind her. "The young man who tutored the princess."

"Of course!" her majesty exclaimed. "Splendid!"

A page was despatched and twenty minutes later, Richard walked into the alley, followed by a dark, curly-haired young man who was probably slightly older than his companion. The young man looked overawed, his dark eyes wide open, though Marian noticed that his eyelid drooped a little over his right eye, giving his face a slightly lopsided aspect, though this didn't detract at all from his handsome appearance.

They bowed low and Richard asked, "Your Majesty?"

"I am pleased to see you again, master Richard."

"Thank you, your Majesty," he replied.

"And your companion?"

"Stephen Arundell, your Majesty," Richard answered for him.

He had not looked across to Marian but she was certain he was aware of her presence. She was certainly aware of him as the fluttering of her heart and an involuntary shiver down her spine evidenced.

"Master Richard," said her majesty, "I vish you both to keep a tally of our scores. How vill you do that?"

"We have brought two counting frames," he explained. "A colour for each lady, and this one will register the units and the second one the tens."

"I see you have six rows of colours and six beads to a row, so my ladies vill choose a colour and make up teams of six. Then the vinning lady from each team vill play one more game to decide the final vinner. How many ladies shall we need for six teams of six, master Richard?"

"Thirty six, your Majesty."

"So how many are wanting?"

Richard quickly counted the ladies present. "Another eighteen, your Majesty."

"I will find them," Marian offered and left the room, followed by Lady Anne Boleyn.

When they returned with the final five, who included Lady Joan Dereham and her sister, Alice, the game was well under way and the laughter and chatter of the ladies was evidence of their enjoyment.

It took all morning to complete the competition and establish the winner, providentially the Queen herself, before she led her ladies back to the hall for refreshment, indicating that the two young men were included in the invitation. After the light meal, the Queen retired to her chamber to rest and her ladies left in small groups to follow her example.

Marian saw her chance and took it as she knew it might not come her way again.

"Richard, you have been ignoring me."

He gestured to his companion, who obligingly also left the hall, leaving them alone.

"No, Lady Marian, I have not but our paths have not crossed since my arrival here."

"'Lady Marian' again, is it?"

"Yes, my lady. It always was."

"Not when you kissed me in the schoolroom –"

"That was dishonourable of me –"

" – and would have done so again in the scriptorium if matters had turned out differently," she interrupted him.

His stern expression relaxed. "Yes, I would have," he confessed with the ghost of a smile at the memory, "but you must accept that our stations in life preclude any understanding between us."

"Oh, Richard, don't be so stuffy! Here is my hand. Take it as an earnest of our affection for each other."

Richard made no move to grasp the hand she was holding out to him.

"Take it, Richard! It will not crush your fingers!"

"My fingers may not be crushed, my lady, but the affection between us has already crushed my heart. You should not toy with my feelings, it is not worthy of you. We can never be more than distant acquaintances. I know it and so should you. I ask you to respect that."

He bowed and turned to leave.

Marian was fuming over his rejection of her advance. She knew she had overstepped the bounds of propriety and her frustration and humiliation made her lash out at him.

"It is a pity your master has no such respect!"

Richard turned back. "Lord Bathampton? He hasn't – since the incident in the scriptorium – he hasn't...?"

"No, nothing since, but only because I give him no opportunity."

"Be careful, Marian –"

"Richard, you just called me plain 'Marian'."

He flushed. "I apologise. It won't happen again."

"Then I am sorry for it. Oh, Richard, Richard! Don't keep me at such a distance. Do you not love me?"

"You know that I do."

"Then kiss me."

"Marian –"

"If you won't kiss me, I'll kiss you. Like this."

She covered the space between them and raised her face to his. When he still resisted, she stood on tip toe and placed her lips firmly on his, forgetting all her resolve to resist her 'bodily passions'.

Immediately, his arms went round her and he was kissing not only her lips but her cheeks and hair and ears and eyes. Her arms went round his neck of their own volition and they were locked together for several moments, totally immersed in each other's need of the other. Then, just as suddenly as he had taken her in his arms, he wrenched himself free and strode out of the hall.

Marian was stunned at the suddenness of the passion that had arisen between them. She had betrayed how she felt about him and had been left in no doubt about his feelings towards her. As for the future …

He was right. She had to face the fact that, for them, there *was* no future.

# CHAPTER 17

The King's party returned late in the afternoon with a great deal of ribaldry, noise and confusion. The King and his men dismounted, tossing reins to the waiting grooms, laughing and calling to their fellows, greatly dishevelled and some covered in mud where they had been thrown. The spaniels were running around the horses' hooves, barking and growling, still greatly excited.

The King strode into the hall accompanied by Sir William and his son, the rest of the party following, calling for flagons of ale and wine and victuals to eat, all of which had been prepared in readiness.

The Queen crossed to her husband and touched him on the arm to ask if they had had a successful day's hawking.

"Never better!" he roared and waved an arm towards the birds, small mammals and several hares strung by their feet from poles and carried into the hall as evidence before being taken to the kitchens.

"Sir William's birds were magnificent but he had to admit that the royal birds were superior. You should have seen –"

"I am sure you all wish to discuss the day's sport," the Queen interrupted him, "so I and my ladies will leave you to your feasting and take our refreshment elsewhere."

Sir William came over to Marian, who was standing with Lady Dereham.

"Will you have a care for the needs of her majesty and her ladies? The King will likely not retire until the early hours of the morning."

"Do not fret, Sir William," Lady Dereham said. "Marian and I will take charge of everything."

"And, once the meal has been cleared, instruct Mistress Malmesbury to take her young women out of the way to the kitchens. I cannot trust these men in their cups to behave with the respect I would wish in my home."

"I understand, Sir William," said Lady Dereham.

"Sire, the King seems much pleased with the day's sport," Marian observed.

"He is very happy," Sir William agreed and winked at her, "especially as his birds were more successful than mine. I believe we will all sleep away tomorrow."

"And we ride out on the day following," Lady Dereham reminded him. "There is little time left to us."

*Little time to do what?* Marian wondered but was too busy to think more about the remark.

When the drinks and meal had been served, Mistress Malmesbury took her army of young women to the safety of the kitchens, not before time, and left the men to their devices.

Hours of carousing in the great hall meant that no one on the upstairs floors slept very much until, as dawn broke, one by one the company stumbled their way to bed or fell asleep where they sprawled.

Marian crept down at first light to make sure she was not needed on duty. With her sleeves rolled up, the housekeeper was busy directing servants as they tended the fire then swept, dusted and polished. The floor and tables where food and brown ale had been liberally spilt were scrubbed, taking care not to disturb those who were lolling on the tables, lying flat on the benches or comatose beneath.

In spite of Sir William's endeavours, there were several women among the company, both ladies and their maids, as drunk as their lords.

"Marmy, do you need me?" Marian asked her.

"No, my lady. Go back to bed. I doubt any of your guests will be up and about before late afternoon. If you are needed, I will send a message."

"Thank you, Marmy," said Marian, yawning her way back to the staircase. "I'll look in on Lady Dereham and give her the good news."

At Lady Dereham's door she knocked quietly and, on receiving no reply, knocked again, louder. There was still no reply. She turned away but, on impulse, tried the latch and peeped round the door. Lady Alice was snoring gently in her bed but the second bed had not been slept in. Puzzled, she closed the door and returned to her own bed, and was soon fast asleep.

When she awoke, it was getting dark and her maid was bustling around her chamber. Confused, Marian asked what time and day it was.

"Three of the clock two days after Christmas Day, my lady. You have slept all day, as have your guests, but they are beginning to stir and cook is requesting your presence below. I am here to help you wash and dress."

Feeling refreshed but slightly disoriented, Marian left her chamber and walked along the corridor towards the staircase. As she reached the bust of Sir William's grandfather on its alabaster pillar, she heard the door to Stephen Tower creak open and shut. She presumed that Sir William was coming down from his quarters to the great hall to supervise arrangements for the evening and prepared to welcome him but saw with surprise that it was a woman approaching.

Embarrassed, Marian swiftly concealed herself in the curtained alcove behind the alabaster pillar, not wishing to spy on the lady her guardian had been entertaining in his chamber.

Looking straight ahead, her hair dishevelled, her coif swinging in her hand, her cheeks flushed, and wearing the gown she had worn the previous evening, Lady Dereham passed within inches of Marian without noticing her and gained access to her chamber.

Marian emerged from behind the pillar, staring at the door through which the lady had disappeared, experiencing a pot pourri of emotions – confusion, embarrassment, indignation – and jealousy? She had been brought up to believe that she would be mistress of Forrester Hall one day. That some other woman might oust her from that position by marrying her guardian was not the plan and could not be tolerated.

She found Philip and voiced her fears but he only roared with laughter.

"Were you spying on them, Marian?"

"No, of course not!"

"My father is a dark horse, I must say, and good luck to him! I wonder whether he invited her into his bed or she invited herself. Shall I tell him you saw her?"

"No, no, please not Philip. It is his house, after all, and he should be allowed to do what he likes in his own home. It's just – oh, Philip, Lady Dereham of all people!"

Philip pulled her to him and kissed her above her breasts. She pushed him away.

"Philip, behave!"

"Marian, when?"

"I have already told you - when we are married and not before."

"You are such a little prude! But maybe, maybe, I shall be glad when the time comes. And don't worry about my lady Dereham. I know my father and have a fancy she isn't as secure in his regard as she imagines she is. Don't fret about it. You'll be mistress of Forrester Hall in time, Marian, no question of it. We've just got to wait to grow up a little."

Marian thought she had felt very grown up yesterday when Richard was kissing her and she was returning his ardour.

She turned as one of the maids addressed her. "My lady, the steward wishes to speak to you urgently."

"Of course."

"How important you have become, sister," Philip grinned. "I won't keep you from your duties. Tonight's banquet must be the best before the court leaves us on the morrow."

His eyes twinkled as he placed his curled forefinger under her chin and raised her face so that he could kiss her on the lips.

"Off you go and I'll see you later at the high table."

Marian followed the maid to the kitchens. The steward was pacing up and down the stone corridor, wringing his hands in distress.

She was immediately alarmed. "What's the matter, John? Is something amiss?"

"My lady, oh, my lady! We have no ale!"

"What do you mean, we have no ale? We have plenty."

"No, mistress. We are on the last barrel! None has been delivered by the monastery today."

"But of course it has! They have been delivering every day since the court arrived. Of course there is ale."

"No, my lady, none has been delivered today. Did you order it? Did you make a mistake perchance? Forget that their majesties were not leaving until tomorrow? I tell you, we have none once we finish this last barrel."

"That is not possible! Of course I didn't forget. I ordered it, I know I did."

"What is to be done?"

"You must despatch a messenger to the monastery at once and arrange for the usual quantity to be sent up. There is just about time before the King sits down to eat. Then report to me that this has been accomplished."

"Yes, my lady."

The steward scurried away to carry out her orders.

Marian was at a loss to understand what had happened. Of course she had ordered the ale. She wouldn't make a mistake like that. The thought that the King could have been waving around his empty silver mug and calling for another barrel to be tapped during this evening's meal sent hot and cold shivers through her. What profound disgrace for Sir William and shame heaped on her own head for not efficiently arranging the affairs of the household as expected of her.

The steward found her an hour later to report that the cart conveying six barrels was on its way.

"The order was cancelled," he told her.

"Cancelled? By whom?"

"No one knows but a messenger arrived at the monastery this morning to say that the ordered barrels of ale would not be required."

"I don't understand," Marian said.

"Neither do I, my lady," confessed the steward, "but it is evident that you did order the ale and somebody cancelled it."

"I'm so grateful that you realised in time."

"I leave nothing to chance. It is my usual routine to check the cellars."

"Sir William shall hear of your diligence."

"Yes, my lady. Thank you, my lady."

Marian pondered this extraordinary incident and could come to no conclusion – at least, the only possible explanation, that Lady Dereham had cancelled the order to discredit her before Sir William, the King and Queen and their whole court, was so ludicrous that she dismissed the thought immediately.

# CHAPTER 18

*Place: Greenwich Palace*

*Date: March, 1525*

After the great success of the Christmas festivities at Forrester Hall, the King and Queen and their entourage travelled on to The Vyne in Hampshire, the home of his Lord Chamberlain, Baron Sandys and his family, and thence to all the great houses in the home counties. Sir William, Philip and Lady Dereham were required to join them.

The dust sheets at Forrester Hall were replaced, a skeleton staff was left in charge as before, and Marian returned with an escort to Greenwich Palace.

The Christmas snow had melted away and the weather in early January, though wet, did little to hinder the royal progress. However, when it began to snow heavily again at the end of the month, Princess Mary received news that the company had spent longer than intended at two estate houses and was much delayed.

During the prolonged absence of their majesties, the schooling of the young princess progressed. Marian was again at her side during their lessons, and the two girls grew to regard each other with great affection. Marian was aware that the princess had few friends, certainly not of her own age, and she was filling a gap in that young, royal but lonely life.

Without the close supervision of the Queen, the nursemaids in charge of the princess relaxed their vigilance and the two girls roamed around the palace and in the gardens wherever their fancy took them.

During inclement weather, they played board games or hide-and-seek and blind man's buff with the ladies-in-waiting, rode hobby horses along the galleries or rocking horses in the nursery. On brighter days, they bowled iron hoops, spun wooden tops and played tag in the gardens.

One afternoon at the beginning of March, after an energetic game of shuttlecock, one of the nursemaids came to collect the princess and take her back to her chamber to rest.

"We have news," the nursemaid said with great excitement. "Their majesties will be arriving back at the palace in three days' time. You will be pleased to see them, will you not, your royal highness?"

"Yes, indeed," replied the princess, her eyes shining at the prospect. "We have missed them, have we not, Lady Marian?"

"Yes, we have. I am so pleased for your royal highness. Will my father be with them, do you know?"

"The court arrives home tomorrow, Lady Marian, to prepare for their majesties' return so your father will be here then. Lord Bathampton is already back in the palace, I understand."

She took hold of the princess's hand and escorted her from the garden. Marian waved them goodbye then gathered up the shuttlecocks and wooden bats. She also found a little wooden peg doll that the princess had discarded when their game began. She picked it up and went to sit on a bench to regain her breath and cool down. It was there that Lord Bathampton found her.

He had approached so stealthily that she was not aware of his presence until he was standing before her. He removed his hat and offered her a courtly bow.

"Lady Marian, I have been looking for you. No, please don't run away. I have news for you."

Marian, who had jumped up in agitation when he addressed her, sat down again.

"News, sire?"

"Yes, of your betrothed and Sir William."

He placed his hat on the bench, swept his cloak to one side and sat beside her, so close that she moved away a little. He smiled and, placing his hand on the pommel of his sword hilt, stretched out his left leg so that it was crushing the folds of her skirt.

She and the princess had dressed informally that afternoon, without farthingales, the better to run across the grass and jump for the shuttlecock, and the pressure of his leg against hers sent an involuntary shudder through her. She moved her leg away. He sighed.

"Lady Marian, you are young – so young and so beautiful. My dearest wish is to make you happy. I could, you know, if you would only let me explore the pleasures beneath your gown. We have opportunity before your stepfather returns tomorrow. He told me to keep away from you – did you know that? But we have all night – all night to touch and taste and devour. I have been patient, so very patient –"

Marian sprang up. "Not another word, sire, I will not listen to another word! Till now I have kept silent about your persecution of me but my guardian and Sir Philip shall hear of this second offence!"

Lord Bathampton also rose to his feet. "Your guardian, Lady Marian, is far too distracted to worry about any dalliance you may be enjoying. I rather fancy that Lady Joan is keeping him fully occupied these days – and nights. And as for Sir Philip – Sir Philip is enjoying the attentions of Lady

Alice. I can vouch for the pleasures that little minx offers. She will spread her legs for anyone –"

The wooden bat struck him across his face with such force that he staggered backwards, bellowing in pain. His hand shot up to his nose and blood began to redden his fingers.

Dropping the bat, Marian fled.

# CHAPTER 19

Gaining her chamber, she flung herself onto the bed and pummelled the pillows with both fists as if it was that man's head, face, chest, and genitals she was battering, at the same time sobbing and crying in shame. When she had exhausted her anger and disgust, she fell on to her back, breathing heavily, perspiring and emotionally drained.

Sleep brought her some relief, though how long she slept she was not sure. On waking, she washed all over in cold water and changed into another gown, wondering whether she dare leave the chamber to face whatever consequences lay ahead. It would be her word against his. How she wished that Sir William had returned and she could feel his fatherly arms around her and listen to his wise counsel.

Pulling back her shoulders, she decided that skulking in her chamber solved nothing and she would have to face the outcome of her action. After all, his lecherous reputation was well known, though not discussed openly, while no scandal attached to her name.

With trepidation, she made her way to the women's quarters where the ladies-in-waiting who had been left behind by the Queen were occupied as usual, their conversation only of the returning court and a regretful end to their idleness.

The evening meal passed without incident and everyone retired early in readiness for the rigours of the following day.

It was not until her maids were preparing her for bed that there was any hint of the gossip she feared.

"What was that you said?" she asked on overhearing their whispers.

"No one saw it happen, my lady," one of the girls replied as she slipped the nightgown over Marian's head, "but there are rumours that Lord Bathampton has fallen down a flight of steps and broken his nose."

"Are you sure?" Marian spoke so sharply that the girl looked at her in surprise. Recovering her composure, she explained, "I saw him earlier in the day and he appeared quite well."

"All I've been told is that one of his squires sent for a physician late this afternoon."

The other girl giggled. "If you ask me, someone pushed him, with good reason – begging your pardon, my lady, but some of us has cause."

After brushing Marian's hair the usual one hundred and twenty times and helping her into bed, they pulled the curtains around her and left the chamber, still giggling and whispering their suspicions.

Next day, the court returned, as planned. Marian did not see her step father or brother. Neither was there any sign of Lord Bathampton.

The King and Queen returned on the day following and life settled back into its normal busy routine.

The ladies-in-waiting newly arrived with their majesties had much to report. Their progress through the counties surrounding London had been impeded by the snowstorms, much to everyone's discomfort, especially their unfortunate hosts, who had experienced great difficulty in feeding the company when supplies from surrounding villages could not be delivered.

Added to all this gossip was the news that Mary Boleyn, Anne's sister, had not returned with them but had been granted permission to go home because she was pregnant again.

There was much whispered speculation when Anne was not present that the King and not her husband, Sir William Carey, was the baby's father; he had probably also fathered Mary's first child, Katharine, now about a year old. However, his majesty was not acknowledging either child.

This was not the case with young Henry Fitzroy, son of one-time lady-in-waiting Bessie Blount. On his sixth birthday in June he was to be created earl of Nottingham and on the same day would receive the honour of a double dukedom, Greenwich and Somerset.

None of this could be gossiped about in the hearing of her majesty, who had been unable to give the King a male heir to the throne. Seven pregnancies and several miscarriages had produced three boys, one of whom, Prince Henry, had lived, but all festivities had been cancelled when he died at seven weeks.

On many occasions her ladies had found the Queen on her knees in the chapel or in tears in her chamber and, although she gave many other reasons for her distress, they were shrewd enough to guess the real reason.

Her last pregnancy had occurred seven years ago and now she was 40 years old, it was unlikely she would conceive again. It was no secret that for several years the King's eyes had been roving in the direction of other, younger women at court.

Another subject of gossip was the suggestion that Thomas Boleyn, Mary and Anne's father, was to become the Earl of Ormond.

"For services rendered," one of the ladies reported, "but rendered by whom? Father or daughter?" There was a ripple of laughter, though all whispering ceased whenever Anne joined the company.

She had news of her own to impart. Marian entered the room where the ladies were gathered in the middle of their conversation.

"His majesty demanded to see him," Marian heard her say, "and it was as had been reported – nose red and swollen, cheek black and blue and one eye almost closed. The surgeon said it will all heal naturally but i'faith it was a glorious sight to behold!"

"Are you speaking of Lord Bathampton?" asked Marian.

"None other. He fell down some steps. His majesty told him not to return to his duties until his injuries had healed."

"We are praying that they heal before his marriage."

Everyone stopped what they were doing and stared at the speaker, who shifted uncomfortably in her seat.

"Marriage?" asked someone. "Did you say marriage?"

Lady Joan Dereham nodded. "Had you not heard?"

Denials were voiced and heads shaken.

"What do you know that we don't?" Lady Jane Seymour questioned, her paintbrush poised half way to the canvas.

"Yes, how do you know? Who is he marrying?" demanded Lady Anne. "He cannot marry without the consent of the King."

"He has the consent of the King and of Queen Katharine."

"Then who?" demanded Lady Anne again. Marian waited. Had he tried to seduce her when he was heavily engaged to be married? Was he even more vile than she thought him?

Lady Dereham paused then sat up straight, her hands clasped in her lap, as if preparing for confrontation. "My sister, Lady Alice."

Everyone gasped in disbelief.

"Your sister?" "When was this arranged?" "Why?" "Are you speaking truly?"

As no answer was forthcoming, Lady Anne changed tack. "When is the marriage to take place?"

"Soon. In a week or so."

The news was greeted with an uncomfortable silence. Lady Dereham stood.

"I thought you should hear it from me," she said. "I have to go now. There is much to be arranged."

The door closing behind her preceded a crescendo of speculation.

"What has the girl done to deserve that fate?" Lady Jane asked, wiping her brush clean with a cloth, her painting discarded.

Lady Anne said what was in all of their minds. "It's obvious, isn't it? Why is any marriage rushed?"

Marian sat, stunned to silence, remembering that only a few days ago Lord Bathampton had spoken so disparagingly about his bride-to-be. Where was the love in that relationship? Surely Lady Alice could have no desire to marry him!

Then Marian thought of Philip. Did he know? Did he care? It suddenly occurred to her that she need no longer be concerned about that young lady and Philip. Their dalliance would have to come to an end – but what an end! In spite of relief for herself, she felt very sorry for Alice. No one deserved Lord Bathampton.

The marriage took place ten days later in the royal chapel, which had been decorated with white flowers and trailing greenery and was heady with the perfume of roses, lilac and lily-of-the-valley. The gold cross on the altar and gold communion plate gleamed above the white altar frontal and rich mahogany of the altar rail.

Cardinal Wolsey was already standing in the sanctuary, a gold mitre on his head and dressed in a magnificent white and gold cope, a white stole round his neck that reached to the floor, with a cross embroidered in gold on each fringed end.

Those who had arrived in good time were seated on chairs but many were forced to stand wherever they could find space or climb the stairs to the gallery.

Sir William, Philip and Marian sat behind their majesties and had a clear view of the proceedings. Marian was annoyed when Lady Dereham, the bride's sister, sidled into the seat next to Sir William and engaged him in a whispered conversation while they awaited the entrance of the groom.

Ten minutes before the appointed time, Lord Bathampton, accompanied by his cousin, walked down the aisle and stood before the altar, waiting for the bride to arrive.

Although Marian had imagined, informed by all the gossip, how Lord Bathampton would look, she was shocked by the reality. Some of the bruising was obviously healing but still disfigured one side of his face and his eye was still swollen and only half open. What horrified her, though, was the injury to his nose, which was now bent crooked halfway along the bridge. His appearance revolted her, though she was conscious that she had been responsible for it.

When the organ sounded the fanfare for the arrival of the bride, he turned to look back towards the west door and his eyes met Marian's. She recoiled from that murderous glare and was relieved when Sir William sheltered her by moving between them for a better view of the bridal party. She supposed at the time that this was a chance movement but later had cause to question her supposition.

Heavily veiled, the bride, on the arm of her father, a portly man with a very grave expression, began to move very slowly along the aisle. Four attendants followed – her younger sisters, dressed in delicate green and carrying green and white posies.

Her gown of pure white with a long train, encrusted with pearls and rhinestones, was very beautiful. She carried a posy of white roses and lily-of-the-valley in her gloved hands.

On reaching the bridegroom's side, her father had to remove her arm from his, so reluctant was she to let go of him. When she peeled off her left glove and gave it, and her posy, to the eldest of her sisters, Marian saw that her hands were shaking and was surprised to feel her own eyes brimming with tears of compassion. This young girl didn't deserve this marriage, whatever foolishness she had committed.

"Dearly beloved, we are gathered together here in the sight of God…"

The service began but Marian could not concentrate on any of it. She stole a look at Philip, standing next to her, his gaze fixed steadfastly ahead and his face expressionless.

"Wilt thou have this Woman…?" "Wilt thou have this Man…?" "With this ring I thee wed…"

Cardinal Wolsey pronounced that they be Man and Wife together and added, "You may kiss the bride."

The time had come for the newly-wed Alice, Lady Bathampton, to lift her veil back over her coif and reveal her face for the first time. Then the truth about this marriage was evident. Her pretty face was blotched, her eyes red and swollen from crying.

Marian heard a strangled sob. She looked at Philip again and saw tears wetting his cheeks. Sir William coughed to cover his embarrassment. Marian reached for Philip's hand. He did not move but she was conscious of his fingers gripping hers. She could only guess how she would feel if it was Richard standing at the altar, marrying someone he didn't love. Or – the thought suddenly struck her like a dagger plunged into her heart – how he would feel if he was watching her marrying Philip.

After the ceremony, when the brief speeches and feasting were over, the bride and groom left for Lord Bathampton's estates near the ancient city of Bath. Their majesties excused themselves and left the assembly. The guests abandoned their pretence of merry-making and began to creep away surreptitiously, so the musicians ceased playing.

Philip was one of the first to leave. When Marian rose to make her way out, Sir William put his hand on her arm.

“Marian, my dear, there is something I want you to know. We will speak of it now and then never refer to it again.”

“Yes, sire?” Marian asked, sitting down again and wondering what he could possibly need to say to her.

“One of the ladies-in-waiting to the Princess Mary came to see me privately. What she had to say surprised me greatly. Mayhap you have some inkling of what that was?”

“No, sire,” said Marian, even more bewildered.

“If what she says is true, she collected her royal highness after you had had a game of shuttlecock.”

Marian nodded, feeling her cheeks beginning to redden.

“It seems that the princess left her doll behind and was insistent that this lady should return immediately to collect it. The young lady was greatly distressed at what she heard and saw. Do you understand what I am saying?”

Marian nodded, unable to speak because of her embarrassment, guilt and confusion.

“Marian, had this happened before? Had he approached you in this way before?”

Again Marian nodded miserably. Sir William took her hands in both of his.

“You told me you were afraid of him but why didn’t you tell me the whole truth?”

When she couldn’t reply but just clung to his hands, he continued, “My dear, I can only ask your pardon for failing in my duty to protect you from that vile man’s attentions. I plead your forgiveness.”

Marian flung her arms round his neck, his distress releasing her tongue. “Oh, Father, there is nothing to forgive. There is nothing you could have done to prevent what happened.”

He stroked her hair and whispered, “What a brave young lady you are! We are well rid of him now, are we not? And Marian –” He paused and she heard the suppressed laughter in his voice. “The bat was well played – very well played indeed!”

# CHAPTER 20

*Place: Greenwich Palace*

*Date: May, 1525*

Marian felt a great sense of relief at the absence of Lord Bathampton, even if it would be for a short while only. She was also very glad that Alice was out of the way.

Since the wedding, Philip had become very withdrawn and uncommunicative.

"Philip, will you walk with me along the Thames path?" she asked him one afternoon, trying to coax him out of his dark humour. When she received no reply, she ventured, "Philip, dear, you will forget Alice in time."

"That's all you know!" he retorted and walked away.

The ladies-in-waiting had to drag out of her the reason for her low spirits.

"He'll come round," they advised her, "just be patient. He's well out of that sticky web; it would have afforded him no favours."

"Be your usual sweet self, Marian," added Lady Anne, "and he'll soon discern where his happiness lies."

A month later, she heard that Lord Bathampton was back at court and, yes, his new young wife was with child. Marian didn't encounter him and was thankful for it.

She found solace in the schoolroom, keeping young Princess Mary company during their lessons. Occasionally, her majesty came to check on her daughter's progress and always professed gratitude for Marian's loving care.

One morning there was a flurry of excitement when his majesty strode through the door of the schoolroom, closely followed by the Queen and Lady Dereham.

The princess was playing a melody on the virginals, on which she was very accomplished. Standing over her and correcting her from time to time was one of the king's chief musicians, Philip van Wilder.

She jumped up from the stool and ran to her father, who held out his arms to her. The tutor bowed low and Marian curtsied.

"Please do not allow me to disrupt the lesson," the King said. "See, I will sit here with the ladies and we will listen."

"Yes, Father," the princess said, returning to her stool.

It was picture perfect, to Marian's eyes. The little girl, in her dark green and russet gown, regained her seat, raised her hands and laid them delicately on the black and white keys, the colours of which were reflected in the ebony and ivory decoration of the piano's frame.

The tutor, unflustered, used to playing for the King in his privy chamber, instructed her to return to the beginning of the piece, then raised his baton before lowering it as an indication that she should begin.

The princess needed little correction, her much-rehearsed melody being played almost faultlessly. As she came to the end and placed her hands in her lap, head bowed, the King jumped to his feet and applauded loudly, his enthusiasm shared by his queen and her lady-in-waiting.

"That was well played, daughter," he said, sitting again. "Now, shall we hear Lady Marian play?"

Marian stammered in confusion. The tutor came to her rescue.

"I regret, your Majesty, that Lady Marian has little expertise on the instrument. She will play for you if you wish but –"

"Of course, your Majesty," Marian concurred, "but I think you will regret it."

The King slapped his thigh in delight and laughed loudly, causing the Queen to smile.

"Very well, but I will not allow you to refuse to sing for me. Queen Katharine tells me that my daughter's voice and yours blend in pleasing harmony. Now, what shall you sing for us?"

"The Merry Greenwood," the princess suggested and came to stand at Marian's side. Marian smiled down at her and took her hand.

"And will Master Jeremy accompany you?"

"Most certainly, sire," he replied and took up his lyre.

On the count of "Six, seven, eight", they began to sing and he to play, the King beating time with his hand on his thigh.

As they repeated the chorus, he joined them in his rich baritone and all three finished with a great flourish – *"The very merry green green wood!"*

"Splendid! Splendid! Was it not, my dear?" The Queen nodded delightedly. "Mary," he said and drew his daughter onto his lap and kissed the top of her head. The Queen was radiant and Marian thought she had never seen them as a family together looking so happy. Even Lady Dereham had a smile on her usually dour face.

"And what shall we give our little princess for giving her father so much pleasure? What do you suggest, your Majesty?"

"Allow our daughter to decide, sire."

"Well, Mary?"

"Your Majesty, I would like the first letter of my name – it's M, you know – hanging on a chain round my neck."

"Then you shall have it!" the King boomed and, kissing her once again, released her and gave her a tiny push towards Marian. "Continue with the lesson, Master Jeremy. The Queen and I are well pleased. Now we must go about the business of the court. Come, Katharine."

With a further flurry of bows and curtseys, the royal party left the room.

The necklace arrived three days later, brought in by Lady Anne, who with Marian watched the princess unlock the red leather jewel box and take out the King's present. All three exclaimed with delight.

From a string of pure white pearls hung a solid gold letter 'M' which in turn had three drop pearls hanging from it.

The princess held it up to the light before Lady Anne took it from her and fastened it, looping it twice round her neck. The little girl stroked the gold letter reverently.

"It is a sign of the King's great love for you," Marian told her.

When the princess and those with her had vacated the room, on a whim, Marian picked up the little bell that stood on the table and rang it loudly. The summons was answered immediately by a page.

"Yes, my lady?" he asked.

"Please take a message to Lord Bathampton and say that her majesty has requested a horn of green ink for her royal highness. Say that she has specially asked that master Richard Mordaunt should attend the princess. Say she has asked specially for master Richard as no other scribe is sufficiently accomplished to fulfil the task her majesty has in mind. Do you understand?"

"Yes, my lady."

"Repeat the name."

"Master Richard Mordaunt, my lady."

"Exactly so. The ink is required immediately. All right, off with you. I will wait here until the ink arrives."

When the page had left the room, Marian busied herself tidying the papers on the table, idling her fingers over the keyboard before shutting the lid of the virginal then wandering around the room, peering out of the window, patting her hair in place and smoothing down her skirt.

When the knock came at the door, she jumped.

"Enter!" she called out, trying to still her thumping heart beats by breathing deeply.

Richard came in. "My lady," he said, bowing, "her majesty requested green ink?"

"No, I did, Richard," she replied.

Both fell silent.

"Have you nothing to say to me?" she asked.

He placed the ink horn in the stand on the table. "Why do you torment me so?"

"You torment yourself, Richard, because you refuse to speak the words that are in your heart." When he still remained silent, she continued, "Very well, let me speak them for you. *'I love you, Marian.'* What's difficult about that? Then I will say, *'And I love you, Richard.'* There, 'tis said."

She would have moved round the table to stand at his side but there was a knock and a page put his head round the door.

"Beg pardon, my lady, but the princess is asking for you. She wishes that you join her on the butts for archery practice."

"I'll be there in seconds," Marian told him and he withdrew.

Frustrated and desperate, Marian went across to Richard and took his hand.

"Richard, in three days' time, Friday, there will be no moon. I know that, because we have been learning about the heavens. I will be in the knot garden at eleven of the clock and we can sit and talk there. Please come, Richard. You will, won't you?"

He hesitated then said, his voice gruff, "Marian, I am such a fool when you plead so. All right, I'll be there, by the yew tree."

Of a sudden, he took a step towards her and put his arms round her, his lips very close to hers.

"And you don't have to say them for me, Marian, I am quite capable of saying them myself. I love you. I will always love you."

This time, she had no need to ask him to kiss her and when their lips at last parted, she laid her head against his shoulder and sighed deeply, pushing away all thoughts of Philip.

"You must leave," he reminded her, "and go shoot your arrows into the bullseye – that is, if you can first pull them out of my heart."

"Do they pain you?" she asked.

"Exquisitely so."

"Then I'll leave them there, so you don't forget me."

"Forget you?" He laughed. "When I am so miserable all the time? Forget you?" He laughed again and kissed her again. "My lady Marian, you have no idea! Now you must go."

She arrived at the butts flushed and excited. When Lady Anne commented on her appearance, she made the excuse that she had been hurrying so as not to keep the company waiting.

Her first arrow flew straight and hit the bullseye. Nobody could believe it, especially Marian herself. For the remainder of the lesson, she was unable even to hit the board and her arrows were left strewn about the grass.

# CHAPTER 21

Marian arrived at the yew tree as the clock in the courtyard struck eleven. As she had predicted, the night was moonless and darkened even further by a low bank of cloud.

Richard was already waiting for her. He drew her to him and guided her to the back of the twisted trunk and pulled her down onto the grass beside him.

His kisses were gentle and she relaxed in his arms, her head on his chest, her lips not far away from his, offering him a pleasure in which he frequently indulged.

She told him about Lord Bathampton's unwelcome approach after the shuttlecock game and that she was responsible for his broken nose. He began to laugh aloud and she put her fingers over his lips.

"Sshh! Someone may hear us."

"There's nobody else about. Were you at his wedding ceremony?"

"Yes. Alice looked wretched." Then she told him about Philip's black mood. "I think he must really love her."

"Then she has a strange way of treating him, if that is so. She is soon to be a mother. Had you heard?"

"Everyone has heard that piece of news," Marian replied. "Is Lord Bathampton very pleased about becoming a father?"

"Not at all. He growls at anyone who mentions it."

"Hush!"

"What is it?"

"I thought I heard voices."

Both were silent and Richard wriggled closer to the yew tree's trunk and pulled her to him and held her very tightly.

"I wish I could stay here forever," she said.

"Hush!" he whispered in her ear. "I hear them now, a man and a woman."

They stayed quite still as footsteps approached along the gravel paths, very slow steps as if the owners were in no hurry.

The voices were little more than whispers and at first the listeners were unable to hear what was being said as one answered the other. However, as they drew nearer, the man said quite clearly, "Walking with you by my side affords me the greatest pleasure, mistress."

Marian recognised the voice but couldn't quite place it.

"May I take your hand?"

There was a slight pause then a further request, "May I kiss the tips of your fingers?" Another pause. "You must know, my lady, that I would rather kiss your lips if you would allow me that greatest honour and pleasure."

"Then you have my permission, your Majesty, and gladly I give it."

Marian gasped and Richard quickly placed his hand over her mouth.

There was another, longer, pause before the King said, "My bed awaits us, my lady."

"Forgive me, sire, but I will not be the cause of your adultery so your bed will continue to wait. But if you were no longer married to the Queen…"

There was a deep sigh and the footsteps moved away and presently there was silence once more.

"The King!" gasped Marian when Richard had removed his hand from her mouth.

"It was indeed," agreed Richard.

"But who was the lady?"

"You know who it was, Marian. You know who it was."

Marian fell silent then.

"We must go," said Richard, scrambling up and pulling her up with him. "'Tis treason we are hearing and that puts us in great danger. Marian, we must forget what we have heard. Forget it all, do you understand? I will take you back and you must not let anyone see you. Marian, do you understand? Say that you understand!"

"Richard, you're frightening me!"

"That is well. You need to be frightened. You must not say a word to a soul. Forget any of this happened."

"I cannot forget meeting you here."

"Well, perhaps not that part, but all the rest."

At the door of the palace, she turned to him and took his hands. "Richard, it seems that, whenever we meet, bad things happen."

"They are signs that there can be no loving between us, ever. Go back to Philip and make him happy, Marian. I think he needs you, too."

"But, Richard –"

"Marian, for pity's sake, go!"

He kissed her on the cheek then opened the door and pushed her through it. He disappeared into the darkness as the clock in the courtyard struck midnight.

# CHAPTER 22

*Place: Greenwich Palace*

*Date: Beginning of June, 1525*

Marian was awakened next morning by the excited chattering of her maids. Still half asleep, she crawled across the bed and peeped out from between the hangings.

"Is it time to rise already?" she asked, squinting at the sunlight pouring through the windows of her chamber.

The two maids were very apologetic as they pulled back the bed curtains and helped her off the bed, placing her feet in the carefully positioned cream silk slippers and guiding her arms through the sleeves of her cream chamber gown.

"Oh, my lady, have we awakened you? We are so sorry, but there is such news to relate this morning!"

"What news is that?"

"It's about Princess Mary."

Marian was alarmed. "What about her? Has something happened to her?"

"Not to her, my lady," one of them replied.

"But to her necklace – the one his majesty gave her."

"The pearl necklace with the 'M' pendant?"

"Yes, my lady –"

"It has been stolen!" they chorused.

"Stolen? But how is that possible? When did this happen?"

They told her, as they poured cold water from a ewer into a basin and began to disrobe and sponge her down. The princess had placed the necklace on a small table by her bed, on the other side of the bed curtains, when she retired for the night – her ladies-in-waiting had seen her do so. As usual, someone had peeped in on her every hour, on the hour. The necklace was still there at eleven o'clock but by midnight it had disappeared!

"Her ladies immediately called others into the chamber, which was searched from top to bottom, but the necklace was nowhere to be found," Marian was told.

This was the only topic of conversation at breakfast as the ladies conjectured who had stolen the necklace and how and when. Whoever it was (and everyone was under suspicion) they could not wear it or pass it on to anyone else, as the necklace was so personal and distinctive as well as being very valuable.

On arriving in the schoolroom later that morning, Marian could see that the princess had been crying and tried to comfort her.

"I'm sure it will be found, your royal highness, and the culprit will be soundly punished. Your father will see to that."

Princess Mary nodded. "His men-at-arms are searching the palace," she said. "If it is here, they will find it. They are searching every room."

The remainder of the day passed uneventfully and it was during their handwriting lesson the following morning that there was an unexpected intrusion.

A small party of the King's men-at-arms burst into the schoolroom, accompanied by two of the Queen's ladies-in-waiting, apologising to the tutor.

"Lady Marian, you are requested to come with us!"

"Certainly, but why?" Marian asked.

"Our orders are to bring you with us, not to answer questions!" barked the officer in charge of the party. The two ladies with him looked highly embarrassed.

"Please excuse us, your royal highness and master tutor, but our instructions are to take Lady Marian with us," said the officer. "This way, my lady."

Before she could comprehend what was happening, Marian was propelled from the schoolroom, calling over her shoulder to the princess not to worry, she would return immediately.

With the officer leading the way, a man on each side of her, holding her arms, but not too tightly, and the ladies bringing up the rear, one of them in tears, Marian was marched along corridors and down a flight of stairs to a small room in the women's quarters. Here the officer saluted and withdrew with his men, closing the door behind them.

"What is this all about? What have I done? If you know, please tell me!" Marian entreated the ladies-in-waiting. She knew both of them and they knew her but they had obviously been instructed not to treat her with any familiarity.

The one who was greatly upset would not raise her eyes from the floor. The other, an older woman, gave an answer that frightened Marian.

"We are not at liberty to say. You will learn soon enough, my lady, if you don't know already."

"I know nothing. I cannot understand why I am being treated in this way."

"We are to vait here. Now please sit and quieten yourself."

She indicated a chair that stood against the wall. When Marian hesitated, she commanded her again to sit and Marian did so.

As she sat in silence, she watched the older woman pacing backwards and forwards across the floor. The younger girl continued to weep.

"For all the saints, take control of yourself!" railed the older woman. "Her majesty will be here soon and will not want to hear that noise!"

"The Queen?" queried Marian. "Why is the Queen coming?"

"I asked you to keep quiet!"

Marian was not used to being spoken to in this manner and was greatly disturbed but did as she was told.

It seemed an age before there were voices outside the door and the Queen swept in, accompanied by two more of her ladies. Marian jumped up and curtsied, fearing that the stormy expression on Queen Katharine's face was an indication of her mood.

"Leave us, ladies," the Queen commanded. "I wish to speak to Lady Marian alone. Please vait outside."

The ladies curtseyed and left the room, leaving the door slightly open.

"Shut that door!" she shouted at them. The door was closed.

"Now, Marian," the Queen began, "you know why you are here?"

"No, your Majesty, I do not."

"Then you should. Do not lie to me."

"I'm so sorry, your Majesty, but I truly don't know."

The Queen sighed deeply and slumped into a chair by the fireplace. She indicated that Marian should sit opposite her.

"Marian, of all the ladies at court, I thought I could trust you."

"But you can, your Majesty."

The Queen waved aside her profession of loyalty.

"Ve have been kind to you, have ve not?"

"Yes, your Majesty. Very kind."

"And ve entrusted our daughter to your care. You have spent much time together and ve thought you loved her as ve do."

"But I do, your Majesty. Please tell me what I have done to displease you."

"This."

The Queen opened the palm of her left hand, displaying her daughter's pearl and gold necklace.

"This is the cause of our anger, Lady Marian."

"Princess Mary's necklace! Then it has been recovered."

"Yes it has been recovered – in your bedchamber! Now how do you explain that, my lady?"

Marian sprang from her chair.

"No, your Majesty, that is not possible!"

"Sit down!"

Marian sat again and apologised. She felt the colour draining from her face.

"That cannot be, your Majesty. How can that be?"

"Because you stole my daughter's necklace! Can you deny it?"

"Yes, your Majesty, I do deny it. I would not do such a thing. How can you think that of me? I would never steal anything and certainly not from her royal highness. I love the Princess."

"Then you have a strange vay of showing it!"

"May I ask where it was found in my bedchamber?"

"Where you thought no one would look – in the varming pan. The men-at-arms were very thorough in their search."

"Please believe me, your Majesty –"

"Then explain how the necklace got there!"

"I cannot, but if that *is* so, someone must have placed it there to discredit me in your eyes, your Majesty."

"It has certainly done that, young lady. Ve had such faith in you with your vinning vays and bright smile. To say that ve are bitterly disappointed is an understatement. If you are innocent of the theft, as you claim, prove it."

"How can I? But wait –"

"Are you giving me orders now?"

"No, your Majesty, of course not."

Both were silent then Marian ventured to speak again.

"My maids told me that the necklace disappeared between eleven of the clock and midnight."

"That is so."

"Then that is proof that I couldn't have stolen it because I was – I was –"

"You were?"

At that time she was in the knot garden – with Richard – at the same time as Lady Anne – at the same time as the King! The words that would have proved her innocence choked in Marian's throat.

"Vell?" asked the Queen icily.

"Please, your Majesty, may I see my father?"

"I suppose so. He vill have to be informed of your treachery and consulted about your removal from the palace. I vill have him sent to you when it suits us. In the meantime, you vill remain here under guard during the day and taken to your chamber under guard every evening until it is decided what ve shall do with you."

She clapped her hands and her four ladies-in-waiting entered the room. She delegated two of them to stay with Marian and left with the other two. Marian knew that news of her incarceration and the reason for it would soon be the talk of the court.

She felt too stunned to weep. Who could have engineered this? Who wanted to have her removed from the palace? Who envied her that much or hated her that much or gained that much by discrediting her? Who?

Then she remembered the incident at Forrester Hall when the order for ale from the monastery had been cancelled. There was only one person who was in the vicinity on both occasions – Lady Joan Dereham!

Marian sucked in her breath and brought her hand to her mouth and gnawed on her knuckles. The ladies looked at her in surprise then looked away.

There were heavy footsteps outside the door, a barked command, the stamp of feet and the rattle of halberdiers, then silence, and she knelt on the floor with her head on the seat of a chair and could not hold back the tears.

# CHAPTER 23

For the next two days, Marian was kept under close guard. Her meals arrived on a tray twice a day. The maids who looked after her at bedtime and woke her in the morning were changed every day, as were the two ladies-in-waiting who kept her company.

Apart from them, she saw and spoke to no one. When she again pleaded to see Sir William, they shook their heads apologetically and sat concentrating on their embroidery.

During the morning of the fourth day, she heard the stamp of feet outside the door, a voice raised in challenge and then a whispered conversation, at the conclusion of which the door was flung open and Sir William strode into the room, his expression grim.

"Father!" Marian cried and ran to him. Immediately, his arms went round her and he dismissed the ladies, instructing them to wait outside until they were recalled.

When they had gone, Sir William led her across to a couch and sat holding her tightly, as he had done when she was a child and Philip and she had been fighting. Now she laid her head on his chest and gave full vent to her anguish.

When she had calmed a little and he had dried her face with his kerchief and could make himself heard above her sobs, he asked, "Now, Marian, what is all this about?"

With her face buried and her words muffled, she protested, "I didn't steal the princess's necklace, really I didn't, Father. You must believe me!"

Sir William put his hand under her chin and lifted her face and regarded the green depths of her misery-soaked eyes and said, "Marian, look me straight in the eye and tell me that you didn't steal that necklace."

Her look was steady and she never faltered. "Father, I didn't steal that necklace. I didn't steal the necklace. I didn't. I didn't."

He dropped his hand and sat back, the lines on his forehead clearing and the muscles in his face relaxing.

"I believe you, Marian, I do indeed, but there remains the question: if you didn't, who did, and how did it get into the warming pan in your bedchamber?"

"Father, I don't know how or when it was hidden in the warming pan but I think I know who put it there and why."

He waited for her to continue but she hesitated, remembering her surprise at seeing a certain lady emerging from the door leading from his chambers on the morning after the Christmas Day feast.

"Sire, do you remember when the order for ale at Forrester Hall was cancelled and how disastrous that would have been if the King had called for more when our cellars were empty, and how incompetent that would have made me look?"

He nodded. "We never got to the bottom of that."

"Because we never decided who would have benefited if I had been shamed. Who would, sire? What gentleman – or lady – would have been advantaged if I had been disadvantaged?"

Sir William shook his head in bewilderment.

"And in the matter of the necklace – who discovered and reported its loss?"

He looked at her intently.

"Who, sire?"

Again Sir William shook his head. "One name springs to mind but I cannot believe it of her. Why, Marian? Why do you think –?"

"Father, only you know the answer to that."

He remained silent.

"And, sire, I have an alibi that makes it impossible for me to have been anywhere near the princess's bedchamber between eleven and twelve o'clock that night."

He leaned forward and took her hand. "My dear, why didn't you say so immediately? Why didn't you tell her majesty?"

"Because clearing my name incriminates others and I cannot do it."

"But you must, Marian, you must. You cannot have this cloud hanging over your head for the remainder of your life. Philip cannot bring you to Forrester Hall as its mistress with this accusation unresolved. You must declare your alibi, whoever else it involves. You must!"

"Sire," began Marian slowly, "I was in the knot garden between eleven and twelve that night."

"What were you doing in the knot garden? Did anyone see you there?"

"I was there because I was meeting someone."

"Who, my dear?"

"You are going to be very cross with me. It was – it was –"

"Yes?"

The answer came in a rush of words. "Richard Mordaunt – you know, the young man who partnered Lady Alice during our dancing lessons."

"I remember. He is one of Bathampton's scribes. But what were you doing in the knot garden with Richard Mordaunt?"

Marian didn't answer. He let her hand drop back into her lap.

"You weren't – Marian, you haven't compromised your maidenhood with a – a servant? Tell me that is not so."

"No, sire, no! I have not been unfaithful to Philip and never would be!"

"Then what were you both doing there?"

Marian had not the courage to tell him the whole truth.

"Sire, he loves me." When she saw the look of disgust on her guardian's face, she rushed on, "He is an honest young man and would do nothing to betray my trust in him."

"We'll let that pass for now. Be sure I will address that matter later. But I must say it is no alibi, Marian. If he loves you, as you seem to imagine, he will confirm anything you say. That is no alibi."

"But there were other people in the garden, sire, who could vouch that what I am saying is the truth."

"Other people saw you? I'faith, the place was as busy as Hampstead Heath on a saint's day! Tell me their names and I will obtain your alibi."

"They didn't see us and we only heard them, but we recognised their voices."

"Their names, Marian."

"Sire, it was his majesty and – and –"

"That's nonsense! Why would the King be skulking about in the knot garden at that time of night? You push my credulity too far, daughter!"

"I tell the truth. The lady with his majesty was – was – Lady Anne Boleyn. And we heard some of their conversation."

Sir William jumped to his feet.

"What nonsense is this that you are expecting me to believe?"

He began to pace the room, wringing his hands and at intervals banging a clenched fist against the wall panelling. Finally, he stopped pacing and stood before his ward.

"Marian, you are talking treason! Do you realise that, you foolish child?"

"I know that, sire. I understand that."

"You must have been mistaken."

"No, there is no mistake. That is why I could not tell the Queen."

"I cannot believe –"

"Father, why don't you ask Lady Anne?"

"Because she will deny it."

"Even if she does, she will have to admit to herself that I am innocent of the theft, and she may consult the King."

"That could put you in grave danger, Marian, grave danger. However, for my own satisfaction, I will ask Lady Anne to see me and I will tell her of your imaginings. I will gauge her response."

"I do not think she will say or do anything to hurt me, Sir William. She and I are friends."

"Now you are being naïve."

"And Richard, sire?"

"I will take my complaint to Lord Bathampton and let *him* deal with this – this – scribe."

He pronounced the last word with such contempt that he could not have hurt her more had he struck her across the face with his gauntlet.

She was also very afraid of Lord Bathampton's probable revengeful treatment of Richard and agonised that she had caused the situation because of her insistence on their secret tryst, so compromising the honour of both of them. But if they had not met, she would not have an alibi – an alibi she could not use.

"I will seek out Lady Anne immediately."

So saying, Sir William strode to the door and opened it. He growled at the two ladies waiting outside and told them to return and make sure that Marian was well guarded – there must be no opportunity that afforded her escape.

The soldiers returned to their positions and Sir William disappeared along the corridor.

Neither of the ladies-in-waiting spoke to Marian for the remainder of the day and she was glad when bedtime came and they escorted her to her bedchamber.

It was another two days before she received any news at all. That morning, she was delighted to wake up to find her own two maids ready to help her bathe and dress.

"You're back!" she exclaimed.

"And pleased to be so, my lady."

"Am I no longer under guard?"

"The men-at-arms have been withdrawn," she was informed. "We have been ordered to escort you to the room where you were imprisoned, where you will await Sir William."

How Marian hated that room but she composed herself and sat quietly, hands folded in her lap, waiting for her guardian to come and explain what had transpired.

He came into the room after about ten minutes. She went to greet him but he walked past her and indicated that she should sit beside him on the couch.

"What news, sire?"

"Marian, I must say at the outset that I am very disappointed in you. I cannot believe that you have disregarded all the rules of propriety and have been meeting that young man – a common scribe – behind my back, behind Philip's back."

Marian hung her head. "I meant no disrespect to you or Philip, Father."

"Did you not consider that you were compromising the honourable name you bear, your father's name – which, I would remind you, will one day be changed to my family name?" He did not wait for a reply but continued, "Fortunately, your meeting was in secret and a secret it will stay! Do you hear me?"

"Yes, Father," she said contritely, then a thought struck her. "So you *do* believe me, that I *was* in the knot garden and could not have stolen the necklace?"

Sir William relaxed his rigid posture a little. "In that, at least, there is no dishonour. I have had private audience with Lady Anne and related to her all that you told me. She denied it, of course, and forbad me to repeat your faerie tales to anyone. They carry with them the legacy of death. She asked me to pass on that warning to you. It was not an idle threat, Marian. She was deadly serious."

"She would not cause me any hurt, sire – she is my friend," Marian insisted again.

"Marian, you still have so much to learn, so much, about people, about life – especially life in King Henry's court. However, I do believe that Lady Anne will not cause you mischief if it can be avoided."

He sighed heavily and continued, "However, I wish to make sure you are out of harm's way. I have instructed your maids to pack a travelling case and you will leave within the hour. I hope that 'out of sight' will mean 'out of mind'."

"Leave? Leave for where?"

"For Forrester Hall. Philip and I have permission from his majesty to follow on horseback."

"Are you being dismissed the King's service, sire?"

"Not dismissed – just released – for the time being, yes. I hope he will see fit to recall me when this matter has quietened down."

"The matter of the stolen necklace?"

"The stolen necklace is of little importance. There are matters of greater import that will develop in his majesty's own time and he cannot risk any whispers before that time. As a family, we pose a problem in that direction, but I believe his majesty values my service and will reinstate me when he is ready."

"Princess Mary will miss me, and I her, and my friends will query my disappearance now that I am pronounced innocent of the theft."

"Friends can become enemies, Marian, in the wink of an eye if it suits them, if it suits their advancement at court, if it suits their standing in the eyes of the King."

"And Lady Anne –"

Sir William stood. "Lady Anne will not be coming to say goodbye. However, I do believe it is because of her that your name has been cleared. Her majesty has been informed that the discovery of the princess's necklace in your bedchamber was not theft but someone playing a practical joke, though in very poor taste. The Queen has accepted this version of the incident and all accusations against you have been dropped by order of the King."

"And what of Richard Mordaunt, sire?"

"It seems someone forewarned him and he has absented himself from Lord Bathampton's service."

"He has gone? Where has he gone?"

"Wherever he has gone is of no concern to us. His name is not to be mentioned in my hearing from this day forward. Is that clear?"

"But Father –"

"Is that clear?" Sir William thundered.

Marian hung her head again and nodded.

"It seems to me, young lady, that we should not wait until Philip is eighteen before you marry and the ceremony should take place very soon."

Marian's head shot up and Sir William silenced her intended protest with a dark look of anger. He had never glared at her in that way before and she was acutely aware of the loss of esteem in which he had always held her.

"I'm so sorry," she mumbled, her eyes filling with tears.

"Growing up is an exciting adventure," he said, "but it can be extremely painful and sometimes we get it all wrong. Hush now, Marian, hush. I am here to protect you – with my life if needs be."

At that moment, there was a discreet knock at the door and Princess Mary entered, quite alone.

"Your royal highness," said Sir William and bowed low while Marian curtseyed.

The little girl ran across to Marian, who crouched to receive her in her arms.

"The King has forbidden my mother to visit you before you leave, Lady Marian, so I have come instead."

"Where are your ladies-in-waiting?" asked Marian, aghast that the princess should appear on her own.

"We are playing hide-and-seek and I have given them the slip, but I can't be long," the princess explained. Before Marian could interrupt, she hurried on, "Lady Marian, I knew you hadn't taken my necklace! When Lady Dereham was telling everyone that you had hidden it in your warming pan, I knew it couldn't be true. Do you know what I think?"

"No, tell me."

"I think that she stole it and hid it so that you would get the blame."

Marian looked across to Sir William, who would not meet her eyes, then back to the princess.

"You must not say that to anyone else, your royal highness, because it may get you into trouble."

"How can I get into trouble when I am the princess? I will be queen one day, my mother says so, and then I will never get into trouble again, no matter what I say."

Marian laughed. "But you are not queen yet. So promise me you will never repeat that to anyone."

"I promise. But Lady Marian, I don't want you to leave. I will miss you so much!"

"And I will miss you, your royal highness, but I have to go. We will see each other again, and that is a promise. Until we do, I want you to work hard at your lessons. Now you must run back to your ladies or you really will be in trouble."

She kissed the princess on the forehead and the little girl hugged her round the waist then ran to door, turned and waved, and was gone.

Sir William followed her to the door.

"It is time you went to your chamber, Marian, and collected together everything you need for the journey. I will send servants to carry your bags down to the stable yard and stow them safely in my whirlicote. Be quick, Marian, as I would have you away from here before his majesty can change his mind about your leaving."

Marian nodded and followed him out of the room.

# CHAPTER 24

*Place: Forrester Hall, Berkshire*

*Date: 10th July, 1525*

It was Marian's fifteenth birthday and her wedding day. She sat before her mirror and regarded her reflection as her ladies dressed her hair, for the last time allowing it to flow freely down to her waist. Tomorrow she would wear it tightly braided in a bun to let it be known that she was now a married woman and no longer a virgin – except that she would still be a virgin as Sir William had made Philip promise that he would not couple with her for another year.

"Her body is not yet fully developed," he told his son, "and we would risk losing her and the baby if she became pregnant while still so young."

Philip had assented to his father's wishes and had accepted with ill grace the stipulation of two separate bedrooms until this time next year. When out of earshot of his father, he had mumbled something about fulfilling his needs elsewhere.

Marian was far less concerned about her year-long enforced virginity and hoped that, during that time, she would find some semblance of peace when she thought about Richard, of whom she had had no news since his precipitate departure from court.

When her hair had been tamed and was tumbling down her back like a stream in full sunshine, she stepped into her farthingale then raised her arms so that her ladies could help her on with her wedding gown.

"You are so beautiful, my lady," they agreed and Marian wished that Richard could see her now.

Her gown was of pure white satin with a heavily gold-embroidered under skirt and under sleeves, a square neck and stomacher that finished in a point below her waist. Her pumps were also of white satin. On her head they placed a circlet of wild flowers and she carried white roses and peonies and green trailing ivy.

When she slowly descended the stairs towards Sir William, who was waiting for her in the hall, he suddenly had to blow his nose and muttered that the perfume from the flowers had caused him momentary discomfort.

She tucked her arm into his and together they walked towards the front door and out into the sunshine. All the staff were dressed in their Sunday best uniforms and were forming a guard of honour as she and Sir William descended the steps. The whirlicote was awaiting them and, once they were comfortably seated and her ladies had made sure that he was not creasing her gown, they were driven the short distance to the little Norman church.

The wives of their tenants had been busy all the previous day decorating the interior with lilies and other blooms from their gardens and the heady perfume filled the nave and chancel.

Waiting for them was Philip and, when he turned to greet her, he too seemed to be having difficulty with his breathing. Marian smiled at him and her step father released her, and in no time at all there was a gold band on the third finger of her left hand and they had become man and wife. Then Philip was kissing her in front of the whole congregation and whispering in her ear, "Marian, I am already regretting my promise to my father."

Tables had been laid in the gardens of Forrester Hall for the wedding feast and there was great good will and merriment as the speeches were made, the toasts drunk to Sir Philip and Lady Marian Forrester and the food was consumed in quantity. Then the musicians struck up and everyone joined in the dancing.

When the full moon was high in the sky and the last guest had gone to bed, husband and wife mounted the staircase hand in hand, accompanied by Sir William, Philip's attendants and Marian's ladies. Outside the door of Marian's chamber, Philip put his arms round his new wife, gave her a chaste kiss, sighed deeply and turned towards his own chamber door.

Marian knew that this arrangement could not possibly last a whole year.

However, tonight she was very tired and, having dismissed her maids, was soon fast asleep.

# CHAPTER 25

Sir William, supported by Mistress Malmesbury, while very gently introducing Marian to her new responsibilities and duties, allowed the young couple to fill their days with pleasureable pursuits.

So they played chess, cards, dice and board games, sang and danced together, and played hide-and-seek with their attendants indoors when the weather was inclement.

When it was fine and sunny, they walked with the dogs through the grounds, rowed a boat on the lake, went fishing, competed against each other at archery, practised their skills with the falcons and rode out with the hunt. In truth, they were encouraged to do everything together except share a bed.

At first, both accepted Sir William's wishes but this arrangement increasingly frustrated Philip and he became more and more irritable. Sometimes they found themselves unexpectedly alone and out of sight of everyone and then he would kiss her passionately on the lips and tell her how much he longed to make love to her, and then kissed the swelling of her breasts where they were revealed above the neckline of her gown, only to draw back in haste when someone approached, as they always did.

On these occasions, she hadn't wanted him to stop and he left her with her breasts throbbing and tightening and the remembrance of his hands all over her and strange feelings in the pit of her stomach.

Sometimes, afterwards, he went missing for hours on end, saying he had urgent business in the village. Marian found a little relief from her emotional and physical turmoil by setting off on brisk walks round the estate.

Whether or not Sir William noticed their increasing frustration Marian wasn't sure but the list of duties assigned to both of them lengthened so that they had very little time to dwell on their situation.

She found the transition to mistress of the Hall very difficult to handle and often longed to cuddle up on Marmy's lap, as she had done when a child, and pour out her problems. These were no longer about grazed knees but about wanting Philip's arms around her at night and her confusion because she still loved Richard but Philip was here and Richard wasn't.

One of her responsibilities, under supervision, was arranging the menus and making sure that cook ordered whatever was required, as she had last Christmas when the King and Queen brought the court to Forrester Hall.

She was also charged with making sure that her beloved Marmy and staff carried out their duties efficiently, and was given the responsibility of hiring servants and sometimes dismissing them.

In general, the older servants were sympathetic and helpful and tactfully steered her away from making foolish decisions but one or two, probably resenting her authority when she was younger and less experienced than they were, encouraged her into making humiliating mistakes.

There was the time when one of them recommended as scullery hand a woman from the village who was suspected of being a witch, though she did not mention this to Marian. When Marmy found out, she would not allow the woman to set foot in the Hall and reprimanded Rosie, the girl responsible.

Everyone hoped that was the end of the matter but one morning all the milk curdled and one of the kitchen cats was discovered stretched out behind the chicken run, having died of a rat bite. Marian felt to blame.

On another occasion, when this same girl was sent to the mill with Marian's order for flour, she omitted to point out that the quantity requested was four times the amount usually required so that explanations and apologies had to be tendered and several sacksful sent back. Again, Marian felt to blame.

When Marmy realised what was happening, she summoned the culprit to her room and closed the door. No one knew what was said, but Rosie left the room in tears and caused no further trouble.

"I was on the point of dismissing the girl," Marmy told Marian afterwards, "but thought better of it as I guessed you would not want her to lose her position. But I warned her that she would be closely watched in future and, if there was another similar mishap, she would be sent on her way without a letter of satisfaction."

Marian said she felt responsible for all the incidents.

Marmy smiled indulgently. "You'll learn, my dear, as she has to. We all have to learn."

One afternoon, to escape her humiliations in the kitchens, Marian decided to cool off in the gardens. A grassy avenue among the trees led to a small arbour where there was a sundial in the centre and a bench beneath a wooden trellis arch overhung with pink roses.

She was standing by the sundial, looking at the shadow cast by the gnomon and calculating the time as half past three, when she heard a noise, and looking up saw Philip approaching.

"Philip!" she exclaimed, pleased to see him. "I came out to cool down. It's so hot in the kitchens. I thought you had gone to look over the new stallion father bought."

"That's where I'm supposed to be," he said, coming over to her and putting his arms around her waist and nuzzling his lips into the back of her neck, "but I saw you leave by the back stairs and thought I would follow you."

She turned round in his arms and lifted her face to his and he kissed her with such hunger that it surprised them both. Drawing her over to the bench, he dragged her down beside him then began to kiss her again as if his life depended on it.

She was dressed much more simply than when at court and it was not long before her bodice was unlaced and bodice and shift pulled down to her waist.

"My father is talking nonsense when he says your body is underdeveloped," Philip commented. "He hasn't seen what I'm seeing!"

The bench was uncomfortable so he picked her up and took her into the grass, beneath the trees. He could not stop kissing her as he told her how much he wanted her. When he entered her after only a matter of minutes, at first there was a frightening pain that made her cry out, but then such a rush of pleasure that she felt herself drowning in a rising flood of sensations. All she could do was clutch at him as he moved inside her, willing him never to let her go.

His desires had been frustrated for so long that he was not soon satisfied and it was only after his fourth ejaculation that he fell back on the grass, his energy spent.

It had all taken place so quickly that Marian could not fully comprehend what had happened to their bodies. She sat up and lent across him, gasping for breath.

"Philip, I didn't know – I didn't know –"

He jumped up and began to rearrange his clothing.

"Well, you know now. And there'll be no more nonsense about separate beds after this. I shall tell my father plainly that it is too late and there is no advantage in keeping us apart any longer." He paused. "That is, Marian, if you want me as much as I want you."

"Philip – husband – that would please me very much. And Philip, you won't need to go down into the village again, will you?"

"What village?" he asked as he helped her to dress, kissing her as he did so. "All I need is here, Marian. You have all I need."

# CHAPTER 26

*Place: Forrester Hall, Berkshire*

*Date: August, 1525*

Philip went to see his father straightaway and they were closeted together for half an hour, at the end of which time Sir William asked to see Marian on her own.

"Marian, my dear, you have been like a daughter to me. If my wife had been spared, she would be speaking to you now, but there is only me, so I am having to say what she would have said."

He paused and Marian waited patiently for him to continue, embarrassed at what she guessed was to come but knowing that he always had her welfare uppermost in his heart.

"Philip has told me that you have come together as a man and his wife should and has told me in no uncertain terms that he will not countenance your having separate beds from now on. He is a hot-blooded young man – as I was at his age –" Sir William allowed himself a moment's reverie and smiled indulgently to himself before abruptly bringing his thoughts back to the present, "– and it was very foolish of me to think that the situation could continue for another year."

Marian hung her head to hide her blushes.

"However, I wanted to make quite certain that this is what you also wish. You are so young and it was not my intention – but circumstances have altered all that. You have always loved each other as brother and sister and I believe now that he loves you as his wife and I trust that you can respond to that love."

Marian guessed that he was, by a circuitous route, referring to her erstwhile interest in Richard.

"Sir William, please do not trouble yourself on that score. We have made each other very happy."

"Splendid! I just wanted to hear it from your own lips. I was wrong to keep you both celibate when your affection for each other was so obvious. You have my blessing and tonight you and your husband will share a bed, as you should have done from the start of your marriage. Come and give this foolish old man a kiss."

"Gladly, Sir William."

Marian clasped his hands in hers and kissed them then kissed his cheek.

"I bless you, sire, and I am sure that my own Father is blessing you from heaven."

That night, the young couple were not escorted to bed as previously. In fact, there was no one in sight as they mounted the staircase, hand in hand, and entered her bedchamber together.

Marian was longing for all that she had felt beneath the tree to overwhelm her again, to have Philip all to herself, to feel him inside her again, to be united in desire and body so that they were one and not two people. To her surprise, this time was even more intimate as she responded to Philip's need of her before they went to sleep and again when they awoke in the morning.

"I must keep busy," he told her at breakfast, "or I will be getting in your way all day in the hope of a kiss or something more."

The weeks passed and they were surrounded by the glorious autumn colours of the September trees and bushes. It was difficult for Marian to realise that it was only a year ago that she and Philip had been introduced to court, so much had happened since then.

Occasionally, Sir William would receive a letter brought by horseback from Sir John Knollys, his friend at court. Then he would regale them with gossip and rumour that was rife at the time, though Marian had the impression that he did not always read them the whole content of his letter and wondered what caused the frown to appear on his forehead. At those times, she would go to him and put her arm round his shoulders, and he would quickly fold the letter and tuck it into the leather pouch hanging from his belt, then pat her hand absentmindedly.

The days drew towards Christmas and preparations began for the festive season. This year, there would be the family only at home, in contrast to the previous Yuletide.

The daylight hours became shorter and the nights longer, not that Philip or Marian complained about that. The temperature dropped and ice formed round the edge of the lake and across the surface of the puddles.

It was on such a day that one of the servants noticed, when passing a window on her way to tend the fire in the great hall, that a whirlicote was heading their way at breakneck speed.

Hearing the excited exclamations and conjectures as the news was passed from one to another, Marian hurried to the hall and sent a serving boy to find Sir William. He arrived as the vehicle pulled up outside the entrance, the horses' breath suspended as clouds of vapour and their snorting and snuffling evidence of the speed at which they had been drawing the carriage.

Marian was surprised. No one was expected and the vehicle had no coat of arms emblazoned on the bodywork. As the driver descended and placed a stool at the side of the passenger compartment, Sir William joined Marian at the open front door.

"Are you expecting a visitor, sire?"

"No, Marian. I am as puzzled as you are."

Now the driver was helping the occupant out of the carriage, taking great care to keep in place the furs that enveloped whoever it was, which were impeding his or her descent.

The figure moved towards the entrance steps, began to climb, then suddenly and unexpectedly collapsed. Immediately, Sir William ran down the steps and, helped by the driver, raised the visitor to her feet and guided her – for a woman it was – up the steps and into the warmth of the hall. He then sent John, his steward, to find Philip.

Marian was still unable to discern who was amongst the furs until the visitor sat on a chair and Mistress Malmesbury removed her hood.

"Alice!" exclaimed Marian, utterly perplexed but noticing on her cheek a red weal that was turning purple and beginning to close her eye.

"Lady Alice!" Sir William repeated.

"I've left him!" she exclaimed in great agitation.

"Lord Bathampton?" asked Marian, knowing it was a silly question.

Alice raised one hand to her cheek. "Because of this. I couldn't take it any more."

"He beats you?" asked Sir William incredulously and she nodded.

"Please forgive me but I didn't know who else would give me shelter," she said. "I remembered how happy we were here last Christmas. I didn't think, I just hired a carriage and came. I know he'll follow me!"

"If he comes, he will not be admitted," Sir William reassured her and turned to Marian with a look of appeal.

"Marmy, please prepare a bed chamber for Lady Alice," Marian instructed their housekeeper. "Have a fire lit and a warming pan placed in her bed and ask the maids to take up hot water."

The housekeeper nodded and was about to attend to her duties when they heard the strangest sound coming from the depth of the furs, like the mewing of a kitten. Mistress Malmesbury came back.

"I recognise a baby's cry when I hear one," she said.

"You've brought your baby with you?" asked Marian in disbelief.

Alice nodded. "I couldn't leave him."

Sir William asked gently, "May we make his acquaintance, my lady?"

Alice pulled away the furs to reveal a tiny face puckering up and about to cry. Sir William seemed mesmerised.

"I remember Philip at that age. He is a very handsome little fellow."

The baby let out a wail. "He needs feeding," his mother remarked.

"Then my maid will take you up to your room," said Marian, conscious only of the needs of mother and baby, that is, until she heard footsteps on the flagstones and stiffened as Philip crossed the hall.

"You sent for me, Father?"

Sir William turned towards him.

"Philip, we have an unexpected guest – two guests, in fact. Lady Alice Bathampton is here – with her son."

Philip stared at the bundle of furs cossetting mother and baby.

"Alice?"

"Hello, Philip."

"She has run away from Bathampton," Sir William explained. "If you look at her face, you will see why."

Philip gasped. "He did that to you?"

Marian interrupted. "Tomorrow, Alice, we can have the nursery prepared for your son but tonight he will have to share your bed."

"Thank you. I am very grateful." She stood and, as Philip was still staring at them, asked if he would like to hold her son. Seemingly embarrassed, he declined but she extricated the baby from the furs and offered him to Philip anyway.

He took the bundle, reluctant and awkward, but studied the little pink face before handing him back to his mother.

"Marmy, please make sure that all their needs are met," Marian instructed the housekeeper. "When they are refreshed, cook shall send up food for Lady Alice, if that is what she wishes."

The young mother profusely thanked her hosts again and followed a maid up the stairs while the housekeeper left to gather together a small army of servants to carry out Marian's instructions.

Sir William turned to Philip and Marian.

"This situation is most distressing," he said, "and has nothing to commend it. Come to my study and we will discuss the matter in private."

When they arrived there, Sir William threw more logs into the flames and indicated they should sit on either side of the hearth. He drew up a chair facing the fire.

"Now, what are we going to do about this unexpected – and may I say, potentially dangerous – situation?" he asked. "I cannot in good conscience send her back to her husband."

Marian and Philip were silent. She remembered his distress at the marriage of Alice and Lord Bathampton and could not guess now the thoughts in his head nor the emotions in his heart – of which she was very afraid – but she knew that the future of their marriage and her own happiness lay at risk if this scheming young woman stayed under their roof.

"We can't give her sanctuary for long!" she blurted out then added in justification, "Lord Bathampton is sure to come looking for her, as she said."

"Those are my thoughts exactly," she was relieved to hear Sir William agree. "Well, Philip? You have said nothing so far."

"We can't send her away, Father. Where would we send her – and the baby? We can't turn them out in this weather. Perhaps after Christmas we can think further on the matter."

"No, son. I am sure her husband will be here before then. This is the obvious place to come looking."

"Whyfor?" Marian asked sharply but was ignored.

"If he arrives and they are still here," continued Sir William, "we cannot refuse to send her back. If they are not here, that is the end of the matter."

"But, Father, where will they go? For humanity's sake –"

*For humanity's sake or for your own sake, Philip?* Marian wanted to ask him but said nothing. The three of them sat in silence, gazing into the embers, each busy with their own thoughts.

Marian wished away the daylight hours so that she could get Philip into bed and make him forget any ideas he had about Lady Alice Bathampton, in the same way that she was pushing all thoughts of Richard to the recesses of her mind. He was still there somewhere but there was no room for three in a bed and at the moment she had her head full of Philip.

Sir William rose and crossed to a table on which stood carafes of red wine. He chose one and filled three goblets which he brought to the fireside.

"I have an idea," he said and raised his goblet, "but let us first drink to our guests. To Lady Alice and her son."

Philip raised his goblet. "To Alice and her son."

Marian thought she would put the record straight and added, "To Lady Alice Bathampton and their son."

The wine slipped down Marian's throat with ease and she felt a little calmer.

"What is your idea, Father?" Philip asked.

"I will visit Mother Superior tomorrow and ask if she will give them sanctuary in the monastery. Where they go after that need not worry us."

The suggestion received Marian's whole-hearted consent but Philip was a little less enthusiastic.

"But we should be told what becomes of them."

"No, son," his father replied. "Once they leave here, their whereabouts will be no concern of ours."

"But, Father –"

"No concern of ours," repeated his father emphatically.

Philip opened his mouth to protest again but Marian forestalled him.

"Philip, listen to Father. He speaks wisdom. It will be better for all of us if Alice and her baby leave here as soon as possible and we do not know where they have gone. In that way, we can truthfully answer Lord Bathampton that we have no knowledge of their whereabouts."

They ate together in the hall that evening. Lady Alice had left her son asleep in her bed, watched over by Marmy, who was in her element in having a baby to care for after the intervening years since Philip and Marian were children.

Alice looked tired and pale, and Marian made sure that this was remarked upon so that everyone encouraged her to retire early, which she did.

Later, in bed, Philip was reluctant to make love to Marian. However, by now she knew exactly how to arouse him, and did so, determined that he should not have time nor energy to think about Alice. After their love making, she lay close to him and stroked his face and whispered how much she loved him until he fell into a deep sleep.

# CHAPTER 27

Early next morning, Sir William rode down to the monastery, missing breakfast in his haste to speak to Mother Superior as soon as possible.

Alice appeared at the table looking much rested after her night's sleep, and in high spirits, saying she had fed the baby and he was now fast asleep on her bed.

Her presence again unsettled Marian, who was looking all the time for any signs of intimacy between her and Philip. The pair were friendly but not unduly so and Marian scolded herself for her lack of trust in her husband.

After breakfast, he asked to see the baby again and took Marian with him, holding her hand tightly all the way to the guest chamber as if to keep his grip on reality.

She felt her antagonism dissipate as she looked down at the tiny boy sleeping peacefully on the large bed, his face pink and untroubled, his breath coming and going quietly and easily. She looked up at Alice and saw again the weal on her face and knew of a certainty that they could not send her back to Lord Bathampton.

"Alice, I am so sorry," Philip said and Marian's heart hardened again. Why was he apologising? If the girl had not, as Lord Bathampton had so graphically described, "opened her legs" for him, she would not be in this situation.

"There was nothing you could do about it," Alice replied and laid a hand on his arm.

"That's about the sum of it," Marian said peevishly. "I don't know why you feel the need to apologise, Philip."

Philip looked at her and put his arm round her shoulders.

"I do believe my wife is jealous, Alice. We intend to wait awhile before we start a family, is that not so, Marian?"

Marian drew close to him so that he would feel the warmth of her body against his.

"Yes, indeed."

"Then I hope that Nature does not have other ideas, as she did for me. She can be very unpredictable, so be warned."

Sir William arrived back several hours later. He did not appear again until the evening meal, after which he invited the three young people to accompany him to sit by the blazing hall fire. He moved a table between them and placed on it a document.

"Children," he began, "– begging your pardon, Lady Alice, but none of you is more than that. We all know the situation – the mark on the lady's face says it all. It is true that the marriage ceremony is sacrosanct and adjures wives to be subject to their husbands in every respect, 'forsaking all others', but the Bible also adjures husbands to treat their wives as if they were as dear as their own bodies. Clearly, this is not happening in the marriage of Lady Alice and Lord Bathampton."

He paused and looked at his guest. "I know I should send you straight back to your husband, Lady Alice, but I cannot do that in all conscience and I am sure that our Lord would not wish me to do so. I may be mistaken in that but I do not think so."

"Thank you, sire," Alice mumbled.

"However, young lady, you and your little son cannot stay here. This is one of the first places your husband is likely to look and you would have to go back with him."

"Please, sire –" she began but he held up his hand to silence her. Marian took hold of Philip's hand and held it tightly as if she was afraid he might be trying to slip away from her.

"This morning, I rode down to the monastery to confer with Mother Superior. I explained to her the position, all of it, and kept nothing from her. She understands it all. I must say that was a great relief to me." He turned to Alice. "My dear, she is willing to allow you and your son to live among the nuns."

Alice remonstrated. "Sire, I cannot take up life in a nunnery. I have too much living still to do."

Sir William smiled. "We are not asking you to take the veil, Lady Alice, but to stay for a while where your husband will not be able to lay a finger on you – she will make sure of that."

Alice heaved a deep sigh of relief. "And may I visit Forrester Hall sometimes?"

"No, that will not be possible. You will stay there, out of sight, for as long as the Reverend Mother considers appropriate, then she will arrange for you to travel onwards to another nunnery or perhaps stay incognito in a secret house in the country. We will not be informed of your whereabouts and you would do well not to inform anyone at court – not even your sister, Lady Joan."

"That will be very hard for me to do," Alice objected.

"It is that or be returned to your husband as any betrayal would place the Reverend Mother in a very difficult situation."

"Then I have no choice, sire."

He pushed the parchment scroll towards her. "Mother Superior has had this document drawn up and has signed it. We wish you to read it carefully and then add your signature. It says in effect all that I have told you."

"When do we leave here?"

"Tomorrow, before it is light."

"I had hoped to stay longer."

Sir William repeated, "There is no 'longer'. Tomorrow, before light."

Alice nodded. "I will do as you wish."

"Then we will leave you to read and sign. Come, Philip and Marian. Let us leave my lady to do as I have asked."

As the three of them left the hearth, Sir William spoke to his son.

"Philip, I would not be surprised if Lord Bathampton arrives tomorrow, seeking his wife. I believe it will be a difficult day and I shall need your support. We must also keep Marian out of sight as he will be even more enraged if her presence reminds him of the injury to his nose."

Philip snorted in derision.

"My son, it may be comical to you but I doubt that my Lord Bathampton finds the memory so amusing. I cannot send him on his way without refreshment but I do not want him to lay eyes on Marian. Marian, my dear –"

"Yes, Father?"

"You must keep out of his way all the time he is here."

"Yes, Father, of course."

"Now there is no reason for either of you to linger down here any longer. I'm sure the maids will make sure that Lady Alice reaches her bedchamber safely. She will also need her sleep if she and her baby are to leave so early in the morning."

"I had hoped to talk to Lady Alice to find out all that has happened at court since we left," Philip objected.

Sir William looked across to Alice, who had raised her head at Philip's last remark. Marian felt she needed to intervene.

"Come, Philip," she said and whispered in his ear, "Would you rather converse with Alice or come to bed with me?"

He brightened visibly and took her hand as they mounted the staircase, leaving Sir William to take possession of the document and instruct the maids that they should ensure that Lady Alice and her son were safely ensconced for the night.

# CHAPTER 28

By the time Marian came down to breakfast next morning, Alice and her son had gone. She was greatly relieved to find that this was so and went in search of Philip. She found him breaking ice on top of buckets of water and helping to muck out the stalls in the stable yard, a chore that he was undertaking with great energy but not much enthusiasm.

In answer to her question, he replied that mother and baby had left with Sir William before dawn, as arranged, and that his father should be returning soon.

He arrived home not long afterwards and confirmed that they were safely out of sight in the nuns' wing of the monastery and, though the accommodation was by no means luxurious, it was more comfortable than the cold, bare cells that the nuns inhabited. Lady Alice would be expected to attend at least one service every day but Mother Superior would be lenient with her because of the needs of the baby.

"The nuns are quite besotted with the little man already," Sir William informed them, "and will be sorry when they leave."

"How soon?" asked Marian.

"Soon," came his reply, "but we will not be informed of the day or the destination or be given any news of them from now."

Philip looked anxious but secretly Marian was very glad to hear the news.

After breakfast, Sir William retired to his study, Philip returned to the stable yard and Marian went about her duties. She decided to write a letter to her erstwhile friend and mentor, Lady Anne Boleyn, to ask after her health and for news of the court, especially Princess Mary.

It was about three of the clock two days later when another whirlicote was sighted approaching along the drive. Sir William sent Marian and Philip upstairs then stood in the hall, awaiting the arrival of their expected guest.

It was not long before Lord Bathampton strode into the hall, pushing aside the steward, who was preparing to welcome him.

"Where is she? Where's my wife?" he shouted as he approached Sir William.

"Lord Bathampton, this *is* an unexpected pleasure," Sir William said calmly. "Welcome again to Forrester Hall."

"If she's here, I'll smoke her out, Forrester, with or without your permission!"

Philip, listening from concealment on the gallery above, clenched his fists and would have started down the staircase to defend his father, but Marian laid a placatory hand on his arm and whispered that Sir William was quite capable of dealing with the bully.

"You are speaking of Lady Alice, of course."

"Of course I am speaking of Lady Alice – my wife, Forrester, my wife! She has run out on me."

"I am not surprised, having seen the bruise on her face."

"Ah, then she did come here! I knew that this was where she would make for! What lies has she been telling you?"

"That it was not the first time you had hit her. I do not think that was a lie."

"Just bring her to me and I will take her and that bawling baby home!"

"She *was* here, Bathampton. We fed her and gave her a room for the night then I sent her away and I don't know where they are now."

"I don't believe that you sent her away!"

Before Marian could stop him, Philip was bounding purposefully down the staircase.

"My father speaks truly, sire. They were here and they have gone."

"Ah, so now the whelp comes to defend the old dog. I might have known you wouldn't be far away. And that wife of yours, Marian, the strumpet who did this to me!" He indicated his crooked nose. "I have a score to settle there! Where is she?"

"She is safely out of your reach, Bathampton, and now I will ask you to leave and go find your wife, if you can, she having been long gone," Sir William replied.

"If I can't find her, I'll be back and I'll tear down every brick until I do!"

"What makes you think she would seek sanctuary here?"

"It's here that the brat was conceived, was it not? During the festivities last Christmas?"

*"Really?"* thought Marian, listening from above.

"I must ask you to leave," insisted Sir William.

"I'm not ready to go yet!"

"Oh, but I think you are!" said Philip. "If you wish to make a nuisance of yourself, we have lads half your age who will assist you on your way."

Lord Bathampton looked about him, saw several of the staff closing in, and turned on his heel.

"If you will wait in your carriage, I will ask cook to pack up a few victuals for you. I would not send you out in this weather without sustenance," Sir William offered.

The front door banged behind the intruder and Sir William motioned to one of the maids to carry his message to the kitchens. Twenty minutes later they heard the whirlicote leave.

Later that day, Marian thought over what she had heard, most anxious about his threat to settle the score with her. She must ensure that she was never alone with him again, not that that was ever likely to happen.

Then she thought about the surprising revelation that their baby had been conceived last Christmas. Strange, she hadn't noticed Bathampton taking a special interest in Alice during that holiday. The only man, young or old, who had been paying court to Alice was… The only man, young or old, who had been paying court… The only man…

Had been Philip! They had spent so much time together that Sir William had had several arguments with his son.

Then realisation hit her like a thunder bolt! It must be Philip who had fathered Alice's baby! Pictures began playing through her mind – Philip's distress at her marriage to that monstrous Lord Bathampton – Philip holding the baby – Alice standing close and cooing to the little boy over Philip's shoulder. How blind she had been! How stupid! How incredibly stupid!

Then all the pieces of the jigsaw fell into place – Alice finding herself pregnant but Sir William deciding that nothing, not even a pregnant girl, should get in the way of Philip's marriage to Marian. So Alice had to be disposed of and had been banished into the arms of Lord Bathampton. She had also been sacrificed as an offering to keep his lordship quiet about his lecherous advances to Marian.

Marian didn't like Alice very much but she did not deserve to be treated in this way. And Marian, unknowingly, had gone along with the convenient arrangement.

So, did Philip love Alice? He had just let her go a second time, supported by Sir William. In effect, they had betrayed Alice and they had lied to herself, and that was hurting her more than any other aspect of the ugly arrangement.

That night, she went up to bed before Philip and directed her maids to go with her into the room she had used when they were first married. When they left, she locked the door.

Philip came to find her and rattled the door handle. When he couldn't get in, he began pleading with her to come back to their bedchamber.

"Go away, Philip, go away!" was her only response.

His entreaties became even louder then, until he was shouting to her through the door and banging on it with his fists.

His father tried to persuade her to come out, without success, then tried to reason with Philip, arguing it could all be discussed calmly in the morning, but Philip would not be mollified and Sir William eventually went up to his own chamber in Stephen Tower.

After about an hour of this behaviour, during which time no one could sleep, Philip gave up and went to bed, leaving Marian weeping into her pillows.

# CHAPTER 29

Next morning, none of the household staff had a smile or cheery word to say to anyone else and went about their duties with dark circles under their eyes and sombre expressions.

Sir William enquired about his son and was told that Philip had roused his groom at dawn, ordering his horse to be saddled, then had galloped off across the fields at a foolhardy speed.

He returned in the late afternoon, hot and bad tempered and thrashing his riding crop against his leather boots. His father sat him down and told him that the present situation could not continue.

Marian had not left her chamber all day and had allowed no one in, refusing all offers of food relayed through the locked door. She would not even converse with Sir William and had asked him please to go away.

"Do you know why she is behaving in this way, Philip? It is so unlike our sweet-tempered Marian. Do you think she suspects?"

"I can think of no other reason, Father."

"Then this is another result of your dalliance with that irresponsible young woman! I warned you no good would come of it. For all the saints in heaven, why couldn't you keep your buttons done up? Now you are paying the price and not only you but the rest of us and especially your wife."

Philip said nothing but flung his crop from him, sending it spinning across the hall.

"Son, that's not going to solve anything," his father reproved him. "I suggest you go upstairs and have a wash in cold water and change your clothes, so you no longer smell like your palfrey. Then come and find me and we'll go together to try to talk reason into our Marian. If it is as we suspect, she is hurting, Philip, and with good reason and all the hurt is laid at your door."

An hour later, they were standing together outside the chamber into which Marian had retreated.

Sir William knocked gently. There was no reply. He knocked again, a little louder.

"Marian, my dear, it's your father. Philip is with me."

"Go away!"

"Marian, you can't stay in there forever. You've got to come out some time."

There was no reply.

"Marian, sweetheart," pleaded Philip, "please unlock the door. We need to talk about this."

"Talking won't make it any better, Philip. Nothing can make it any better. I've been so foolish, not to have seen it before she came here, rubbing my nose in your mess. You must have thought me so stupid! Have you been laughing at me all this time – you and her?"

"No, Marian, no! Please come out so we can talk about it."

"I want Marmy. Please, Sir William, send for Marmy."

"Stay here, Philip," his father said. "I'll go myself and find her. Stay here and for the sake of Our Lady and all the saints, tell her how much you love her!"

When he had gone, Philip stood with his forehead pressed to the door and his hand on the latch.

"Marian, Father's gone to find her. Please come out. I want to put my arms round you and ask you to forgive me. I regret what I did so much. It is all my fault."

"Yours and hers. It takes two to make a baby. He *is* yours, isn't he?"

"Yes, he's mine."

"You will want to find her and go to her, I daresay, and him, and become the family that you are."

"We are not a family. We never were. She belongs to Bathampton now, though in no way would I send her back to him – and nor would you, I am certain."

"Do you love her, Philip?"

"I thought I did, once, but she has never given me what you have given me. She gave me her body, willingly – too willingly – too knowingly, but you came to me as fresh as a spring flower and gave me your heart. I know I am weak, Marian, but I do love you, wholly and sincerely."

There was a movement on the other side of the door.

"Is Marmy here yet?"

"Not yet."

Neither of them said anything then until the arrival of Sir William with the housekeeper, who was carrying a mantle.

"Marian, I've brought Marmy, as you asked."

There was a click as the door was unlocked and slowly, very slowly, it began to open to reveal Marian standing there, her fair hair wild about her face, her eyes a deeper green than ever behind wet lashes, her clothes dishevelled where she had lain in them all night and day.

Sir William pushed the door wide open and Marmy went to Marian, wrapping the mantle about her and pressing her very tightly against her full figure.

"Oh, my dear, my dear," the woman said. "Come, let me take you to your bedchamber and see you washed and comfortable between the sheets. Then you must eat and drink a little."

"I'll stay away if you wish it, Marian," Philip offered despondently.

"No, please don't leave me. We have much to say to each other, Philip. Please stay with me."

"I'll never leave you," he promised and Marian knew that he meant it.

# CHAPTER 30

*Place: Forrester Hall, Berkshire*

*Date: A year later – October, 1526*

Marian sat close to the low-burning fire in the hall, her feet on a footstool, her hands folded comfortably in her lap and her back and head resting against the cushions that Marmy had placed there for her. She was lost in a light sleep.

Passing through the hall on his way out, Philip stopped to kiss her gently on the cheek. She stirred and opened her eyes.

"And how is my lady-in-waiting?" he asked, sitting on the footstool and laying his head on her stomach. "And how is my son and heir?"

"We are both well," she said, stroking his hair and allowing the soft blond strands to intertwine round her fingers. "So you have quite decided that the baby will be a boy?"

"Quite."

"You may be in for a big disappointment."

"No matter. If she is as beautiful as her mother, I shall have no cause to fret and we can always have a son next time around."

"You expect a lot, Sir Philip," Marian teased him. "There may not be a next time around."

"You can say that when you know I love you so much?"

"Then kiss me again."

He kissed her distended stomach then stood and bent over to kiss her on the lips. She laughed and pulled him down towards her, her arms round his neck.

"Again!" she commanded and he willingly obeyed.

"Where are you going?"

"To meet Father. His whirlicote has been seen on the road. I thought I would ride out to welcome him home."

"Then go with all speed. Tell him we await him with great impatience. I long to hear all that has been happening at court since his recall by King Henry."

"As do I."

Almost an hour later, Sir William strode into the hall, black velvet hat in hand, his cloak billowing around him. A manservant relieved him of both.

"So good to see you back, Sir William," the man said. "Lady Marian awaits you by the fire. I will bring you a jug of ale."

Sir William thanked him then walked across to where Marian sat. She would have stood to embrace him but he gently pushed her back into the chair and raised her hand to his lips.

"How are you, my lady, and how is my grandson?"

"We are both well, sire, and so pleased to see you home."

"And glad I am to be home."

He began to stamp one booted foot at a time on the flagstones and lustily swung his arms across his chest.

"That October wind shows no mercy," said Philip, who had followed him into the hall.

"But see, I have had the fire made up," said Marian.

Father and son stood with their backs to the hearth until Sir William realised they were shielding the heat from Marian and moved to sit on a couch, where Philip joined him.

"Father, what news of court?" Marian asked. "I do so long to hear it."

"There is much to tell and I have many messages for you, but I am unable to speak at length until I have warmed my throat with the ale I was promised."

Marian waited patiently, at peace now that both her husband and Sir William were here to take care of her, and watched as they drank a jug of ale between them and called for another.

"Sire, you need to rest," she told her father-in-law.

"Yes, I do, but I would not have you wait any longer before imparting my news. I much regret having to tell you, and you will not believe it, though I vouch for the truth of it, that his majesty is seeking an annulment of his twenty-four year marriage to his lady Queen."

Marian and Philip both gasped in surprise.

"Is he really so displeased with her majesty?" Marian asked.

"He has become obsessed with the need to produce a male heir to secure the Tudor dynasty and, at her majesty's advanced age, the clock is ticking against the probability."

"If the marriage is annulled, what will happen to Princess Mary?" Marian asked.

"The Princess will become illegitimate."

Marian and Philip were silent as they digested this news.

"Furthermore," continued Sir William, "he has convinced himself that the lack of a male heir is his punishment for marrying his brother's wife, even though the Queen insists that the couple were too young to consummate the marriage before his brother's early death. Some sycophantic priest has directed him to a passage in Leviticus, which he is quoting: *If a man shall take his brother's wife, it is an unclean thing and they shall be childless*".

"But he is not childless, he has Princess Mary," Marian objected.

"The quotation suits his purpose, nevertheless. It suits his purpose admirably."

"Purpose, Father?" asked Philip.

"Yes. He has looked on another lady at court and they are making no secret of their liaison. If he were not King, it would be quite shameful, behaving thus under the nose of his wife, but he is King and cannot be gainsayed."

"Will you tell us her name?" asked Marian.

"I think that you of all people know it already."

"My Lady Anne Boleyn?"

"'Tis so. You were not mistaken when you said you saw them together. It was for that reason I had you leave court, when their relationship was not general knowledge, and not for that trumped-up charge about the necklace."

"His holiness Pope Clement will never allow an annulment," Philip declared.

"I agree, he will not," said Sir William. "Indeed he will not."

"So what will happen?" asked Marian. "Ohh!"

Both men looked at her with concern and Philip hurried across to her chair.

"No need for alarm," Marian assured them. "Your son just kicked me."

Philip grinned and stood with his arm round her shoulders. "So what will happen?" he reiterated.

"I cannot guess but the King will not be frustrated. He is not accustomed to being opposed. We can only wait and see."

Sir William crossed to the hearth again and warmed his hands.

"And the messages, Father?" asked Marian eagerly.

"The first from that same lady, Anne. She says that, if the wind blows fair – and we understand what she means by that though it cannot be openly stated – she wishes you to return to court to become her lady-in-waiting."

Marian clapped her hands together, contemplating the offer, then looked down at the swelling beneath her waist and up into Philip's blue eyes.

"She is proffering me a great honour, is she not, and if I were free I would clasp it with both hands, but I have a husband and will have a child in two months' time and I cannot foresee that it will be possible."

"I have another message, from the princess, who says that she misses you very much but she is doing well at her lessons and her majesty is very pleased with her."

"And her father?"

"He does not see so much of her these days. He is cutting himself off from both mother and daughter."

"Are there more messages?"

Sir William hesitated. "There is something else –" He stopped in mid-sentence, then continued, "I have one or two letters in my pack and will give them to you on the morrow, Lady Jane Seymour's among them. Now, if you will excuse me, I will go to my rooms and refresh myself, then meet you later at table."

Marian thought that his going was abrupt but decided it was because he was weary from the two-day journey and needed to rest.

"There's something he's not telling us," Philip said.

Marian had ordered hot soup to begin the evening meal and cook had prepared a satisfying thick pea pottage with newly-made bread. Sir William cast all gentility to the winds and voraciously dipped portions of bread into the pottage until his bowl was empty and wiped clean. The remainder of the meal – brawn and bacon, pigeon pie and carp from the monastery ponds – disappeared in like fashion. Wiping his lips on his napkin at the end of the meal, he congratulated Marian on her table.

While he was eating, she and Philip had been trying to coax any undisclosed news from him but he would not be drawn. However, when they were once more seated around the fire and Marian announced her intention of going to bed, and he could delay no longer, he laid a hand on her arm and asked her to stay a while.

"I have further news and I want you both to hear it."

He paused for a long while and Marian and Philip waited patiently.

"Is it bad news, sire?" Philip asked at last, looking at his father with concern.

"I fear that it is. I have to tell you both that Lady Alice has returned to Lord Bathampton and has become subject to him again as his wife."

"And my son?" The words were Philip's immediate reaction and he looked apologetically at Marian for having uttered them. Defensively, she bent forward and hugged her stomach.

"Your son is here, Philip," she admonished him.

"Her baby is with her," Sir William replied.

"But why would she do that?" asked Marian in disbelief.

"I hear she decided that she was better off with her husband than living on charity in some convent, however kind the nuns were."

"But he beats her!" Marian objected.

"That is a husband's privilege," Sir William observed.

"Is the child safe?"

"I believe so, Philip. He is passed off as their own and Bathampton is very proud of the boy, from all accounts."

"His welfare concerns me," Philip said, a worried frown on his forehead.

"Then it should not," Sir William told him. "You gave up all right to the child when you allowed that strumpet to marry into the Bathampton dynasty and take your son with her. You chose a better path by electing to marry Marian, which was the destiny of both of you."

"You're not regretting it, are you, Philip?" Marian asked, looking at him directly, willing him to reply in the negative.

"No, no, of course not. How could I, my darling? How could I, especially now that you are carrying our child?"

"'Tis well said, son, and very sensible. I wished not to tell you both but didn't want you to hear it from other lips. Now I am away to my bed and I suggest you do the same."

He rose from his chair and placed a hand on Philip's shoulder then went across to Marian to kiss the top of her head.

"You are both so young," he said. "Be kind to each other."

He left them then and mounted the stairs. Philip and Marian sat quietly for a while, both absorbed in their private thoughts. Marian was thinking about Lady Anne, guessing that she would not be popular among the Queen's ladies and the rest of the court for her act of betrayal, though no one would dare voice such an opinion. Marian could not begin to imagine the humiliation that the Queen was feeling.

She wondered if Philip was thinking about Alice and their son, now a year old, who would be brought up believing that Lord Bathampton was his father.

"Come, wife," said Philip, rising and taking her hand to help her up from the chair. "The passion is in me to make love to you, if we can manage it and you will not be fatigued by it."

"Philip," she laughed, "we will manage it."

# CHAPTER 31

*Place: Forrester Hall, Berkshire*

*Date: November, 1526*

A month had passed and Marian was becoming more and more uncomfortable. Philip was being most solicitous and spending as much time with her as he was able, but Sir William had returned to court three weeks previously and overseeing the upkeep of the old Hall and the estate and the smooth day-to-day running of the establishment kept them both very busy.

One mid-morning, as Marian was leisurely pacing the length of the long gallery, as she was wont to do each day for exercise, she heard galloping hooves approaching. Going to the window, she saw a fine blue roan being reined in at the entrance and a young man bending low in the saddle to hand a letter to the servant who came down the steps to meet him. Having fulfilled his errand, the messenger turned his horse and returned the way he had come. The servant retraced his steps and entered the hall.

Marian wondered who had sent the letter and what news it contained but the incident was forgotten when Marmy came to find her to report a crisis in the kitchen. One of the kitchen maids had clumsily knocked over a pan of boiling water and cook's arm had been scalded. Marian went at once to the kitchen and found cook at the sink with her arm in a bowl of cold water and in much pain.

She despatched a lad from the stables to ride at once to the village and bring back the apothecary.

"Do not delay," she told him. "The black clouds presage a storm."

While they awaited the arrival of the apothecary, she asked Marmy to find Philip and tell him what had happened.

The housekeeper eventually returned, saying that she couldn't find Sir Philip anywhere and no one seemed to know where he was.

The apothecary arrived ahead of the rain. He was a tall, gaunt man with a kindly manner. He went immediately to the kitchens, gave instructions for the table to be cleared at one end and tipped onto it a collection of snails that he had brought in a sealed pot. Marian watched, fascinated, as he gently spread cook's arm with slime from the snails before making sure it was securely bandaged then sending her to bed to rest.

By now it was raining hard. The whirlicote left, taking the apothecary back to the village, a groom driving the horses and the lad from the stables sitting beside him. Only then did Marian go looking for Philip herself. As he was nowhere to be found, she surmised he was overseeing work somewhere around the estate though it was strange that the storm had not brought him to seek shelter.

When the vehicle returned, it was late afternoon and getting dark and still no sign of Philip. Marian was becoming concerned. None of the household staff could explain his absence so she despatched one of the servants to the stables to ask whether one of the horses was missing.

The servant returned with the lad who had been sent to fetch the apothecary.

"Oh, my lady," he said, standing before her with head bent and rubbing his hands together in a most nervous fashion, "I am so sorry."

"There's nothing to be sorry about," Marian said. "You did well."

"But being sent to the village, and the upset with cook, then having to take the gentleman back home, made me quite forget that I had a message to give to your ladyship. I beg forgiveness, my lady."

"Message from Sir Philip?"

"Yes, my lady. I am so sorry."

"Then give it to me now."

"I saddled his horse for him this morning and he asked me to tell you that he would be home before dark."

"But why didn't he tell me himself?"

"He was in a great hurry, my lady."

"Hurry? He said nothing about it at breakfast. Hurry to go where?"

"He didn't say, my lady."

Marian glanced towards the rain-lashed windows, one of which was rattling under the force of the wind. She was about to speak when the silhouette of a clump of trees in the distance was revealed by a lightning flash followed by a loud clap of thunder overhead.

The servant who had brought the stable lad to her ventured, "I may be able to shed some light here. A messenger came this morning with a letter for Sir Philip. The man said he came from The Vyne."

"I know of it," Marian observed. "It is where their majesties visited with the court after leaving us last Christmas. But why a message was sent from The Vyne, I cannot imagine. Thank you. You may go now, but please send Mistress Malmesbury to me."

That good lady came immediately and, taking Marian by the hand, led her towards a chair by the fire, settled her among cushions, and sent for a shawl to put around her shoulders.

"Marmy, I am so worried," Marian said as she snuggled into the warmth of the shawl.

"You should not fret, my lady. You would not want Sir Philip riding home through this weather. He will be staying the night at The Vyne, I am certain of it. And when he arrives home in the morning, he will explain everything to you."

"The baby is very active tonight," Marian said, rubbing her stomach, "and my back aches so."

"Then it's bed for you, my lady, and a gentle massage with warm oil and hot towels, and warming pans between the sheets. Stay here by the fire and I will find your maids and make sure that everything is carried out as I have suggested, begging your pardon, my lady."

"Oh, Marmy, you don't have to beg my pardon for an instant," Marian said. "You have always been like a mother to me."

"And to think you will soon be a mother to your own little one," the older woman said, smiling down affectionately at her lady.

# CHAPTER 32

The storm blew itself out overnight and the morning dawned bright but with a mist over the downs, concealing details of trees and habitation.

The mist cleared during the morning but still Philip had not come home.

"I'm going to The Vyne to find him," Marian decided. "Hopefully, I will meet him along the road."

"Are you sure, my lady?" Marmy sounded very worried.

"Yes, I'm sure," Marian said. "I will not have him absent another night and not know the reason why."

"Then take one of your maids, I beg of you, and two grooms to drive the carriage. I will pack up some food and drink for the journey and prepare hot bricks for your feet and furs for your comfort."

"You fuss so, Marmy," Marian laughed, but allowed all these preparations to be made before she set off after the mid-day meal.

The whirlicote bowled along at a steady rate but the ruts in the roads were full of water and not always visible to the drivers so that there were many jolts and jars on the journey. Marian was in much discomfort and was continuously massaging her stomach.

"My lady, is there anything I can do to relieve the pressure?" asked Betty, the maid who had come with her, who was a mother herself.

"My back aches so," Marian complained.

"Then, if you will pardon the intrusion, let us share the furs so that I may rub your back and you may lie against me for my body to protect you from some of the rough journeying."

Marian was glad of the wise advice and mistress and maid spent the remainder of the three-hour journey cuddled together in the furs.

When Marian felt she could not endure another minute, the groom shouted that The Vyne was at last in sight and they would be at the entrance in another fifteen minutes.

In less time than that, they were trotting along the drive and onto the circular sweep of the entrance. The two-storey mansion had been built for Baron William Sandys, chamberlain to King Henry. It was constructed of brick with stone surrounds to doors and windows, wings jutting out at each end of the principal reception rooms and a tower or two with pointed roofs.

Marian, however, was in no mood for admiring the architecture and, on being assisted from the carriage, walked purposefully, if a little slowly, to the entrance. Her maid pulled on the rope and sent the bell clanging and echoing loudly throughout the house.

The wooden, studded entrance door was opened by a manservant in a fine blue satin uniform trimmed with silver lace and ruffles.

"Good afternoon, my ladies," he greeted them politely. "Won't you please come in and state your business. I regret that his lordship is not at home but Lady Elizabeth Sandys is, if you wish to see her."

The two women stepped inside and he closed the door.

Marian was in great discomfort and not a little pain, she was fatigued and thirsty and in no mood for polite niceties.

"I have come seeking my husband, Sir Philip Forrester," she said. "Is Sir Philip here?"

"I believe so, my lady," the servant said, somewhat anxiously, Marian thought.

"Then may I see him?"

The servant hesitated.

"Now?" asked Marian, politely but very firmly.

When the servant still did not move, Marian opened her mouth to demand that she see Philip when a young woman's voice reached them from halfway down the staircase. The soft carpet had concealed her approaching footsteps.

"Thank you, Adam," she said. "I will speak to the ladies."

The servant bowed and departed.

She continued her descent. Marian judged her to be in her mid-twenties, a very serious young woman – at least, she looked so now – though her introduction was friendly enough.

"Lady Marian Forrester, I believe?"

"Yes, my lady, but I have not had the honour –".

"I am Lady Elizabeth Sandys, daughter of Baron Sandys. I am pleased to make your acquaintance."

She dropped a curtsey and Marian did likewise, though more awkwardly.

"I have come seeking my husband."

"Yes, so I heard."

"I believe he is here."

"Yes, he is."

"But why so? He left Forrester Hall yesterday morning with never a word to me, leaving only a message that was late in its delivery. I have been waiting this long time for his return but he has delayed and still no word. I do not understand why he came and what is keeping him here."

"We cannot speak freely in the hall, my lady, and I see you are in some discomfort. Pray come into the library, you and your maid, and I will send for some refreshment, and explain everything to you, though it is difficult for me as a go-between."

"Go-between? Between whom?"

"Come," Lady Elizabeth said and led the way towards a door across the magnificent hall.

Half way across, they encountered a young man, probably in his early twenties and a little younger than Lady Elizabeth, riding crop in hand, who looked at them in surprise.

"Lady Forrester, may I present to you my brother, Sir Thomas?"

Marian barely noticed him but curtsied politely, "My lord."

"My lady," he said and swept her a courtly bow, dropping his riding crop as he did so.

"Really, Thomas, you are so clumsy!" Lady Elizabeth scolded him.

Reaching the door to the library, she guided her guests through it and left him staring after them.

They were in a large room whose walls were covered from floor to ceiling with glazed book shelves that contained thousands of books. There was a polished table running the length of the room with chairs placed round it, others were positioned round the fireplace, and several globes of the world were standing in their wooden frames about the room. The long windows, draped with dark blue velvet curtains, looked out onto the driveway, where their whirlicote was still standing, the horses fidgeting in the traces.

When they were seated, Lady Elizabeth rang a bell and sent a servant to bring bread, cheese and wine.

Marian looked at her hostess expectantly.

"This is very difficult for me," Lady Elizabeth said, "as I am not party to any of the circumstances except that unwittingly I have been drawn into the melée."

She paused then continued, "You may remember that two years ago, after spending Christmas at Forrester Hall, their majesties brought the court here. At that time, I made the acquaintance of Lady Alice Dereham."

"Alice!" Marian exclaimed. "I might have known that this had something to do with her!"

"Hear me out, please," Lady Elizabeth asked and Marian nodded and fell silent.

"We became quite close in our affections during the time she was here. Later that year, she married Lord Bathampton and bore a baby son, who I now know was not his."

Marian withheld any comment in the presence of her maid.

"As you know, Lady Alice ran away from her husband because of his harsh treatment of her and came for shelter to Forrester Hall. Sir William put her in the care of the nuns at the monastery."

"But she went back to her husband."

"That is true. However, she found the marriage intolerable and has run away again. Knowing that her husband would go looking for her at Forrester Hall, she came here instead."

"She's here?" echoed Marian.

Lady Elizabeth nodded, "With her son."

"And she sent a message to my husband to come to her aid?"

"No, I sent the message as I was very anxious. You see, she was threatening to kill herself and the baby if your husband didn't come to her. I believe I am right, am I not, that the baby is his?"

Marian looked across to Betty and nodded, unable to speak.

"It's all right, my lady, I had guessed," volunteered her maid.

"So where is my husband now?"

"He is with them and has been pleading and arguing with her all night."

"How does she intend to carry out her threat?"

"She has not been specific but has mentioned walking into the lake, jumping from a tower, taking poison –"

"And my foolish husband has been taken in by her histrionics?"

"It seems so."

"So what is she asking from him to prevent her taking one of these drastic actions?"

"She is asking him to take her away with him."

"And leave me and our unborn baby?"

The other woman nodded.

"Lady Elizabeth, I do not wish to seem ungracious, but it is coming on to rain again and we have a three-hour journey home. I would be much obliged if you would ask Sir Philip to attend on me – now! There is much I have to say to him!"

Lady Elizabeth rang the bell again and asked the servant who answered to request Sir Philip's presence in the library straight away. The servant left and the three women sat quietly, without conversation.

It was not long before the door opened and Philip came into the room. He stared in surprise to see Marian sitting there.

"I did not know you were here!" he exclaimed.

“I have come to ascertain the reason for your absence, husband, and having heard it, to ask you to escort us home immediately.”

He went across and knelt by her side, taking her hand in his.

“Marian, my darling, Lady Elizabeth will have told you the reason for my delayed return.”

“She has and I am asking you to take us home.”

“I cannot while Alice is behaving in this alarming way and threatening to harm herself and the boy.”

“Oh Philip, cannot you see what she is doing? She is playing you for the fool that you are, running to her as soon as she lifts her little finger. Of course she won’t do anything drastic. She hasn’t the backbone for it! And what about *our* baby? Do you not think that this six-hour journey to save our marriage could cause us both harm?”

He stood. “Oh, Marian, I am so sorry. How are you feeling?”

“I couldn’t feel worse. Philip, I want to go home.”

“And I will take you home, dearest –”

“Now, Philip, now!”

“I must plead with Alice one last time –”

“Philip, I forbid it! Either you are married to me or you are not. If you won’t leave with me now, our marriage is over!”

“But Marian, darling –”

“Over, do you hear? Come Betty, please take me to the carriage. I do not feel at all well.”

“When is your baby due?” their hostess asked.

“In a month’s time, but I am not sure that he will wait that long.”

“Sir Philip, you must take your wife home. I will explain to Lady Alice. She loves that child and I do not think she will do anything foolish.”

“Your arm, Philip, if you please. We should be on our way. I fear there is another storm brewing.”

Defeated, Philip extended his arm to his wife and led her from the room. At the front door, they expressed their thanks to Lady Elizabeth and walked towards the whirlicote.

Before handing Marian in, Philip looked up. Following his gaze, Marian saw Lady Alice, the toddler in her arms, looking down at them from an upper window.

Exultantly, Marian gave her a cheery wave and entered the carriage. Without a word or gesture, Philip followed. As soon as Betty had seen them both comfortably settled, she also climbed in and sat opposite them, and the conveyance moved off.

# CHAPTER 33

The rain was falling heavily now and Marian thought she had never felt so miserable in her entire life. She didn't know whether Alice would carry out her threats but guessed not. Anyway, there was nothing she could do about it. Her first consideration was for this new life that was growing inside her, seemingly impatient to be free of its confinement, and her marriage that was being constantly challenged.

She was so fatigued, physically and emotionally, that she succumbed to sleep in Philip's arms.

It was pitch black when she awoke and stirred. The wind and rain seemed to have eased.

"Are you awake?" Philip whispered and, when she answered in the affirmative, he told her she had slept for about two hours, in spite of all the jolting and bumping, and they were now well on their way towards home.

She could hear Betty's heavy breathing from the seat opposite them and guessed she was asleep.

"Philip, you do love me, don't you?" she asked him.

"Always and always," he replied.

"And Alice?"

"'Twas but a foolish infatuation. I see that now. And I also see how she has been manipulating me emotionally. It won't happen again."

"Thank you, Philip."

"Thank me for what?"

"For keeping your word to my father."

"It was my good fortune, Marian, though it took me a while to realise it. But no more talking. We will soon have you home and in bed."

She was about to snuggle back into the furs when there was a terrified squealing from the horses, warning shouts from the drivers, the whirlicote lurched forward then back again and they were enveloped in a tangle of branches and leaves.

Then the vehicle lurched again and all that followed seemed to happen very slowly. Toppling sideways, Marian felt Philip's weight on top of her as they were thrown into the air and began to fall. There was a cracking sound and a sharp pain in her head then everything went black.

# CHAPTER 34

Marian was confused. Voices, always voices, sometimes loud and demanding, at other times soft and caressing. Then excruciating pain and a voice, her voice, screaming and calling for Philip. Then peace again.

Sometimes the space around her was light, but the darkness always returned. Then she saw Richard and heard him speak her name but, when she reached out to him, he disappeared. A voice intoned, "There's no Richard here. There's no Richard here." And all she wanted to do was sleep again.

Finally, it was Sir William's entreaties, caring and concerned, that were reaching her and calling her home and she opened her eyes.

"Marian," he breathed, "you're back with us at last, thanks be to the Holy Mother."

"Where am I?"

"You're safe now and in your own bed."

He was sitting in a chair by her side and took her hand.

"Where have I been?"

"On a long journey, I think, and out of reach of those who love you, but now you've come home."

Frightening memories began to flash through her head.

"Was there an accident?"

"Your carriage ran into a fallen tree along the road and you were thrown out."

"Was Philip with me?"

Sir William signalled to someone standing in the shadows. The person moved across to the door and went out.

"Who was that?"

"A maid. She's gone to fetch Marmy."

"I'd like to see Marmy. I feel so strange."

"Perhaps a little gruel will help. You haven't eaten for a week."

"Have I been ill that long?"

He nodded. "We thought you were never coming back to us."

"Where's Philip? I'd like to see Philip and tell him that I've woken up. He'll want to see me, I think. He loves me, you know – he told me so. We were quarrelling but he told me he loved me."

"I never doubted it, my dear."

"Will you send for him?"

"After you've eaten, when you feel a little stronger."

She closed her eyes again and Sir William put his arm round her shoulders and lifted her into a sitting position, plumping pillows behind her for support.

"Don't go back to sleep, Marian. You must keep awake. Marmy will have sent for the apothecary. Ah, she's here now."

The little woman bustled into the room, her lined face a picture of joy.

"Oh, my lady, my lady, you're back! I was so afraid you had left us as well. Here, my dear. Will you eat a little chicken broth? It will help ease the pains."

Sir William stood and the housekeeper took his place in the chair. She motioned to a girl behind her, who handed her a steaming bowl and spoon then placed a clean cloth on Marian's chest.

"Marmy, I'm so pleased to see you. I feel so weak."

"It's only natural, my lady, after all you've been through. Now, taste this and see if it's not the best chicken broth in all the world."

She spooned some of the liquid into Marian's mouth, who smiled and nodded and opened her mouth for the second spoonful. The bowl was soon empty and Marian lay back against the pillows with a sigh of contentment and closed her eyes.

Suddenly, they flew open and she cried out, "Where's my baby? I was expecting a baby!"

She flung the bedcovers off and gazed down at her flat stomach. "Where's my baby? I want to see him! Where is he?"

Marmy jumped up, sending bowl and spoon flying to the floor, and threw her arms round Marian. Sir William drew the bedcovers back over her and knelt by the bedside, holding her hand. Marian was conscious that the maid was crying.

"Oh my love, my lady," Marmy was saying, "I'm so sorry. The accident – you were so hurt. They took you to the convent and you gave birth but the little mite couldn't be saved. She died in the arms of the Mother Superior and they have buried her in the convent cemetery."

"I don't want a grave – I want my baby!" Marian shrieked and began thrashing about but was soon exhausted and fell back against the pillows, moaning pitifully.

"Does Philip know? Where is he? Was he disappointed that it was a girl? Where's Philip? Sire, I want to see Philip!"

She saw that tears were now running down Sir William's cheeks as he clasped her hand in his and held it to his breast, and there was no need for any words.

"No, not Philip, too!" she cried, clinging to him. "Please, Mother Mary, not Philip, too!"

All was quiet by the time the apothecary arrived. Marian had not spoken since her appeal to the Virgin.

"She will need a sleeping draught," Sir William told him. "She won't be able to bear it otherwise."

Marian allowed him to raise her lids and stare into her eyes, then feel her pulse and her forehead.

He shook his head helplessly. "I will give her something now to help her sleep," he said, "and leave some for tomorrow night and the night after – but keep it out of her reach. Then bed rest is all that I can prescribe. She must stay in bed for two weeks at least, longer if she is not regaining strength. I will call again tomorrow."

"Thank you," said Sir William, escorting him to the door. "You may rest assured that she will not lack any care that I and my staff can lavish on her. She is very precious to us."

"And, Sir William, may I say again how sorry I am for the loss of your son and grandchild."

When he had gone, Marian said bitterly, "What I have been unable to do, sire, Lady Alice has done for you. You are fortunate in that she has borne you a grandson who lives."

# CHAPTER 35

*Place: Forrester Hall, Berkshire*

*Date: Christmas, 1526*

Marian stayed in bed for three weeks, eating very little, weak and listless, taking no interest in anything but her own misery. However, she made an effort to rise on Christmas Day morning, the day her daughter should have been born. Sir William carried her downstairs to breakfast but still she would eat nothing.

"I would like to go to church," she announced, "to the late morning service."

"Do you feel strong enough?" he asked with concern. "Perhaps another day?"

But she was adamant, saying she needed the comfort of the blessed Virgin, who would understand her plight.

"Then it shall be done," Sir William said and set about organising their outing, knowing that fresh air and the company of sympathetic tenants from the village and surrounding farms could not help but aid her recovery.

Servants bore her in a chair to the whirlicote and her maids helped her climb in and sat opposite her and Sir William, who was fussing over her like a mother hen. One of the maids was Betty, whose leg had been badly injured in the accident but she had been fortunate and it was healing well.

When they arrived, Marian was again carried in a chair to the church entrance in the square Norman tower but then managed to walk on Sir William's arm to the Forrester pew. On either side of the aisle were friendly folk who smiled and nodded Christmas greetings to her, the women standing to drop a curtsey and the men touching their forelocks.

She could not stay the tears that wetted her eyes and cheeks on several occasions during the service but partaking of the bread and wine in communion with her Lord was a great solace to her and she came to the end of the service with a deep inner peace.

They allowed everyone else to leave so that the priest could minister words of comfort, then he too left and disappeared into the vestry.

"Sir William, you buried Philip?"

It was the first time she had spoken his name for three weeks.

He nodded. "While you were asleep. He lies in the churchyard."

“Will you take me to his grave? I would like to say goodbye and thank him for all that he gave me.”

“Are you able to walk there, my dear?”

“Yes, Sir William, if you will help me.”

They left the ancient flint church and made their way across the grass to a spot beneath an old chestnut tree and there stood together, looking down at a mound of earth, freshly dug.

Marian was glad that Philip was not in the Forrester vault. Sir William had decided he was too young to lie in the dark among the mouldering bones of their forebears and should be out in the sunlight where he could be visited at any time.

He wandered away then and left her to say all that she needed to say to her husband. When he returned ten minutes later, she was ready to go home.

It was not a happy Christmas but Marian and Sir William spent it together, comforting each other and cared for by their loyal staff, who would not take the following day as a holiday in spite of their master’s entreaties. Cook, whose scalded arm was almost healed, said they would starve without her dishes and she could not have that tragedy on her conscience.

Throughout the twelve days of Christmas they rested or sat before the huge fire and reminisced about times now past.

Marian was growing stronger by the day and eventually asked Sir William if he would accompany her to the convent so she could see the grave of her daughter. He sent a message to Mother Superior and the visit was arranged.

The monastery of St. Jude was further away than the church and village, set in its own grounds, surrounded by gardens of flowers and areas laid out for growing vegetables, with fish ponds and bee hives in the distance and its own trout farm alongside the little river. The building itself was older than the church, the original part of the monastery inhabited by the monks, a new wing having been built two hundred years ago for the nuns.

Sir William guided Marian to the front door of the nuns’ wing and pulled the rope. A bell clanged inside and soon the door opened and a young nun in a black and white habit peered out.

“God’s greetings, sister,” said Sir William. “We are here to see Mother Superior. She is expecting us. I am Sir William Forrester and this is my daughter.”

“Please come in and I will tell Reverend Mother that you are here.”

The little graveyard was surrounded on all four sides by cloisters where a group of nuns was processing, praying the rosary as they passed the beads through their fingers. Mother Superior, elderly but standing tall and upright, with a demeanour of authority, asked the nun accompanying her to speak to the sister at the head of the procession, which she did, and the procession obediently left the cloisters.

She guided her guests to a very small mound with a wooden cross driven into the grass.

"We would like to have named her but did not know what name you would choose," she said.

Marian hesitated for a little then said, "Margaret. It was the name of Sir William's dear wife and I think that will please you, will it not sire? and would have pleased Philip."

"Then I will make sure she is named on the cross," promised Mother Superior. "May I say again how sorry we all are, Sir William, Lady Marian. The nursing nuns in the infirmary did their very best to deliver her – Margaret – alive when you were brought to us after the accident, but it was not God's will. We are pleased to have her here and promise we will look after the grave as long as we are able to do so. Now I will leave you for a while but I will not be far away should you need me."

"Thank you, Reverend Mother," said Sir William. "Her mother and I are very grateful."

When they left the convent, the bell was calling the monks and nuns for the afternoon service of Nones. They made their way to the front of the monastery, where the whirlicote was awaiting them.

Marian, who had stayed calm throughout the visit, began to sob uncontrollably. Sir William's arms went round her immediately and he drew her to him, stroking her hair and shushing her until her shoulders ceased to heave.

At that moment, Marian had the strangest intuition that they were being watched and, raising her eyes to a first floor window, saw the dark shape of a monk looking down at them. She blinked the tears away and looked again but the shadow had disappeared and she thought she must have imagined it.

# CHAPTER 36

*Place: Forrester Hall, Berkshire*

*Date: February, 1527*

The days that brought them to the middle of February were dark, miserable and snow-laden. All the household staff were at great pains to ensure that Marian was comfortable and had plenty to occupy her mind and her time.

So she learned to make pastry, cook's way, and was given mending to finish when there was no embroidery to hand and her paints had dried up and could not be replaced until the weather improved and someone could go down to the village for the various ingredients.

Sir William spent a great deal of his time closeted with his steward, overseeing the affairs of the estate, its farms and his tenants.

"I plan for its future, as I have always done," he confided to Marian, "but it would seem now to have no future."

When they could venture out, Sir William walked with Marian in the gardens or round the lake. He picked her a bunch of snowdrops and watched as she arranged them in a leather jug and placed them on a small table by her fireside chair. Of an evening, they played chess or cards.

Gradually the colour returned to Marian's cheeks and lips and she was heard to laugh occasionally.

At the end of February, a messenger arrived on horseback from the court. Sir William read the letter, which the King himself had scribed. He sent the young messenger to the kitchens to be fed and asked Mistress Malmesbury to prepare a bedchamber in the servants' quarters.

After their evening meal, he told Marian that he had received a message from the King, which he wanted to discuss with her. He ordered a bottle of the best red wine from the cellar and asked her to join him in their usual place, by the hearth.

When the wine had been poured, Sir William rose and stood with his back to the fire, the letter in his hand.

"The King has written it himself – such an honour," he announced.

"It is no more than you deserve, sire. You have been a very faithful servant to his majesty for so many years."

"Marian –" He began and stopped.

"Sir William?"

"Young lady, I think it high time you ceased calling me 'sire' and 'sir' and addressed me as just plain William!"

"But, sire –"

"No, my dear – William."

"William. It will take a little getting used to."

"There are many things that will take a little getting used to, but may not prove impossible."

"You have not told me what the King has said."

"He writes that he and the Queen trust you are recovering from your ordeal and asks that I return to court."

"Oh." Marian had known that this moment must come. His majesty had been very lenient, she thought, in allowing one of his squires of the body to be absent from court for so long, and said so.

"Very lenient," agreed Sir William, "but then he has been distracted for some time with other affairs, not least his determination to have his marriage annulled."

"That makes me very fearful for Princess Mary," she said yet again.

"I will have to obey his summons, of course," he said. "Marian, will you go back to court with me? In that way, I can continue to look after you, which is all I desire to do. Lady Anne has already offered you the position of lady-in-waiting."

"But as yet she is still herself only a lady-in-waiting and has no authority to ask me to serve in that capacity, not while Queen Katharine is on the throne. I fear it is treason to think otherwise."

Sir William sighed deeply.

"William, I cannot go with you, but I will stay here and be here whenever you come home. You will come home, won't you, and not let Lady Joan Dereham entice you away?"

His laugh was dry and humourless.

"When will you leave?"

"Tomorrow. You will see me off?"

"Of course."

"Then I will say goodnight and see you in the morning."

"In the morning – and William, thank you, thank you for everything."

He inclined his head in acknowledgement of her gratitude then turned and left and she watched him slowly climb the stairs and disappear through the door to his tower.

# CHAPTER 37

Marian slept very little that night and was not able to eat breakfast.

"My dear lady," Marmy admonished her, "you should eat something."

"I don't want Sir William to go," Marian complained. "Why does everyone I love leave me?"

"You must tell him so, my lady," Marmy said. "It grieves me to see you both so unhappy."

"I will, but it will make no difference. He cannot disobey the King."

When Sir William came down the staircase, Marmy dropped him a curtsey and wished him well, promising to look after Marian, then discreetly withdrew.

"All is accomplished," Sir William said. "My valise is in the whirlicote and I must be on my way." He held out his arms to her. "Come to this foolish old man, Marian, and tell him you'll miss him."

She went into his arms and knew the comfort of his embrace and the warmth of his body close against hers.

"William, I don't want you to go," she said.

"Believe me, my dear, if I had any choice in the matter I would not be leaving you, but I have no choice. I will come home as soon as I am able and, in the meantime, will write to you and you must write to me by return."

"Of course."

"Now I should delay no longer."

He kissed her on the forehead and was gone. Marian ran to the window and watched the vehicle that was taking him away until she lost sight of it when it rounded a bend in the drive.

Letters from Sir William brightened the days following his departure. He told her about the affairs of the court – how the developing friendship between the King and Lady Anne Boleyn was becoming increasingly obvious to everyone and his majesty was planning to send his secretary to Pope Clement VII to sue for the annulment of his marriage to Queen Katharine. She, poor lady, was looking increasingly distraught and vulnerable.

He passed on messages of goodwill from the Princess, Lady Anne and Lady Jane Seymour and others of her acquaintance, even from Monsieur, the dancing master, who promised that he would choreograph a dance especially for her as soon as she returned to court.

She filled her days as best she could, making frequent forays to the village, accompanied by her servants, to take food and firewood to families who were in need. On Sundays, much of the day was spent at church services, after which she placed blossom and spring flowers on Philip's grave.

One morning, while sitting at the table in the great hall, engaged in balancing the monthly accounts, a task she enjoyed, the bell at the entrance door clanged and the steward brought her news that there was a young man arrived on horseback who desired audience with her, if Lady Forrester was not busy and would afford him such an honour.

"Who is he, John?" she asked.

"He introduces himself as Lord Thomas Sandys from The Vyne."

"Lord Thomas? I don't think I have had the pleasure of meeting him previously. But yes, I will see him, if only to relieve the boredom of the morning. Please bring him in."

The young man who followed John across to where Marian was now standing was tall with wiry fair hair beneath his soft black hat and eyes that radiated an enjoyment of life. Around a wide mouth that was smiling broadly was the hint of a moustache and beard.

When he reached her, he removed his hat and swept a deep bow, to which she responded with a curtsey.

"Sir Thomas Sandys?"

"Lady Forrester, it is a privilege to speak with you this bright morning – made all the brighter by your presence, my lady."

"I'm sorry, sir, but you have me at a disadvantage. Have we met before?"

"Not met, exactly, my lady. More of a passing acquaintance."

"How so?"

"You were with my sister, Lady Elizabeth, when you called at The Vyne on that most unhappy day. We passed each other in the hall."

"Oh yes, now I remember. You dropped your riding crop."

"That I did. I had preferred you had not remembered. It really was most clumsy of me but meeting you quite unnerved me."

Marian laughed and motioned him to sit down. "How so? I cannot believe that, Sir Thomas."

"It was a most unusual day with all the commotion upstairs. I would have you know that Lady Alice did not succeed in bedding your husband any more than she did me – though she tried." His eyes danced at the memory. "Quite the seductress was that young lady – begging your pardon, my lady."

"There is no need to apologise, Sir Thomas. I am well aware of the allure of Lady Alice – well aware."

"Not surprising, really, when one thinks of her husband, old Bathampton. He looks as though he has been kicked in the face by a horse."

Marian smiled. "Will you take some wine with me, sir?"

"With great pleasure."

Marian rang the bell that stood on the side table and asked the servant who responded for wine and goblets.

"Now, Sir Thomas, what is your errand in coming here? I hope your sister is well?"

"Yes, indeed. She is desirous of asking you to visit with her one day soon and I offered to bring the message in person."

"Thank you for riding all this way."

"I was also curious to see Forrester Hall. It is a very fine mansion. You *will* come, won't you?"

"There are too many memories –"

"She guessed you would find the journey difficult. If it will help you, I am willing to collect you in our whirlicote. My sister is offering for you to stay for two or three nights, when I would bring you home."

Marian hesitated.

"You must say yes, Lady Marian. It would give me – us – so much pleasure to be able to entertain you and overlay the unhappy memories with happier ones."

"Then yes, I am glad to accept. Please thank her ladyship."

"Will today week be convenient?"

"Quite convenient."

While finishing their wine, they talked of inconsequential matters, until Sir Thomas decided that, having delivered his sister's message, he would depart.

After he had left, Marian smiled to herself and realised she was looking forward to her outing to the Vyne the following week.

When the appointed day arrived, she was undecided about what to wear but thought it too early to leave off her widow's black, especially bearing in mind the journey she was taking and the destination. She also decided that it would be more appropriate to keep her face veiled but when she saw from the window the young man who had come to escort her to his home – his youth and vitality, and the energy with which he leapt from the whirlicote and bounded up the steps two at a time – she was ashamed of her decision and bid Betty run with her upstairs and pin on another black hat, the one that sat on the side of her head and was crowned with ostrich feathers.

Feeling altogether differently – a young woman again and not a middle-aged shadow of herself in mourning – she descended the staircase slowly and sedately, not allowing him to guess for a moment that she had been waiting by the window this past half hour.

"My lady," he said and swept her one of his deep bows.

"Sir Thomas," she said, curtseying to him and taking his arm.

His brown eyes shone. "May I say how beautiful you look. Come. My sister is waiting for you."

He escorted her to the whirlicote, with Betty following, and settled her in the seat facing the way they would be travelling, seating himself opposite her. Betty rode by the side of the driver.

The journey was more comfortable than the first time she had travelled to The Vyne, probably due to the slower pace and the conversation with her companion, added to the fact that she was no longer pregnant.

Sir Thomas was very knowledgeable about the land through which they were passing, its trees and wild flowers, and the creatures that called it home – the badgers, foxes, stoats and weasels, hares and rabbits. He explained their usefulness in the chain of life and made the subject so interesting that the hours passed quickly.

"My lady, I fear I have been boring you with my talk of field mice and shrews," he apologised.

"Not at all, my lord. It is refreshing to hear you speak thus of country matters. In my experience, men wish to kill everything that moves."

She was surprised to find that they were once more trotting along the drive approaching his home.

He seemed determined to allow her no time to indulge any dark memories. He took her by the waist to assist her from the vehicle, then gave her his arm and escorted her to the great entrance.

As they approached, the door was opened by a servant who told them that Lady Elizabeth awaited them in the Oak Gallery.

Sir Thomas led Marian along a stone gallery perfumed by the orange and myrtle trees growing there, through a door in an octagonal tower and up a staircase that led to the floor above.

When they emerged, Marian saw that they were at one end of a long gallery with large windows and decorated with linenfold panelling. Lady Elizabeth was walking backwards and forwards at the far end.

When she saw Marian, then her brother, emerge through the door, she gave a cry of delight and hurried towards them, her arms outstretched in welcome. She took hold of Marian's hands and kissed her on the cheek.

"See, I have brought her to you safe and sound," Sir Thomas teased his sister. "We didn't drive into a ditch or get stuck in the mud and I didn't tread on her gown!"

"He has been a most considerate and amusing companion," Marian said.

"My sister thinks I can do nothing right," he complained.

Lady Elizabeth laughed. "How he is going to manage the estate when my father is no longer here, I have no idea," she said. "Now, Thomas, you have earned your keep for today and may leave us."

"So soon?"

"Yes, we have confidences to share – women's confidences – and you can have no part in them. We will see you this evening."

"As you will," he said cheerfully, bowed and left the room by the door through which they had come.

"I'm the elder of the two of us," Lady Elizabeth explained, "but, of course, he will inherit when my father passes on, whereas you, my lady, are managing the Forrester estate on your own, I believe, while Sir William is absent."

"With a great deal of help," Marian admitted.

Her hostess rang a bell. "Your maid is with you?"

"She is waiting downstairs."

"Then you will both be shown to your bedchamber so you can rest and change, then we will have a pleasant conversation before the evening meal. We have much to discuss, I believe. What think you of Lady Anne Boleyn, who seems to have bewitched his majesty? I understand she has been a friend to you?"

"She has indeed," Marian confirmed, "and – somewhat prematurely, I feel – has asked me to become her lady-in-waiting should I return to court."

Lady Elizabeth pulled a face and drew her guest over to the linenfold panelling by the door that she said led to the King's bedchamber.

"Their majesties have visited us on several occasions. See here," she said and pointed to emblems carved into the oak. "The fleur de lys of the King and the Spanish pomegranate, the symbol of Queen Katharine. I fear the panel will have to be replaced if his majesty has his way – as, of course, he will – and he brings Lady Anne Boleyn here as Queen."

# CHAPTER 38

*Place: The Vyne, Hampshire*

*Date: Summer, 1527*

"Elizabeth, you and Sir Thomas have been so kind to me while I have been staying in your beautiful home," Marian said as the two young women lazed on cushioned chairs in the summerhouse, having taken an afternoon tour of the grounds in the late March sunshine. "You must allow me to return your hospitality soon."

Elizabeth Sandys flicked open her silk fan and fanned her face and neck. "That would be delightful and I know it would please my brother."

That evening, walking in the stone gallery, their talk turned to the fate of Lady Alice, who had gone back to Lord Bathampton with her son but had threatened to abscond yet again.

"Marian, this must be very difficult for you," her hostess said sympathetically. "How do you really feel about the child? If it were me, I believe I would be calling down fire and brimstone on that young lady's head."

Marian stopped walking and, frowning, turned to face her new friend.

"In truth, it troubles me that I haven't forgiven her or Philip, though I have tried. But the boy is Sir William's grandson and for that reason I wish them no ill. I do envy her, though, and long for Philip's and my own baby." Tears came to her eyes. "Did you know I named her Margaret, after his mother?"

Next day, on the journey home, Sir Thomas asked to hear all about her life up to the time she had unexpectedly arrived at The Vyne to take her husband home, and was not content until she had related everything pertinent.

"You are a very remarkable young woman," he told her.

"Oh, not so remarkable."

"'Tis God's truth, I have never met anyone like you," he said. "I hope we will become very good friends, my lady."

"I'm sure we shall."

He reached across and took her hands and held them tightly in his.

"That would give me the greatest pleasure."

She allowed him to hold them until they drove over a large hole in the road and both had to cling to the framework of the whirlicote to steady themselves.

When they arrived at the Hall, as before, he held her by the waist to assist her descent then stood looking down at her, his hands still on her waist.

"My lady Marian," he said, "I am loath to let you go until I have made sure you are quite safe."

Marian laughed. "What circumstance would render me unsafe in my own home, Sir Thomas? However, you are welcome to come inside and take some refreshment before your return journey."

She took his arm and they mounted the steps and passed through the entrance, the door being opened by an unseen servant as they approached. Her maid, Betty, followed closely behind.

Marian knew as soon as she set foot inside the hall that all was not well. She could almost smell disaster.

Confirmation was written all over the face of Marmy, who came hurrying towards her, wringing her hands.

"Oh, my lady, such liberties! I'm so glad to see you return, but, oh, they are taking such liberties!"

"Who are? What has happened? You remember Sir Thomas?"

Marmy bobbed a perfunctory curtsey but paid him little heed.

Marian removed her hat and gave it to her maid. "Betty, please find someone to bring us refreshments. Now Marmy, tell me."

"Sir William has come home. He arrived the day you left."

"But that is great news! Where is he?" She turned to her guest. "Sir Thomas, I would like you to meet my father-in-law. Where is he, Marmy?"

"Not such great news, dear lady. He brought guests with him and she is ordering every one of us about as if she was already Lady Forrester and not your own dear self."

"Marian, my dear!"

Marian turned to see Sir William approaching and ran to him, dropping him a curtsey before putting her arms round his waist and giving him a hug.

"Sir William!" she exclaimed, quite forgetting that he had asked her to drop the 'Sir'. "I'm so glad you're home. Come and meet Sir Thomas Sandys of The Vyne. I have been staying with his sister for a few days and he has brought me home."

She took him by the hand and drew him across to where Sir Thomas stood, looking rather bewildered.

Sir William welcomed the younger man, somewhat stiffly, thanked him for escorting Marian home, then spoke to her again.

"Marian, I have not returned alone."

Noticing a movement out of the corner of her eye, Marian directed her attention towards the staircase, and was astounded to see Lady Joan Dereham descending the last few steps and coming towards her, arms outstretched.

"My dear, dear Marian, how I have looked forward to seeing you again after your sudden departure from court, after that most unfortunate incident of the Princess's necklace."

She dropped a curtsey then embraced an unwilling Marian, who was too surprised to say a word.

"And who is this handsome young man with you?"

"May I present Lord Thomas Sandys of The Vyne," Sir William said and she curtseyed again in response to Sir William's introduction and the young man's bow.

"Ah yes, The Vyne," Lady Dereham repeated. "I believe we have cause to be very grateful to you and your sister."

"We?" asked Marian sharply.

At this point, servants arrived with wine and goblets and bread and cheese and Marmy set about guiding Sir Thomas and Lady Dereham away from Sir William and Marian, towards the hearth and seats and side tables.

"William, what does all this mean?" Marian demanded. "Why is she here?" Then suspiciously, "You haven't married her, have you?"

"No, of course not. How could I?"

"What then?"

Marian was beginning to get very angry at the presence of this woman who had been the cause of her flight from court in such humiliating circumstances.

"I had hoped to explain before they arrived –"

"They? Who's they?"

"I came on horseback ahead of them, expressly to tell you, but you had already left."

He drew her arm through his and walked her along the corridor leading to the chapel and through a side door into the rose garden. They wandered between the beds of trees and bushes for a time in silence, the myriad colours and perfume of the flowers calming her spirits while she waited for him to explain.

"This is the position, my dear, and I hope you will understand that I could do nothing other than the action I have taken. You must know the trouble that Lady Alice has been giving her husband – I have hinted at it in my letters to you –"

"I might have known it had something to do with her!" interjected Marian.

"She has caused her husband so much grief, having run away on several occasions, that at last he would tolerate her behaviour no longer and threw her out, with her son, letting the world know that the child was not his but Philip's."

"Oh, William, I am so sorry," said Marian. "Is there no end to the trouble those sisters cause us? Is everyone at court deeply shocked?"

"For better or worse, the scandal has passed almost unnoticed in the shadow of what is happening to the marriage of his majesty and Queen Katharine, because of his pursuit of Lady Anne. He is like a wild man as he lusts after her – begging your pardon, young Marian – but I believe she is playing a very clever game and will not allow him into her bed unless he marries her – rids himself of Katharine, marries her and makes her his Queen – but that is by the by."

"So what has happened to Lady Alice and her son?"

"I had to bring them here."

"Here?" Marian screeched. "To our home?"

Sir William looked crushed but was unrepentant. "What else could I do? She arrived in court, a rejected and discarded young woman, pleading for shelter. Lady Joan came to me – after all, the little fellow is my grandson, my only grandson."

Marian's sob choked in her throat. Immediately, his arm went round her shoulders.

"I'm sorry, my sweet one, that came out of my mouth unbidden."

"But you speak truly, William."

"Now they are here, I know not what to do about them. Marmy has accommodated them so that the little boy has plenty of room to play, and she has taken on two women from the village to act as nursemaids to look after him. He is almost two years old now and very loveable, though truth to tell, I cannot see either my son or his mother in his features."

"So what now? Where will you send them?" Marian saw the shadow that crossed her father-in-law's face and with determination raised her chin. "You must send them away, William. They cannot stay here."

"No, they cannot, you speak the truth."

"If they stay, I will go. Lady Joan has designs on you, William, and if she stays she will not rest until she is Lady Forrester, then there will be no room for me here."

"You are speaking nonsense. Of course you cannot leave."

He stopped and snapped off a beautiful yellow and orange tea rose and gave it to her. She buried her nose in its petals and took a deep breath.

"I will not stay just to keep her out of your bed, William. After all, it would not be the first time, would it?"

He was silent and they continued their walk. Marian wondered whether she had overstepped the line but presently he said, "I believe her strategy is more complicated. I think she has a second string to her bow and is not above sending her sister to me to achieve what she cannot."

"So if the elder sister is not sufficient enticement, the younger one may be?"

Sir William nodded and grinned cheerfully. "If I was younger, I might take full advantage of the situation, playing one sister off against the other!"

Marian looked at him aghast then saw the mischief in his eyes and laughed in spite of her anger.

"And what about Sir Thomas?" he asked. "Is he your suitor?"

"If I encouraged him, yes, perhaps, but I don't want to leave Forrester Hall or you, William."

He sighed. "I cannot see the future, Marian, or what's to be done. Come, let us return to our guests. Now you are home, we must make plain to their ladyships that there is already a Lady Forrester in possession of Forrester Hall and she does not need replacing."

"Though that does not eliminate the blood ties and your feelings for that little boy."

When they returned to the hall, they found an altercation in progress. Sir Thomas came across to them, saying he was awaiting their return before taking his leave and returning to The Vyne.

Lady Alice was close behind him, trying to persuade him to take her with him, saying she felt oh, such affection for his sister, and was absolutely longing to see her again after her great kindness on the last occasion.

Lady Joan was admonishing her for neglect of her son and reasoning with her that it was not proper for her to travel for three hours in a vehicle with a young man and without a chaperone, and Lady Alice was heaping scorn on her sister's head for her suspicious thoughts.

Marmy was standing in the background, wringing her hands again and repeating "Oh my!" over and over.

"Sir William, please talk to my sister," Lady Joan pleaded with him. "It is not fitting that she should leave and neglect her responsibilities to her son."

"Fie!" exclaimed the young woman. "What are two nursemaids for, if not to look after him when I am not here?"

"But you *are* here, sister," protested Lady Joan. "Sir William, please speak to her."

Sir William sighed. "This argument is not of my making," he said, "and I would not involve myself if it were not for the child."

He turned to face Sir Thomas. "Young man, I think it would be better if you were on your way. Mistress Malmesbury, my housekeeper, will ask cook to pack up some food for your journey."

"Thank you, Sir William."

"This way, my lord," said Marmy and led him away.

"Thank you, dear Sir William," purred Lady Joan. "I knew you would decide what was to be done."

"I would like Lady Forrester to meet my grandson," he said to the boy's mother. "May I send for one of his nursemaids to bring him downstairs?"

Lady Alice shrugged. "If you wish," she said and turned away.

Sir William beckoned to Marian's maid, Betty, who was also hovering in the background, and asked her to convey his message to the nursery.

Within a very short time, they heard a childish voice above them and, looking towards the staircase, saw a motherly-looking middle-aged woman coming down towards them, holding the hand of a little boy who appeared very apprehensive. As soon as he saw his mother, he called out to her, pulled his hand from the grasp of the nursemaid, scrambled down the remaining stairs and ran across to her.

"Here's my baby!" she exclaimed and crouched to receive him. "He's a handsome boy, don't you think so, Sir William?"

"I do indeed, Lady Alice. So, tell Lady Forrester your name, young man."

"Tell the lady your name," his mother urged him.

"William," he lisped.

"Now there's a coincidence," Sir William replied. "That is my name, too. I'm your grandfather, you know. Will you come and meet Lady Marian and let her have a good look at you?"

His mother stood. "Please forgive him, Sir William, but he is rather shy of strangers. Perhaps another time. Now, William, it is your bedtime. Off you go with your nursemaid and I will see you tomorrow."

"You will come and wish him goodnight when he is in bed, my lady?"

"I think not. You are quite capable of putting him to bed. I'll see him in the morning."

Marian watched as Alice turned her back on her son and directed her attention to Sir Thomas Sandys, who had just re-entered the hall from the direction of the kitchens. He bowed low to Marian.

"My lady Marian, it is my fervent wish that we meet again very soon."

"And my wish, too," Marian said, curtseying and enjoying the scowl on the face of Lady Alice.

After he had left, the ladies retired to their bedchambers, their maids following. Marian and William were left alone.

"So, what did you think of my grandson?" he asked. "I am very happy to have a little boy in the house again."

A troubled look crossed his face when Marian did not reply. "Marian?"

"William, you say you remember Philip at that age?"

"Very clearly. We were both so happy to have him, Margaret and I."

"Does this little William resemble him?"

"No, I can't say that he does."

"Philip was so fair and Alice has that flaming red hair, but her son is so dark."

"Children do not always follow the colouring of their parents," he said.

Marian nodded assent. She did not wish to upset Sir William, but she couldn't help thinking that the boy reminded her of someone. She wished she could remember who it was but it certainly wasn't Philip. Was it possible…?

Sir William broke into her thoughts. "Marian, you must be tired. Off to bed with you now, and I will see you in the morning."

"Very well. And William, lock your door!"

He laughed and, at the top of the stairs, kissed her on the cheek.

No one else was in sight but she had no sooner closed her bedchamber door when she heard another open and shut.

"Betty, peep and see who it is."

Betty opened the door a crack and looked along the corridor.

"It's Lady Dereham," she whispered back to Marian. "She is talking to Sir William outside the door to his tower."

"Can you hear what they are saying?"

"No."

"What are they doing now?"

Betty shut the door quickly and stood with her back to it.

"She is coming back to her chamber and Sir William has gone through his door and shut it behind him. She looks very cross."

Marian grinned, then saw the knowing look on her maid's face. They both pressed their knuckles between their lips so that their laughter would not be heard.

"I am so pleased, my lady. Sir William deserves someone better."

# CHAPTER 39

*Place: Forrester Hall, Berkshire*

*Date: Summer, 1527*

Marian grew more and more uncomfortable as the days passed and Alice and her sister settled into life at Forrester Hall, giving no sign that they were thinking of leaving any time soon. She had to be very firm to stand her ground as mistress of the Hall and gave orders to the staff that they should disregard any instructions that came from anyone other than herself.

She was also troubled by the enjoyment and inordinate interest that Sir William was taking in his young namesake. Toys that Philip used to play with were brought from cupboards in the nursery and taken to the estate carpenter for repair where necessary. An old rocking horse appeared resplendent in fresh paint and with a new mane and tail of horse hair brought from the stables, and a new length of string was fixed to the nose of a wooden dog on wheels.

One afternoon, Marian found grandfather and grandson sitting on the floor of the nursery enjoying a game of nine men's morris. Sometimes Lady Alice and Lady Joan joined them in the skittle alley. When the weather was dry, there would be a game of 'touch' on the lawns or Sir William would show little William how to spin a top, or bowl a hoop along the drive without letting it fall flat or spin out of reach.

Sometimes the horses were the main attraction and whole afternoons were spent at the stables.

At other times they walked over the fields or around the lake, when Sir William delighted in pointing out to the little boy wild flowers or birds and fish, butterflies and dragonflies, and on one occasion a beautiful kingfisher.

Surprisingly, a large black cormorant had flown in and seemed to want to stay. They watched as it dived beneath the surface of the lake, remained under a long time and eventually emerged with a large fish in its beak, which it swallowed whole. It spread its wings to dry, fanning them in the breeze, their sheen of emerald green rich in the sunlight, then stretched out its neck this way and that to survey its new home. In the excitement of the moment, Sir William seemed not to have noticed that Alice had slipped her arm through his.

Marian looked on, feeling like an outsider in her own home, not knowing how to cope with the two sisters who were making themselves more and more part of the household. If it was not one it was the other laughing at Sir William's witticisms or praising his natural gift of understanding little boys or ingratiating themselves in so many other ways.

"Marmy, I don't know what to do," she confided one evening.

The housekeeper hurrumphed and folded her arms across her chest.

"Sir William is becoming too fond of that little boy," she said. "It's all about him missing his son, and nothing more than that. Strange thing is, Lady Marian, the little boy looks nothing like Sir Philip."

Marian looked at her sharply but said nothing. However, it set her to thinking again and searching her memory. It was true, he looked nothing like Philip, but who did he look like?

She awoke in the middle of the night with the answer. Of course! What a fool she had been not to remember before this. How much distress it would have saved and how much heartache in the days to come!

She got out of bed, drank a beaker of water, and began to pace the room. William would have to be told – or would he? He was so happy these days with little William in his home. Should she deprive him of that? Purely selfishly, it provided the opportunity to get rid of those two scheming sisters once and for all.

She crossed to the casement and looked out over the rose garden to the downs beyond, lit by the almost full moon. The beauty and peace of the scene away to the horizon and the freshness of the night air filled her with reassurance. Of course she would tell him, she could not do otherwise. She would tell him first thing in the morning, after breakfast, but would try to break the news very gently.

However, before she had opportunity to do so, Sir Thomas and Lady Elizabeth Sandys arrived, with apologies for their unexpected appearance. Marian had come down to the great hall to greet them and found young Sir Thomas looking very surprised to find the Dereham sisters and little William still there and appearing so comfortably ensconced. He sent a questioning look to Marian, who shrugged helplessly.

After Lady Elizabeth had been introduced to Sir William and Lady Joan Dereham and formal pleasantries had been exchanged, Sir Thomas contrived to draw Marian apart.

"We were not expecting you, Sir Thomas," Marian said, "though it gives me great pleasure to see you both. What is the purpose of your visit?"

"My sister came to invite you and Sir William to stay with us for a few days, but I came because I could not stay away. I have thought of no one but you since I left here."

There was a peal of laughter from the ladies encircling Sir William and Sir Thomas frowned in annoyance.

"Is there somewhere we could hide?" he asked. "I do so long to be alone with you, my lady."

Marian decided to be generous towards him and said, "Perhaps later. But now I have an announcement to make and I am glad that you and your sister are here to witness what I have to say."

"An announcement?"

"Yes, a very important announcement. Come."

He followed her over to the group.

"Sir William, my ladies, I have something to impart," she told them.

The chatter and laughter ceased and they looked at her expectantly.

"What is it, my dear?" asked Sir William. "You are looking very serious."

"Because this is very serious."

She turned to face Lady Alice.

"Alice, we have known each other for some time and I accept that you knew my husband very well, before you were married and before he and I had married."

Alice contrived to look coy. "We need not rake over the past, Marian. We all know the fruit of my relationship with your husband. He stands before you – Sir William's grandson – his only grandchild, I might add. I have watched them grow very close to each other, which pleases me – is that not so, Sir William?"

The little boy was playing with his marbles on the floor. Sir William bent to ruffle his dark curls and smiled down at him.

"We like each other, don't we, William?"

"Yes, grandfather," the boy said, reaching up and taking the older man's hand before going back to his game.

Marian gulped but determinedly carried on.

"He is a very handsome little boy, there's no question of that, with his dark curls and dark eyes. Think, now, of my husband. He was very handsome, too, but his hair was blonde, blonde and straight, his eyes blue, and his complexion pale, none of which has been inherited by your son, Alice."

"That's easily explained," replied her sister. "He takes after our side of the family."

"But I have met your mother, Lady Joan," interrupted Sir William. "She is white-haired now but I believe in her youth her hair was the same colour as yours and your sister's. It's a very distinctive colour, very beautiful."

"You compliment us, sire," Alice broke in hurriedly. "But you promised little William a morning spent with the horses and he is greatly looking forward to that, aren't you, son?"

The boy looked up and nodded vigourously.

"So I suggest you take him now, Sir William, because I am not sure it is not going to rain later."

"Of course. I want to put him up on a horse I have acquired especially for him. It is justly limbed and has an easy ambling pace and so is quite suitable for the little fellow."

"Then let us repair to the stable yard," urged Lady Joan.

"But I think Marian had something more to say. What is it, my dear?"

Marian gulped. There was no easy way of saying this. It was best that she came straight out with it.

"I am saying that he is not Philip's son."

There was a gasp from Lady Joan then a stunned silence for several seconds, broken at last by Sir William.

"What are you saying, Marian? Not Philip's son? You cannot be so cruel as to suggest –"

"This is ridiculous!" stormed Alice. "Of course he's Philip's son. I'm his mother, I should know who – who –"

"Who bedded you?" asked Marian. "From what I've heard, it was half the men at court!"

"That accusation is outrageous!" stormed Lady Joan. "How dare you suggest such wantonness in my sister!"

"Marian, this is all rather indelicate," Sir William remonstrated. "I think you should apologise to Lady Alice."

"Thank you, Sir William," Alice said and went across to him and began to cry. He put his arms round her, as Marian knew he would out of the kindness of his heart. Alice cried all the louder and Marian became even more incensed. Everyone was staring at her.

Lady Elizabeth said she thought she and her brother should withdraw but Marian asked them to stay.

"If your husband was not the child's father," interjected Lady Joan, "then kindly tell us who was – and prove it!"

Sir William still had his arms round Alice.

"Stephen Arundell," announced Marian.

Alice raised her head from Sir William's chest and stared at her with a look of panic and Marian knew she had hit the bullseye.

"Who?" asked Lady Joan, doing her best to sound surprised.

"He's one of Lord Bathampton's scribes," said Marian. "He came with the court to spend Christmas here."

Sir William dropped his arms and regarded little William, who was quite oblivious of the drama being enacted above his head. "I agree, there is a certain resemblance."

"She's making it all up! It's all in her head! She's quite mad!" asserted Lady Alice, no longer tearful. "She's jealous because the boy is mine and not hers! Because your son, Sir William, took me to bed – and not only once, may I add, and not always to bed!"

"That's enough!" thundered Sir William. "I will not have this disgraceful altercation beneath my roof and in front of my guests!"

"Sir Thomas and I really should retire," Lady Elizabeth offered again, but was ignored.

Sir William turned to Marian. "You have made a serious accusation, Marian, but it is impossible to prove."

"Not so." Marian was determined not to be browbeaten. "You remember Stephen Arundell, William – his dark curls, just like little William's here – his dark eyes. What else was unusual about that young man's face?"

"Unusual? Nothing that I can think of."

Alice moved across to her son, picked him up and cradled him close to her, burying his face in her neck. She seemed to have forgotten all about the visit to the horses.

"He is tired. I really should ring for the nursemaid to take him up for his mid-morning sleep."

"You will stay here, Lady Alice, until this matter is thrashed out," Sir William ordered, his voice as ominous as a thunder roll, his expression as dark as a storm cloud.

Lady Joan came to stand by her sister. "My sister and I have suffered enough without these wicked allegations. We will leave immediately and take William with us. We will not stay beneath this roof a moment longer and will not be returning."

"But we have nowhere to go," wailed Alice.

"Lady Elizabeth," said Joan, turning to her, "you gave my sister refuge once. May we take advantage of your hospitality again, in this emergency, just until we find somewhere for my sister and nephew to shelter?"

Lady Elizabeth looked taken aback. "I – I'm not sure," she wavered.

"Neither am I!" Sir Thomas spoke for the first time since the argument had started.

"Wait!" The command came from Sir William. "There *was* something about young Stephen Arundell's face. He had an eyelid that drooped a little over his right eye. I was so used to seeing it that I had stopped noticing it."

"As you didn't notice William's droopy eyelid?" asked Marian.

Sir William looked at her sharply then turned his gaze to the child. "William, look at your grandfather. Look at me, William."

The little boy slowly turned his head and looked at Sir William. The drooped eyelid was plain for all to see. Sir William gave what sounded like a sob, turned and walked out of the front door. No one else said a word. At last, Marian spoke.

"I want the three of you out of Forrester Hall within the hour."

She also left by the entrance door, intent on searching for William. When she could not find him anywhere and returned to the Hall, the two sisters with the little boy were climbing into the whirlicote that had the Sandys arms emblazoned on the bodywork. Sir Thomas hurried across to her.

"Lady Marian, I didn't wish to leave without saying goodbye."

"You are taking them with you?"

"Lady Joan will return to court immediately. We will give shelter to Lady Alice and the child for a couple of days only, while she finds somewhere else to go." Marian nodded her appreciation of their chivalry, though she thought it was misplaced. Sir Thomas continued, "I am so sorry that we were witnesses to all that."

"I'm glad you were," Marian said, "because you will know exactly what was said and will be able to refute any lies they spread about Sir William and myself."

"My lady, will you permit me to call on you again, soon?"

"My dear Sir Thomas, I think not. I would not have you wasting your time on me. There is no future for us, none whatsoever, but thank you for caring."

"But, my lady, I beseech you –"

"I'm sorry, Sir Thomas. Please bid your sister goodbye for me."

She stood on tiptoe to kiss him on the cheek.

"Now I must find Sir William. He might need me."

So saying, she turned and entered the Hall.

Passing through the door leading to Stephen Tower, she climbed the stairs and entered his study but he was not there. She knocked on his bedchamber door and, receiving no response, raised the latch and peeped in, but he was not there, either.

Descending to the hall, she took the side door to the rose garden and explored the grounds again. Finally, she found him sitting on the bench in the arbour and was shocked to see that he had been crying.

"Oh, William, my dear. My dear, dear William," she said and sat beside him and put her arms round his waist, leaning her head against his shoulder.

"I didn't mean for you to see me like this," he said, "but I've lost Philip all over again."

"I know," Marian said, painfully aware that it was here that Philip had first made love to her. She could see through the trellis and the pink roses the spot beneath the tree where, for first time, when she was only fifteen ... She closed her eyes tightly to shut out the view and the memory of her sexual awakening.

"I had such dreams for that little boy."

"I know," Marian said again.

"I need to be loved," he said.

"You are loved, William. We all love you."

"I speak of a woman's love."

Some foreboding of what was coming caused Marian to draw away from him. His next words came out in a rush.

"Marian, my dear, if I could, I would ask you to marry me, but mother church forbids it as you were my son's wife. So I cannot offer you that close protection. But I want you with me to the end of my days. I cannot bear the thought of someone taking you away from me. If you could love me –"

"But I do love you, William, oh, I do love you!"

"But as a father, eh? Nothing more?"

"This is too soon for me, too soon, and I am not sure it is appropriate."

"I want always to be near to look after you. I am conscious, of course, of the twenty two years that lie between us. But, if ever you felt you could love me as a husband, I can wait for that joy. If ever you came to me with that desire, I would honour you as my wife even though the church had not joined us together and I had not placed a wedding band on your finger. All I ask is that you give my proposal some thought."

Tears stung Marian's eyes and he wiped them away with his fingers.

"I did not wish to make you cry."

"No, William, it just would not do. Supposing I became pregnant – and I could, you know –"

He smiled at the compliment.

"Think of the scandal, the disgrace because we would be regarded as living in an incestuous relationship. You don't need me, William. One day, you will meet a fine lady whom you can marry and who is worthy of you. I have loved you as a dear father and father-in-law, but I cannot enter into what you are suggesting. It would destroy us both."

He sighed then was quiet.

Marian also was silent, her thoughts chasing themselves round and round in her head. Could she possibly go to bed with her husband's father? If she refused this offer, would she lose her status as lady of the manor one day? Where was this imagined fine lady of whom she had spoken? There was no such person – but there might be in the future.

The future… what was her future? If she could not be with Richard, she had no other plans. Did that foreshadow an old age of loneliness? William could save her from all that. Was the idea so repugnant to her?

She looked about her as if the answer was out there somewhere, among the trees, in the grass. The roses swayed above her head and the sun was burnishing the gnomon of the sundial. Perhaps she could ask him to wait a day or two for her final answer. Did she need a day or two? Didn't she know that her answer would be the same then as now?

"Do you still think of Richard Mordaunt?" he asked suddenly, seemingly forgetting that he had forbidden that name to be mentioned in his hearing ever again.

"Yes, often." Caught by surprise, her reply was truthful but laced with so much guilt that she added quickly, "But we have had no contact since I married Philip. I loved Philip, William, and was faithful to him."

That was true, too. Surely there was a vast difference between the deed and the fantasy that had come unbidden, sometimes during the very act of lovemaking?

"I know you were. I am also aware that you and Richard were in love."

"But we were ill matched. I have no idea where he is now."

Sir William took her hand in his and stroked the back of it with his thumb.

"He may be nearer than you think."

It was not until much later in the day that she thought what a strange remark that was for him to make.

Sir William stood.

"We must live our lives the best way we know how, no matter what the heartaches. I will ride back to court tomorrow and petition the Queen to allow you to return. She has told me many a time that she misses your bright smile. That will be best for you and I can keep my eye on you and you on me so that my loneliness does not provoke me into doing something foolish regarding the ladies."

"Of which there are many who would delight to become Lady Forrester."

His eyes twinkled and something of the robust William returned.

"Yes, of which there are many, I'm glad to say."

# CHAPTER 40

*Place: Greenwich Palace*

*Date: September, 1527*

Sir William left for court next day and after Easter Marian found herself again riding through the black and gold crested iron gates and along the tree-lined avenue leading to the east wing of Greenwich Palace.

She had been instructed to report immediately on arrival to her majesty and made her way to the ante-room next to the audience chamber where she and Philip had been introduced to the King and Queen four long years ago. Now, at almost eighteen years of age, she had become very familiar with the ways of the court.

Marian knew that William would be waiting there for her, though she could not see him immediately among the crowd of noisy courtiers and others who had come to petition their majesties about some issue or another.

Several were calling out to acquaintances or importuning the officials, who were endeavouring to impose some semblance of order. This took the form of a constantly changing line with those of pre-eminence at the forefront and those with little hope of being admitted bringing up the rear.

A tussle broke out between two young courtiers and a strident voice was raised in complaint. "Go further back in line? Indeed I will not! Did he slip you a coin? Else why should I lose my place to this ruffian?!"

"If you don't move, you'll lose more than your place!" retorted the steward and made a sharp cutting gesture across his throat with the side of his hand, reminiscent of the bloody axe.

"Seems to be a matter of heads or tails!" guffawed the so-called ruffian. "Tails you win or heads you lose!"

Muttering under his breath, the young courtier who had been ousted walked to the tail end of the line, accompanied by the jeers of those around him.

Marian saw William before he saw her and pushed her way through the crowd to reach him. He smiled broadly when she came up to him and kissed her on the cheek.

"You look magnificent," she whispered to him, admiring his brown and gold doublet with ruby red sleeves and hose, and dark brown boots reaching above his knees.

"And you are becoming more beautiful by the day, daughter," he said, taking her hand and placing it on his arm, "even in your widow's black."

"Thank you for petitioning the Queen for me, William."

"I have instructions to take you to her immediately you arrive."

He spoke to one of the officials and they were placed at the head of the line, the next to receive an audience. This caused those around them to complain bitterly about being pushed further back when they had already been waiting all morning, but the official barked at them and they quietened.

The door opened to allow the exit of an elderly couple. The official entered the audience chamber, bowed low then announced their names, received acquiescence, and beckoned them to enter.

Marian was surprised to see the Queen seated there on her own. Sir William bowed with a flourish of his hat and Marian curtseyed her special curtsey.

"Bring her forward, Sir Villiam," the Queen commanded and he led Marian to the foot of the daïs. She looked up at the Queen and thought how faded her majesty appeared. Her red hair was turning grey, her blue eyes looked tired and had lost the sparkle they once had and her skin at throat and neck was beginning to wrinkle and sag.

"Now, my lady, once again – the Marian curtsey, if you please."

"Yes, your Majesty," said Marian and curtsied as she was asked.

The Queen smiled. "It gives me great pleasure to velcome you back to our court, Lady Marian. I have missed you."

"And I have missed your Majesty, and Princess Mary. May I ask how she is."

"She is vell and looking forward to your companionship again. That was a most unfortunate incident about her necklace but it is all over now."

"Thank you, your Majesty."

"And, my dear child, I have sorrow at the loss of Sir Philip and your baby. I too have had babies taken from me."

Marian bowed her head, unable to answer.

"And as for this latest scandal about the paternity of Lady Alice's son," continued the Queen, "Sir Villiam may have told you that she and Lady Joan Dereham have been dismissed the court. Such disgrace! Ve are most distressed at the sorrow you have both been caused."

Sir William and Marian mumbled their gratitude.

"So," said the Queen, "I am vanting one lady-in-waiting and am offering for you, Lady Marian, to take her place. It means you will have to discard your widow's black."

"Your Majesty, this is such an honour."

"Yes, yes," said the Queen with some impatience, "but this is agreeable to you, no?"

"Yes, your Majesty, thank you, your Majesty, it is very agreeable to me," Marian answered.

"It is vell. You may go now. Lady Jane Seymour is vaiting for you. It is vell. I am very pleased. Thank you, Sir Villiam."

They backed towards the door, which was opened on their approach and closed behind them.

"Oh, William," said Marian, "I cannot believe my good fortune!"

He raised her hands to his lips and kissed them. "It is nothing more than you deserve and her majesty needs around her those who love her."

"I will serve her well."

"To do that, you will have to forget your former devotion to Lady Anne Boleyn. She is not in favour now – with the Queen, that is. She is much in favour with his majesty. Be careful how you tread."

"I will try, William."

"And you know you may always come to me if you are in any difficulty. Now you must announce your presence to Lady Jane."

"At once," said Marian and left him with a smile.

Lady Jane and the other ladies-in-waiting were delighted to welcome her back and she was moved by their genuine grief for her loss. They plied her with questions about the Dereham sisters and their conspiracy to pass little William off as Philip's son, expressing sympathy for Sir William but guessing that the truth must have made Marian very happy.

Shortly after her arrival, she passed Lord Bathampton in a corridor. He bowed and she returned this acknowledgement with a reluctant and stiff curtsey.

"So, Lady Forrester, you have returned and have been vouchsafed her majesty's high favour."

"I have that honour, yes, my lord."

"And we are both alone in the world now, having been duped by that scheming whore –"

"Where is Lady Alice?"

"I have sent her and her bastard child to live with her sister."

He drew close and she could smell the bad odour of his breath.

"I repeat, we are both alone in the world, our beds are cold and we could be of comfort to each other."

Marian stepped back. "Never!"

He grabbed her wrist and held it in a vice-like grip so that she could not pull away.

"You think you are too good for me, don't you, now you are under the protection of the Queen but I still require recompense for this!" He jerked her hand up to touch his crooked nose. "And I will have recompense eventually, make no mistake. Queen Katharine may not always be there to protect you."

"Lady Marian, are you in need of assistance?"

A young squire paused to ask the question as he passed them. Lord Bathampton dropped her hand.

"Thank you, but all is well," she said, rubbing her sore wrist.

"Then may I escort you to wherever you are going?"

Marian's relief was evident in her reply. "I would be very glad of that and am much indebted to you, sir."

Side by side they walked away and Marian did not look back but, until they turned a corner, she could feel Lord Bathampton's eyes fixed upon her.

The next few months were spent learning her duties under the guidance of Lady Jane Seymour. Her previous mentor, Lady Anne, was pleased to see her back but was seldom in the company of the other ladies and seemed distracted when she was.

The reason was endlessly discussed in her absence – the infatuation of the King and his gradual withdrawal from the company of the Queen. Her ladies were greatly distressed at this and did all they could to alleviate her majesty's increasing unhappiness.

So, when on duty, Marian sought to engage her majesty in lively conversation about anything that might interest her.

She committed to memory the proportions of asses' milk and rose water for the Queen's face wash and how to apply lead powder to produce a white complexion and how to bring colour to her cheeks with cochineal and how to pluck then draw her eyebrows with charcoal.

The ladies instructed her in her majesty's preferences for which jewelry to wear with which gown, whether it be diamonds, rubies, emeralds or pearls set in necklaces, brooches and rings.

She also had to learn how to deal with lice in the Queen's hair, brushing it so gently after an application of vinegar that her majesty fell asleep in the chair. Then she would help her sleepy mistress to bed before lighting a camphor candle that would burn itself out during the night and kill the infestation.

But then the sickness known as the English Sweate erupted and began to strike down members of the court for the fourth time in the past forty three years.

Princess Mary was sent away to safety. Lady Anne was given permission to return to her family home at Hever Castle in Kent. When the

King absented himself from court and was believed to have followed her, the Queen was greatly distressed and barricaded herself in her rooms with her ladies for company.

Marian hoped fervently, as did they all, that they weren't imprisoning the fever along with them and they watched each other constantly for any signs of severe cold shivers, the first symptom of the sickness. They were especially vigilant about the Queen and asked many times a day whether she was feeling any aches in her head, neck or limbs. She always insisted that she was quite well in body, if not in heart.

Each day, food, beer and water for washing were left outside the door. The contents of the chamber pots were tipped out of a window. Daily news came by messenger, a young lad who was not allowed entry but who conversed from the other side of the door.

Marian appealed to the Queen for news of Sir William and was granted permission to receive information. She thanked God silently during their morning devotions when she learned that the King had included him as part of the royal entourage that had travelled to Hever Castle.

One morning, there was a different voice on the other side of the door and the Queen was informed that the first young messenger had succumbed to the sickness and was now in the second stage – severe sweating accompanied by a disabling pain in his heart and the strong desire to sleep. If he lasted for the next twenty four hours, he might be lucky enough to survive, but the Queen was informed on the following day that the boy had died during the night, which distressed everyone greatly.

So Marian sang the songs that comforted her majesty and, although she was not as accomplished a singer as some of the other ladies, the Queen seemed to like her renditions well enough.

Gradually, the number of deaths decreased as the infection departed. After three weeks, the Queen herself opened her door and emerged to find her court severely depleted.

Marian went at once to look for William and found him in attendance on the King, who had returned to the Palace. He managed to slip away to meet her in the corridor outside his majesty's suite of rooms but could not stay long to talk as several of the Esquires who had stayed behind had died of the Sweate and those who had survived had to double their duties.

"I am particularly grieved that Sir John Knollys has been taken from us. He was a gentle and kind friend."

"And Lord Bathampton?" Marian asked.

"He has survived," Sir William replied.

"Am I very wicked to say that I had hoped to be grieving for him?"

"Yes," he said and his eyes twinkled, "I perceive that you are very wicked."

# CHAPTER 41

*Place: Forrester Hall, Berkshire*

*Date: May, 1533*

Marian sat on the window seat in her chamber, her arms resting on the sill, her eyes and heart feasting on the view beyond. It had been raining during the night and the air blowing in through the open casement was heavy with the scent of wet grass and the lighter perfume of rain-washed roses burgeoning beneath the window.

She sat, gazing out and lost in reverie, wondering what the future held for her.

Five years had passed since the rampage of the sweating sickness, during which time Marian, now twenty two years old, had become a well-respected member of Queen Katharine's household.

She had retained her friendship with Princess Mary, who was herself seventeen years old. Although not a beauty, she was a very intelligent and accomplished young woman who was preparing to take her place as queen of England one day.

The wrangle between King and Queen had continued during these five years. The Archbishop of York, Cardinal Wolsey, had written to Pope Clement VII, setting out the King's demands that the case for the annulment of his marriage to the Queen should be decided in England, in a court presided over by Cardinal Wolsey himself and attended by a visiting papal legate who had the full authority of the Pope.

To this end, the Pope sent over Cardinal Lorenzo Campeggio. He at once suggested to the Queen that she should enter a nunnery, to facilitate the annulment of the marriage, but she continued to insist that she was King Henry's true wife and queen. To support her claim, she produced Pope Julius II's dispensation for her to marry King Henry following the death of his brother twenty years previously.

Then Wolsey, whom the Pope had made his vice regent in the matter, tried to bully her, threatening that they would separate her from Princess Mary, but the Queen remained adamant.

The requested Legatine Court had begun its session on 31st May 1529 at Blackfriars. Marian was one of the ladies-in-waiting supporting the Queen in court and tears blinded her vision when her mistress had knelt before her husband, pleading with him for justice. The Queen's words, spoken in charming broken English, had burned into Marian's soul:

*"Sir, wherein have I offended you? I have been to you a true, humble and obedient wife, ever comfortable to your will and pleasure, that never said or did anything to the contrary thereof, being always well pleased and contented with all things wherein you had any delight or dalliance, whether it were in little or much. I never grudged in word or countenance, or showed a visage or spark of discontent. I loved all those whom ye loved, only for your sake, whether I had cause or no, and whether they were my friends or enemies. This twenty years or more I have been your true wife. When ye had me at first, I take God to my judge, I was a true maid, without touch of man."*

She asked for the King's permission to appeal to the Pope, which permission he gave. Only then did she rise from her knees, Henry having tried unsuccessfully to raise her twice before. Then she curtseyed and with great dignity led her ladies from the court, ignoring calls from officials to return to her seat.

When the Pope unexpectedly ruled in her favour, her majesty was jubilant and her ladies with her. The King was furious and vented his anger on Cardinal Wolsey, accusing him of betrayal, and had him arrested for treason. The Cardinal died on his journey south from York to attend his trial and Sir Thomas More was appointed Lord High Chancellor in his place.

That was three years ago. Then two years ago, Marian had been very happy to attend the marriage of her beloved William to Lady Susan Knollys, widow of his great friend who had succumbed to the sickness.

At first, she had questioned her acceptance of their betrothal. There was a time when she bristled at the very thought that anyone might supplant her as mistress of Forrester Hall but since then she had witnessed the loneliness and need of Sir William to hold someone close to his heart, closer than she could ever be. Now she rejoiced to see him supremely happy, more so at the recent news of his wife's pregnancy.

Marian closed the casement window. Throwing a cloak about her shoulders, she descended to the great hall and went out through the side door into the rose garden, refusing the offers of her maids to accompany her.

"You have no need to fret about me," she told them. "I have much to think about, much to decide."

Knowing the circumstances in which their mistress was placed, they nodded their understanding and withdrew.

Marian made her way to the arbour of precious memories. She flopped down onto one of the benches, wrapped the cloak about her and rocked backwards and forwards, hoping this would calm the myriad thoughts that were chasing each other round and round inside her head, hoping it would help her come to a decision.

It had taken a tumultuous and distressing four years for King Henry to get his own way following the Pope's unexpected ruling, during which time Queen Katharine had been banished from court to More Castle, taking four of her ladies-in-waiting with her and leaving the remainder in Greenwich. Before she left, she confided to them that her consolation was her strong Catholic faith and the high esteem in which she was held by the people, who regarded her as their true Queen.

Her rooms in the palace had been given to Lady Anne Boleyn.

Henry then brazenly rejected the power of the Pope in England and on 23rd May this year, 1533, Thomas Cranmer, Archbishop of Canterbury, ruled that the royal marriage had never been legal and was being annulled.

Five days later, to everyone's surprise, he pronounced as valid the marriage of the King to Lady Anne Boleyn, which had taken place in secret on 25th January at Hampton Court.

Lady Anne was crowned Queen of England just days later during a lavish ceremony attended by all the nobles of the land, during which over one thousand guns fired a salute from the Tower and from ships in the river. The ceremony was followed by a feast in the great hall of Westminster.

However, during her progress through the streets of London, the people had made it quite plain by their insults and jibes that the new Queen, already two months pregnant, was not at all popular. It was reported by the ladies with her that there were shouts of "Strumpet!", "King stealer!", "The disgrace of Christendom!", "The King's Whore!" and worse.

These happenings devastated Katharine, no longer to be known as Queen but as Princess Dowager of Wales, a title she adamantly refused to acknowledge.

With only a handful of servants, she was transferred to Kimbolton Castle, Cambridgeshire, confining herself to one room except to attend Mass. She was forbidden to meet or communicate with her daughter. The King offered them both better accommodation and permission to meet if they would acknowledge Anne as Queen but both refused.

Marian had been with Queen Katharine throughout her ordeal until the time she was banished and then had stayed on in court to comfort and serve Princess Mary until she too had been sent away. The princess had been deeply humiliated by being pronounced illegitimate and had no hope now of becoming queen.

In the ensuing confusion, Sir William had advised Marian to return to Forrester Hall and await events. Years ago, Queen Anne, then Lady Anne, had expressed the wish to offer her the appointment of lady-in-waiting. That offer had now been made formally and Marian had to decide whether to remain loyal to Queen Katharine or attend upon the new Queen, who had once been her mentor and friend.

She walked across to the sundial and idly wondered how many times the shadow of the gnomon had travelled round the face of the dial since those less complicated days when she and Philip had gone to court for the first time and had met their majesties, when the King was still in love with his Queen Katharine.

She sighed and wished to be somewhere where she could love and be loved without complication and without stint. Suddenly, she had the overwhelming desire to visit her baby's grave.

In no time at all she and her maid Betty were on their way to the monastery so she could petition Mother Superior for permission to visit that little plot in the cloister garden.

She had still not come to any conclusion about her future.

# CHAPTER 42

*Place: The Monastery of St. Jude, Forrestram*

*Date: Early Summer, 1533*

Reverend Mother welcomed Marian with hands outstretched. Of course she could visit the grave of her baby.

As before, nuns were hurrying through the cloisters on their errands or, with heads bowed, were walking sedately in a column, two by two, in silent prayer and contemplation. Several acknowledged Marian, seeming to know who she was and why she was there.

Mother Superior led the way across the grass to the tiny mound of earth. Marian was surprised to see a beautiful granite stone with the single word 'Margaret' engraved on it in black letters. When she asked about it, Reverend Mother said that Sir William had arranged for it to be placed there last year on the fifth anniversary of his granddaughter's death.

As before, Marian was allowed time on her own. She sank onto the grass by the grave, conversed lovingly with her daughter, then struggled with her dilemma but after about half an hour was still undecided about her course of action.

Unwilling to leave the peace of the convent straight away, she did not return by the direct route to the front drive but slipped through a door and found herself in a vegetable garden, startling the monks who were working there, shaded by the wide brims of their straw hats.

However, as the bell began to peal for mid-day prayers, they laid down their garden tools and made their way towards the chapel, leaving her alone. She lingered a while longer, admiring the neat rows of plantings, the absence of weeds and the canes erected so meticulously to support the runner beans.

She was just about to leave when she heard her name spoken.

"Lady Forrester!" and again, "Lady Forrester!" in a voice she had thought never to hear again.

Slowly she turned with his name on her lips but it froze there, unsaid, as she was confronted by a tall young man in a brown habit and brown sandals, hood thrown back, arms crossed and hands invisible inside loose sleeves. The thrice-knotted cord round his waist confirmed his vows of poverty, chastity and obedience.

She stared in disbelief.

"Richard?"

"No longer Richard, Lady Forrester. I am Brother Lawrence now. There's no Richard here."

"There's no Richard here," she repeated, "no Richard here. I have heard that intoned before."

"On the night you were brought into the monastery after your accident. You saw me and, in your delirium, kept calling my name and they had to tell you."

"You were here on the night of the accident?"

"They brought you to us – the driver and your maid, Sir Philip and you – then you went into labour and the nuns took you away to care for you. When you lost your baby, it nigh broke my heart."

"But you – a monk? A monk? Whatever possessed you –?"

"You possessed me, my lady, in body, heart and soul. I couldn't have you so I turned my back on the world."

"But how is it that you are here?"

"I asked to serve my novitiate in this monastery, to serve God here, but in truth – may the good Lord forgive me – I made the request so that I could be near you."

Marian remembered the strange remark uttered by Sir William: "He may be nearer than you think".

"Sir William knows?"

"Yes. He was here on the night of the accident and saw me. I made him promise not to tell you, if you survived."

She took a step towards him but he backed away from her.

"No, don't touch me or I shall be in mortal danger of breaking two of my vows."

"Do you still love me, Richard?"

"Why are you making me say it? Yes, I still love you –"

"And I still love you!"

"But now my loyalty is only to my heavenly King."

Marian spoke with passion. "Then my loyalty is to my Queen! She is far from heavenly – in truth, she is very much of this world – but I will serve her faithfully, nevertheless." So, he had made up her mind for her. "I will soon be returning to court as lady-in-waiting to Queen Anne Boleyn. Goodbye, Richard!"

"Marian!" Now it was his turn to reach for her but she turned and ran from the garden.

# CHAPTER 43

*Place: Greenwich Palace*

*Date: June, 1533*

Marian returned to a different court from the one she had left. Gone were the previous anxiety and distress and in their place was an atmosphere of anticipation, of hope, of new beginnings.

There had been many changes among the courtiers, who were now younger, and there was a great deal of laughter and frivolity in the state rooms and along the corridors. The King was spending more time in the palace, his new wife by his side, and it was obvious that he was obsessed by her.

Their baby was due at the beginning of September and her ladies were instructed by the midwives that she should rest each afternoon and not tire herself with any strenuous activities. The Queen replied that she was in very good health and had plenty of energy, and insisted on partnering the King in at least two measures at the frequent celebrations of their marriage.

The only matter for grief was the excommunication from the Catholic church of the King and Archbishop Cranmer. In response, the King had set himself up as the Supreme Head of the Church of England, a role previously held by the Pope, and the clergy and everyone of note was being required to swear the Oath of Supremacy.

All were doing so, aware of the consequences of refusing, with the exception of Sir Thomas More. Remaining loyal to the Catholic church, he had resigned his position of Lord High Chancellor last year and had refused to attend the coronation of the new Queen. Everyone knew that he was treading on very dangerous ground.

"I am so pleased to have you among my ladies," the Queen told Marian, who was making her comfortable on a couch, plumping up cushions and raising her feet. "I know you will serve me as faithfully as you served the Princess Dowager of Wales."

"I will, your Majesty," Marian replied, removing the Queen's slippers.

"You are very special to me, Lady Forrester – my little Marian."

"Your Majesty honours me," Marian said and curtsied. She no longer gave her expansive curtsey that had so delighted Queen Katharine.

"We have a very special relationship, have we not?"

"Yes, your Majesty."

"You remember the yew tree?"

"I do indeed," Marian replied, "though I was innocent of the identity of your 'friend' at the time."

"It plagues me to lie here every afternoon with nothing to do," the Queen complained. "Please send someone to fetch Master Mark Smeaton, then come and sit with me while he plays his violin. He plays exceedingly well."

"Yes, your Majesty."

Marian was delighted when news arrived that Sir William's wife had been safely delivered of a boy. The King allowed him time away from court to visit his son and offered his congratulations, commenting that he hoped to be in the same position in three months' time. On his return, Sir William asked immediately to see Marian, to describe to her the appearance and attributes of this unique baby.

"He is being christened Philip William," he told her and she smiled with pleasure to witness the happiness of this doting father and knew for certain that she had been right to refuse his romantic overtures to herself. Their relationship now had reverted to the loving father-daughter intimacy they had always enjoyed before Philip's death and both were content to put the past behind them.

The Queen went into labour on 7th September. Three doctors and a team of midwives attended her while Marian, Lady Jane Seymour and two other ladies-in-waiting hovered in the background and the King paced backwards and forwards in the room adjoining her bedchamber. The Queen had promised him a son and the astrologers he had consulted as well as the physicians had foretold the birth of a boy.

When the baby breathed its first gulp of air and began to cry lustily, the King could no longer be restrained and burst into the chamber, intent on seeing his son.

"I want to see the heir to the throne!" he demanded.

"Your M-majesty –" stammered one of the doctors, "your wife is well and so is the baby – but she is a girl."

The King stopped in his tracks.

"Henry, my love," said the Queen, "come and meet your daughter. She is a beautiful baby."

The King came to the bedside and took the Queen's hand. Along with everyone else in the room, Marian held her breath, waiting for his response to this disappointment.

"Are you quite well, Anne?" he asked.

"Quite well, my love, and it will be a boy next time, I promise you."

"You promised me a boy this time."

"Perhaps I did, but I was practising for the more important event."

"Then I am content."

Three days later, the baby was christened Elizabeth after both grandmothers, at the church of the Observant Friars, Greenwich, where her father had been christened. Neither parent was present, as was the custom, but both received the godparents and the returning christening party with great pleasure.

George, second Viscount Rochford, the Queen's brother and a great favourite of the King, had helped carry the canopy over the little princess, and it was he who now placed her in her cradle by the side of the expansive French bed where the royal couple reclined. This was the bed in which the Queen would lie-in for forty days before being 'churched' in the royal chapel and returning to the life of the court.

"Forty days!" complained the King.

"It will soon pass," the Queen reassured him, but looked anxious nevertheless, "then we can set about producing the heir to the throne."

"But forty days!" he repeated and looked about him as if searching for an answer to his sexual dilemma. His gaze came to rest on Lady Jane Seymour.

Marian admired her majesty's determined forestalling of the King's well-known appetites.

"It will give you time to plan your reform of the monasteries," she said, "and how to distribute their considerable wealth and income between the scholastic foundations. That is your wish, is it not, my lord? And I am certain it will take you more than forty days to draw up the steps of your campaign."

"You are right, Anne," the King replied and kissed her. "The systematic reform of the monasteries it is."

Marian's pleasure in the scene before her, of the King and Queen with their baby daughter, revived her grief at the loss of Philip and her own daughter but then came anxious thoughts when she remembered the King's last words. They prompted her to question her majesty next day when she and the other ladies were alone in the bedchamber.

"Reform of the monasteries?" she asked, intent on hiding any personal concern but thinking, of course, of Richard. "I hope your Majesty is not involved in this campaign that the King is planning. You know you must rest, begging your pardon, your grace, but we have had strict instructions –"

"Pooh!" Anne exclaimed in a manner most unbecoming for the Queen of the realm.

Marian laughed and was joined at the bedside by Lady Jane.

“Lady Forrester wishes to know the King’s plans, cousin, regarding the monasteries,” said the Queen. “You have heard him discuss them often enough. You explain them to her. I have not the energy or interest to do so.”

“The King plans,” explained Jane Seymour, “to close all the religious houses, by force if necessary –”

“Friaries, monasteries, convents, priories – all nine hundred of them,” added the Queen, waving a dismissive hand, her head buried in the pillows.

“He will sell their assets, appropriate their income, then endow grammar schools and university colleges, new places of education for the sons of his noblemen, new places of instruction for his Church of England clergy.”

“Is that so, your Majesty?” Marian asked.

“Exactly so.”

“So what will happen to the monks and nuns?”

“What will happen to them, Lady Jane?” asked the Queen.

“His majesty has not said.”

“Will they be thrown out like old shoes, past their usefulness?” persisted Marian.

“Lady Forrester, my dear Marian, what an imaginative turn of phrase you have,” murmured the Queen sleepily. “Old shoes? I will ask his majesty.”

Marian was very concerned at what she had heard and paid greater attention to any conversation around the court that concerned the King’s plans for the Catholic monasteries. The news increased her consternation. The abbots and priors, many of whom had grown fat on the taxes, rents and tithes they imposed, many of them idle and dissolute, were not likely to allow their vast estates to be seized without resistance.

His majesty was cognizant of this and began by closing the smaller establishments, pensioning off the monks and nuns who served there.

Marian reasoned that Henry may be King of England and Supreme Head of the Church of England, but he was not God. She understood that Richard had been sincere in taking his vows, even if God had captured him on the rebound, and he and others like him were worth the Lord’s consideration.

# CHAPTER 44

*Place: Greenwich Palace*

*Date: September, 1533*

With this thought in mind, one evening, when she was not in attendance upon the Queen, she made her way with determination to the royal chapel, to state her case to the Almighty at the foot of his Cross. However, she was not unmindful of her total unworthiness to demand anything of the Lord and her belief in her complaint, however just, had completely evaporated by the time she reached the imposing studded-oak west door of the chapel. Humbled, she quietly opened the door and stepped across the threshold.

It took a while for her eyes to adjust to the gloom so she stood there until she could distinguish the marble font near the entrance and, through the tracery of the ornate chancel screen ahead of her, the gold cross on the altar.

She began to make her way slowly along the aisle of the nave, making no noise on the deep pile of the carpet. Then she heard a strange sound. She stood quite still and listened. Someone was crying!

Marian was not sure what to do. Should she turn round and quietly leave the way she had come? Or should she see if she could help? She decided on the latter course and continued to walk forward, making a slight sound so that the other person, whoever it was, would not be startled.

In the front pew was the figure of a young girl, doubled up over her stomach and weeping copiously.

"Can I help?" she asked softly.

"No!" came the anguished reply. "Go away!"

Marian hesitated again. Perhaps she should leave. But here was a very young person in obvious distress and it may be that she *could* help.

Crossing in front of the figure, which was still doubled up, she sat down beside the girl and stroked her back. The girl sat up and Marian put an arm around her shoulders.

"You can tell me," she said, "whatever it is."

"No I can't, I can't tell anyone."

"I promise it won't go any further."

Marian's voice was quiet and reassuring. The girl said nothing for a while then blurted out, "I'm pregnant, four months pregnant, and soon everyone will know."

"Oh," said Marian. She looked at the girl's hands and saw no wedding band.

She tightened her grip round the young shoulders and moved closer and drew the girl's head onto her shoulder, supporting it with her own. They sat like that for a very long time.

"Do you know who I am?" Marian asked eventually. The girl raised her head and nodded. "You're Lady Marian Forrester, lady-in-waiting to her majesty."

"I don't think I've seen you around the court before. Will you trust me with your name?"

"It's Margery. I'm maid to Lady Agnes Mortimer."

Marian had to think where she had heard that name before then remembered that she was the elderly lady whom Sir William had partnered at the very first ball Marian and Philip had attended at the palace. She was now of great age and lived in one of the grace-and-favour suites of rooms in a far wing of the palace.

"Does Lady Mortimer know?"

The girl began to cry again. "No, but she soon will, then I will be thrown out. My family will disown me and I have nowhere to go. My baby and I will finish up in the gutter."

"How old are you, Margery?"

"Just sixteen, my lady."

"What about the father?" Marian asked the question with little expectation of a hopeful reply.

"I thought he loved me," the girl said, "but I haven't seen him for two weeks, not since I told him. He said he loved me. I know he loved me."

Marian sighed and let that statement pass.

"Perhaps he can be approached," she suggested. "Perhaps his better nature will prevail if someone, perhaps another man, could speak to him on your behalf."

"He can't marry me, if that's what you mean, because he's already married – though his wife is not living with him," she hastened to add. "I wouldn't have –"

Marian was not surprised.

"Is he one of our young courtiers?"

"Oh no," said the girl. "I prefer older men. He is much older than me."

*Why does that not surprise me, either?* thought Marian.

"How did you meet him?"

"He sometimes visits my lady. He came more often after he saw me. He used to bring me presents. He gave me this locket." She fingered a little gold and mother-of-pearl locket that rested in the cleavage between her young breasts. "He kissed my neck and fastened it himself and I have never taken it off. He gave me pretty blue and green bracelets and earrings and pins. He said that they matched my eyes."

"Did Lady Mortimer not question the jewelry?"

"My lady is almost blind now. She wouldn't have noticed. And she doesn't hear when I am being sick. But I haven't worn my jewelry during the day, except for the locket. I wore it at night when we met secretly in the gardens, always in the gardens. He was so kind to me. When he showed me how to make love to him, how to please him, it was all I wanted to do – all I want to do – to please him."

"But you haven't seen him for two weeks?"

"No. Do you think he is ill? Perhaps he wants to see me but can't."

Marian knew she had to do something to help this young and very innocent girl whom she was still hugging so fiercely in an attempt to convey she was not alone in her predicament – but what? She wondered about telling her majesty but decided against it as the news would likely spread throughout the court. But it occurred to her that there was another way, someone else she could approach for help.

"Margery, there may be a way I can help you."

"No, no, not that – I won't have my baby done away with! I want his baby."

"No, no," Marian hastened to reassure her, "I wasn't suggesting anything like that."

"Perhaps you could find out whether he is ill. Could you do that, my lady?"

"Yes, if you tell me his name. I cannot do so unless you tell me his name."

"You won't tell anyone else? I would not have his name sullied because he loved me."

"There is just one other person I will tell, if you allow it, who may be able to help you."

"If you trust that person?"

"With my life."

"Then, yes, I will tell you."

"Could you meet me here at about the same time on the day after tomorrow? I will endeavour to have news for you."

"Yes, I can be here. Her ladyship is in bed and fast asleep at this time. Yes, I can meet you here then."

"It is well." Marian stood. "Now you must go back. And try not to worry. I am sure I can help you." She sounded more confident than she felt.

Margery stood and Marian's heart went out to her. How young she was and how pretty, in spite of her tear-stained cheeks and red eyes. And how callous this 'older man' who had plied her with pretty trinkets and then had taken his pleasure with her as and when the fancy took him, regardless of any consequences.

"His name?" she asked but had guessed the answer before the words were on the girl's lips.

"My lover is Lord Bathampton."

# CHAPTER 45

Marian lay awake that night, thinking of young Margery and her dilemma. She had conceived a plan and lost no time next day in seeking a meeting with Sir William. Her urgent message to him brought the response, relayed by a page, that he would meet her that afternoon on the towpath by the steps leading down to the river.

He greeted her effusively and said how glad he was to see her and she replied that she much regretted that the Queen kept her so busy. After enquiring about Philip William and Lady Susan and learning of the baby's latest accomplishments, they fell in step to walk along the path.

All about them was noise and bustle. It was a warm autumn afternoon. The tide was coming in and sunlight reflected back from the ripples making their determined way towards the shore. Leaves were beginning to flutter down from the trees, the rowan bushes were aflame with myriads of orange berries and they saw a red squirrel busily searching for acorns to hide away in his winter larder.

"Philip and I used to walk this path," Marian reminisced sadly.

Sir William took her hand and drew it through his arm. "Now, what is so urgent that you must see me today, young lady?"

Marian told him about Margery, the young girl she had met by accident in the royal chapel on the previous evening, about her dilemma and the callous lecher who had caused it.

"A sad story," agreed Sir William. "Not unusual, of course, but sad nevertheless. So what do you want me to do about it?"

Marian took a deep breath. "William, would it be possible for you – could you find it in your heart – would Lady Susan – oh, dear, I don't know how to ask you."

Her father-in-law smiled. "You want me to take her in, don't you? Shelter her and her baby at Forrester Hall?"

"Oh, William, would you? Could you? She is so young and so innocent. She would be a companion for Lady Susan, and her baby would be a playmate for Philip William."

He was quiet for a long moment, during which time Marian hardly breathed. They stopped and regarded the activity on the river – the sailing ships loading and unloading their goods at the warehouses opposite, the double-oared wherries ferrying their passengers from bank to bank.

In danger of receiving a bang on the head from an oar, a dog was swimming close to the shore, heading for a stick thrown by a boy of about seven years of age. The boy was bare footed, wearing ragged breeches and a filthy vest that was more absent than it was present.

Marian turned her attention back to Sir William, who was answering her. "It would not be impossible, but I would have to ask my dear wife before I committed us to the responsibility."

"Oh, William, thank you for your compassion."

"You say she has nowhere else to go?"

"She says not."

"I cannot give an answer straight away."

Marian nodded. "She has time before her pregnancy is noticeable."

"Our Lord Bathampton, eh?"

Marian was highly indignant. "He should be made to take responsibility."

"He'll deny all knowledge of the girl, obviously."

When Marian arrived in the chapel on the next evening, Margery was already there, waiting for her. She cried when Marian told her the plans afoot for a safe haven for herself and the baby.

"And, my dear, I have to tell you that Lord Bathampton is not sick or away from the palace. Sir William said he is very much alive and well and carrying out his duties in the usual way."

"Then –"

"Then he has abandoned you with scant regard for your fate or what will happen to his child. I will be very brutal, Margery, and tell you that he doesn't love you, he has never loved you. He was playing the part of a lover to get what he wanted from you and now there are complications, he has turned his back."

Margery's eyes filled with tears again.

"I do not have complications, my lady, I have a baby."

"Don't cry. You are well rid of him. I only wish we could make him pay for his callous treatment of you. I am sure you are not the first young woman he has betrayed and you won't be the last."

Margery picked at a loose cotton on her sleeve. "He will deny it, won't he?"

"Of course," confirmed Marian, "and there is no way we can prove he is the father of your baby."

"But I was a virgin when he first took me."

"I believe you but there is no proof of that."

"There may be something – not proof exactly, but something."

"What is that? Tell me!"

Margery hesitated then shyly said, "There is a mole on the inside of his right leg, near his – near his –"

"I understand," said Marian.

"It is as black as his heart."

"Not proof, exactly," murmured Marian.

"But how else would I know it was there?" asked Margery.

"Mmm, you speak truly."

"And his cod piece is well padded!"

"Really?"

Margery nodded and tried not to laugh but a wicked look came into her blue-green eyes and a grin began to play around the corners of her mouth.

Marian too began to smile and was comforted to realise that Margery's heart was nowhere near broken.

Marian told Sir William what she had learned. He said, "Leave it with me. I will speak to his majesty."

A month later, Margery bid a tearful farewell to Lady Agnes Mortimer and left the palace in the company of Lady Susan, whose compassion had caused her the inconvenience and discomfort of travel to Greenwich to accompany the girl back to Forrester Hall.

True to his word, Sir William explained the situation to his majesty, who had roared with laughter on hearing about Lord Bathampton's mole and said he would make good sport of the information.

One evening in the south drawing room, when most courtiers of the inner circle were present with their ladies, the King said he had a most interesting investigation to conduct, one of great import. The gentlemen and ladies of the court were used to the King's sometimes bizarre sense of fun and waited expectantly for a game of sorts to begin.

Then he called the men forward, about thirty of them, and announced, "I wish you to be witnesses to this event. I am informed that one of the very young ladies of my court – a lady's maid and only sixteen – a virgin at the beginning of my story but seduced and now with child has made an accusation against one of you that needs to be proved or disproved."

Marian looked round the assembled company and saw that several of the men, young and not so young, were looking highly uncomfortable. She hoped that what she suspected was to come would cause some to think twice before pressing their attentions in the future on some unfortunate young woman who was in no position to refuse them. However, tonight was not their night.

The King spoke again. "Lord Bathampton, come forward, if you will." His lordship, looking highly embarrassed, did so.

The King then asked the Queen, who knew what was coming and was smiling broadly, to conduct the ladies to the back of the room, Marian among them. He instructed them to turn their backs. Mystified and questioning, they did so.

"Now my lord, it has been whispered in my ear that you have a black mole on the inside of your right leg, almost in your groin, where no one except your wife should know of its existence."

The ladies, their backs still turned and straining their ears, could hear the spluttered denials of Lord Bathampton.

"We wish to know whether this is true or a figment of the young lady's imagination. There is only one course to prove this accusation, one way or the other – my lord, remove your codpiece."

In the ensuing silence, the ladies heard Lord Bathampton's objections and one or two turned their heads, only to be reprimanded by the Queen.

The King repeated the order and they then heard a shuffling of feet as presumably the men gathered round his lordship to have a better view. There was a pause and then the King roared with laughter and slapped his thigh, followed by the laughter and guffaws and ridicule of the men.

"And she said your codpiece was padded, and so it is!" chortled the King.

There was such an uproar among the courtiers that the ladies did not hear the King's command for them to turn round and take their places alongside their menfolk again but the Queen turned anyway and went back to sit by her husband and the ladies followed suit.

Marian caught sight of Lord Bathampton, scarlet-faced, his scowl rendering his face even more ugly, drawing his cloak around him and shrinking into it as if for protection, and was almost sorry for the man as he left the room.

She had noticed before that the King could be very cruel. Everyone knew that his majesty indulged himself wherever his fancies took him and he and most of the men, especially the young ones, had well-padded codpieces. However, he was the King and could say and do as he wished.

Marian looked for William but he was nowhere to be seen. She knew he was there at the outset of this charade so presumed he had discreetly absented himself so as not to have to take part in bringing low this proud, if heartless, man.

The story spread throughout the court and Bathampton was forced into paying a monthly allowance to the young lady concerned, which was increased once their daughter was born.

Marian was gratified at the outcome but realised that his lordship would surely discover who was the cause of his utter humiliation and she had thereby given him yet another compelling reason to seek revenge.

# CHAPTER 46

*Place: Greenwich Palace*

*Date: Autumn, 1534*

Before the birth of Margery's daughter at Forrester Hall in February 1534, the Queen was pregnant again. The King was so delighted that he ordered from his goldsmith a silver cradle decorated with Tudor roses and precious stones and this now stood in a corner of the Queen's bedchamber. She was spending a great deal of time in the royal chapel, praying for a son, her ladies with her.

Spring and early Summer passed happily, the ladies-in-waiting once more protecting and pampering her majesty, with everyone enjoying the smiles and sunny demeanour of the King.

Then one day in July it was all over. Lady Jane Seymour found the Queen in great pain on the wooden floor of her solar, blood oozing from beneath her skirts. Her medics and midwives were sent for immediately but, before they could transport her to her bedchamber, a miscarriage had occurred. It was whispered that the baby boy was malformed.

The King did not come near his Queen for many weeks, and was rumoured to be taking his pleasure elsewhere, which caused her more distress than the loss of the baby.

Her ladies were with her day and night, fulfilling her every desire except the greatest, the presence of the King. The Queen went into a deep depression and had no interest in her appearance, saying she did not care whether she lived or died. Gradually, however, aided by the love and care of her ladies and the daily presence of little Princess Elizabeth, she was drawn out of the pit into which she had fallen and began to ask what was happening in court and whether it was raining, as she might take a turn in the gardens.

At the Queen's request, Marian and Lady Jane accompanied her on her walks, each holding an arm to lend their support. The warm autumnal colours surrounding them and the busyness along the river revived the Queen's spirits.

"I must look like an old woman," she said.

"We can do something about that, if your Majesty is ready to take your place in court again," Lady Jane reassured her.

Marian agreed. "Your Majesty, you must entice the King back into your bed. After all, if he wants an heir to the throne, where else can he go but into your bed?"

The Queen raised her eyes from the ground and looked more energised than she had for a long time. "You speak the truth Marian, my dear."

"He was besotted with you once and he must be so again," Marian persisted. "You must make it happen."

So the Queen took up again the full life of the court. She was looking more radiant than ever and it was not long before her relationship with the King was back on its previous footing and the prayers in the chapel were resumed. Marian seldom returned to Forrester Hall as she and Sir William could meet and talk together whenever they wished. After his trips home to see his wife and son, he brought her news of the estate farms, village and church as well as tidings of young Margery and her daughter, who had been christened Agnes, after the old lady.

One communication that arrived by messenger, which caused her much distress, was of the death of Marmy, who had succumbed to a fever from which she had not recovered. Marian could not bear to attend the burial in Forrestram churchyard but sent messages of love and sympathy to the staff and family of her beloved housekeeper.

With Sir William away and much to think about, not least the continued rumblings that threatened the future of the monasteries, Marian had taken to walking in the gardens or along the towpath on those evenings when she was not required by the Queen.

Life was passing her by with no husband, no lover, no child to distract her and, in the absence of Sir William, she was conscious of being very lonely.

In the evenings, the light from the moon when the clouds cleared and from the candles shining through the palace windows cheered her. The warm aroma of honeysuckle, though often overlaid with less delightful smells emanating from the river, delighted her. The friendly slap, slapping of the waves against the mud banks when the tide was high, comforted her.

The men who earned a meagre living from the great river and the nearby royal shipyards relied more on the times of the tide than the time of day. She grew accustomed to hearing their shouts and was glad of their company, although they were unaware of her passing in the shadows.

Feeling her loneliness acutely one night, she had the sudden urge to join the few children who, using the light of the full moon, were still squelching barefoot in the mud, searching for anything that could be sold.

Disregarding any feelings of impropriety, she lifted her skirts off the ground and ran to the stone steps leading down to the river. She sat on the top step and removed her shoes and hose then gingerly made her way down. At high tide, the last step would have been under water but at low tide, as now, there was a short distance between its cold, slippery surface and the mud. She jumped and her bare feet sank into the mire and the murky water came up over her ankles.

She experienced such a sense of freedom, of being a child again, careless of the problems at court and of life in general, that she laughed aloud and began stomping around in the mud, not succeeding in keeping the hem of her gown out of the brown gooey mess.

The children nearby were startled by her antics and ran away from this strange apparition, which made Marian chuckle all the more. Then her toes touched something hard and cold and she realised the danger in which she was placing herself as visions of deep lacerations, foul-smelling infection and amputated limbs filled her imagination. She made a hasty retreat.

Slipping occasionally, she climbed to the top step and retrieved her shoes and hose. Her feet were too tender to be walking on stones and she had no intention of going barefoot back to the palace.

A voice spoke. "You come from up there?"

Startled by the question, Marian looked down. At the bottom of the steps stood an urchin, whom she recognised as the boy she had seen throwing sticks for the dog. He was looking at her with great interest as if she were another species which, she realised, she was in his eyes.

"If you mean the palace, yes, I do."

"You the Queen?"

"No."

"She your friend?"

"I am her lady-in-waiting."

"Wotcha waiting for?"

Marian didn't know what to say so replied simply, "Many things."

"Me, too," the boy said.

"What sort of things?"

"I want my mother home."

"Where has she gone?"

"Dunno. She went away when my baby sister came. Father jumped into the river and drownded." Marian was appalled and asked, "When did you last eat?"

"Two days afore this."

Acting on impulse, she unlaced her shoes again and held them out to him. He hesitated.

"Go on, take them," she said. "They're leather. You should get a good price for them. Don't sell them too cheaply."

The boy came slowly up the steps as if in a dream and took them from her.

"Thanks, lady. They'll think I stole 'em."

"But you didn't."

"Not this time I didn't. Thanks, lady."

Hugging them to his chest, he ran down the steps and squelched away to her right.

Left alone, Marian realised that she would have to walk back in her stockinged feet after all and stood. Buoyed up by the gratitude of the boy and his wide grin, she decided to end the evening by doing what every little boy and girl longs to do and that was paddle in the fountain.

Accordingly, she made her way gingerly to the marble basin where the god Neptune rode aloft, trident in hand, in a chariot pulled by six horses with fish tails. The horses were straining against their seaweed reins, water pouring from their mouths and splashing over four beautiful mermaids and six fat cherubs, one of them trumpeting on a large conch shell. The scattered moonlight was polishing the marble until it gleamed.

At intervals round the basin's rim were flat surfaces so that visitors could sit, facing away from the fountain, and admire the acres of gardens before them.

Marian sat, removed her stockings and shuffled around to face the fountain. Holding onto the edge of the seat, she bent forward, her bare feet dangling, and began swishing her silken hose in the water. However, the stockings were in a sorry state and would need a proper washing. She laid them next to her on the rim of the basin.

Then she leaned back and pulled her skirts above her knees, her feet dancing this way and that in the clean, cold, energizing water. She began laughing out loud in sheer exuberance.

The laugh died in her throat as an arm came round her neck, strangling her so that she could barely breathe. A knee jabbed into her spine and she was wrenched backwards, tumbling off the seat and landing on the grass on her back, her skirts up around her thighs.

Her assailant dropped onto his knees, towering above her. She didn't know who he was because his face was concealed by a black cloth; his coat and doublet were also black and a black cloak billowed about his person.

Without a word, but grunting with the effort, he forced her legs apart then fell on her, pinning her wrists to the ground and forcing his legs between hers. She screamed and he slapped her face hard before snatching her wrist again.

"Please don't! Don't!" she screamed. "No, no!"

He raised himself a little and snarled, "Oh, yes, yes, my lady!"

She could see that his penis was red and erect and quivering with the excitement of what he had in mind to do to her. Then he fell on her and viciously drove into her again and again until she thought she would pass out.

In the distance, she heard shouts, men's voices, and felt herself roughly raised and thrown. When water closed over her head, she did pass out.

# CHAPTER 47

Marian did not recover full consciousness until next morning when, following nightmares about helplessly trying to run from her tormentor, she stopped tossing about and screaming and woke to find herself in bed in her bedchamber, her maids fussing about her, straightening covers, smoothing pillows, feeling her forehead, and Lady Jane Seymour bending over and quietly talking to her.

At first she thought her nightmares would dissolve quickly now that she was awake. But then she became aware that she was sore and bleeding, she had pain in her lower back and thighs and saw the bruises on her arms and wrists. Marian realised that her nightmares were real.

"Jane –" she whimpered.

Lady Jane took her hand. "You've had a terrible experience, Marian, but it's over now and you're safe here with us, and he's in irons in the Tower. Do you remember what happened?"

Distressed, Marian turned towards her friend. "I don't want to remember!"

Jane knelt by the bedside and put her arms around her friend. She laid her cheek against Marian's.

"You don't have to speak about it now, but we will need to know. The Queen has already been here this morning to see how you are."

Marian was silent for a long time while Jane held her close, then asked, "He's in irons in the Tower? Then you know who he is?"

"Yes, we know – and I think you know, too."

"Lord Bathampton?"

"Who but him? Everyone else loves you, Marian. Did he – did he – her majesty wants to know if –"

Marian was surprised that she wasn't crying but her anguish was lying too deep for tears.

"Yes, he did, again and again. He was like a crazed dog! I thought he would never stop but we heard men's voices and he got off me."

"And tried to drown you! He threw you into the fountain."

One of the maids brought a small table to the bedside and another a large bowl of warm water. They fetched a cloth and a phial of scented oil.

Marian lay back on the pillows as they began carefully to wash her all over in an attempt to clean and remove from her skin not only the lingering odour of her attacker and the grime from the river but also to start the process of banishing the attack from the forefront of her memory.

"Who rescued me?"

"That's the strange part. We don't know. One of the watchmen ran into a boy who said the kind lady was being murdered where the horses were spitting out water. The watchman would have given him a whipping for being anywhere near the palace but he heard your screams. He blew his whistle to raise the alarm and they found a couple of rough men in the water, dragging you out, and two more pinning Bathampton to the ground."

"The boy?"

"A scruffy little urchin. He said he had been following you so saw the attack and ran to get his father. He was clutching a pair of leather shoes, which he must have stolen from you because yours were missing, but he ran off before anyone could catch him, and the men disappeared, too. They should have been apprehended but everyone was more concerned in bringing you to safety and taking his lordship into custody."

"What will happen to him?"

"That all depends on the Queen. You are one of her ladies and should be inviolate, especially from one of the King's men."

"That boy –" said Marian. "He hadn't stolen them. I gave them to him. He said his father had 'drownded' in the Thames after his mother died."

"His father was very much alive!" smiled Jane. "I was told that, once they got his lordship onto his feet, the boy's father floored him again with one punch."

Marian didn't leave her bedchamber for a month. She would have emerged sooner but the Queen was adamant that she should not resume her duties until her bodily injuries had healed and her mind was at peace. Her young body healed quickly but not so her fears and anxieties.

Her majesty sent to Forrester Hall for Sir William and he returned as soon as Marmy had been buried.

Before going to see Marian, he obtained the King's permission to visit Bathampton in the Tower of London.

He was not accorded a cell on the upper floors of the Tower with the important political prisoners but was incarcerated beneath in the dank and acrid dungeons.

A gaoler led Sir William down a steep flight of stone steps. Their only light was a flaring torch the man lowered to guide their feet then raised again to the roof whenever the low arches threatened to knock them senseless.

When the tide was high, water seeped in across the beaten earth floor and lay there, stagnating. Sir William shivered, not only because of the cold and the permeating atmosphere of evil but because of the dreadful stench in which Lord Bathampton was lying. He heard the sounds of tiny scurrying feet in the darkness beyond the torchlight.

The prisoner was dressed in the clothes in which he had been arrested and was using his cloak as bedding, but he was unwashed and unshaved and his bucket had not been emptied.

"My lord, I am appalled to see you in such sorry circumstances, but you have brought this upon yourself. If you expressed some remorse, you might be moved to a more congenial cell."

"I cannot express what I don't feel," growled the prisoner. "If I was out of this accursed place and again met Lady Marian in the dark, I would still take my pleasure in her. She put up a very satisfactory fight – as energetic as she could with me on top of her – but I took her nevertheless. I took her many times. You should try her, William – or perhaps you have?"

His visitor drew back in disgust and spat on the floor. "Let's go," he said to the gaoler and they returned the way they had come, goaded by the jibes of the prisoner, leaving him again in utter darkness.

"Being down here for a while will soon cool his ardour," commented his guide as they retraced their steps. "We won't be bothered by him for long. His sort don't last. All bluster and no stamina."

Once in the fresh air again, Sir William inhaled several deep breaths, thanked the gaoler, gave him a coin, then proceeded by rowing boat along the river to Greenwich palace.

He spent many hours over several days listening to Marian's delusions of guilt for the attack, her fears for the future as she questioned her self-worth, her depression and despair. He spoke quietly, offering love and reassurance, until at last she said that, with support, she was ready to face the world again.

Once back at court, she felt that all eyes were upon her, that courtiers were pointing her out – "That's the lady-in-waiting who..." – but gradually realised that this persecution was of her own imagining. Although at all times watchful of those around her, she eventually relaxed and began to accept each day as it came along. Ministering to her majesty left little time for introspection.

# CHAPTER 48

"We will watch his majesty jousting tomorrow," the Queen decided. "He is a formidable contestant but doesn't always win."

Early next afternoon, Marian and three more of the Queen's ladies, including Jane Seymour, escorted her majesty to the tilt yard.

Flags were flying and the breeze was disturbing long lines of bunting as they took their seats on a daïs beneath a yellow awning. The four judges were seated below them, courtiers on each side, and opposite them the spectators who had paid to gain entrance.

The anticipation of a first-class tournament was high. Marian was caught up in the euphoria and, when she clapped her hands in sheer excitement, looked up to find the Queen smiling down at her.

Between them and the paying audience were the lists, two corridors of sand separated by a wooden barrier, along which the contestants would approach from opposite directions. Marian admired the self-confidence of the knights. They were excellent horsemen, well able to control their mounts while balancing the heavy lances in a horizontal position before striking their opponent in an endeavour to unhorse him.

The wooden barrier, or tilt, relieved the riders of the task of guiding their horses and protected their mounts from injury. Deliberately targeting a horse was forbidden and brought instant dismissal from the joust.

Two teams were taking part. The Red team, led by the King, sported red and grey caparisons over their horses' armour, which was replicated in the colours of their grand guards, the shields bolted to their left shoulders and the target for their opponent's lance. The plumes surmounting their helmets were red, as were the pennants carried by their squires, the young knights in training. The Black team was similarly decked out in black and yellow.

After several trumpet blasts from the four heralds in attendance, the King was called forward. He sat high and proud on his horse, his lance held upright. The heralds played a grand trumpet voluntary, which sent shivers down Marian's spine, and the two opponents rode forward to the lists, lowering their lances to the horizontal position. The horses stamped and snorted as they waited for the marshall to lower his flag. When the jousters received the signal, they moved forward.

Their slow canter escalated into a gallop. Crash! The wooden lances clashed viciously. Neither lance broke and both riders wheeled at the end of the lists to make a returning pass, each using a fresh lance handed to him by his squire.

This time, the King slammed his lance against his opponent's grand guard, almost toppling him from his horse, which earned his majesty five points.

After four passes, neither rider had unseated the other and the score was even, eleven points each.

Then it was the turn of the second rider in each team. They provided an even greater dramatic spectacle, one black knight being unhorsed, so earning his opponent ten points, and both reduced to finishing the combat with a sword fight.

The exciting display lasted two hours, with a break inbetween to allow horses and riders to refresh themselves, during which time the royal party was brought ale and sweetmeats.

The King was not in the final play-off between the two highest scoring champions, but he had ridden well and was as enthusiastic as everyone else in congratulating the final winner in the opposing team.

That knight was Sir Henry Spencer who, laying his helmet and gauntlets aside, accepted his award from the judges, a silver shield to display above his horse's stall. Then, pulling off the yellow and black favour from the top of his helm, he presented it on one knee to Lady Edith Woodford, one of the Queen's ladies. Edith, with a delighted smile that brought dimples to her cheeks, placed a garland of flowers about his neck. Then he gallantly kissed her hand.

Everyone cheered and clapped and agreed it had been a most pleasant way to spend an afternoon, in the warm autumn sunshine, in good company and with the added spice of the presence of their majesties.

That evening, there followed a sumptuous feast, at which the baby princess Elizabeth was brought in by her nursemaid and shown around to the assembled company, who admired her pretty ways. Queen Anne took the infant in her arms into one of the dances but, when the child cried, returned her to the nursemaid with some alacrity and the princess was taken back to the nursery.

Marian had continued her lessons with the dancing master so she knew all the court measures and danced every one with a different partner.

Determined to suppress the nightmare of her recent experience, she enjoyed the company and easy conversation of the young courtiers. She thought of them as friends for the most part and was not interested in any romantic attachments, realising that she was probably popular because she had the ear of the Queen and, as night follows day, therefore the ear of the King.

One of her admirers was George, the Queen's brother. He had recently been appointed Lord Warden of the Cinque Ports and Constable of Dover Castle, the highest appointments in the realm. Having been unhappily married to Jane Rochford for ten years, he was a known womaniser.

A poem written about him and bandied about the court recorded that "*I forced widows, and maidens I did deflower*". Marian told him plainly that she was one widow he was not going to force. When he laughed and asked whether, then, he could expect her to come to him willingly, she raised her eyebrows and said nothing but determined to speak to the Queen.

She did so as soon as the opportunity arose, pleading that, although she recognised the qualities of the viscount, which were many, and without doubt he was very handsome, her recent experience with Lord Bathampton had left her at this moment unable to respond to the advances of any man, even though he was her majesty's own brother. The appeal was effective and she was no longer troubled by that young man.

The royal Christmas was to be spent at Hampton Court, thirty miles upstream from Greenwich and a day's journey by boat. The palace had been 'given' to the King by the late Archbishop of York, Cardinal Wolsey, when it was obvious that he was falling from favour.

The King had put in place an expansive building programme and the great hall had been completed recently, along with a large tennis court. Still under construction was the gatehouse to the second, inner court, above which were apartments being prepared for her majesty. The Queen was much pleased with her new palace.

Reluctantly, she granted permission for Marian and Sir William to return home for Christmas, Marian to recuperate further and Sir William to spend time with his wife and son.

Marian was pleased to be home, although Christmas was not the same without Marmy. Lady Susan had taken on a new housekeeper, a very pleasant woman, anxious to please, and none of the arrangements went awry.

Philip William was almost a year old and Margery's daughter, Agnes, a little younger. Both were standing without support and Philip had taken his first tentative steps, much to the delight of Sir William who was watching when it happened and called everyone to witness this miracle.

Although so young, Margery was proving a very attentive lady's maid and a capable mother, under the guidance of Lady Susan and Philip William's nursemaids and wet nurses, and would not let them perform any duties for her daughter that she could perform herself.

Lady Susan was even allowing Marjery a follower in the person of a likeable young lad who worked in the stables and lived in the village. She confided to Marian that a marriage between the two would solve many problems.

The traditional Christmas festivities were meticulous. As usual, a party of villagers arrived at the Hall to decorate it with greenery then welcomed the arrival of the yule log. The Christmas morning service for the family and the Hall's servants took place in the chapel and was followed by the feasting and dancing. Sir William and Lady Susan had invited friends and acquaintances from among the local gentry, landowners and farmers and were gracious and benevolent hosts.

Marian was delighted to see how happy the couple looked but also admitted to being a little envious.

On the day after Christmas Day, Marian rode down to the monastery to take Mother Superior a gift of meat pies, patés, preserves and sweetmeats, all beautifully prepared and cooked in the Hall kitchens, together with several bottles of fine wine, for which the Reverend Mother was very grateful. She asked Marian to walk with her in the cloisters, which Marian was pleased to do.

At first they walked in silence, Marian wondering why she had been accorded such an honour, but she had not long to wait to divine the reason.

"I am greatly burdened," confessed Reverend Mother, and certainly sounded as if this were true. "Parliament has passed the Act of Supremacy, declaring the King 'the only head of the Church of England on Earth', so ousting Pope Clement from that exalted position."

"Yes," Marian agreed, "I know of it."

"He is ordering all those in holy orders to take the Oath of Supremacy. This I cannot do."

"To refuse is very dangerous," Marian warned her with concern. "To refuse is treason."

Mother Superior nodded in agreement. "And we all know where that will lead."

Marian said nothing but her emotions were in turmoil. On the one hand, her duty and loyalty were to her King but, on the other, she recognised the dilemma in which the Reverend Mother was placed. Her integrity would not allow her to swear allegiance to a religious principle in which she could not believe.

The elderly woman was adamant. "I cannot take the Oath, neither will the Abbot."

"You must," Marian insisted.

"We are in good company," said Reverend Mother. "Sir Thomas More, one time Lord High Chancellor of England, is also refusing."

"He cannot hide from the King," Marian said, "but you could, Reverend Mother, if you left before Thomas Cromwell makes his visitation."

"I could not leave my daughters to their fate."

"If they swear the Oath –"

"They won't."

"Some might. Some do, with persuasion."

Neither needed to articulate the elements of *persuasion* – at best, the temptation of a lifetime's pension; at worst, torture or the threat of death by one of many cruel methods.

"Lady Forrester, you are at court and close to the Queen. You must hear what is in the wind. Will his majesty go so far as to take his revenge on the Holy Father, who has excommunicated him, by sacking all the monasteries and acquiring their lands and property?"

"I have heard that is in the mind of his majesty."

"Lady Forrester –"

"Reverend Mother, do not ask me anything more. You must recognise that my loyalty is to his majesty, the King of England, and Queen Anne."

"And he must recognise that *my* loyalty is to his majesty, the King of Heaven, to the blessed Virgin Mary, the Queen of Heaven, and to the Holy Father."

They had made a full circuit of the cloisters and Mother Superior stopped walking and faced Marian.

"I understand your position and would not lead you into danger, Lady Forrester. We must trust the Lord, whatever the future holds."

"Please be careful, Reverend Mother."

"I promise that I will not take any unnecessary risks. Now you must do what you came to do and visit your daughter's grave. It has been a pleasure, as always, to converse with you. Please take my blessing to Sir William and his family."

"I will," said Marian and bowed her head as her companion left.

Over the grave of her daughter, Margaret, she silently prayed that the King would stay his hand and that this monastery and all those who lived and worked in it, monks and nuns, would be kept safe.

Before leaving, she looked for Richard, but whether or not he was aware of her visit, she saw no sign of him, not even a shadow at a window.

A week after Marian and Sir William returned to Greenwich Palace, the weather changed and it snowed continuously for several days so that travel was unwise, if not impossible, over the layer upon layer of pristine white carpeting and the high snowdrifts.

Those at court whiled away the hours by playing board games or charades, listening to virtuoso violinist Mark Smeaton and the other court musicians or the boy choristers, or singing bawdy songs struck up by the court jester.

At other times, they sat and conversed round the huge fires that the servants were constantly tending. The servants were also engaged in stuffing with rags any cracks and holes through which the icy north wind was gaining entrance and the heavy brocaded curtains were kept drawn across doors and windows in an endeavour to keep draughts at bay.

One evening, when the King and Queen were keeping company together in the French drawing room, where many of the court were also gathered, Sir William sought out Marian and whispered, "I have to speak to you."

He led her away into a dark corner at some distance from the firelight and glow of the lamps.

"What is it, William?"

"I have some disturbing news. You'd better sit down."

He pulled a heavy chair over and, puzzled, she sat.

"What is it? What's the matter?"

"It's about Bathampton."

"Is he dead? His gaoler told you he wouldn't last long in those conditions."

"No, he's not dead. The King has released him."

"What?" Marian's voice rose to a screech and she clapped her hand over her mouth. Fortunately, there was such a hubbub in the room that no one took any notice. "Are you sure?"

"Yes. Has the Queen not told you?"

Marian shook her head.

"The King decided he had been taught a lesson. He also said that Thomas Cromwell has work for him to do and needed his scrivener back in office."

"What work?"

"My guess is that Cromwell wishes Bathampton to accompany him on his visitations to the monasteries and friaries. He will need help in assessing their holdings and the worth of their goods and ornaments. We must pray for the safety of the monastery at Forrestram."

The chill that ran down Marian's spine on hearing this news was colder than anything the blustering north wind could hurl at her.

# CHAPTER 49

*Place: The Monastery of St. Jude*

*Date: January, 1535*

There was no luxury at the monastery of St. Jude, adjacent to the village of Forrestram, sited on land owned by Sir William Forrester.

The monks' individual cells contained simply a bed, chair, table, bookshelf, a wooden cupboard, a washstand and a chamber pot. There was one small barred, glazed window but no heating.

The monks ate three meals a day in the refectory, during which time they practised silence while one of their number read to them from holy writings.

Within the complex was an infirmary where the elderly brothers and sisters could receive the care they needed. This nursing care was available to anyone in the village who fell sick or was injured, the fate of many during their working day, and to any traveller who fell ill in the vicinity of the monastery and needed their ministrations.

Theirs was not a closed order and the monks and nuns were familiar figures among the local people, bringing baskets of food to those who had little means of feeding their large families. They also taught the children to read and write when their pupils were not needed to work in the fields or help with household chores.

Rising at 5 a.m., much of their time was spent in both chapels as they observed the nine offices of the day. Interspersed between the services were periods of study, private prayer, work, visiting, recreation and rest.

Two days after Mother Superior had had the conversation with Marian, she visited by arrangement the Abbot and they were closeted together for a long time, parting only when the bell began to toll for the office of Vespers at six o'clock.

After supper, when the table had been cleared, Reverend Mother asked the sisters to forego their recreation hour as she had something of serious import to say to them before it was time for Compline, the last service of the day. They remained in their seats and listened respectfully while she stood.

"My dear children," she began. "We all know that times are changing in our land. His majesty has turned his back on holy mother church and has set himself up in place of the Holy Father, for which act he has been excommunicated." She crossed herself and so did the sisters. "He has exalted himself as the Supreme Head of the Church in England in place of Pope Clement and has commanded that everyone consents to the Act of

Supremacy. Failure to do so will attract fearful consequences. Need I spell it out for you?"

Some of the sisters looked unsure so she said, "Non-compliance will be construed as treason and the punishment for that is death – not always instant death."

Greatly troubled, she sat, clasping her hands in her lap to stop them from shaking. "I have to tell you that the Abbot and I are in agreement that neither of us will in all conscience sign that Oath. Neither will we flee. We shall stay here until the soldiers come for us."

"When will that be, Reverend Mother?" asked one of the sisters.

"It will not happen until Thomas Cromwell has visited us to make an inventory of all that we possess and has asked us to sign the Oath. There is no knowing when that will be. He certainly will be unable to come until the snow clears, which gives us time to muster our courage and prepare our response."

"I am greatly feared, Reverend Mother," confessed one of the young nuns.

"We are not placing any obligations on your shoulders," Mother Superior continued. "Each of us must pray for herself and her sisters – that each of us will make the response that our Lord requires of us. Take your time, in prayer, to search our Lord's will. It may be, of course, that only the Abbot and myself will be interrogated but, whatever transpires, remember what Saint Paul wrote to the Christian church in Corinth: that God had told him, *My grace is sufficient for thee: for my strength is made perfect in weakness.*

"Reverend Mother, it doesn't always seem like that," said the young nun.

"But it is so, my child, and we must have courage, faith and hope, and they will come only through much prayer and fasting."

She stood again. "However, whatever happens, holy mother church will rise from its destruction and will prosper again, and we must be good stewards of our possessions for those who come after us. Sir Thomas will find some of our treasures but there is no need for him to find them all. Once the snow clears and the ground can be dug, we shall bury the most valuable in the fields, leaving only the items of lesser value for the vicar-general to find. The monks will take the same measures with their valuables. They will be buried together." She looked around the table. "I have no need to tell you that secrecy is of the utmost importance. For that reason, only one or two will be involved. The rest of you need know nothing about what is happening so close your eyes and shut your mouths and let the good Lord provide."

# CHAPTER 50

In the monastery refectory, Abbot Johannes was saying something similar to the brothers.

"I am putting Brother Alphonsus in charge of the operation. He was a lawyer before taking his vows and has a good business head on his shoulders. He will draw up a list of our earthly treasures. All that the rest of you will know is that a list of the monastery's wealth has been compiled in preparation for the vicar-general's visit."

Next day, Abbot Johannes summoned Brother Alphonsus to his study and they spent several hours preparing a list of the monastery's removable wealth.

Heading the list was the solid silver communion plate given three hundred years previously by an ancestor of the present Lord Forrester. The set consisted of two engraved and decorated chalices to hold the communion wine, plus covers, two patens for the bread, two flagons, two candlesticks for the altar, a collection plate and a magnificent crucifix. There were several more sets – one silver plated, one of pewter, one of base metal and a very plain pottery set. There were also several very old icons, a small gold-plated crucifix fixed to the wall above the pulpit, a set of Stations of the Cross inlaid with ivory and pearl and a couple of oil paintings of the Virgin Mary with the baby Jesus on her lap.

To the list were added the priestly vestments in rich fabrics, embroidered and decorated with semi-precious stones; the white and gold altar frontal for the great festivals and the coloured frontals for each season in the church's year; a generous supply of 'fair linen cloths', coverlets and veils for the Lord's table and the linen for cleaning the communion vessels.

"Brother Alphonsus, we will continue tomorrow," decided the Abbot as he closed the leather-bound book in which he had been listing and describing each item. Brother Alphonsus inclined his head in acknowledgement and left.

Once back in his cell, Alphonsus drew the chair up to the table and sat in thought, his head resting in his hands.

It was obvious that the Abbot was intending to conceal from Thomas Cromwell the most precious of the monastery's goods and vestments and it was his understanding that the most valuable items from the nunnery would be hidden with them. The Abbot had mentioned digging a pit in the fields behind the village, from which they could be retrieved when the monastery was resurrected in years to come, as he was sure it would be.

Brother Alphonsus was not so sure. The King seemed to have severed all connection with the church in Rome for all time – his marriage to Queen Anne, his erstwhile mistress, and the annulment of his previous marriage to Katharine, the Roman Catholic queen from Spanish Aragon, ensured it was so.

The Abbot had stated that, whatever the outcome, he was unable to betray the Holy Father and holy mother church and would never sign the Oath of Supremacy. Of course, the King had ways and means of making men and women change their minds, but he thought that the Abbot was foolhardy enough to go to the stake or the block rather than sign. Mother Superior had decided to take the same path.

Alphonsus could not help but admire them for the stance they intended to take but at the same time considered them stupid when their names scratched on a piece of paper would ensure their freedom.

He had no such scruples. His signature, if required, would be appended in a matter of seconds and so, he imagined, would most of his brothers. He did not know about the sisters.

What then would become of the hidden treasures when the lives of the Abbot and Mother Superior had been obliterated, when those who at present inhabited the monastery had gone their own ways and the buildings had been destroyed? What then of the hidden treasures? Who would know of their existence let alone where they were concealed?

Before making his way to the chapel to join his brethren for the service of Compline, he had made up his mind what to do. As the chest and its contents would be very heavy, he would obviously need help to carry it to its place of burial, which act would have to take place at the dead of night. He would require a second plan, one that would not come easily to him but one that it would be vital to carry out if his secret was to be kept safe.

Finally, the snow began to ease off, then melt in the winter sunshine, leaving the landscape covered in slush that eventually disappeared until all that was left was mud and puddles.

"If the weather has also changed for the better in London," said the Abbot to Brother Alphonsus, "it is likely that Cromwell will be setting off on his visitations without further delay. It is time for us to put our plans into operation."

While waiting for the snow to cease, he had not been idle and had ordered the brothers in the carpentry workshop to construct a strong chest, sealed against ground moisture, and to deliver it to the chapel when requested.

That chest now stood by the west door and was receiving the items being collected by Brother Alphonsus, as directed by the Abbot. Packed neatly, each item wrapped in protective wool, was the entire solid silver communion plate. Following now was a bag of gold coins from the safe, a gold pectoral cross, the oldest icon, a bejewelled stole, and various other precious artefacts – "But not too many," stipulated the Abbot. "The absence of any of these must not be noticeable. The vicar-general is not to be underestimated as a fool."

On top went the leather bound book listing all the goods and ornaments that the abbey possessed.

"I have been busy making entries in a second book," he explained, "that makes no mention of the items in the chest. That is the book we shall show to Cromwell."

"Will he not be suspicious, Father, that the book is newly written?"

"I shall say, my son, that I drew it up in anticipation of his visit, which is the truth, of course."

They were interrupted by the arrival of Mother Superior and one of her nuns with their few treasures, and soon the chest was full, the lid closed and the padlock fitted and locked.

"You must go, Reverend Mother," he said and the nuns left.

"Obviously, it is too heavy for you to carry or drag yourself so I have asked Brother Barnabus to aid you," said the Abbot. "Now we will conceal the chest in the vestry. After Compline, you both will return to your cells as usual, to allay any suspicions, then return after half an hour and remove the chest. A horse and cart will be waiting for you and at that time I will tell you where to bury it."

"Yes, Father," nodded Brother Alphonsus.

The plan went ahead as the Abbot had directed. An hour after the brothers had retired to their cells, Brother Alphonsus was seated on the cart in the stable yard, reins in hand. Brother Barnabus was sitting on the chest in the cart, two spades at his feet. Thomas, one of the stable lads, who was being paid well to work late, was standing at the horse's head, stroking its muzzle. The Abbot made sure that he could not overhear their whispered conversation.

"The hiding place?" Brother Alphonsus asked.

"The Gospel according to Saint Matthew, chapter 13, verse 44 –"

Brother Barnabus knew his Bible. "*The kingdom of heaven is like unto treasure hid in a field,*" he quoted.

"Exactly. You know the old oak tree on the incline above the village?" Both brothers said yes, they knew it. "From there, pace thirteen steps north and forty-four steps east, then repeat, thirteen north and forty-four east. Bury the chest there."

"I will, Father," Brother Alphonsus promised.

The Abbot said a brief prayer for the success of their mission and they were on their way.

The horse's hooves had been muffled with rags. Fortunately, it was a dark night, with threatening snow clouds covering the moon. Alphonsus, driving slowly to prevent the cart from creaking too loudly, was fully occupied with the task in hand and said very little.

Barnabus, who was being swayed and jolted most uncomfortably on his hard seat, was glad of the silence. He fidgeted nervously with the little wooden crucifix at his neck, praying earnestly for a speedy execution of their mission and that this act of treason, in which he was fully implicated though not from choice, would not be discovered.

To his dismay, the cross suddenly came away in his hand. The leather cord had finally worn through. It had been fraying for some time but he had been reluctant to replace it. His young brother had carved the little crucifix and had knotted it around his neck before Barnabus left home for the monastery. That was the last time he had seen his brother, who had fallen sick and had gone to an early grave.

He was about to tell Alphonsus about the mishap when they drove over a particularly rutted part of the lane, which upset the horse and rocked the cart from side to side. He could have been mistaken but he thought Alphonsus uttered an expletive.

Barnabus crossed himself, almost losing his balance and falling off the chest in doing so, and decided to say nothing. He placed the crucifix on the floor of the cart and hoped that the breaking cord was not an ill omen.

Before they reached the village, Alphonsus turned the horse along a track then jumped from the cart to open the gate into a field. After a few minutes they had reached the oak tree that the Abbot had mentioned. Alphonsus secured the horse by tying the reins round a low branch and together they lifted the chest from the cart to the ground.

"I will pace out the steps," said Alphonsus, "and mark the spot with my cloak, then come back for you and the chest."

So saying, he turned to his right and began to pace out thirteen steps.

"Brother Alphonsus," whispered his colleague urgently, "the Abbot said north; you are pacing to the south."

"I know what I am doing," growled Alphonsus. "Stay there."

Bewildered, Brother Barnabus watched him take thirteen steps then turn to his left and pace towards the east until he was lost in the darkness. Moments later he was back.

"Right, the spot is marked. Take the handle that end and we'll carry it between us. First pass me a spade and you carry the other one. Tell me if you need to put the chest down and take more breath."

"But Brother Alphonsus –"

"Just do as I tell you."

They lifted the chest by its handles and began to struggle with it across the field.

"But you have not carried out the Abbot's instructions," insisted Brother Barnabus. "You have walked in the opposite direction."

"Do you think I am going to bury all this treasure where he says, where its whereabouts could be discovered under torture? No, *I* shall know where it is and that is all that matters – and you, of course."

"If you are tortured –"

"I won't be. I will sign the Oath of Supremacy, if pressed. What about you?"

"I cannot sign. I cannot betray holy mother church."

"So, if you are tortured?" asked Brother Alphonsus.

"I need to take breath," the other monk panted and they lowered the chest to the ground. He paused, breathing hard. "I would pray to stand firm but how can anyone know what he will say under torture?"

Alphonsus grunted and they picked up the chest again and struggled on to where his cloak lay on the ground. Both were used to digging graves and soon their efforts were rewarded with a pit large enough to take the chest, indeed deep enough to take two chests, one on top of the other.

"Why so deep?" Brother Barnabus asked as he began to spade loose earth back into the hole.

The clouds had momentarily drifted away from the moon, which was giving them more light by which to finish their task.

He raised his head as Alphonsus moved round the hole towards him, spade in hand.

"My brother, what is amiss?" he asked, seeing the spade raised high in both hands. "What are you –?"

His question was cut short as the spade came swinging through the air and hit him with full force on the side of the head. He staggered, dropping his own spade and raising his hand to his temple, which was bleeding profusely. The second blow came with even more force behind it and the young monk fell backwards into the hole, landing on top of the chest.

"You have your answer for the depth of the hole," Alphonsus muttered grimly and began pushing back into it the mounds of earth they had dug out, hiding both chest and body.

When the hole was filled and the reserved top layer of grass had been laid over it and banged down with the spade then stamped on, and Alphonsus was satisfied with a job well done, he went back to the oak tree and threw the spades into the cart. He released the horse, climbed up, took the reins and drove back to the monastery.

On the way, he stopped by a stream to wash the dirt off the spades, trusting that any blood would be washed away with it.

Back at the monastery, he handed horse and cart over to Thomas, made his report to the Abbot then, after briefly visiting the cell of Brother Barnabus, went to his own cell to sleep before rising for the morning service of Vigils at 5.30 a.m.

As soon as Brother Alphonsus had left the yard, the boy loosed the horse from the harness and settled it in its stall for the night then manhandled the cart into the cart shed. As it tipped forward onto its shafts, he heard something slither down the boards until it came to rest behind the driver's seat.

Curious, he took a torch from its sconce and discovered a small wooden crucifix, a miniature figure of Christ on the Cross with a halo around His head.

He recognised it at once as belonging to Brother Barnabus. The story was well known. The monk always described the crucifix as his most precious possession because his young brother had carved it for him when he entered the monastery and had died shortly afterwards.

The lad liked Brother Barnabus, who always had a pleasant word to say to him, unlike Brother Alphonsus and some of the others. So he decided to deliver the crucifix straight away and not wait till morning as the monk might need it for his devotions before going to bed. There might even be a coin awaiting him for his good deed. The monks had taken a vow of poverty but occasionally there was a coin to be had for running an errand.

Accordingly, he left the yard and hurried across to the main building. A candle was burning in the window of the Abbot's study and he guessed that the brothers were seated in there, reporting on the night's work, whatever it was.

He knew where the cell he was seeking was situated and made his way there. On arriving, he knocked quietly on the cell door, just in case Brother Barnabus was inside and not with the Abbot. When he did not receive a reply, he lifted the latch and peered round the door.

His eyes were quite accustomed to the darkness by now and he was able to make out the few objects in the room. He laid the crucifix on the bolster and withdrew, thinking he would explain to Brother Barnabus next time he saw him.

Of course, the non-appearance of the monk at Vigils was questioned by the brethren. After the service, the Abbot despatched one of them to inspect his cell, thinking he had overslept, but the monk returned with the news that Brother Barnabus was not in his cell, though obviously he had spent the night there because the blanket on the bed had been thrown back, the piss pot had been used and there was mud on the floor. However, he was nowhere to be found. The Abbot summoned Brother Alphonsus to his study.

"Have you any explanation for the disappearance of Brother Barnabus?" he asked. "Tell me again what happened last night."

"As I reported to you, we carried out your instructions without mishap," the monk lied, "and Brother Barnabus came back to the monastery with me. I drove the horse and cart round to the stables, where Thomas was waiting for me, then came to report to you. As far as I know, Brother Barnabus went straight to his cell to sleep."

"Did anything happen between you, was anything said, that can throw any light on his disappearance? Was he ill, for instance?"

"No, Father. There was nothing – except – except –"

"Except what, my son? Tell me what you are thinking."

"We were talking about signing the Oath of Supremacy and how that was not a possibility for either of us, and what if we were taken by the soldiers and tortured? Would either of us be able to hold out under torture or would we offer information about the burial of the chest to secure our freedom? I said that none of us knows how he would react – the King's torturers can be very persuasive – and Brother Barnabus said he was greatly troubled. He said he was not a brave man and the pain and humiliation might be too much for him. That is all."

"Hhmm," murmured the Abbot. "Would that conversation cause him sufficient anxiety to run away, do you think? Did you not remind him that the grace of God is sufficient in all circumstances?"

"I did, Father, but that promise seemed of little comfort to him."

"Very well. We must pray and wait with patience. He may yet return to us. God grant him and us that comfort."

"Amen, amen," intoned Brother Alphonsus, crossing himself, amused that he had got away with that interrogation very easily. Now all he had to do was act normally as if nothing untoward had happened last night.

# CHAPTER 51

Thomas Cromwell, vicar-general, arrived at the monastery two weeks later. His entourage was first seen a mile away from the village. Calmly, the Abbot made his rounds of all the areas in which the monks were working – the kitchens, library, refectory, infirmary, stables and gardens – and prayed with each group for integrity and courage. He was returning from the trout farm when the procession of outriders, mounted escort and following men-at-arms with their squires began lining up in the driveway, a protective wall around the vicar-general and his staff in their whirlicotes.

The Abbot hurried to greet his prestigious visitor and escorted the company to the refectory for refreshment. From there they made their way to the chapel and, without wasting any time, over the course of the afternoon, every item listed in the duplicate leather bound book was inspected and assessed as to its value.

"And this is the extent of your acquisitions?" asked Cromwell suspiciously.

"We have never been a rich monastery," replied the Abbot truthfully. "Most of our treasures have been given by grateful travellers who have fallen ill while in the vicinity and have been cared for in our infirmary."

"What about Sir William Forrester? Does he not give alms, Abbot?"

"Sir William worships at the parish church when he is at home. He allows us to occupy his land free of rent and that is his not inconsiderable contribution to our ministry here."

"Make a note of that, Bathampton," Cromwell ordered his scrivener, who was seated at his side. Lord Bathampton nodded and made a note in the book then closed it.

"We will have a look round, with your permission, Abbot." Abbot Johannes bowed his head in agreement. "While we are thus engaged, a messenger will be sent to Forrester Hall to announce our intention of passing the night there. We have no wish to spend an hour longer here than necessary. Your hospitality, Abbot, will leave much to be desired if your cells resemble others we have seen. Tomorrow, we will interview the brothers. I believe that you have a nunnery attached? Then we will speak to Mother Superior and the sisters as well."

Next morning, Cromwell and his retinue rode in from the direction of Forrester Hall, looking well fed and well rested.

He ordered that a table should be set up in the chapel. The brothers had gathered at the usual time for their morning service and sat waiting but the Abbot was not allowed to celebrate the Holy Mass. Instead, the vicar-general addressed them from the pulpit.

"You all know why I am here," he began. "I am here in the name of his majesty, King Henry VIII, appointed by God as Supreme Head of the Church of England. Yours is not a wealthy monastery, as some are, with taxes and tithes to collect, which makes it all the easier to dismantle, as it will be, as soon as is expedient."

There was a general murmur of dismay and disapproval from his hearers and he held up his hand for silence.

"Before you all retire to the refectory for breakfast, my scrivener will leave a copy of the Act and Oath of Supremacy on the table here, which your Abbot and all of you will be required to sign before you gather for mid-day prayers. We have a list of you so there is no escape. This afternoon, my scrivener, Lord Bathampton here, will interview each of you who has not done so."

Brother Lawrence was one of the last to enter the chapel and was standing at the back. He had been listening to the vicar-general and, although he had registered that a man was seated at the table, he had not paid him any attention. Now, however, he had been made to pay attention and drew in an audible breath at the announcement of the name – Lord Bathampton!

"What ails you, brother?" asked the young monk standing next to him.

"I know him," Brother Lawrence muttered. "I used to scribe for him at court."

"Then you might receive lenient treatment."

"I very much doubt it."

Thomas Cromwell was bringing his speech to a close. "The documents will remain on the table until our next visit," he said, "to give any of you who decide not to sign time to review your decision. Needless to say, not to sign will be regarded as treason with its attendant consequences." He turned his head to where the Abbot was standing. "I am sure that your Father in God will be the first to append his signature."

With that remark, he turned and descended the steps and walked out of the chapel, Lord Bathampton and his attendant bodyguard shadowing him.

Abbot Johannes did not follow his monks into breakfast but stayed in the chapel, on his knees in prayer. He knew that, whatever happened, he would not leave the monastery but would stay, as the captain of the King's flagship *The Mary Rose* would stay with his ship if it was sinking. He imagined that Mother Superior felt the same way. Neither would sign the Oath and neither would run from the consequences, with God's help.

However, he could not lay that obligation on his children's shoulders. He would give his blessing to whichever action each brother decided to take, whether it be to sign or not. At heart they were of the Roman Catholic faith and that is where their loyalties would lay for the rest of their lives, he felt sure. He very much doubted that it mattered one way or the other to Thomas Cromwell.

Crossing himself, he rose to his feet and went to the refectory. Cromwell and his men had left to inspect the gardens, fish ponds and trout farm so the Abbot had opportunity to confide his thoughts and decision to the young monks seated at the table. They listened to him in silence and he left them to their heart searching and retired to his cell.

After he had gone, the monks finished their breakfast of bread and ale and eggs from the monastery's chickens then most of them made their way to the chapel to sign the document lying on the table.

To their surprise, the scrivener was already seated there with two soldiers in attendance, observing each young man as he signed, and surprisingly, handing each one a pouch of coins retrieved from a leather bag at his feet.

"You see, the King is not ungracious to those who are loyal to him. Regard this as your pension from the hands of his majesty. Go and find work elsewhere, marry, start a family."

"My lord, we are not allowed –"

"To have carnal relations?" Lord Bathampton laughed. "You are now. Make the most of it! Go and find yourself one of the nuns before your brothers get there first!"

The monk to whom he was speaking blushed bright red and left.

At the end of the line of brothers, Richard was watching all that was being said and done. He was surprised to see Brother Alphonsus appending his name to the document. Until now, Alphonsus had asserted many times that he would not do so, no matter what the consequences. In fact, he had made a great show of his loyalty to Rome. Now he was signing, even saying something that made Bathampton laugh, before holding his hand out for his pouch of coins and hurriedly leaving the chapel as if the scrivener might change his mind and call him back.

As yet, Richard was not certain whether or not he would sign. He believed in God and would continue to worship and pray, and asked himself whether it really mattered whether the pope in faraway Rome or the King at Greenwich headed the church in England.

He recognised that the situation had arisen only because the pope would not allow the annulment of Henry's marriage to Katharine so that he could marry Anne Boleyn. All that had more to do with men than with God. If truth be told, God had caught him, Richard, on the rebound and progressing from lay worshipper to a brother in a monastery was all to do with his hopeless love for Marian.

By now, he was second in line at the table. He pulled his cowl over his head in the vain hope that Bathampton would not want to see his face, but it was not to be.

"Push back your cowl, monk," said his lordship, looking down at the list of names before him. "You must be Brother Lawrence."

"I am, your lordship."

"And are you going to sign the Oath, as have your brothers? You will be rewarded if you do."

"It is not the reward that will move or stay my hand," Richard said, "but my conscience."

Lord Bathampton looked up sharply at the sound of his voice.

"I know that voice and that face! Richard Mordaunt, I do declare!" he chortled and thumped the table with his fist. "So this is where you have been hiding yourself all this while! How long has it been since you left the court?"

"Ten years."

"A great deal has happened during those years."

"We do receive news of the outside world from time to time."

"Of course, through Sir William. You will know then that I married young Alice Dereham, who was with child, so that his precious son – may he rest in peace – could marry his sweetheart, Lady Marian – you remember Marian? But that whore, Alice, had us all fooled. The baby wasn't Philip Forrester's leavings after all. How about that? I need never have married her. They made it worth my while, though, so little harm done."

Richard said nothing.

"Coincidence, your coming here to this monastery, in the grounds of Forrester Hall. I always had the notion that you and Lady Marian – but, of course, you were only a scribe and now you are only a monk. That young woman needed a mature man to handle her, none of your pale sons of insignificant fathers. She got her man in the end – I made sure of that. She cried 'rape' but she was willing enough – willing and pleading for it each time. I went to the Tower for it but I'm out now, by the grace of the King, and I reckon it was worth it."

"You – you – raped Lady Marian?"

"Was that one item of news that Sir William didn't divulge? I wouldn't call it rape, just the fulfilling of desires that she didn't know she had. I taught her what it is to have a real man between her legs, and I would do it all over again given half a chance."

Richard was across the table with his hands round Bathampton's throat in seconds. His attack was so unexpected and was delivered with such force that his victim fell against the back of his chair, toppling it over and sending him crashing to the floor with Richard sprawling on top of him, his hands still gripping his throat.

Immediately, both soldiers were upon them and hauled the attacker to his feet, holding him fast while two of the brothers assisted Lord Bathampton and righted the chair. The victim was left spluttering and gasping for air, his own hands massaging his neck where moments ago Richard's fingers had been trying to throttle the life out of him.

"Ah," he said, once he had recovered, brushing himself down, "so that's the way of it, is it? I can't say I'm surprised. I saw how you always looked at her. Will someone fetch the Abbot? He shall hear about this. Then we shall decide what to do with you!"

Richard knew it was useless to struggle and stood quite still in the grip of his captors.

One of the monks went to fetch the Abbot, who came without delay and received a vindictive report from Lord Bathampton, who was still rubbing his neck, which was turning dull red and showing the white imprint of Richard's fingers. The Abbot was puzzled as he looked from one man to the other.

"My son," he asked, "is this true? Did you try to murder his lordship? I cannot believe it of you."

"He's not going to admit it," said Lord Bathampton, "but there are plenty of witnesses. I want him put under guard in your prison cell until I have been able to discuss the matter with the vicar-general."

"We have no prison cell in the monastery," the Abbot told him.

"His own cell then with a guard at the door. You two men –"

He spoke sharply to the soldiers and they stood to attention. "Yes, sir?"

"Take him away and remain outside his cell. I will make sure you are relieved in two hours. Abbot, please lead the way."

The Abbot, looking greatly troubled, nodded and led Richard and the soldiers out of the chapel.

When they reached Richard's cell, the Abbot went inside with him while the soldiers stood guard outside. He asked for an explanation of what really happened, so Richard told him.

"You had provocation, my son," the Abbot said, "but that was no excuse for giving way to your anger. I will plead your cause to the vicar-general but, from what I know of the man, it will have little influence. I fear they will take you with them back to court for judgement and punishment. Lord Bathampton is, after all, one of the King's men and on his mission."

Thomas Cromwell and his entourage again spent the night at Forrester Hall and left early next morning, calling at the monastery on the way to take Richard with them. They had confiscated one of the horses from the Hall's stables and tied him to it. He rode uncomfortably between two of the armed escort, wondering what fate awaited him.

# CHAPTER 52

*Place: Greenwich Palace*

*Date: February, 1535*

The first that Marian knew of Richard's return to Greenwich was when Sir William came looking for her and told her the news. He found her in the blue drawing room, where she was retrieving rubies and diamonds that had rolled all over the floor when the Queen had broken a necklace earlier in the day.

On learning of the arrest, he had visited the young monk in the room in the north tower where he was under guard.

"How is he?" asked Marian with concern.

"Well enough, considering his plight."

"You say he tried to throttle the life out of Lord Bathampton? But why would he do that?"

"Because his lordship was tormenting him about what he had done to you."

Marian paled and would have dropped the precious stones if Sir William had not taken them from her. She clasped her fists against her heart.

"So Richard knows. I would rather he didn't. I would never have told him."

She paused and Sir William waited quietly while she regained control of her breathing.

"Do you think I would be allowed to visit him?"

"Why don't you ask the Queen to petition the King?"

"Yes, I will do that."

For several days, Marian sought an opportunity to speak to her majesty and finally plucked up courage while helping to prepare her for bed one evening. She had been picking up the Queen's discarded clothing and paused with a gold-embroidered shoe and two stockings in her hands, watching as Lady Jane Seymour hunted for the other shoe, while another of her ladies smoothed ass's milk on the royal arms and another massaged her neck and shoulders.

"Your Majesty," she tentatively began.

"What is it, little Marian?" the Queen asked, her eyes half closed as she relaxed under her ladies' ministrations.

"I have a favour to ask of your Majesty."

"Well?"

Marian took a deep breath. "I have a friend who is under guard in the north tower for attacking Lord Bathampton."

"You have such friends, Marian?"

"He is not a criminal, Majesty."

"How is that?"

"His lordship was boasting about what had happened between us and my friend attacked him in anger."

The Queen opened her eyes.

"Come nearer. I would hear more of this."

Marian passed the shoe and stockings to Edith Woodford and came over to stand before the Queen. She curtseyed.

"Now, Marian, let me hear of it."

"Your Majesty, you may not remember Richard Mordaunt, one time scribe to Lord Bathampton."

"Your dancing partner? Yes, I remember him. I also recall that you had wayward feelings for him at the time – but you were very young."

"And I married Sir Philip."

"You did indeed, Lady Forrester. So what became of your scribe?"

"Your Majesty, he entered a monastery, ten years ago."

"For love of you? Why, that is most romantic, is it not, ladies?"

The ladies smiled and nodded and giggled a little.

"But he is now imprisoned in the north tower? So how did that come about?"

Marian repeated all that Sir William had told her.

"And he tried to kill him? It is unfortunate that he did not succeed. Bathampton is a vile man. So, what do you want me to do about it, my Marian?"

Marian curtseyed again and lifted her eyes to meet those of the Queen in the large mirror backing her dressing table.

"Your Majesty, if the King knew the truth of the matter, would he not release Richard – or Brother Lawrence, as he is now?"

"His majesty has no option but to punish him for the attack on one of his body men. I cannot think that he will release him."

"But might he not show mercy if *you* asked him, your Majesty? He would listen to you."

"I fear that I do not have the ear of the King as I once had, Marian. However, I *will* ask him, in view of the provocation."

"Oh, thank you, your Majesty," Marian exclaimed and impetuously knelt and took the Queen's hand and kissed it.

The Queen looked down at Marian's fair head bent over her hand.

"Lady Forrester, he was a scribe and now he is a monk. It is not seemly that you show so much passion on his behalf."

Marian rose to her feet in confusion, her face pink.

"I am sorry, your Majesty. It is as you say."

The Queen motioned her ladies to cease their pampering and said she was ready for bed.

Two of them knelt with her to accompany her in her nightly prayers, which always included the petition that she might become pregnant with an heir to the throne.

*Little chance of that while they sleep in separate beds*, thought Marian.

They made her comfortable beneath the sheets while other ladies glided round the room, tidying up in preparation for the morning's routine. They all wished her a good night's sleep then went round again, blowing out all the candles except one, and left the chamber.

The days passed without any indication from the Queen that she had spoken to his majesty about Richard, and Marian had almost given up hope when one afternoon as they strolled in the gardens in the March sunshine, with the daffodils resplendent along the borders, the Queen whispered to Marian, "The King will not entertain the idea of releasing Brother Lawrence, but he will allow you to visit him in the circumstance of the reason for the attack. You must know that Lord Bathampton is pressing for the young monk's execution."

"That cannot happen! It must not be!"

"What will be is whatever the King decides, Marian. You will have no say in the matter. So I would advise you to visit him as soon as possible."

"I will, your Majesty, and thank you."

# CHAPTER 53

With anxious steps, Marian followed the serjeant-at-arms into a wing of the palace she had never entered before. Their footsteps echoed along stone floors of corridors that seemed endless, without drapes at the windows or any adornment along their narrow, cheerless lengths.

At last they reached a heavy oak door, which the serjeant unlocked. Once through it, he went before her up a winding flight of stone steps to the floor above. On a landing at the top of the stairs a thick-set man sat at a table, idly gazing out of a small window while digging out dirt from beneath his nails.

At the sight of the serjeant, the man jumped to his feet, a bunch of keys jangling from the belt at his waist. The two men exchanged a few words, the serjeant saluted Marian and descended the staircase, saying he would wait for her on the other side of the door to escort her back to the Queen's quarters.

The gaoler unhooked the ring of keys from his belt, selected a large one and opened the nearest door.

"You got a visitor," he announced and stood back to allow Marian to enter the room.

A figure in a monk's habit was seated at a table with his back to her, his quill pen busy scribing on a scroll of parchment by the flickering light of a candle. He lay down his pen and stood immediately and turned towards the door. The only natural light in the room came from a small window high in the curved wall and at first the prisoner seemed not to know who it was standing there before him.

"Got to lock you in," the gaoler apologised. The door swung shut and Marian heard the grating of the turning key.

"Brother Lawrence," Marian said.

"Lady Forrester?" His voice rose in surprise.

"Richard."

"Lady Marian."

"Richard," she repeated, not knowing what else to say.

His voice softened. "Marian."

"I am so sad to see you here."

"Don't be sad, my lady. They are treating me well enough."

"Are you in good health?"

"I am being fed and am able to wash and sleep." He indicated a bowl of water in an iron frame and his cot bed. "And I have work to do. Come, take the chair and I will sit on the bed."

When she did not move, he held out his hand. She took it and he guided her to the chair. She sat and looked up at him.

"Richard, I know why you are here, why you attacked him."

"Marian, I could not bear it, what he was saying about you. I still cannot bear it when I think – that he should have –"

Marian laid a hand on his arm. "Please pray for me, Richard, as I pray for you. Six months have passed and by the grace of God he did not impregnate me." She shuddered. "He is an evil man and no good will come of it, in the Lord's good time. Yes, I have suffered greatly, as have you, but the Queen and her ladies have been very kind and I have recovered somewhat, as you see." Her voice quietened. "Though I still feel tainted."

He sat on the end of his bed and looked at her, framed by light from the candle. "I perceive you as lovely as you always were."

"Richard, there is no need for you to suffer on my account. Have they said what is to happen to you?"

"My gaoler says he has had no news."

"Did you know Bathampton is pressing the King for your execution?"

Richard nodded gravely. "I had heard of it."

"His majesty has allowed me to visit you and I will not stop pleading with the Queen to petition for your release."

Shivering, she stood and paced the room while he watched her.

"It is so cold in here."

He interrupted her. "Have you any news of the monastery?"

"None, so far."

"Then I must hold to my vows."

"Richard, please tell me what is in your heart. I read it in your eyes every time you look at me."

"My lady, I cannot. I am not free."

"We were free once. We danced together. Have you forgotten?"

"How could I? And have you forgotten the reason I entered the monastery?"

Marian hung her head. She had married Philip and there was no going back.

The door opened and the gaoler peered in.

"Time's up, my lady," he said.

"I cannot leave you here, in the cold and dark." Despair was threatening to overwhelm her.

"The room is no longer cold, nor dark, Lady Forrester."

"I am glad of it, Brother Lawrence," she said and turned and walked through the open doorway. The gaoler locked the door behind her.

From a velvet purse hanging from her waist, she took a coin and pressed it into the man's hand.

"Please do everything you can to make him comfortable," she said.

The gaoler looked at the gold shining in his palm as if he could not believe his good fortune, then nodded.

"Everything I can," he agreed and, escorting her down the stairway, unlocked the door at the bottom and ushered her through, where the serjeant-at-arms was waiting to escort her back to all that was familiar.

She went up to her bedchamber, splashed her face with cold water, then lay on the bed, trying to quieten the turmoil in her breast and the thoughts tumbling around in her head. There was no escaping the fact that she loved Richard and so desperately wanted to be enfolded in his arms but he wasn't within reach and was never likely to be.

She dozed a little then got up and went to find the Queen's ladies who were not on duty.

They were twittering excitedly to each other in the large chamber where they gathered for relaxation but stopped abruptly when they saw her approach. Aware of her visit, they would not be satisfied until she had told them all about conditions in the north tower and her conversation with her monk-cum-knightly defender.

"He is in great danger from Lord Bathampton and I must get him out of there," Marian insisted, absentmindedly picking up someone's embroidery and crushing it in her hands. "I will speak to the Queen again, if she will allow me."

"I doubt that her majesty has the ear of the King at the moment," confided Edith Woodford, gently retrieving her embroidery. "You will not have heard what happened while you were absent."

"The entire court is talking of it," said another of the ladies.

"Talking of what?" asked Marian.

The young woman next to her paused dramatically before blurting out, "Her majesty walked into the King's private rooms and discovered Lady Jane Seymour sitting on his lap, whereupon she had a screaming fit."

"She has taken two of us with her and has locked herself in her bedchamber and won't come out," Marian was told. "She has sent Lady Jane home and their majesties are not speaking."

"They will have to communicate sooner or later, if the King wants a legitimate heir," another giggled.

Marian said she was sure the Queen would get round him. "She has always done so in the past."

# CHAPTER 54

*Place: The Monastery of St. Jude*

*Date: April, 1535*

When a company of the King's men arrived to demolish St. Jude's monastery, only the Abbot and Mother Superior were in occupation.

They watched helplessly and in great distress as sledge hammers, picks and shovels, iron bars and other weapons were employed without conscience or respect by the men who went lustily about their business.

Systematically, all the beautiful furnishings in the chapel were torn down and thrown into a farm cart; anything of intrinsic value was removed; and sacred statues, pictures, icons, furniture, tapestries and books were destroyed. Many of the precious scrolls were purloined to use as bungs in beer barrels.

Then the gangs of ruffians brought in for the purpose, who seemed to be enjoying themselves, turned their attention to the secular buildings. Decorations and glass were smashed, tiles destroyed, supporting columns attacked with sledgehammers again and again until they collapsed, bringing ceilings down with them. Even the lead on the roof was stripped and loaded into one of the carts.

After they had destroyed the nuns' cloisters, they surveyed the plot in which Marian's baby daughter and many elderly nuns had been buried. Mother Superior was present to warn them of God's wrath and terrible punishments in the next life if they disturbed the peace of the dead, buried in consecrated ground, and that was the only area left untouched.

The Abbot took to wandering around the grounds as if without purpose and without hope. One morning, he arrived in the stable yard and for a while watched the lads mucking out the stables.

"Then they have not yet released the horses, Thomas. Thankfully, normality is here, and peace."

"Yes, Father Abbot."

The Abbot continued to watch the lads at work, his thoughts obviously far away, his fingers fidgeting with something he was holding. Thomas stopped, pitch fork in hands, and stared.

"Father Abbot, is that the crucifix that belonged to Brother Barnabus?"

The Abbot looked confused for a moment then looked down at the object in his hands. "Is it? Yes, probably. I picked it up from my desk this morning before the sledge hammers arrived."

"Begging your pardon, Father Abbot, but I hears that Brother Barnabus has run away."

"It would appear so."

"He never would've left without his crucifix."

"But leave it he did, probably because the cord had frayed – see here."

"So where was it found?" Thomas pulled at his forelock in deference. "Begging your pardon for asking, Father."

"The brothers I sent to his cell to find him saw it on his bolster in the morning. The cord must have broken during the night and he didn't notice it had fallen from his neck."

Thomas remained silent.

"What troubles you, Thomas?"

"Father, I found the crucifix in the cart when Brother Alphonsus brought it back that night. Yes, the chord was broken. I took it to Brother Barnabus's cell straight away, thinking he would be searching for it, but he was still with you, in your study, so I left it on his bolster."

"But he did not come to my study with Brother Alphonsus that night. I understood he had gone straight to bed."

"Then I don't know where he was. All I knows is that he wasn't in his bed."

"But he did sleep in it that night because the blanket was rumpled and thrown back, or so it was reported to me."

"Then he would've found the crucifix on his bolster. He wouldn't have slept on it all night, would he, Father?"

"I think not. But if he did not rumple the blanket, who did? Who would have used the piss pot and left mud on the floor? Here is a mystery that I will have no time to solve now."

Several days later, the monastery lay in ruins, open to the sky, its former glory now just heaps of rubble strewn within its broken walls.

When all had been accomplished to the satisfaction of Lord Bathampton, who had supervised the destruction, the company packed up their tents and belongings and rode out, taking the Abbot and Mother Superior with them. Both may have been trembling at the thought of the fate that awaited them but they continued to hold their heads high in defiance.

Bathampton, well pleased with all that had been accomplished, was the last to leave. With his escort he rode into the stable yard to give orders that the horses should be brought out from their stalls and hitched together in preparation for their journey to London. A couple of old horses and another that was coughing were left where they were.

"Hey, you boy!"

Thomas came forward in response to Bathampton's shout.

"Yes, my lord?"

"What's your name?"

"Thomas, sire."

"Don't be afraid, Thomas. No one's going to hurt you. I'm leaving these three nags behind. They wouldn't last the journey. Take them to Forrester Hall and say that Lord Bathampton requests that they take care of them."

Thomas looked crestfallen.

"I suppose this means that you'll have no more wages."

Thomas nodded.

"Then tell them I said they should employ you. Here!" He rummaged in his saddle bag and threw Thomas a pouch of coins. "Take this for your trouble."

Thomas caught it. "Thank you, sire."

Lord Bathampton turned his horse's head as if to leave then hesitated and turned back. He had lingering suspicions in his mind and decided to chance one last throw of the dice.

"Thomas, I see that you are an intelligent lad." Thomas grinned and smoothed down his smock. "I judge," continued my lord, "that you know a lot about what goes on in the monastery. You see the monks come and go and must notice anything that happens out of the ordinary. Is that not so?"

"Yes, your lordship, that's about right."

"Have you noticed anything out of the ordinary in recent weeks?"

"No, sire," Thomas replied.

"Any strangers visiting? Anything that has happened that is different from the monks' usual routine? Anything you have noticed but can't explain?"

"No, sire," said Thomas. Then his face brightened. "Except –"

"Except?" Lord Bathampton prompted him. "What did you notice that perhaps no one else did?"

"I did not understand about Brother Barnabus running away and leaving his crucifix behind."

"Tell me," Bathampton encouraged him. "Why was that so strange?"

"Well, sire, he would not go anywhere without his crucifix. His brother made it for him, you see, when he came into the monastery, then died weeks later, and Brother Barnabus wore it all the time."

Bathampton's common sense told him that a missing monk leaving his crucifix behind could not possibly be of interest, but his instincts told him otherwise.

"Tell me everything, Thomas, and there'll be another pouch of coins for you."

So he learned about the missing Brother Barnabus and his crucifix with the frayed cord, the rumpled bed and used piss pot and mud on the floor.

"Mud?" queried his lordship.

Then he heard that the crucifix had been found in the cart, which had been brought back by Brother Alphonsus with muddy wheels late at night when all the brothers were asleep in their cells. Thomas remembered then that both spades were clean as if they had been washed, when he would have expected them to be muddy as well, because they must have been used to bury the chest.

"Chest?" Bathampton could barely keep the excitement out of his voice. "Did you say chest?"

"Yes, my lord," confirmed Thomas. "Brother Barnabus was sitting on it when they left, but they didn't bring it back."

"Do you know what was in the chest, Thomas?"

"No, sire, but it was very heavy because I helped load it onto the cart."

"And where is Brother Alphonsus now?"

"He left with the other brothers, sire, before you came to knock down the monastery."

"Alphonsus? Yes, I remember him. A very confident fellow. Does it seem to you, Thomas, that Brother Barnabus never came back to the monastery that evening?"

"I did wonder about that, my lord."

"Thank you, Thomas, for that information. This is for your honesty."

This time, he did not throw the pouch at Thomas but leaned down from the saddle and gave it to him.

"It seems that we must find this Brother Alphonsus and ask him what really happened that night."

"I never liked Brother Alphonsus," Thomas volunteered. "He may not tell you."

Lord Bathampton laughed delightedly.

"Don't concern yourself about that, Thomas. We have ways. Every liar tells the truth in the end."

With that, he turned his horse's head again and with a cheery wave to his informant, led his company from the yard and onto the road for their ride back to London.

# CHAPTER 55

*Place: Greenwich Palace*

*Date: April, 1535*

Meantime, the Queen was appearing at the side of the King on all formal occasions but was still denying him access to her bed and would not relent and go to his chamber. The King became increasingly frustrated and was heard to remark that the whole kingdom obeyed his every word except his harridan of a wife.

When he left Greenwich with his entourage and was gone for several weeks, it was rumoured that he was spending time at Wulfhall in Wiltshire, the home of Jane's parents, Sir John and Lady Margery Seymour.

It was not long before the Queen was sending a stream of messengers to Wulfhall. For a week there was no response but then a man arrived at Greenwich with a message from the King for the Queen. She replied immediately and from then on the arrival and departure of the messengers were daily occurrences. Finally, the King himself came striding into the palace, calling for his wife.

For two days the Queen's ladies and the Esquires to the Body of His Majesty were required to do very little for the royal couple, who were spending all their time in the King's private chambers, but at length they emerged and the court resumed its usual routine.

One of the King's pressing duties was deciding what to do about Sir Thomas More, who was still refusing to take the Oath of Supremacy. The King could not be seen to weaken, not even for a man of good reputation. There could be no exceptions.

Accordingly, Sir Thomas was arrested and tried, convicted of high treason after only fifteen minutes and sentenced to be hanged, drawn and quartered.

For a year he languished in the Tower, during which time he was visited on several occasions by Thomas Cromwell. He could have signed the Oath at any time, together with the Oath of Succession, proclaiming Anne as Queen and her children as legitimate heirs to the throne, but adamantly refused, insisting that Katharine was the king's true wife and the pope the head of the church.

The king relented in that he changed the means of death to beheading and, on 6th July 1535, Sir Thomas More was executed on Tower Hill and his body buried in an unmarked grave. His head was displayed on a pike on London Bridge – the fate of all traitors.

It was rumoured that, on receiving news of the execution, the king had scowled at Queen Anne, accusing her of being responsible for Sir Thomas's death.

Whatever the truth of that, happily, in the same month, the Queen announced to the world what her ladies had kept secret for several weeks, that her monthly flow had ceased and she was pregnant again. Her physicians and soothsayers predicted that this time the expected baby was the long-awaited heir to the throne, and there was great rejoicing throughout the land.

Now the King watched over his wife with extraordinary solicitude. She was not allowed to carry anything, not even a shawl, and whenever she sat, a footstool was brought for her feet and cushions were placed behind her back and head.

Marian was glad to see her so happy and the King in such good humour, not least because she had decided to speak to the Queen again about the release of Richard. She had not been to see him since her first visit but often sent trusted servants to enquire about his health and welfare and to take a bag of coins to whichever gaoler was on duty, to make sure that he lacked no comfort that she could provide.

It was one of these servants who came back with the news. Marian was in conversation with one of the Queen's jewellers, arranging for the replacement of a stone that had been dislodged from a sapphire and diamond ring, when she became conscious of the man hovering in the background. She dismissed the jeweller with an instruction to return the repaired ring on the following day, then turned to speak to the man she had entrusted with the latest bribe to Richard's gaoler.

"Michael, you wanted me? What is it?"

The servant bowed low and held out the purse of coins.

"Lady Marian, I did not deliver the purse because he has gone."

"Who's gone?"

"Brother Lawrence, my lady."

Fear restricted her throat as she croaked, "Where has he gone?"

"I could not find out, my lady. All the doors in the tower were unlocked and the door of his cell was wide open. All of his things had gone and there was no sign of him anywhere."

"Not to the scaffold? Please God not to the scaffold!"

"Oh, no, my lady, have no fear about that. I found one of the men who had been guarding him – he was swilling beer in the guard room – and he said that the monk had been released."

"Released?"

"That's what he said, my lady."

A surge of hope rose in Marian's breast.

"Thank you, Michael. Take this for your trouble."

"Thank you, my lady. Very grateful."

He bowed and left.

She had to wait two days before the opportunity arose to speak to the Queen. Her majesty had replaced the repaired ring on her finger and was holding her hand up to the light from the chandelier in her bedchamber, turning it this way and that to catch the sparkle.

Breathlessly she said, "Your Majesty."

"What is it, Marian? I must say, he has done a splendid job in matching up the stones. One would never know that the diamond is not the original. Well, what is it, my Marian?"

"Richard – Brother Lawrence – he is no longer a prisoner in the north tower."

"I know it. The King has released him. Did I not tell you?"

"No, your Majesty."

The Queen winked at her and whispered in her ear. "His majesty is very pleased with me at the moment and will do whatever I ask. So I asked him to release Richard, and he has."

"Your Majesty, I don't know what to say."

"I thought it would please you, though I don't approve of your intense interest in that young man – I never have. He is out of your life now. Let it rest there."

But Marian could not let the matter rest there. She needed to know where he had gone and a few anxious days later contrived to speak to her father-in-law. A banquet followed by dancing had been arranged to celebrate the royal couple's good news and Marian sidled up to sit next to Sir William in the great hall.

"Marian, my dear, what a pleasure to see you. We so seldom meet these days."

"Their majesties keep us both busy, William. Tell me, how is the family at Forrester Hall?"

"Everyone there is well and I have received the welcome news that my dear Susan is in the same condition as her majesty."

"Oh, William, I am so happy for you. Please send her my sincere good wishes when next you write."

Sir William acknowledged her request with a bow of his head.

"And young Marjery?" Marian continued. "How is she and her baby?"

"All is well there, also. My wife depends on her exceedingly. And her baby daughter is a happy playmate for our son."

"William, had you heard that the King has released Richard from his imprisonment?"

"I did hear some mention of it. Lord Bathampton is not best pleased but there is nothing he can do about it."

"His lordship would have sent Richard to the block if he had had his way."

"Then it is just as well that he did not."

"Since the Queen has fallen pregnant, the King is not denying her anything."

Sir William looked astonished. "You petitioned the Queen?"

"Endlessly, and of course, she remembers Richard from the days of our dancing classes when Philip and I first came to court."

"Do you know where Brother Lawrence is now?"

"No. I hoped you might have news. He has just disappeared."

"To his great advantage, I would say, in view of Lord Bathampton's desire for his death."

"But I need to know where he is, that he is safe."

Sir William patted the hand that was gripping his sleeve.

"I am sure he is quite safe. Now please release my arm, my dear. I do believe you are restricting the flow of blood."

"Oh, William, I am so sorry. It's just –"

"It's just that you are taking too much interest in that young man, Marian, as you always have. It is not becoming in a lady of your standing."

"Please don't lecture me, William."

Her troubled eyes looked up into his and she saw the familiar twinkle in them.

"I would not dream of it," he said. "But here comes a partner to request your hand for the next dance. The master of ceremonies has just announced the name but I didn't quite catch what he said."

"You tease!" Marian laughed. "Of course you did!"

"Did I? Then it must be the dance that Monsieur choreographed especially for you. Its name has quite slipped my memory."

"Then I will remind you, William," said Marian, delighting in the game he was playing with her. "It is titled *Marian's Measure.*"

"Why, so it is. *Marian's Measure*. And here is your partner. Enjoy your freedom, Marian, and don't worry about our young friend. I am sure all is well."

"Oh, I do hope so," she answered and turned to smile at the young courtier who was bowing and proffering his arm.

# CHAPTER 56

*Place: Greenwich Palace*

*Date: Early January, 1536*

The Christmas festivities were over. They had been as exuberant as ever but the Queen had paced herself, had danced very little, and had slept a great deal. She was eating well and was growing more contented and happier as her belly swelled. With two months still to wait until her confinement and the baby making its presence felt by energetically moving around inside her, the physicians pronounced both of them in excellent health.

The only cloud on the royal couple's horizon concerned news from Kimbolton Castle, Cambridgeshire, the present home of the Princess Dowager of Wales, Katharine of Aragon. A few days previously she had written a letter to the King. The Queen was contemptuous.

"Imagine her effrontery," she complained to her ladies, "in addressing him as her 'most dear lord, king and husband'. Husband, indeed!"

"Please do not upset yourself, Majesty," pleaded Edith Woodford. "It is not good for the baby prince when you get so upset."

"But I want to tell you all what she wrote."

"Then please lie down and let us massage your stomach with aromatic oils, Majesty," pleaded another.

"And I will massage your legs and feet, if you will permit me," offered another.

They all knew that, if the Queen was ill or, God forbid, miscarried while they were on duty, it would not go well for any of them.

"Marian, come and hold my hand. I know you will listen to me."

Marian came at once and sat on a chair by the side of the recumbent Queen and held her hand tightly and gently stroked her cheeks.

"We will all listen, your Majesty," she said quietly, "if you will promise not to upset yourself. You are the rightful Queen, wife to the King of the realm. He loves you very much and you are bearing his son, the future heir to the throne. You must do nothing to endanger the precious life within you. Calm yourself and tell us quietly, begging your Majesty's pardon."

"You have always been my friend, little Marian."

"As you were friend to me when I first came to court, your Majesty."

The Queen nodded and said, more calmly now, “Katharine said he should remember to safeguard his soul instead of pampering his body. She said she forgives him and prays that God will pardon him also. How dare she? How dare she!”

Her voice was rising again.

“Hush, my Queen, hush,” said Marian soothingly, stroking her arm.

“Then she beseeched him to be a good father to Princess Mary – that bastard Mary.”

“Begging your Majesty’s pardon, you will understand that request, being a mother yourself,” Edith Woodford ventured.

“Yes, I suppose so, but she then had the immodesty to say that her eyes desired him above all things and signed herself Katharine the Queen. The Queen! She signs herself so! I am the Queen, am I not? There is only one Queen of England and I am that Queen!”

“Hush, hush, Majesty,” Marian whispered again. “Of course you are the Queen. Everyone recognises that.”

“Not everyone, Lady Marian. The papists do not. She wrote that the hour of her death was drawing on – how can she possibly know that? But I hope it is true! Oh, I do so hope it is true!”

On 8th January, the King received news that Katharine of Aragon, his first wife and one-time Queen of England, had died the previous day.

The Queen had the grace to weep among her ladies in her private chamber, in spite of her protestations of relief. However, both she and the King decked themselves in yellow from top to toe, insisting that yellow was the Spanish colour of mourning, though few believed that it was so.

They took two-year-old Elizabeth with them to church that morning and sent for her to join them in the great hall in the evening, requiring her nursemaids to parade her before the court. Everyone admired the young princess’s natural regal bearing and endearing baby talk and commented on the happy anticipation of seeing her and her long-awaited brother growing up together.

For the following two weeks, while a funeral was in preparation at Peterborough Abbey for the Princess Dowager (which the King had no intention of attending), there was a light and relaxed atmosphere at court. The King was heard to be humming to himself as he walked the corridors and attended to the business of the kingdom, the ladies smiled more readily, the gentlemen laughed at silly jokes, and the Queen looked radiant as she basked in the solicitude and approval of her husband.

Such was the mood on the morning of the twenty-fourth of January, the day of the joust held in honour of the little prince yet to be born.

As before, the Queen sat with her ladies on a daïs, protected now by a canvas shelter, the judges below them and courtiers on each side. All were wrapped in layers of furs to keep out the bitter winter chill.

The King was again leading the Red Team and the Queen drew attention to her brother, George, waiting in line in the opposing Black Team.

The blast from the trumpets quietened the crowd, a judge read out the rules appertaining to that occasion, the King rode forward, the trumpet voluntary announced the beginning of the tournament, the marshall lowered his flag and the joust began.

At the half-way interval, tension was rising as the Black Team was ahead of the King's team by ten points. Neither team had yet unhorsed an opponent.

Sipping mulled wine, the Queen speculated on the final outcome of the tournament and sent one of her servants to lay a wager in favour of the King's team as eventual winners, because she could not wager otherwise.

"However," she whispered to Marian, who was sitting next to her, "if Black Team win and my brother is champion knight, as he is likely to be, I believe he will present his favour to you," and she laughed at her lady-in-waiting's confusion. "Come now, I have noticed the way he always looks at you and am sure that your acceptance of it would warm his heart on this cold day."

When the marshall indicated that the riders were again ready to defend their honour, the trumpets blasted, the spectators quietened and the next two opponents approached the lists and waited, lances held horizontally. The marshall lowered his flag and the second half of the tournament began.

Each team had earned another five points before all eyes were turned on the third pair of riders.

"'Tis my husband and my brother pitted against each other," the Queen commented, looking anxious. "I wish it were not so."

The marshall's flag dropped and the two riders approached each other, their horses' canter having escalated to a gallop by the time they drew abreast. Viscount George Boleyn's lance made contact with the King's but neither snapped. However, the King's lance had slammed against his opponent's grand guard and the young man was almost unseated, gaining Red Team five points.

At the end of the lists, both riders accepted new lances from their squires and turned their horses for the return attempt. The atmosphere around the arena was intense and Marian was conscious that the Queen was holding her breath.

This time, the riders kicked their horses into a gallop from the outset and closed in on each other at great speed. Their lances entangled but Viscount George's hit home before they had passed each other.

The crowd watched as initially the King seemed to withstand the blow but then he began to sway in the saddle as his horse carried him to the end of the list, and he dropped his lance. Finally, he fell heavily, landing on his back, his horse on top of him.

The crowd emitted a concerted gasp then there was not a sound in the whole arena and no one moved.

The horse struggled to its feet and trotted away, breaking the silence, then there was a frenzied flurry of activity as people rushed to the King from every direction. Someone raised his head and shoulders and pushed up the vizor while shouting orders, a groom ran towards them with a bucket of water that was slopping over the rim, and the crowd gathering around him were shouting and gesticulating at each other. A tall man pushed his way to the front of the crowd and Marian recognised him as one of the physicians on duty.

She was suddenly aware that the Queen had dropped her furs, had left her side and was descending the steps. She and the other ladies in the escort scrambled after her and ran with her to her husband.

The crowd made way for her to kneel beside him, which she did with great difficulty due to her condition. She took his hand, the gauntlets having been removed, and instructed a young man to take off his helmet.

The King lay quite still, his eyes closed, not responding to anyone. In no time at all, a stretcher was brought, he was laid upon it, and an anxious procession made its way from the tilt yard to the nearest door of the palace and with difficulty to his bedchamber, where he was lifted off the stretcher and laid upon his bed.

The Queen was beside herself, crying and speaking his name, without response.

"Your Majesty," said one of the King's esquires who had joined the group, "'twould be better if you would allow your ladies to escort you outside. Ladies, please."

The Queen protested vehemently.

"We will call you the minute he opens his eyes," promised Sir William, who was also in attendance.

"Come, your Majesty," her ladies implored her, "you must give the physicians space to examine his majesty. You can do no good here. Come away, your Majesty."

The Queen struggled to remain.

"You must not cause the little prince any distress," Marian cautioned her. "Please let us escort you outside. They have promised to call you the moment the King regains his wits."

At the mention of their baby, the Queen quietened and allowed her ladies to take her from the room into the anteroom, where they made her comfortable on a couch and proceeded to massage her shoulders and head, her stomach and arms, and brought her a posset which they would have her take. When she wanted to get up and pace the floor, they restrained her.

The waiting group received constant news of the condition of the King. Lord Bathampton reported that he had no broken bones but there was an ugly gash on his left leg. Still he was not responding to their blandishments.

Marian turned her back on his lordship as she could not bear to be near him and he returned to the bedchamber without further comment.

At the end of about an hour, Viscount George Boleyn was escorted into the room. He had washed and changed. He looked panicked when he heard that the King was unable to speak, knowing he was responsible for his majesty's plight, and said he feared that he had killed him, but was greatly relieved to hear the physician's report that the King was breathing normally.

It was a full two hours before Sir William slipped out of the bedchamber to report that the King was beginning to come round and was calling for the Queen. She went to him immediately and knelt by the side of the bed and took his hand, murmuring endearments. He made no response and she looked over to the physicians, who were standing on the other side of the bed in whispered conference.

"Keep talking to him," one of them advised and came across to wipe the King's face with a cold-water cloth. He moaned quietly.

"Your Majesty, your Majesty," his physician said to him, "her majesty the Queen is here and is greatly concerned for you."

"Speak to me, Henry," the Queen was pleading. "Dearest, please open your eyes and speak to me."

"We will bleed him again," the physicians decided and proceeded to do so from a vein in his uninjured leg. The only sound in the room was the murmur of the priests who had been summoned to pray.

After a great while, the King moaned again and moved his head and opened his eyes.

"Oh, my dear, you're back with us!" the Queen exclaimed.

"What happened?" he asked.

"You were knocked from your horse and have not been awake for two hours. I was so worried about you."

He closed his eyes again.

"Ladies, we must make him comfortable now and he must rest," said one of his physicians. "Lord Bathampton, please escort the Queen and her ladies from the room."

"Assuredly," he replied and offered his arm to the Queen to help her rise, then ushered her and her ladies from the room, softly closing the door.

"Lady Marian." Drawing close, he managed to whisper to her, his mouth very near her ear. "I think of you by day and dream of you by night. It is my constant hope to be to you again what I was in the past."

Appalled, Marian drew away and turned on him a look expressing all her contempt and fury. His lordship appeared unmoved.

"I would sooner be dead," she hissed at him.

"Say not so," he replied. "And what of Brother Lawrence? Would you say the same to him? I fancy not. So where is young Richard?"

"He's where you'll never find him!" She hoped that this was true.

"So he has abandoned you to the attentions of such as myself? How ungallant! But then, of course, he has taken a vow of chastity. Such a pity. He will never know what delights he is missing."

Before Marian could answer, he turned and went back into the King's bedchamber. If she had been a man, she would have slapped his face with a gauntlet and challenged him to a duel, but she was not a man, and did not know how to show how much she loathed and despised him. She wanted to scream, to cry, but the Queen was calling for her and all she could do now was attend to her majesty and go with the other ladies to the Queen's rooms and calm her so that she could sleep.

# CHAPTER 57

*Place: Greenwich Palace*

*Date: 29th January, 1536*

The King was kept in bed for three more days. He was then allowed to take up his normal duties provided he did not tire himself or further damage his injured leg.

There was a strange atmosphere in court on the morning of the second day of his recuperation, the day of the funeral of the Princess Dowager, Katharine. The King decided to ride out into the surrounding fields and woods and was allowed to do so by his physicians as long as he took several attendants with him and the horses were not spurred to any speed above a brisk trot. At first, he remonstrated at this restriction but then saw the sense of it and agreed.

When selecting the men who should ride with him, he very obviously passed over his brother-in-law, Viscount George Boleyn, who had unseated him. The Queen expressed her regret to her ladies but said nothing to her husband.

Her brother requested an audience with her during the morning and confessed himself greatly distressed at causing the King's injury and his majesty's apparent anger at the incident. He did not say so but it was clear to the Queen's ladies that he was very fearful of the consequences as he pleaded with his sister to mediate between them.

When he left, she became extremely anxious. Her ladies persuaded her to rest. She agreed, saying she did not feel at all well, so they made her comfortable on her bed then quietly left the chamber, hoping that Marian and Edith Woodford, who were in attendance at her bedside, would be able to persuade her to sleep.

At about the time that the cortege left Kimbolton Castle for Peterborough Cathedral, bearing the Princess Dowager Katharine to her burial, the worst of everyone's nightmares happened.

The Queen was very restless, turning this way and that in an endeavor to sleep, then the pains began. She cried out and sat up, clutching her belly, and called for her ladies to support her, then to help her off the bed.

Her screams and the shouts of Marian and Edith Woodford brought the other ladies scrambling into the bedchamber but all they could do was watch in horror as the blood began to pool at her majesty's feet and she went into labour.

There was nothing that they or her physicians could do except carry her back to bed and hold her when the pains were at their height. The prayers of the priests in the background were of no avail and the Queen was delivered of a dead son two hours later.

When it was all over and she had been washed and carried by stretcher to another bedchamber, there was not a sound to be heard in the whole of the palace except the anguished weeping of the Queen and her pitiful questioning over and over, "What will become of me? What will become of me?"

Her ladies wondered that, too.

A messenger was sent to find the King. He strode into the chamber hours later, his eyes glittering dark and merciless, his voice without pity for the distress of his wife.

"So, madam, you have failed again! You have born a dead prince! I have no need of a Queen who cannot bear live sons. This is a monstrous act of ineptitude and not to be tolerated!"

So saying, he left the room with as much ill grace as he had entered it and the Queen and her ladies did not see him for two weeks.

They were as much distressed as their Queen as they tried to comfort and console her and attend to her every need, but a new and terrible humour was with her now as they witnessed her fear.

She asked them to try to contact her brother and have him come to her but they were given to understand that the King had expressly forbidden any contact with him or with her daughter, Elizabeth. The King's withdrawn affection for George was evidenced when an expected honour, the Order of the Garter, was denied him and given to another.

The Queen took a long time to recover from the miscarriage and moved around her suite of rooms like an aged woman, often with trembling limbs. Her ladies walked with her in the gardens but her pallor remained, her eyes grew lacklustre and every morning and evening her brush captured handfuls of falling hair.

They tried to keep from her the news that Lady Jane Seymour had returned to court and had been given a suite of rooms well away from the Queen's, but she heard the gossip and her agony and fear increased by the day.

Winter passed and Spring came again but there was no sunshine in the Queen's rooms and her attendants felt isolated from the rest of the court. They heard, if she did not, that Lady Jane was now accompanying the King on many of his royal appearances and was at his side, taking the place of the Queen, at official functions.

One event of great happiness occurred in March, though the ladies thought it prudent not to inform the Queen, and that was the birth of a healthy daughter to Lady Susan, wife of Sir William. In a note delivered to Marian, he asked her to rejoice with him, though they could not meet at this time of constraint between his lord and her lady.

Towards the end of April, musician Mark Smeaton was arrested, accused of being the Queen's lover. The Queen was appalled at the suggestion but surprising news came that he had confessed to the liaison.

Sir William contrived to speak to Marian, to warn her to distance herself from the Queen, but Marian replied that this was not possible and, even if it were, she could not betray the lady who had been her friend for so long and who trusted her.

It was he who suggested that the confession had been extracted under torture. As the young man was merely a commoner, torture was permitted.

"And this will not be the end of it," Sir William said before leaving.

Another courtier, Henry Norreys, Groom of the Stool, was arrested for the same reason and vehemently denied his guilt. The accusation against him was that he visited the Queen in her bedchamber and his assertion that he had been courting one of her ladies-in-waiting at the time was disregarded.

His arrest was followed with the imprisonment of Sir Francis Weston and then William Brereton, a Groom of the King's Privy Chamber.

The Queen was distraught and her ladies with her. These men were friends, innocent of anything more than mild flirtations with her majesty, and the women were distressed to contemplate the fate towards which this manhunt was heading.

Thomas Wyatt, a poet and friend of the Boleyns, was next to be taken but he was later released, probably because he was a friend of Thomas Cromwell, the man thought to be behind the accusations. Sir Richard Page was another victim but further investigation could not implicate him sexually with the Queen and he too was released.

There was nothing anyone could say or do to hold back the ominous tide that was surging towards her majesty. It was very evident that the King was determined to rid himself of Anne. Imagining how he intended to do so was a black cloud hanging over the whole court.

Finally, George Boleyn, the Queen's brother, was arrested and accused of treason following two incidents of incest. She said it would be laughable if the situation were not so serious.

Serious it was. On 2nd May, they heard a great commotion approaching the Queen's rooms, the marching of heavy boots along the wooden floor of the corridor, shouted orders then the stamp of feet coming to attention. There was the rattle of the circular iron handle as those outside attempted to gain entrance, without success as the door was locked. Then the barked command to open the door in the name of the King, and a heavy thud as a halberdier crashed against it.

The Queen, surprisingly very calm now, signalled to one of her women to unlock the door. She did so and stepped back hurriedly as a captain and six of his men marched into the room and approached her majesty. She did not move and the captain, appearing very uncomfortable about the task he had been instructed to carry out, stood to attention in front of her and bowed.

"Your Majesty," he said, "I have orders from his majesty the King to arrest you and take you to the Tower of London. A barge awaits you. I pray your Majesty will come willingly as I have no wish to use force."

The Queen stood regally before him and drew herself up to her full height.

"I am ready to go," she said.

Two of the guard moved to stand behind her, two others came to stand on each side of her and two preceded her, the captain leading the way.

"May we accompany her majesty?" Marian asked. "She will need us with her."

"My instructions are that she goes alone," the captain replied.

"Your Majesty –" Edith Woodford began but the Queen cut her short.

"Do not fear for me, ladies," she said. "In all things I wish to please my lord, the King. Pray for me."

With that, the party departed as noisily as they had arrived, leaving her ladies in shock, some rendered speechless, others sobbing.

In the ensuing days, all they could do was busy themselves tidying her rooms and making sure they were cleaned and aired, so that everything would be welcoming on her return.

They did manage to obtain permission to send her a change of underclothes and gowns and, among the folds, Marian concealed a note of love and affection, begging her grace to keep her spirits raised, to take strength in the knowledge of her innocence, and to pray daily, as they were doing.

Sir William informed Marian that the Queen had written the King a letter expressing her loyalty and affection for him, pleading the cause of the men wrongly imprisoned and asking for herself a lawful trial at which she could express her innocence.

On 12th May, the four men were tried in Westminster Hall before a jury that included Anne's father, Sir Thomas Boleyn. William Brereton, Sir Francis Weston and Sir Henry Norreys maintained their innocence and only Mark Smeaton pleaded guilty but all were convicted of high treason because of their adultery with the Queen. The sentence for each was to be hung, drawn and quartered.

The verdicts rendered her majesty's guilt a foregone conclusion.

On May 14th, the Archbishop of Canterbury, Thomas Cranmer, declared the marriage of Henry and Anne 'null and void'.

On May 15th, the Queen and her brother were tried separately in the Tower before a jury of twenty seven peers. She was accused of incest, adultery and high treason and furthermore that she and her 'lovers' were plotting the King's death so that she could later marry Sir Henry Norreys.

Unanimously, the jury found both of them guilty. The punishment for a woman was being burnt alive at the stake.

Mercifully, the King commuted all the sentences to beheading. He sent for an expert swordsman from France to carry out the execution of Anne rather than have a queen killed by a common axe.

# CHAPTER 58

*Place: Greenwich Palace*

*Date: May, 1536*

Marian's hands shook as she held the letter she had received that morning from the Queen and read it aloud to Edith, whom she had summoned to her chamber.

"My dearest Marian and Edith," it began. "My husband, my lord and my King, has acceded to my request and will allow two of my ladies to keep me company here in the Tower until my forthcoming execution. It is my wish that you, Lady Marian, and Lady Edith Woodford should be those two ladies. If you love me and believe you could endure incarceration in this dreadful place, please come to me with all haste."

There followed instructions about clothing and other items to bring with them and the request that they send their answer by return.

"What say you, Edith?" Marian asked her.

"Need you ask, Marian? Of course I will go to her as you will, no doubt."

Marian nodded agreement and words were unnecessary as they embraced and shared their tears before calling their maids to help them prepare for the journey.

Marian immediately sent the messenger to find Sir William and acquaint him with the situation. Both ladies were very surprised and grateful when he arrived early on the morning of their departure, ahead of their escort, and insisted on accompanying them to the Tower. Of course, he had had to petition the King for his clemency in this matter and had received his majesty's permission to do so.

"Oh, William, dear," Marian said on his arrival, "we shall be so glad of your company."

The other ladies gathered to send them off with tears and good wishes and messages of love and support for the Queen, whom they knew they would never see again.

It was the morning of the execution at the Tower of London of the Queen's brother and the four young men convicted with him.

With trepidation, Marian and Edith, who had formed a firm friendship in recent months, followed the captain of the guard and Sir William along the bare corridors towards the tower where Richard had been imprisoned but they turned right there and came to a door leading out to the towpath, well away from the central part of the palace. On the bank of the river was a flight of rough wooden steps leading down to a small landing stage where a wherry was awaiting them.

The two boatmen took from them the bundles containing the clothes the Queen had requested and their own changes of clothing as well as packages of food for the journey down river, then Sir William and the captain of the guard helped them climb into the boat. Once all were seated, the boatman put out into the strong current.

It was a warm and sunny morning, for which the passengers were very grateful.

Marian felt as though her whole world was crumbling about her but was ashamed for thinking about herself when the Queen, her friend, was facing the ignoble end of her young life, convicted of crimes and sins of which she was not guilty and of which Marian was sure God would not hold her accused. The guilt lay (dare she admit it, even to herself?) with the King and those who toadied up to him – in other words, all the members of the court, who feared their fate if they did not.

She felt a movement by her side as Sir William held out his arm towards her, inviting her into his embrace. Without hesitation, she cuddled up to him and felt again the love and protection he had offered her since she had been a little girl.

She was aware of Edith sitting bolt upright on the other side of him, and he must have noticed also, because his other arm was extended and, without hesitation or embarrassment, she too moved over to share his comforting compassion.

Sir William made some light comment about his unexpected good fortune in holding two ladies in his arms and the lighterman rowing the wherry said he would gladly change places if the gentleman would take to the oars, and he would not charge for this extra duty.

The captain of the guard then said he would fight him for the honour, and there was a great deal of laughter among them, which lightened the mood. All in the boat were aware of their journey's end.

After a while, the ladies were able to leave the shelter of Sir William's arms and take notice of their surroundings. At first, in the lower reaches of the river, traffic was light and they passed the time of day with the pedlars and tradesmen trekking along the towpath and the cart drivers bringing their goods to the London markets but as they drew nearer to the capital, the river became the great highway it was known to be.

They passed one-, two- and three-masted ships with their prows directed towards the sea, taking advantage of the current. Others were tied up at various wharves and jetties, unloading their cargoes of wool, timber, iron, paper, tallow, hides and much more.

Sir William pointed ahead and they saw, on the northern bank, the great edifice of the White Tower with its four sturdy projecting towers at each corner, dwarfing everything around it.

Ahead was London Bridge built over nineteen arches, with shops and houses, some seven stories high, built against both parapets. The ladies shuddered to see, displayed on pikes, rows of the severed heads of traitors, tarred and boiled to preserve them. Later they would be thrown into the river.

Their wherry needed to cross to the further bank and the passengers marvelled greatly at the skill of their oarsman. Ignoring the uncouth shouts and commands and orders and warnings as smaller craft narrowly missed colliding with them and with each other, their boatman kept his eyes darting in every direction and his wits about him as he rowed them safely through the melée.

By this time, Marian and Edith were greatly discomfited. Their black velvet gowns were wet with dirty river water, the passengers having been rocked and splashed on numerous occasions. Marian reflected that his majesty had little concern for his Queen's ladies and if it had not been for the good humour of Sir William, the captain and the two boatmen, all of whom were understanding of the circumstances, she and Edith would have been very distressed indeed.

"I promise you," said Sir William, "that for your return journey –" He paused, realising the import of his remark, then continued, "– for your return journey you will not be subjected to this tedious river trip. I will have a carriage at your disposal if I have to drive it myself."

They did not enter the precincts of the fortress through the infamous Traitors' Gate, as Marian had expected, but through a smaller entrance at the side of the curtain wall. A challenge from a man-at-arms on the battlements was answered by the oarsman with a shouted password and the portcullis was raised by means of a winch turned by a yeoman of the guard on the other side of the wall.

They passed through the archway and so into the greensward between the two curtain walls, where they alighted at a small jetty and the boatmen said they would wait till the captain of the guard and Sir William returned.

The two gentlemen and two ladies, who were trying to keep the hems of their gowns away from the damp grass and mud, crossed a wooden drawbridge that would be high above water level if the moat was purposely flooded. A second password gained them entrance beneath another portcullis into the inner ward, where they were met by a yeoman warder, who would not allow the two gentlemen to venture any further.

Sir William passed their bundles to their official escort and adjured the ladies to be of good courage and of cheery disposition, for the sake of the Queen, and to give her majesty his high regard and farewells.

With great apprehension and eyes full of unshed tears, they promised to give her majesty all that she needed in her final hours. Edith curtsied and the hem of Marian's gown fell in the mud as she gave Sir William a last hug, then they turned to follow their escort.

The Queen was imprisoned, not in the cells, but in some comfort in the rooms she had occupied before her coronation.

To say that she was delighted to see them is an understatement. She opened her arms wide and embraced them both, a familiarity that was never allowed in court.

"Your Majesty, we are both wet and muddy," Marian apologised.

"'Tis of no matter," the Queen assured them. "You have brought the gowns I requested?"

"They're in the bundles," Edith replied.

"Then I will change at once and so will you, after you have taken some refreshment."

She rang a bell and a servant attended on her and was ordered to bring ale and bread and cheese for the ladies. They shared the meal, frugal but sufficient, while sitting on benches at a plain wooden table.

Then her majesty said she greatly desired to wear the blue gown so they retired to her bedchamber. This was sparsely furnished, a large four-poster bed taking up most of the space. Two small truckle beds had been placed on either side for Marian and Edith.

They washed the Queen as best they could from a basin of cold water then helped her into clean underclothes and her gown, which was deep blue over a pale blue underskirt. Its square neck was encrusted with pearls and diamonds, the pattern being repeated on her outer gown where the edges left her slim waist and fell diagonally to the floor.

Marian brushed and dressed her long hair and was concerned to find, among the dark brown, shades of grey that had not been there before. She reminded herself that it was of little consequence now and her breast tightened at the thought.

She then fastened her majesty's head dress, fashioned in the French style she had always worn since returning to England from the French court. The pattern of pearls and diamonds was repeated around the edges, alleviating the sombre black satin base. Edith fastened round her neck her favourite pearl necklace – a copy of Princess Mary's but with a gold letter B supporting the three drop pearls.

"You may consider it strange," the Queen mused, "that I wish to dress for my gaoler as I would if I had audience with my King."

She looked down at the swathes of brown and gold now lying on the flagstones, the gown in which she had been arrested two weeks previously.

"You may discard this one and the others you kindly sent," she said. "I will have no further need of them."

"Do not say so," pleaded Edith, tears welling up in her eyes.

"Edith, my dear, I speak truly. It is unlikely that his majesty will change his mind during the next three days, having installed Lady Jane Seymour in his heart and I have no doubt in his bed, where I once reigned. He has, however, relented over the manner of my death and I am to be beheaded, not burnt alive at the stake. I hear that he has sent to France for an expert swordsman. That is of great comfort."

Marian marvelled at the Queen's composure and wondered at the effort it must take for her to speak so calmly, as if it were not her own death she was discussing but someone else's.

However, while her two ladies were changing their own gowns, replacing black with black, the Queen spoke very softly, asking that they would go with her to the block and support her should she grow faint or show any signs of fear.

"Will you be able to accomplish that for me, my dears?" she asked and said she would not be able to face her death without them by her side.

Their reassurances were fervent and sincere. Marian thought her heart would break and wondered whether she would have the fortitude to fulfil her promise but knew that she must. She looked across at Edith and guessed her thoughts were running along the same lines.

"Then, my dears," continued her majesty, "you must forget all this folly and go on to live your own lives. I suspect that Lady Jane will request that you become her ladies-in-waiting – she would be foolish not to do so when you have given such loyal service in the past."

"She has already asked us, your Majesty," Edith confessed.

"And I trust you have acceded to her request?"

"I cannot," Marian blurted out. "I have loved and served you, your Majesty, and cannot on a whim change my loyalty to one who has taken everything from you."

"As I took everything from Queen Katharine and, I fear, as someone will take everything from cousin Jane if she cannot bear a living son. Have you told her you do not accept?"

"Yes and I have begged leave to return home to help Lady Susan manage Forrester Hall and the estate. She has much to do there as well as raising two young children without their father."

"Lady Susan is a very fortunate woman. But you must give time and thought to your own happiness. Find and marry Richard. Ah, those dancing lessons! What happy days they were, little Marian. His majesty loved me then."

Marian could feel her cheeks burning and stammered something inconsequential. The Queen looked at her and smiled.

"You love Richard, do you not?"

"Yes, your Majesty," Marian confessed, her answer barely above a whisper.

"Then what matters that the young scribe is now a monk? Fie! Sir William told me that the monastery has been destroyed by Cromwell and the monks and nuns have been pensioned off."

"That is so, your Majesty."

"Then seize your happiness, Marian, while you can. The opportunity may not be there forever. It is no longer there for me. Now come and read to me, Edith. A dark humour is upon me and I have need of comfort."

Edith picked up the Bible that was lying on a side table and looked at the Queen questioningly.

"The twenty-third psalm, Edith – *'Yea, though I walk through the valley of the shadow of death, I will fear no evil'*."

During the night they could not sleep for the sound of the Queen's anguished weeping, which Marian thought was the most terrible sound she had ever heard. They both crawled into bed with her and one or the other held her close all night until, in the early hours of the morning, she managed to sleep and they too could doze until she needed them again.

Next morning, Marian requested that the Queen might walk a little in the grounds and assent was given.

For an hour, they tried to put aside all thoughts of the coming horror and walked and chatted as lightheartedly as they were able, barely conscious of the two warders walking discreetly several paces behind them.

On the way, they met the ravenmaster and assisted him in feeding the ravens from a large bag of seeds and watched as he gently held one a prisoner so as to clip its wing.

"They must not be allowed to fly away," he said, "or 'twill bring about the end of the monarchy." Then he clapped his hand over his mouth and flushed as red as the trimmings on his dark blue tunic and stammered his apologies to the Queen. She graciously begged him not to distress himself and said ruefully, “The Queen is dead. Long live the Queen.”

So that day passed and the next and brought greater distress as her majesty’s fear increased and at times she became hysterical, pacing round and round her rooms, thrashing her arms about and kicking any piece of furniture that impeded her passage.

Her ladies pleaded with the gaoler for a forgetfulness potion and he brought a phial containing a concoction of mistletoe berries and valerian sprigs, so that her last day passed more calmly.

Towards evening, the Archbishop of Canterbury arrived to administer the blessèd sacrament of bread and wine in a short service of Holy Communion. During her confession, she admitted her many sins in the sight of God but insisted again and again that adultery, incest and treason were not among them.

When he had gone, she asked her ladies to pray with her for the salvation of her soul. She was then desirous to talk and they listened for several hours about her childhood and the years spent in the French queen’s household then returning to England and falling in love with the handsome and virile young King.

She fell asleep mid-sentence and Marian and Edith eased her down onto the pillows and pulled the covers up round her chin, to make her comfortable during her last night on this earth.

# CHAPTER 59

They woke early. Now her majesty was calm and every inch a queen.

"My dear ladies," she said as they dressed her with trembling fingers, "if I falter, you must support me. This is the last loving service you can render me while I am alive."

Over her crimson kirtle they fastened a grey damask mantle trimmed with ermine. Discarding the rounded French style, she chose to wear an English, gable-hood headdress.

"Because my heart and I are English, are we not?" she asked them.

When dressed to her satisfaction and the approval of her ladies, they sat in silence to await the arrival of the escort that would take her to the scaffold. Mercifully, it was not long before there was a knock on the door and, upon her invitation, the chief yeoman warder entered and bowed deeply.

"Your Majesty, we are ready," he said simply in a voice that was gruff and sought unsuccessfully to conceal his reluctance to perform his duty. This was, after all, the first occasion on which a queen of England had gone to the scaffold.

"And I am ready, too," the Queen said. "And, sir, I wish to thank you for the kindness with which you and your men have carried out your duties here. I greatly appreciate your unfailing consideration to me and my ladies."

The warder bowed again. "It has been a privilege to serve you, your Majesty," he said and stood back so that she, followed by Marian and Edith, could exit the room.

In the corridor, they were met by a contingent of six more yeoman warders and the chaplain. The chief warder and two of his men led the way, the remaining four in the rear, the chaplain last of all.

Keeping to this formation, the men slowing their march to accommodate the gentler pace of the ladies, the party left the Queen's lodgings and skirted the western wall of the White Tower, making their way towards the crowd gathered on Tower Green.

A low whisper of voices reached them across the grass, like the passing of a breeze through the trees in summer.

As the party slowly approached, those who had come to watch the execution fell silent and self consciously moved away to open up a pathway to the scaffold.

The yeoman warders stood to attention, their weapons held at an angle over their shoulders, while the Constable of the Tower, Sir William Kingston, bowed low, the white feathers of his helmet falling over his face. He then proffered his arm to assist her majesty to climb the steps, her ladies and the chaplain in close attendance.

The Queen walked to the edge of the platform and surveyed the waiting crowd, at the front of which the King's men stood in defiance – Thomas Cromwell and his cohorts, among whom Marian noticed the hated Lord Bathampton.

Her eyes returned to her majesty, poised and composed, regal and beautiful as all awaited her final words – a final confession, a reiteration of her innocence, regret at the circumstances that had brought her here – what?

Without faltering, she began: "*Good Christian people, I have not come here to preach a sermon; I have come here to die. For according to the law and by the law I am judged to die, and therefore I will speak nothing against it. I am come hither to accuse no man, nor to speak of that whereof I am accused and condemned to die, but I pray God save the King and send him long to reign over you, for a gentler nor a more merciful prince was there never, and to me he was ever a good, a gentle, and sovereign lord. And if any person will meddle of my cause, I require them to judge the best. And thus I take my leave of the world and of you all, and I heartily desire you all to pray for me.*"

A low moan rose from the crowd and some of the women turned away or fell to their knees, covering their faces with their hands. There was not one ribald catcall or shout of jubilation, or encouragement to "get on with it" as there were at most other executions.

The Queen stood and allowed Marian and Edith to remove and lay to one side her mantle and necklace then take off her headdress, so that her long dark hair fell around her shoulders. They helped her tuck it all into a black cloth cap, away from her neck.

She turned to Marian, who handed her a leather purse of coins with which to pay the executioner. He fell on one knee and begged forgiveness for the deed for which she was paying him. Graciously, she nodded her assent.

Then she indicated that she was ready to be blindfolded and the executioner's assistant handed Edith a black cloth for this purpose.

"Thank you, Edith, dear," Anne said. "Marian? Where are you?"

"I'm here, your Majesty," Marian choked, not wanting this nightmare to be happening but at the same time wishing it were all over.

"Then help me down and lay my hands on the block."

They assisted her to kneel on the straw and guided her hands to the block so that she could place her head in the correct position. Then she clasped her hands behind her back and relaxed her shoulders forward.

The swordmaster's assistant waved Marian and Edith away and they retired to the back of the platform where they fell into each other's arms and turned their heads away but could clearly hear their Queen's pleas to God the Father and the Lord Jesus to grant her mercy and receive her soul.

Around them, most of the waiting crowd had sunk to their knees. There was not a whisper to be heard in that hour, not yet nine o'clock in the morning – no hooters nor whistles from the river nor even calls from the ravens to disturb the deep, unnatural silence. Even the chaplain had ceased his murmuring.

Then there was a dull thud and it was all over. The French swordsman, engaged for his expertise, had severed the head of Anne Boleyn with one blow.

The date was 19th May, 1536.

As Queen of England she had reigned and as Queen of England she would always be remembered.

# CHAPTER 60

"I wish I were travelling with you," said Sir William wistfully as he helped Marian into the whirlicote that had arrived yesterday to take her home. "Give my best love to Lady Susan and tell her I will be with her as soon as I am able, and give young Philip William and my daughter a kiss from their father."

"I will, William," promised Marian, "be sure I will."

Once on the road, Marian lay back against the cushions and sleepily listened to the chatter of Betty and Polly, who were sitting opposite her. They had slept overnight in the vast servants' quarters at the palace and could talk of nothing else.

When they had exhausted all they could think of to say in the matter, Marian asked them whether they had not been nervous, travelling all the way from Berkshire on their own.

"A little, my lady," Betty, the elder of the two, had replied, "but the drivers had orders to take care of us."

"I am very tired," Marian told them. "I wish you to speak quietly to each other, as I have many sorrows to bear, though I do anticipate a happy homecoming."

"They are all waiting for you, my lady, with great love. We were told to tell you that."

Marian smiled then closed her eyes and became prisoner to her thoughts.

It was only six days ago that the Queen had been beheaded, the previous Friday, and she wanted to be well out of the way before the marriage of the King to Lady Jane Seymour took place in four days' time. Jane would become consort as there had been no mention of a coronation. Marian just wished to hide away in rural Berkshire, at Forrester Hall, where affairs at court could not affect her.

The hours following the execution had been a nightmare. The onlookers had crept away in silence and those on the scaffold had milled around for a while, not knowing what to do next. The King had made elaborate plans about the conduct of the execution, even to having the scaffold draped in black velvet, but no instructions had been given about the disposal of the Queen's head and body, which lay there, where they had fallen.

For a while, Marian and Edith held on to each other, both in tears and trying not to look, but knowing that they were responsible for what happened to the Queen now. Gratefully, they welcomed the arrival of several more of her ladies, who had brought white cloth for her shroud.

Supporting each other, they had neatly folded the Queen's grey mantle and had given it and her necklace to the executioner as part of his fee. Anything she had left in the Tower would be claimed by the Constable.

They had then carried out the macabre and gruesome task of wrapping the body and head separately in the cloth. No coffin had been provided and they were not being allowed to bury her in consecrated ground. However, the chief yeoman warder remembered that he had accepted a delivery of bow staves on the previous day, which had arrived in an elm chest, and he despatched four of his men to empty the chest and bring it to the scaffold.

When his instructions had been carried out, her ladies reverently laid the Queen's body in the chest, her head at her side as the cavity was not long enough to do otherwise. The lid was fastened and six warders carried the chest to the nearby chapel of St. Peter ad Vincula.

Distressingly, the burial party had to wait until the afternoon before they could carry out their task. No provision had been made for disposing of the Queen's remains and workmen had to be found to lift the stone slabs in front of the altar, where she was to be laid to rest close to the grave of her brother, George.

Workmen eventually arrived with picks, spades and shovels and the stones were carefully removed. When she had been interred, the slabs were replaced and concreted in again and the area swept clean. Marian and the other ladies then left the chapel with heavy hearts, knowing that no marker would be placed there to show where the Queen lay.

Marian's eyes now filled with tears behind her closed lids as she prayed. Some escaped and ran down her cheeks. Her only consolation was that she had always lovingly served her lady well and had been a source of comfort to the Queen while she was awaiting death. Now she had to put the past behind her and concentrate on the future – but what future? She fell to wondering where Richard was and what he was doing.

As before, they stopped mid-day at The Bear at Maidenhead. Once on the road again, she was dozing after a satisfying meal when she was conscious of Betty speaking with some urgency.

"Lady Marian, Lady Marian!"

She opened her eyes. "What is it?"

"It may be nothing, my lady, but we have glimpsed a rider on a big brown horse, through the trees. He has been keeping pace with us since Maidenhead."

Marian looked out but could see nothing untoward. They had travelled about five miles from Maidenhead and had just passed through the small village of Knowl Hill. The trees surrounded them thickly on both sides and it would be possible to ride a horse through them without being seen from the road, or what passed for a road in this dark leafy world.

"Are you sure?" Marian asked them. "You're not imagining apparitions, Betty?"

"Oh no, my lady. Polly saw him, too."

Marian did not want the girls to notice how anxious she felt but anybody about his legitimate business would surely ride along the road and not skulk in the trees. She decided not to alert the drivers until she had seen the horseman for herself. At the moment, there was no sign of him.

Then, without warning, there were frantic cries of "Whoa! Whoa!" as the driver desperately pulled on the reins and brought the horses to a standstill, both neighing loudly in protest. The whirlicote dragged its wheels along the surface of the road then lurched to a sudden stop.

The girls screamed as they fell on the floor on top of each other. Marian, who had managed to retain her seat, leaned out of the carriage and demanded to know what was happening.

They had rounded a bend and he was there, sitting astride his horse in the middle of the road, his black cloak falling behind him over his horse's rump, just far enough ahead to allow the horses drawing the carriage to pull up. The driver was cursing and trying to quieten the pair while his companion was shouting at the lone rider, asking in God's name what he thought he was about and please to get out of the way so they could continue their journey.

"All in good time," the stranger shouted back, "but first I would speak with Lady Forrester."

"What do you want with me, sire?" Marian responded and would have stepped out of the carriage but for her maids who, having scrambled to their feet, pleaded with her to stay where she was.

The rider prompted his horse forward, closing the gap between himself and the carriage. She was surprised to notice that the horse was black and not brown as the girls had reported.

"Lady Marian," he called again. "Do you not recognise me?"

She did then and recoiled in fear and loathing. "Lord Bathampton!"

"Yes, my lady, it is I. Now, won't you step down and join me, and allow these good people to go on their way to Forrester Hall?"

“No, I will not!” Marian was surprised that her voice sounded so steady and resolute when she was trembling with fear.

The second driver scrambled down from his perch and began to walk towards Bathampton. He was a tall man, thickly set, and looked as though he meant business, but Marian’s tormentor swung himself out of the saddle and drew his sword from its scabbard. The driver stopped and looked back uncertainly but his companion was still trying to settle the horses.

“Just walk across to me, Lady Marian, and your people can go on their way without the need for bloodshed.”

Marian did not know what to do. She did not wish to be responsible for causing a fight, which the unscrupulous Bathampton would win, leaving the innocent driver dead, but she could not put herself into the hands of that man, whose intentions she did not doubt.

“Come, Lady Marian,” he called to her. “I am willing to shed blood if needs be.”

*“If blood is to be shed, I vow it will be yours!”*

The unexpected challenge rang out from their left and, as all eyes turned in that direction, from the shelter of the trees and bushes emerged the head of a large, handsome bay with a black mane and a white stripe running from forehead to muzzle.

When the horse had cleared the trees, they saw, sitting upright in its saddle, a rider dressed in dark green with a cloth covering the lower part of his face. Only his eyes were visible and they were fixed on the man standing in the road, brandishing his sword.

On approaching Bathampton, the rider sprang from his horse, threw the reins over its back and drew his sword. The driver withdrew a few paces, putting a greater distance between himself and the two men now confronting each other with such menace.

Marian stepped out onto the road, ordering the two girls to stay where they were. Bathampton unfastened his cloak and let it fall to the ground, kicking it out of the way.

For a few moments, the men, with swords raised, circled each other, assessing the other’s potential. The mystery rider was the first to close in and the two swords began to flash in the sunlight.

It seemed to Marian that Bathampton was at a disadvantage because he had been completely unprepared for such a challenge, but as the fight began, he regained his focus.

He was the heavier opponent and his blows were deadly but the mystery fighter was obviously younger, certainly lighter and more agile as he blocked the other man's attack time after time by parrying right and left.

Both men were determined and skilled as they lunged forward or were forced to retreat, their swords clanging echoes each time they crashed against each other. For a while the outcome was in the balance.

Gradually, however, Lord Bathampton seemed to tire and, though he made a valiant effort, at last he was outclassed and buckled under the determined onslaught of his opponent. The newcomer pressed forward, broke through Bathampton's defence and slashed his sleeve, leaving a long gash in his upper right arm. He cried out in pain, dropped his sword, fell on his knees, and the fight was over.

Marian's rescuer kicked the sword into the grass verge, sheathed his own, and came across to the injured man to see what damage he had inflicted. The wound was bleeding profusely.

The two girls had disobeyed Marian's instruction and had joined her on the road to watch the fight. The spectators stood silently as the victor picked up Bathampton's cloak, tore off a strip then bound it firmly over and round the injury. He signalled to the two drivers to come over and help him lift Bathampton back onto his horse and place his feet in the stirrups, then walked it round to face the direction of London and put the reins into the man's left hand.

"On your way, my Lord Bathampton," he said in a gruff voice that was obviously disguised. "Crawl back into that hole you crawled out from and don't come anywhere near my lady Marian again."

A slap on the rump sent the large black horse trotting back along the road with its rider slumped over its neck. The mystery swordsman then climbed back into his saddle, inclined his head respectfully towards the three young women, who were standing in the road as if turned to stone, pulled his horse's head round and was soon lost among the trees.

"Who was he?" asked Betty in awe. Polly just gaped in the direction of the undergrowth that had swallowed him up, the branches still quivering from the disturbance.

"I don't know," Marian replied, "but I intend to find out! Back in the carriage with you."

She had to turn Polly round physically and push her back into the whirlicote.

"Let's be on our way, driver, lest there be any more delays."

"Yes, my lady."

He touched his hat and both men climbed onto the driving seat, only too pleased to resume their journey.

# CHAPTER 61

*Place: Forrester Hall, Berkshire*

*Date: End of May, 1536*

Homecoming was so sweet for Marian. She could hardly contain her joy as the first sight of Forrester Hall came into view in the folds of the downs, and when the whirlicote drew up at the entrance to the mansion, she was across the drive and up the steps before anyone could open the door.

When it was finally flung open by John in response to her urgent knocking, Lady Susan stood in the hall, her arms outstretched. Marian fell into them and the two women hugged each other with pleasure, until Marian felt a small tug at her kirtle, and looking down, her eyes met the blue-eyed gaze of a very small boy.

"You must be Philip William," she said, bending down to his level. He nodded gravely. "My name's Marian."

"This is such a happy day," said a girlish voice and there was Marjery with Susan's new baby in her arms and her own daughter by her side. Marian recoiled slightly when she saw the likeness to Lord Bathampton in the little girl's features but hoped her reaction hadn't been noticed and said, with genuine sentiments, what a pretty little girl she was. Then she had to peek at the baby and asked what names she had been given.

"Susan," replied her mother, "and her second name will be Marian."

"Marian?"

"It is my husband's wish, and we are asking if you would stand as her godmother."

"That would give me so much pleasure," Marian said.

"She will be christened as soon as Sir William returns. But now you will need to rest and refresh yourself, then we shall have something to eat."

"And I have a story to relate – an incident that occurred while we were on the road."

"I look forward to hearing it but you must rest first. Betty, go with her ladyship and make sure she has everything she needs. You're in your old room, my dear."

"Oh, I am so happy to be home!" Marian exclaimed and followed Betty up the staircase, reflecting that she had never expected to be sleeping anywhere else but in her own room.

Over the next few weeks, she determined to make her homecoming as easy as possible for all concerned. In past days, she had been in charge of the Hall and all its affairs when Sir William was away and now had to accept that his wife had taken over that role.

She told herself that, though routines had changed and matters were executed differently, it did not mean that one way was right or another wrong. The results justified the methods.

This was a hard lesson to learn but learn it she must if there was to be harmony in the Hall. And harmony there should be, for the sake of her dear William and his family, whose home it had become. As children, it had been her home, and Philip's, but now it was theirs.

She soon learned that she was surplus to requirements. Whatever help she offered was politely refused, which was very frustrating for Marian. Recent events at court and the execution of the Queen still caused her much anguish and she needed to keep her mind and hands busy to prevent the flow of dark memories.

However, young Philip William and Agnes, Marjery's daughter, were always ready for her attention and regarded Rian – they could not pronounce all three syllables of her name – as an additional playmate.

"Rian," said Philip William one morning, "See horses?"

"If your mother says you may go to the stables then, yes, I will take you both."

Neither mother had any objection so Marian, hand-in-hand with the young pair, took them round the back of the Hall and across the gardens and paddocks to the stables.

There was a great deal of activity in the yard. The grooms welcomed them respectfully and Marian assured them that she would not let the children get in the way of their work or too near the horses.

"They'll be safer and cleaner, my lady," advised a young man who was trimming a horse's hoof, "if you took them to see the horses in their stalls."

Marian took the hint. "Come, children, let's go and see where the horses eat and sleep."

There were two lines of stalls opposite each other with an aisle between that was being swept clean. Several of the most inquisitive animals came to look out over their stable doors, which delighted the children. Under the watchful eye of Thomas, the young man who had once worked at the monastery and who was now wielding the broom, they stroked the horses' muzzles and fed them with carrots.

They had spent twenty minutes with the horses and were about to leave when Marian noticed one that was feeding from a net stuffed with hay. It was flicking its beautiful black tail across its brown rump.

"Hello, you're a handsome fellow," she said.

Thomas leaned on his broom. "That's Jason," he told her, "the master's favourite. Come, Jason, come and meet the lady, and see what I has for you."

The bay turned and looked at the carrot being held out towards him then ambled over to the stable door. Marian's heart quickened. There was no mistaking that white stripe running from forehead to muzzle.

"Does anyone else ride him except the master?" she asked.

"No, my lady."

Marian looked at him sharply but he continued to fondle the horse.

"Come, children," she said, gathering them to her, "let's go back and you can practise bowling the ball in the skittle alley."

"I knocked down four," Philip William boasted to Agnes.

"That's because you're a boy and stronger than her," Marian said, "but she can spin her top longer than you can spin yours."

Once back in the Hall, Marian sent the children to the skittle alley with two of the maids and went in search of Susan, who was writing letters in her drawing room.

"Susan, I hope I'm not disturbing you."

The older woman looked up as she blew on her letter to dry the ink. "Not at all. Come in. You look very flushed, Marian – are you feeling quite well?"

"I've just had an amazing revelation!" she said. "We were at the stables."

"Oh?" asked Susan, laying the letter on the writing table.

"And we saw Jason."

"Sir William's horse?"

"Yes, the bay with the white stripe running down to its muzzle."

"He's very handsome, is he not?"

"Susan, it's the same horse that my mystery knight was riding the day Lord Bathampton held up our carriage."

"Really? How can that be?"

"I don't know how it can be, but it is."

Marian had questioned Susan several times about the mystery rider and she had denied all knowledge of him. Now Marian watched her nervously fingering the pendant at her neck.

"I only know what Sir William tells me."

"Which is?"

"Marian, my dear, you must ask him. If he has not told you, he does not want you to know. It is not my place to speak against his wishes."

"But Susan –"

"Patience, Marian. He will be home soon. He writes that the King does not need him during his extended honeymoon at Hampton Court and has given leave for him to come home until summoned to return. I caution patience but am impatient myself to have my husband home again. Then you will be able to ask him."

"I shall!" replied Marian, then smiled. "I, too, will be glad to see him."

When Sir William arrived, she was last in line to receive his greetings. Even Marjery and her daughter took priority. She tried not to mind but was very conscious that, whereas once she had received all his love and attention, he now had a wife and children who came first. That morsel was very hard to swallow.

Just as soon as she could, she whispered that she would like to speak to him alone as soon as possible. Sir William's days were filled with administration of the estate, which had not been dealt with quite as he would have wished, and it was several days before she received his invitation.

"Come up to my study in Stephen Tower this afternoon, while my wife and the children are resting," he said, "and we can talk."

"Like old times, William."

He must have heard the wistfulness in her voice because he smiled and patted her hand. "Life changes, Marian, and we must change with it."

"I'm finding it so difficult," she complained when she was seated opposite him and they were alone. "I want to help Lady Susan and take some of the responsibility off her shoulders but she won't let me. I offer and she politely refuses, every time. William, I used to run the estate with the assistance of the steward, and now I'm not allowed to lift a finger. I sneaked a look at the household accounts. I'm sure there are mistakes but I'm not allowed to point them out."

"Marian, my dear, she is the lady of the house now. I know she has a lot to learn but please be patient with her. Is this the discussion you wanted to have with me?"

"No, William. I took Philip William and Agnes to the stables."

"Ah, you saw Jason – my delight. Such a magnificent beast, such a noble head."

"A noble head with a white stripe running down its nose."

Sir William drummed his fingers on his writing table, disturbing a document that floated to the floor. Marian picked it up and saw that it was a letter giving a neighbour permission to hunt over Forrester land, and very elegantly scribed. She replaced it on the table.

"You know very well, William, what I am asking you. It was the same horse that my mystery knight was riding when he accosted Lord Bathampton on the road and nicked him in the arm with his sword. The same horse, William, yet your wife denies all knowledge of my knight and you are going to do the same."

"If I do, my dear, it is for your own safety – and his. I witnessed Bathampton's return to Greenwich – the entire court heard about it. He was breathing fire and brimstone and will try to exact his revenge once his arm has fully healed. Fortunately, it is taking some time for the surgeons to accomplish that, in spite of bleeding him regularly."

"Hopefully they will miscalculate and drain out all his blood."

Sir William laughed. "I doubt that very much, however earnestly you wish it. They will bleed him until they have adjusted the humours in his body and his arm heals."

"Who was he, William, my rescuer?"

"Marian, you are not listening to me. Bathampton will have his revenge and I fear it will not be long before he pays us a visit. He will have the authority of Cromwell to search out the swordsman and take him back to court to stand trial for some trumped-up charge that carries the death penalty. When he comes, it will be better for you if you know nothing about the young man."

"Did you send him as my guardian angel, William?"

"I thought Bathampton would make a move once you were far enough away from the protection of myself and the Queen."

Marian flinched. "But the Queen –"

"I refer to Lady Jane Seymour, who is now Queen in all but title as the King has not yet arranged her coronation. She is very fond of you."

"Then I *do* have you to thank for my knight."

"Let it rest there, Marian, and we will say no more about him. And I will find you something to do for me on the estate."

Two days later, he asked her, "How would you like to assist the forester in looking after the trees? One was struck by lightning during that fierce storm some weeks ago and requires felling, and there are always others dying and new saplings needing light and space. Would you like that?"

"Yes, William, I would, and it will get me out of the Hall and from under your wife's feet."

"Then I'll ask Matthew to begin your instruction, though it will take a lifetime to learn all that there is to know."

What began for Marian as an interesting idea developed into an obsession. She wandered through the copses and woodland with Matthew, surprised by the many clearings lit by the sun when moments later they were plunged into gloom as tall trees with their broad leaves shut it out.

The forester could have been taken for one of the faerie folk the villagers whispered about as they sat round their firesides on dark evenings. He was short in stature, his legs bowed since childhood, so that his gait was unbalanced and awkward. He had very dark hair streaked with grey, a wrinkled face and swarthy complexion that contrasted darkly with his unexpectedly very bright, blue eyes. And what he did not know about trees and woodlands could have been written on an acorn.

He taught her to regard the ancient trees with awe – the smooth, grey bark of the ash; the silver birch named because of its silvery trunk, with leaves shaped like arrow heads; pussy willow with a bark that contained a natural pain killer; and the smooth trunk of the lime tree whose young leaves were edible. She knew the shape of oak leaves but learned to recognise the pattern of the oak's bark with its deep grooves and ridges.

During one of their forays into a wood, they surprised a young doe grazing in a clearing. The deer bounded away in fright and Marian was following its path when she came upon a small barn. On further inspection, she saw that it was a shelter, presumably for a horse, as it had fresh straw bedding and a hay loft and a collection of buckets, pitch forks, rakes and brooms in one corner.

"What is this barn used for, Matthew?" she asked as he followed her through the open door.

"Sometimes a horse needs a quiet space of its own," he explained, "away from the other horses, if it's sick or about to go into labour or just needs rest and quiet."

"It's well hidden," she remarked.

"Has to be or we'd get all the passing vagrants setting up home here."

# CHAPTER 62

*Place: Forrester Hall, Berkshire*

*Date: July, 1536*

Sir William was summoned back to Greenwich Palace at the end of June and had been gone less than a week when Lord Bathampton arrived with an entourage of servants and men-at-arms, bearing in his leather satchel papers that allowed him to search Forrester Hall from cellars to battlements.

Someone sighted his party when still some distance away and raised the alarm so that, when he banged on the door, those within were prepared for his unwelcome arrival.

John, the steward, opened the door to him.

“Is your mistress at home?” he demanded without courtesy.

“Lady Susan Forrester? Yes, she is,” John answered. “I will announce your arrival. Who shall I say is calling?”

“You have a short memory, steward. I spent Christmas here with his majesty and his whore of a wife but, true, it was a while ago – twelve years, in fact – and we have all aged in that time.”

“I do remember you, my lord. You came again when you were searching for your wife, Lady Alice, and also stayed here when engaged in destroying the monastery.”

“So, you are not such as a fool as you make out. Please announce me to Lady Susan Forrester.”

John turned away to carry out this errand but Bathampton stopped him.

“Stay. Before you do so, please to inform me, is Lady Marian Forrester here?”

“Yes, my lord, Lady Marian is here.”

“Aha, all the better.”

Marian heard this exchange from where she stood on the landing above the hall. She was afraid of this man but knew she had to face him at some time and better to do so in company than when on her own. When John returned to conduct him to the drawing room in which Susan had decided to meet him, she ran down the stairs and slipped into the room as John left.

Susan was sitting in a chair, her embroidery on her lap, and rose when Lord Bathampton entered. Marian moved across to stand by her side. His lordship could not have been more charming and bowed very low but his eyes were fixated on Marian, who would not curtsey, before they shifted across to Lady Susan.

"My ladies, what pleasure it affords me to greet you once again in your beautiful home. I have been anticipating my sojourn here with some impatience."

"Why, sir," Susan replied with great dignity, "I do not recall having invited you to stay with us."

"Do I discern a note of displeasure, my lady?" he asked. "Perhaps Lady Marian is better pleased to see me here?"

"I believe that Lady Marian has greater reason than anyone to wish you absent. Lord Bathampton, you and your men have never been welcome here. Please state the reason for your visit during my husband's absence."

"Sir William's absence is of no import one way or the other. I came as soon as the injury to my arm had healed which, I am pleased to say, is now the case."

He unfastened his satchel and extracted a sheaf of papers which he spread out on an adjacent table.

"You will see, my lady, if you care to inspect them, that I have letters here from Thomas Cromwell to search this house from top to bottom and the surrounding lands –"

"To what purpose? To find what exactly, my lord?"

"Not 'what', Lady Susan, but 'who'. And do not expect me to believe your very charming act of innocence. Lady Marian, you at least cannot pretend ignorance of the reason for my being here. You were on the road and witnessed the aggression of that fellow."

"My memory is somewhat at variance with yours, my lord," Marian countered. "I seem to remember that it was you who were the cause of the confrontation and he wounded you in a very fair fight because he was by far the better swordsman."

Lord Bathampton flushed. "He had the advantage. He was much younger – and I want to know who he is."

Marian sat, then looked at him with disdain.

"You must find out elsewhere because I have no knowledge," she answered him. "I wish I did know so that I could thank him for protecting me that day."

"You cannot expect me to believe –"

"You may believe what you like but I too have been unable to discover his identity."

"Then I shall have the pleasure of informing you when we catch him, as catch him we shall."

"Surely, your being ousted in a sword fight is not reason enough to arrest a man?" Marian asked.

"It is not, I agree," Lord Bathampton said, gathering together his papers and returning them to his satchel, "but by the time we apprehend him, his crime will have escalated to – how about treason? I am sure I could cobble together a case for treason."

"And the punishment for treason is the death sentence?" Susan asked, though she knew the answer.

"Certainly. He will be hung, drawn and quartered."

He paused to allow this statement to take effect.

"Lady Susan, I will require a room while I am staying here, as will my servants – in the West Tower, perhaps. I have a fancy to occupy the room in which his majesty slept. That will suit me excellently. My men-at-arms can be accommodated in the stable block."

Marian thought of Jason, the beautiful bay horse, and involuntarily gasped, which did not pass unnoticed by his lordship.

"So, Lady Marian, that does not please you? That sets me to wondering why."

He turned again to Susan.

"Now, my lady, please give your orders for our accommodation so that I may make myself presentable for our mid-day repast."

Susan moved across to the table and rang a bell. John must have been listening outside the door because he entered immediately and, having received his orders, preceded Lord Bathampton from the room.

He had not once mentioned Marjery. He must have known she was living under this roof with her daughter, his daughter, but he had chosen to ignore the fact.

Marian was very disturbed by his presence and must have shown it in her expression.

"Don't look so anxious, Marian," Susan smiled. "We have been expecting this visit and William has well prepared us all."

# CHAPTER 63

Their unwelcome guest had changed out of his travelling clothes by the time he joined the ladies for their mid-day meal.

Marjery refused to eat at the same table and asked to take all her meals in her chamber.

She was adamant that Agnes should not meet her father so the children stayed in the nursery on the floor above, their nursemaids being instructed to keep them there until Bathampton had left.

After the meal, he lost no time in assembling his men and setting them about their task. Susan watched for a while then retired to her room to rest, leaving Marian to monitor proceedings.

The men were nothing if not meticulous in their search for anything that would lead them to the identity of the unknown assailant and his whereabouts. Some were sent to the servants' quarters to question the staff minutely but they eventually returned, reporting that they had discovered nothing.

The remainder began in the hall, lifting loose flag stones, peering up inside the cavernous chimney, knocking on walls to discover their integrity, rummaging through drawers in tables, removing cushions.

Under the direction of the housekeeper, servants went round behind them, putting everything back as it had been, to cause Lady Susan as little distress as possible when she came downstairs.

Systematically, the men combed every room, even the chapel, leaving not a loose board unturned, not a wooden panel untapped, not a rug that wasn't dragged out from beneath furniture nor a receptacle uninspected, even taking down tapestries and large framed portraits of Sir William's ancestors. As well as looking for hidden rooms or priests' holes, the search was designed to cause as much distress as possible to everyone in residence at the Hall.

Marian was very surprised when one of his men brought Bathampton the large family Bible from the chapel and placed it on the table. Bathampton began to turn its pages.

"How well do you know the Scriptures, Lady Marian?" he asked.

"Tolerably well," she replied, mystified.

"Then are you able to quote to me St. Matthew, chapter 13, verse 44?"

Marian confessed that she could not.

"Then let me enlighten you. The verse reads, '*The kingdom of heaven is like unto treasure hid in a field*'."

"I bow to your superior knowledge," she said, wondering where this conversation was leading.

"It is knowledge that I acquired," he said, "from my mentor, Thomas Cromwell, and he obtained it from a very helpful monk from St. Jude's monastery, Alphonsus by name. He squealed rather much before he confessed but he *was* being racked at the time."

Marian shuddered and Bathampton apologised with obvious insincerity for upsetting her delicate sensibilities. She remarked that she did not know what any of this information had to do with her and then he told her plainly how Abbot Johannes had planned to deprive his majesty of some of the monastery's wealth but happily the plan had been discovered and he had that morning despatched four men to retrieve a buried chest.

He then told Marian to accompany him to the stable block so that she could show him what obviously she had not wanted him to discover. Marian was comforted to know that Betty was following them at a distance and was not concealing her presence.

They arrived to find men searching there also and the grooms endeavouring to calm the horses, most of whom were unnerved by this disruptive activity.

Surreptitiously, she looked over to Jason's stall and was relieved to see a very large draught horse sleepily peering out from the stable door, philosophically surveying the chaos around him. Jason had been spirited away and Marian guessed where he was being hidden.

Her suspicions were confirmed when she saw Matthew, the forester, sitting at a lathe, busily fashioning a length of walnut into an elegant goblet. She caught his eye and raised her eyebrows. He grinned, placed a forefinger to the side of his nose and winked, then turned his attention back to the job in hand. Looking frustrated and puzzled, Bathampton eventually returned to the house.

He was even more angry when one of his men came to report that they had dug where he had directed – thirteen paces east of the large oak tree and forty-four paces north, then had repeated the pattern – but had found nothing and, yes, they had dug all round the area but, again, nothing.

"So, Brother Alphonsus, you have had the last laugh and have taken your secret with you to the grave, for all the good it will do you," Bathampton muttered.

"And Abbot Johannes?" asked Marian.

"Obdurate to the end but the old man died well," Bathampton answered with grudging respect, "as did Mother Superior at the stake. Stupidity, when a signature would have saved them both."

Thankfully, he did not go into further detail and Marian did not enquire. She prayed now that their souls might rest in peace.

His lordship went to bed immediately after the evening meal and the ladies retired not long afterwards. Marian locked her door and wedged a chair beneath the handle.

# CHAPTER 64

She awoke from a troubled night's sleep, wondering what the day would hold and wishing William would come and put a stop to this invasion of their home. Lord Bathampton was adamant that the mystery swordsman had taken shelter at Forrester Hall and was like a man possessed in his determination to find him and take him to London to stand trial. She was aware that his obsession was fuelled by the alcohol he had consumed since his men had broken into Sir William's stock of wines, ales and beers in the cellar.

When Marian left her chamber, Bathampton's men were already working their way through the rooms on the second floor. She ate a hurried breakfast then went upstairs and found his lordship rifling through all her drawers and cupboards, handling all her intimate clothing. The sight sickened her. How she loathed that man!

"I doubt you will find your quarry in my bed, my lord," she observed. "Please leave my chamber this instant."

Caught in the act, he had the grace to lower his eyes and stepped out on to the landing, ordering two of his men to take over where he had left off.

At that moment, they heard the excited squealing of children's voices at the other end of the corridor and Philip William and Agnes came running towards them with their nursemaids in hot pursuit. The children stopped short when they reached Marian and her companion.

"Who are you?" asked Agnes, looking up at Bathampton with eyes wide with interest and of the same steel-grey colour as his.

He studied her for a moment then the truth dawned on him.

"I believe I am your father," he said.

"Agnes hasn't got a father," Philip William told him. "My father lives with King Henry."

"Does he now?" Lord Bathampton responded.

The two nursemaids approached and curtsied nervously and asked leave to take the children back to the nursery.

"Wait!" he said and knelt on one knee so that his face was on a level with the children's innocent gaze. "I think you're very clever children and know everything that happens here. Are there any secrets you can tell me?"

"Cook hides the marchpane from us," Philip William volunteered, "but we know where she puts it."

Agnes nodded agreement.

"Splendid! Do you know any more secrets?" he persisted. "Is there someone here who hides away because he doesn't want to be seen?"

They thought about this very seriously for a moment then Agnes asked, "Like the man who lives in the wall?"

For seconds no one spoke. Lord Bathampton rose to his feet.

"Yes, child, like that man."

"Agnes, you're a naughty girl to tell such faerie stories!" one of the nursemaids scolded, grabbing her by the arm. "You must come back to the nursery!"

"Leave her!" Bathampton commanded.

"But, sire, she talks such nonsense," said the nursemaid. "Let me take them back –"

"I said to leave her!" he thundered and the girl faltered and took a step backwards, relinquishing her hold on Agnes's arm.

"Where does he live?" he asked Agnes in a softer tone. She pointed to the curtained alcove behind the bust of Sir William's grandfather on its alabaster pillar.

"In there," she said.

"Then that's where we shall look," he said, his voice still velvety soft. "What a clever little girl you are. I must remember to tell your pretty mother so."

He moved across to the wall behind the curtains and began tapping the panelling. At first the sound of his knocking was dead, as against a solid wall, but then the sound changed and echoed beneath his knuckles.

"Here!" he exulted. "Now all I have to do is find the catch that opens up the entrance."

He continued to tap the panelling then felt around with his fingers.

"Ah, seemingly a knot in the woodwork," he said. "And if I press it –"

Without a sound, a section slid along behind the rest of the wooden panelling, leaving a space just large enough for a person to squeeze through.

"So!" he said. "All is revealed."

Marian was astounded. She had lived here all her life and had no notion that there was a secret aperture behind this wall. She guessed that, as always, William had been protecting her by keeping her ignorant of the fact.

She realised now that Bathampton had grabbed Agnes's hand, and protested.

"I may need her," he said, "but to set your mind at ease, you will come with us."

Marian hesitated, not wishing to compromise her own safety by leaving the security of the landing. At that moment, she remembered again the horror of being close to him in the darkness. However, she could not allow him to take Agnes into the secret passage without supervision so summoned up all her courage and reluctantly followed. She reasoned that he had another prey in his sights this time and was not thinking about her.

"I need a light. You, girl, bring me a lantern!" he called back to the two nursemaids who were peering through the opening. One of them scurried off and returned with a candle lantern which he held high as he felt his way along the passage.

It followed the line of the corridor then widened. The lamp lit up a small area that housed a truckle bed made up with a bolster and coverings and a chair and table with the remains of a meal on it.

The passage then continued until it came to a curved wall which was obviously the wall of Stephen Tower. Leading upwards was a flight of stone steps that wound round the outside of this wall. There would be no indication from the gardens that there was a wall within a wall.

Unsteadily, Lord Bathampton began to mount the stairs, dragging Agnes after him, not caring that sometimes the little girl was on her knees. Marian followed, trying to help her as best she could.

They came to a flagstone forming a level platform in front of a door. His lordship opened the door, which revealed yet another door. When this was pushed open, they found themselves emerging through a section of the bookcase in Sir William's study. Marian was amazed yet again. She had been in there many times without having an inkling of the hidden doorway.

Now, everything appeared to be as Sir William had left it. His large mahogany desk stood in the centre of the room and on it a wooden tray containing a pile of scrolls. An hour glass, sealing wax, ink wells, a pot of quill pens, a pen knife and a candle in a holder were tidily arranged to one side of a writing slope.

Various chairs were placed around the room and a very large globe of the known world stood in a wooden frame to one side of the fireplace. Sir William's high backed, swivel chair was turned away from the desk and was facing the fireplace.

As they stood by the bookcase, surveying the room, Marian noticed a slight movement. The chair began to revolve very slowly. As it did so, first a hand, then an arm and then the whole person came into view. Marian would have recognised her knight with or without the green cloth that covered the lower part of his face.

"You!" she exclaimed, delighted to see him but apprehensive about the conduct of this meeting.

"I believe you have been searching for me, Lord Bathampton," he observed, his voice disguised as previously. Bathampton, also taken by surprise, was momentarily nonplussed and let go of the child's hand. Agnes ran to Marian and peeped out from behind her kirtle.

"Well, you have found me, my lord. So, what is your intention now? I am greatly interested to know."

"It's the hangman's noose for you!" replied his lordship, having gained control of his tongue. "You'll not get away a second time!"

He drew his sword and quickly covered the distance round the desk but the young man was too quick for him and dived through the gap beneath the desk and was out through the open door in the bookcase, closing it behind him.

Bathampton bellowed in anger and tried to follow but fumbled with the catch that opened the door. When he found it, Marian, with Agnes still clinging to her, sprang in front of him to block his way but he pushed them both aside.

As he again grabbed Agnes by the wrist and dragged her through the second door, which was still open, Marian had no option but to follow, stumbling after them both in the darkness.

The staircase climbed ever higher. Then from above came a blast of fresh air and a door banged shut. Still they climbed and eventually Lord Bathampton reached the door and pushed it open. They emerged from the brick base of a false chimney stack and found themselves on a flat roof, blasted by a strong wind that was twisting Sir William's flag emblazoned with the Forrester coat of arms round and round its flag pole. Bathampton let go of Agnes. The young man had vanished.

"Rian, we're on the roof!" the child exclaimed and ran over to the parapet, fortunately protected by battlements. Marian ran after her and pulled her away.

"Be careful, it's a very long drop down to the ground."

It was indeed a long way down into the front courtyard, where Bathampton's men were coming and going as they searched grounds, outhouses and stable blocks.

Around them, the rolling downs of the county enfolded the fields and woods of the estate and, in the distance, the church tower marked the site of the village.

"So much for your protector! He's made a run for it!" proclaimed Bathampton, irritation on his face and in his tone.

"But how?" asked Marian.

"Across the roof – look, there's a door into the West Tower. He'll have taken that way down!" He sheathed his sword. "He won't get far."

"I'm cold!" Agnes complained.

"She's cold," Marian repeated.

"Then let her go back the way we came."

Marian took her by the hand and led her to the door in the false chimney stack.

"Go carefully," she warned and was about to follow when Bathampton moved between them and shut the door. Agnes screamed from the other side.

"She'll fall in the dark!" Marian protested and tried to side-step him so that she could open the door again but he blocked her way.

"Open the door!" she commanded but he laughed and moved towards her.

Marian realised the danger in which she was placed as he approached her, affording no chance of escape. He swung her round and forced her back against the chimney stack and pressed himself against her, taking her face in his hands so that she couldn't turn her head away.

"My beautiful Lady Marian," he said, his breath alcohol-laden, his breathing heavy and laboured. "You will kiss me."

"No I will not!" she said, trying to twist out of his grasp.

"Oh, but you will," he insisted and lowered his lips onto hers in a kiss so passionate that she could barely breathe. Behind her, Agnes was crying and pounding on the closed door.

Outraged and terrified, Marian stamped on his foot with all the weight she could muster, which caused him to release his grip on her head but his arms went round her waist and he pulled her to him, so close she could feel the quickening beats of his heart.

"I will have you, my lady, whether you wish it or not! I have never taken a woman on a rooftop before, but there is a first time for every pleasure."

While he was breathlessly whispering all this, one hand had reached down to draw up the hem of her kirtle and was travelling with it up her leg. She was desperately trying to push his hand down.

"'Tis of no avail," he told her.

In desperation, Marian continued to struggle, pounding her fists against his chest and kicking out at his legs. He was unable to hold on to her and became so exasperated that he hit her hard across her face, jerking her head to one side. Before she could recover from the blow he had his hands around her neck and began to squeeze until she thought she was about to pass out. Her vision was filled with his face, red and angry, ugly with thwarted passion.

"Conscious or no, alive or dead, I will have you anyway!"

*"That you will not!"*

Marian recognised the voice but in that moment could not think whose it was. Bathampton turned, letting go of her neck.

"So it *is* you!" he exclaimed.

Now that he had discarded the cloth that had concealed his face and had resumed his natural voice, Marian realised what she should have known all along.

"Richard!"

His anger rising, Bathampton threw himself at the young man but Richard stepped aside and turned to meet the next attack.

Released from the weight of his lordship against her, Marian took a step forward and, behind her, Agnes fell through the doorway. She picked herself up and together they watched the two men wrestling each other, Richard showing superior strength and mobility until Bathampton hooked his leg around the younger man's ankle and brought him to the ground. Now in control, he began to kick him viciously as he lay on the ground before sitting astride him and punching him in the face.

Marian mustered what strength she could and rushed to Richard's aid, pounding his attacker's back then throwing her arm round his throat and pulling his head backwards.

With this intervention, Richard managed to free himself and got to his feet but Bathampton also scrambled up, throwing Marian off his back as he did so. Then, turning, he caught hold of her and, using her as his shield, began backing away towards the parapet. Agnes was clinging to Marian's kirtle and would not let go, in spite of Marian's pleas.

The trio retreated until they backed up against the battlements. Richard came towards them but Bathampton drew his sword with his free hand and held it close to Marian's throat. Richard perforce stayed quite still.

Through one of the crenellations, Bathampton bellowed down to the men in the courtyard but the wind caught his shout and blew it back at him. He took another step backwards until he was almost sitting on the base of the crenellation and hurled his sword down through the opening.

The sword landed at the feet of a man-at-arms, who swore as he jumped out of the way and looked skywards. Bathampton shouted an order to come up, which the man must have understood because he signalled to two of his comrades and they ran to the entrance.

Richard took advantage of his opponent's momentary lack of attention and started forward but Bathampton was quick to respond. Pushing

Marian away from him so that she fell to the ground, he grabbed Agnes and hoisted her on to the base of the crenellation, holding her there with one hand.

"Come no nearer," he warned, "or she goes over."

"You can't – she's your daughter!" Marian shouted at him, scrambling to her feet, but he laughed insanely.

"Will you rescue her, my lady?" He moved Agnes a little further towards the edge. "Why don't you try it?"

Checking her urge to rush to save the child, Marian's gaze moved from Agnes, close to the edge of eternity, to the face of her captor and felt completely helpless. Was he vile enough to cause the death of his own daughter? Surely not, but she could not be entirely certain so she stood quite still.

Perhaps he was not sure, either, because he reached into the pouch hanging from his belt and pulled out a small flagon. Removing the glass stopper with his teeth, he drained the flagon then hurled it out through the opening. They heard it smash in the courtyard below and the curse of a man who bellowed up that it had missed him by inches.

Richard also was not moving. All they could do was wait until the soldiers arrived, when he would be arrested.

She looked at him and he held out a hand towards her. She moved across to him and his arm went round her waist.

"How touching," Bathampton said. "Make the most of it. You won't have her for long and then I will."

They continued to wait, no one moving. At long last, the three soldiers crashed through the door at the top of the West Tower.

"Arrest him!" Lord Bathampton barked.

When they did not move, he shouted at them, "Do as I say – take him prisoner!"

The men rushed at the couple, elbowing Marian out of the way, and took hold of Richard's arms.

Seeing Richard immobilised, Bathampton let go of Agnes. Released from his grip, she teetered, unbalanced, on the edge of the crenellation but thankfully fell inwards, towards them, onto the concrete roof, and began to scream.

"Shut the brat's mouth or I will!"

Marian ran to quieten Agnes at the same moment that Bathampton threw himself at Richard, and the pair collided. Marian was able to regain her footing but Bathampton struggled to stay upright. He tripped over Agnes where she crouched and, with arms flailing wildly, stumbled backward through the crenellation and disappeared. His scream reverberated around the rooftop. Then they heard a sickening thud and Bathampton was silenced for all time.

For a moment, no one moved or made a sound. Even Agnes stopped crying. Then the soldiers dragged Richard across to the opening and gazed down before turning to each other, ashen-faced.

When they released their hold, Richard crossed to Marian, whose arms were round Agnes.

Seeing him walk free, one of the men seized Richard again.

"You are still under arrest," he said mechanically.

"On what charge?" asked Richard.

The man looked helplessly at his companions, who shook their heads.

"As there is no charge for me to answer, I suggest that you retrieve the body of your master and prepare for your journey back to Greenwich," Richard said. "You saw what happened. There was no foul play here and that is what you will report back to Thomas Cromwell."

The men nodded, completely at a loss now that there was no one to give them orders, and crossed to the door through which they had emerged.

When they had gone, peace descended on the rooftop. The only sound was the flapping of the Forrester flag in the high wind.

# CHAPTER 65

Gathered round the table in the hall, no one was speaking. Lady Susan sat with her head in her hands. Marjery was cuddling Agnes on her lap, Philip William sitting between her and his mother. Marian and Richard sat close to each other, holding hands under the table.

Around them, servants and soldiers were crossing and recrossing the hall, preparing for the journey back to Greenwich. They had wrapped the smashed body of Lord Bathampton in a sheet and it was lying on the floor of a whirlicote.

"If only William were here," wailed Lady Susan at last.

"He will come," Marian reassured her, "as soon as he hears the news."

John, the steward, poured copious amounts of wine and beer until the leaderless entourage had left and everyone had calmed down a little, then it was time for Richard's explanations.

"When I was released from prison and left the court, Sir William offered me concealment here, for which I was very grateful. When you left court, Marian, he was very concerned that Bathampton would intercept you once you were some distance from Greenwich so I kept pace with you for most of the way, staying out of sight, though you tell me that your maids spotted me on the road from Maidenhead."

Marian nodded.

"It was as Sir William feared and the wretch stopped you at Knowl Hill. You know what happened."

Physically and emotionally drained, she nodded again, unable to speak.

"Sir William knew the man would not rest until he had me in chains, standing trial on some fictitious charge, so I took up residence in the secret passages, or 'in the wall', as Agnes innocently said. There is no more to tell – you know the rest."

Sir William arrived home a week later to stay indefinitely.

"His majesty has been gracious enough to grant me a pension so that I can stay at home with you, my dear, and manage the Hall and estate," he told his wife. "He said I had served him faithfully and should take a well-earned retirement, especially in view of recent events. However, he has asked me to bring young Philip William to court when he is sixteen, as I did his half-brother, so that he can one day take my place as an Esquire to the Body of His Majesty."

"And what of the Queen?" Marian asked.

"She thrives," he reported. "The King spends much time trying to impregnate her with an heir to the throne. She sends you her regards, Marian, and wishes you as much happiness as she has. Which brings me to a very important issue – your marriage."

"Marriage, sire?" Marian answered, her heart leaping at the thought.

"Now, now," smiled Sir William, "none of that coy girlish innocence with me! I know you too well, my Marian! You are aware that Richard has asked me for your hand in marriage, are you not?"

"Yes, William."

"And I promised to give him my answer this evening if he would attend on me. Where is he, by the by?"

"He's waiting up on the landing," she said, smiling up to where Richard was leaning over the balustrade.

Sir William looked up and beckoned the young man down. He raced down the stairs and stood by Marian's side.

"Silly question, I know," said Sir William, "but is this what you want, Marian?"

"Above all else," she replied.

"And you think he will make you happy?"

"I am sure of it."

"And you, Richard?"

"I will do everything in my power to take care of her, Sir William."

"Then I suppose I have no option but to give my consent."

Marian flung her arms round her dear William's neck and kissed him fervently on the cheek, then hugged Lady Susan, while the two men clasped hands and beamed at each other and the ladies.

"And they will live on the estate," Lady Susan questioned, "won't they, William, so that we shall see them often?"

"It is all arranged," he confirmed.

Marian smiled broadly and curtsied to him.

"You are most gracious, sire."

Then she turned to Richard. "Is Sir Villiam not gracious, my lord?" she asked mischievously.

"Your révérence leaves much to be desired, Lady Marian," William returned gravely, entering into the fun of the charade. "I am sure you could do better than that."

And she did, carrying out the action as she repeated the instructions the dancing master had taught her twelve eventful years before.

*"Take hold of* your *skirt with both hands, slide your foot to the right, left foot behind right foot, no wobbling, bend low – lower – look down at the floor, then chin up and smile!"*

And Marian gave Richard, with Sir William by his side, the most radiant smile that had ever set fire to those green eyes, born of her overwhelming happiness in the presence of the two men she loved most in the whole world.

THE END

Lightning Source UK Ltd.
Milton Keynes UK
UKHW010601291118
333132UK00001B/34/P